REVENGE

OSGUARDS: GUARDIANS OF THE UNIVERSE

By

Malcolm D. Petteway

Homecoming
Revelations
Armageddon
Revenge

REVENGE

BOOK FOUR
OF
OSGUARDS: GUARDIANS OF THE UNIVERSE

MALCOLM DYLAN PETTEWAY

Rage Books LLC
www.ragebooks.net

Osguards: Revenge

Edited by:
Karen M. Petteway
James Barnes

ISBN: 0984364536
EAN-13: 9780984364534

Printed in the United States
Rage Books LLC
www.ragebooks.net

"Like an unchecked cancer, hate corrodes the personality and eats away its vital unity. Hate destroys a man's sense of values and his objectivity. It causes him to describe the beautiful as ugly and the ugly as beautiful, and to confuse the true with the false and the false with the true."

—Martin Luther King, Jr., Strength to Love, 1963.

PROLOGUE

The stars of the Tandor Galaxy in the Gigantur cluster shone with the brilliance of gold, filling the heavens with billions upon billions of twinkling angels of light. In sector sixteen, in the midst of this radiance, poised two starship fleets of destruction, like football teams ready to do battle in a stadium filled with bright eyed spectators.

On one side, the last remnants of the Tuit military in the Tandor Galaxy, two white cone-shaped firestars and three smaller versions of the firestar called fireships, spread in a challenging attack formation, weapons charged and locked on to each ship on the other side. Facing them, were two black arrow-shaped Universal Science Security and Trade Association of Planets (USSTAP) star protectors and two smaller version of the star protectors called star cruisers.

"This is the First Osguard, Kang Sario, of the Gigantur Association of Planets onboard the *Star Protector Moryugh*," shot the hail from the lead star protector. "We are on a diplomatic mission, and you are hampering our progress. Please state your intentions." Kang Sario stood on the bridge of the *Moryugh*, impatience soaking his eyes. He was six feet tall, and had the body of a professional wrestler. His short hair was reddish, almost orange in places and slicked back. His skin color made him look Middle Eastern; however, his vampire canine teeth added a different flavor to his appearance. His rugged features told a story of a man who lived a hard life, even torturous at times. The vibrato of his voice confirmed he was not a man that played games. He was a serious person with no time to waste, and at the moment, the five ships in front of him presented a waste of his time.

"I say again, this is First Osguard, Kang Sario, of the Gigantur Association of Planets onboard the *Star Protector Moryugh*. Please stand down or we will interpret your actions as hostile and take appropriate action." Sario looked to his communications officer, and beckoned him with his eyes for any news. None came.

1

"Let me try," Prime Ambassador Jingen Tou, who was sitting behind him requested.

Sario tilted his head in thought, and then turned toward Tou to regard her for a moment. Tou had dark hair highlighted with streaks of gray. She was a mix of Tuit and Gigantur. She had the yellowish tint in her eyes of a Tuit and the hint of the canine teeth from the Gigantur race. She was slim and cut like a long distance runner. She said she hailed from Betli in the Tandor Galaxy. Betli was a planet that supported the former Tuit Consortium and that suffered greatly during the Tuit Revolution. It was the Tuit seat of power throughout the Gigantur Star Cluster. Tou arose from nowhere to lead the revolt on her planet in the last days of fighting. Until then, Betli was a Tuit stronghold in the Tandor Galaxy, one of the last holdouts, and no one ever heard of Tou. Somehow Kang Sario who was the leader of the revolt throughout the Tandor Galaxy and now sat as the First Osguard, forged a relationship with Tou's forces that helped changed the course of the revolution. Kang remembered it was an uneasy relationship at times, but without Tou's help the revolution in the Tandor Galaxy would have lasted several more years and could have been lost. Even though he was unsure of her agenda, he supported her rise to power as the prime ambassador of the Gigantur Association of Planets.

"Go ahead," he shrugged, "it can't hurt."

Tou motioned for the communications officer to open hailing frequencies once more, "Commander of the Tuit ship, this is Prime Ambassador Jingen Tou. Please state your intentions."

The airwaves cracked as a feminine voice began to pierce the air. "Ambassador Tou, this is Kimlin of Vexul, First Daughter of Gigantur Cluster. I will speak to you and not that lolwe who has taken on the mantle of our sworn enemy."

"Then speak," Tou commanded.

"In private...what I have to say is not for the ears of a lolwe."

Tou signaled for the connection to be severed and turned back to Sario. Disgust ruled Sario's face and distrust anchored his body.

"I don't know about this," Sario grunted.

"Look, as long as she's talking, she isn't attacking us," Tou tried to rationalize to him. "Let me use your office and give me a private secure link to Kimlin and I will stall until you can figure something out. Who knows, I may be able to negotiate her surrender."

"Surrender?"

"Yes, her surrender." Tou reiterated. "Osguard, those ships out there are probably the last of the Tuit Consortium in our space. She is outnumbered and outgunned by all military strategies. If she attacks us, she is signing her own death warrant. After all, you *are* the First Osguard and I *am* the Prime Ambassador."

2

"Well maybe she's thinking taking us out will set our government back several years and she will be able to use that time to gather enough resistance to reclaim this space for the Tuit Consortium," Sario pushed back.

"If she attacks, she will fail...you will make sure of that. I just want to negotiate for her life and the lives of the women on those ships."

"Tou, I'm glad you have so much faith in me."

"Hasn't there been enough killing in the last eight years. Please give me a chance. I am a diplomat, let me do my job. If I fail, then you can do your job as a warrior."

"Tou..."

"Osguard, I can do this. Besides, what do we have to lose?"

"Tou..."

"I'll be in your office," Tou said, and then turned and exited the bridge.

"Tou...you crazy—" Sario caught himself and let his thoughts die in midstream. "Secure link, private mode and patch it into my office," he grunted to the communications officer.

"Kiza!"

***

"So Tou of Betli or should I call you Lermi of Betli," Kimlin's said through the link. The Artificial Intelligence (ARIT) projected a young brunette on the holographic view screen, fairly attractive, slim and no older than nineteen.

"Okay, you know who I am...so what?" Tou pushed with bitterness. "You're the twentieth person to claim the mantle of First Daughter of Gigantur since the Tuit Consortium self destructed eight years ago. How old were you then...ten...eleven?"

"It doesn't matter," Kimlin hissed, "I am the First Daughter now."

"Listen kid," Tou continued rebuffing Kimlin's claim, "You're way over your head on this one. Why don't you just calm down and let's talk about your future here."

"Lermi, your time on Earth has softened you. You were once a proud warrior sister, a command daughter of the fifth level. What happened to you?"

"My eyes were opened," Tou confessed. "After I escaped Earth and returned home, I learned of the treachery the Consortium's second daughter committed and of the blind stupidity of the First Daughter of Fire in leading us into war with USSTAP—"

"Lies...all lies," Kimlin screamed. "Miam was a great warrior who would have led us on to victory over the dogs of USSTAP and those damned Osguards, especially Michael Genesis." She then paused and squinted as if to beam her hatred through the link at Tou. "It was Tisha and that fumbling idiot, Rina of Jaywick that caused the Consortium to self-destruct. But you...you had a chance to bring us together and lead us when you returned. Instead you sided with our enemies and the lolwes they released. Why?"

"I told you, my eyes were opened. I no longer believed in what the Consortium was about or what they were doing. Besides, our hatred of USSTAP was based on a lie, on a misunderstanding, one born from stubbornness. Haven't you seen the HVP yet?"

"No," Kimlin bellowed, "and I won't. It's all lies. I believe the daughters and my ancestors, not some fairy tale made up by our sworn enemies."

"Kimlin," Tou pleaded, "Please don't be so blind, let me show you."

"No...you're responsible for too many of my sisters' death for me to listen to you now. In fact, I am here to carry out justice. You are a traitor to the Consortium and I hereby sentence you to death with the lolwes and dogs you have decided to lay down with."

Tou's eyes widen. She had lost the argument without even entering it. The fact that Kimlin knew her true identity threw her off her diplomatic game and bounced her onto her warrior backside. "Kimlin...Kimlin...what are you planning on doing?"

"Good-bye bitch!" Kimlin's projection then faded into smoke.

Tou slapped her communication collar, also known as CC, and screamed, "Now...now...now!"

***

With those words a circus of activity swirled like a tornado. The four USSTAP built ships slammed through the speed schedule in reverse, backing up from the fight at MOP two, disappearing from sight in a blink of an eye. The Tuit ships fired their shockdel plasma cannon at the echo, which was once Sario's fleet. At the same time, three USSTAP built galaxy cruisers, looking like black bats with red seams, popped out of stealth mode ten, negative one half on the galactic plane, under the Tuit ships and let loose a barrage of pagenay ray, kwainique gun and coronet cannon weapons fire on the Tuits' underside. The pagenay blue rays sliced through the blackness of space with the ferocity of a sun's energy, the kwainique gun, also known as K-gun, and the coronet cannons shot invisible balls of energy that ripped and shredded anything in its path like a bullet hitting a balloon.

Usually the Tuit ship's protective field would withstand such an assault, but its protective field was not as strong at the tribolemincic core energy converter that hung on the ventral side of the ship on the last third like a male appendage. The core needed the extra coldness of space to keep it within operating range. Additionally, if the core was placed inside the ship's hull it would contaminate the artificial atmosphere with abnormal radiation.

4

This was a weakness of all Tuit ships that they failed to or were unable to correct during eight years of battle.

The weapons fire created a red blotch on the protective field near the tribolemincic converters like a rash, weakening the protective field. After twenty seconds of the assault, the galaxy cruisers let loose six Asher torpedoes each. Asher torpedoes had nuclear-tipped warheads with the equivalent force of all three energy weapons put together. The Asher torpedoes were used less, because their energy did not dissipate with distance, as did the particle generator array, K-guns or cornet cannons. If the Asher torpedoes missed their targets, the resulting damage could be worse than intended. However, these javelins of death punched through the protective field at the red blotches and connected with the converters like wrecking balls. The missiles connected and the glass frame exploded with the force of an F-8 tornado. Faint orange mushroom clouds made a brief appearance before the vacuum of space swallowed them, taking the Tuit ships and their crew to the bowels of hell.

"Remind me to thank Michael Genesis for giving us the galaxy cruisers," Sario whispered to his Centurion of Operations."

"When you meet him, see if you can get some galaxy protectors for you and the other Osguards," his CO recommended with a smile of relief. "That should about round out the power needed to clean up space around here."

"I'll see what I can do," Sario huffed, sitting in his command chair. "Now see what you can do about rounding up the fleet, and getting those cruisers back in stealth mode, before we find ourselves staring down the barrel of another First Daughter of something."

"Kiza!"

Chapter 1—Like Father...Like Daughter

Michael David Genesis, the leader of the Universal Science, Security and Trade Association of Planets, sat in the command chair of his galaxy protector, the *Neraka*. The ever present burn in his hazel eyes was now accompanied by nearly three decades of experience, levied by war and diplomacy. He sported his boxer built muscular frame like a model. He was confident, strong and sturdy, exuding the mantle of leadership.

The *Neraka* was traveling back to Millmum Capitol Station, the seat of the Milky Way Galaxy and effectively all of USSTAP. The black slitanium coated ship sailed through space like a bat through the night. The engines that spread like wings were concave and ran the entire length of the ship on each side. The ship flared in the stern where it contained a launch and receiving bay for its space fighters and space transports. The bow was arrowhead shaped, which sat on top of a pear shaped bridge.

At first Osguards and Centurions sired these massive powerboats of the heavens. However, since the Tuit war Michael resurrected the guardian ranks of Nolvar, Solvar and Vanguard and ordained them to sire the galaxy protector fleet of starships. Along with the galaxy cruiser, star cruiser and star protector, the galaxy protector spread USSTAP influence throughout the Virgo Star Cluster as the acknowledged authority of the cosmos.

"Approaching Millmum Capitol Station," Major Jacoby announced from the pilot station.

"Thank you Major Jacoby. Proceed with standard docking procedures," Michael responded.

The sight of the majestic diamond station filling the view screen was like coming home to Michael. It gave him a feeling of familiarity...of warmth, but most of all, it gave him the feeling of security.

He watched as his crew performed the docking procedure without error and without interruption from him. In ten minutes, the gentle bump, signifying the docking to ring position one, vibrated throughout the ship. It was like a mother's kiss, welcoming her child back home. After sixth months on patrol, it was the warm kiss he missed.

The command bridge door slid open behind Michael and the Centurion of Medical Science, Michelle Katherine Genesis, his wife and mother to his three children stepped on deck.

"Osguard," she called, being as professional as possible as always.

"Yes, centurion," Michael said with a smile, standing and moving toward her.

"Well, we're home," she announced, stepping next to him.

"Yeah, I guess we are," he sighed. "You think Eddie missed us this time?"

Michelle shrugged her shoulders, "I hope so. But I'm sure our parents spoiled him to no end."

"Mom said they will meet us in our quarters on station," Michael said with a gleam in his eyes as he motioned to the view screen. "I can't wait to see him," he finished. Then he turned to Michelle, "Are you ready?"

"Hell yeah, I'm ready."

"Mitchell, you have the bridge. Standard debarkation," he told his Centurion of Operations, Mitchell Deacon.

"Tiah!" Mitchell responded, accepting the responsibility with inner glee.

Without further conversation, Michael and Michelle left the bridge and made their way to the ship's main exit. They emerged onto the docking port where Admiral Tirana Ritchen, his former Centurion of Operations and now the station's sire awaited them.

"Osguard," she called.

Michael and Michelle had already seen her and were gravitating toward her through the crowd of welcoming family members and friends. The debarkation process was orderly and efficient, considering the galaxy protector housed two thousand crewmembers. And for every crewmember, there was at least an average of three people waiting to see them. Some people exercised prudent judgment and opted to meet their loved ones somewhere other than the docking port, which thinned the crowd and accelerated the process. After fourteen years of doing this with the *Galaxy Protector Neraka* and fifteen years on the *Galaxy Cruiser Justice*, Michael had become use to the debarkation process, but the crowd was still a little unnerving.

"Osguard," Tirana called once more.

Michael and Michelle waded through the crowd, bumping shoulders, crushing arms and stepping on toes. Michael and Michelle raised their hands above their heads, so as not to accidentally touch anyone inappropriately.

Two minutes later, Michael and Michelle reached Tirana and with a simple head nod from Michael, they began their trek from the docking port toward their quarters. Soon they escaped the commotion as they wandered into the bowels of the station's passageways. The women flanked Michael, Tirana on the right and Michelle on the left.

"Osguard," Tirana said for the third time, "the unity chamber is just about ready. The technical team is running several last minute tests, but so far, everything checks out okay."

"Well, nice to see you too admiral," Michael teased. "How was my patrol, you ask? It was mostly uneventful. But there was this one planet in the Angel Solar System. I think we can…well you can read the report."

"Sorry sire. I'm just so excited about Unity. It has to be the biggest thing that has ever happened in USSTAP in over one hundred universal years."

"Maybe," Michael said, trying to hide his doubt.

They approached the coaster doors. The ARIT sensed their presence and signaled for the closest coaster to answer their request. Two seconds later the doors opened and they stepped in.

"Deck L–one," Michelle ordered, usurping any attempt of Tirana's to abscond with her husband. Michael smiled, approving Michelle's show of authority over the situation.

The doors whispered shut, and the low hum of the coaster filled the air as it floated on the electromagnetic coils through vacuum tubes led by the station's ARIT transportation management system.

"Well," Tirana continued, "the Chaktun Science Academy did a wonderful job with the unity chamber. Our technology team thinks the unity chamber will be the most unifying piece of equipment since the gate portal."

"How about the galaxy protector?" Michelle shot back.

"Don't get me wrong, Michelle," Tirana rebounded. "The galaxy protector is probably the most important technology ever invented to keep the peace. But I'm talking about unifying the universe. I'm talking about instantaneous communications, not just from galaxy to galaxy, but from galactic cluster to galactic cluster. That is what I mean. Communication is the key to understanding, and understanding is the key to unification. This is the first time ever we will be able to communicate with all six known clusters."

"Slow down, Tirana…slow down," Michelle surrendered. "I understand what you mean, now!"

"Okay. I understand as well," Michael intervened. "What time is the first unification chamber meeting?" The authoritative voice of a leader resounded in his question.

"Thirty-eight universal hours," Tirana responded.

The coaster stopped and the doors jetted opened. "Deck L–one," the ARIT announced.

"I'll inspect the unity chamber in fifteen universal hours," Michael told Tirana. "I've used this technology several times before, but that was with the virtual conference chamber chair…and I'll tell you, that took some getting used to. I'm sure there are some quirks in this update." Michael added with some pain in his voice.

"Tiah!" Tirana snapped.

Content that his wishes were understood, Michael and Michelle stepped out of the coaster toward their quarters. "Later!" and the doors closed behind them.

The decks that housed the living quarters were absent the artistic collage that the rest of the station boasted. There were no combat operations painted on the wall, no starships in battle, or weapons garnished. The coloring was lighter and livelier…more of an off white pastel coloring. Psychologically, it helped shake off the strain of work, and stripped the darkness of space from the soul.

To Michael, it meant he was closer to seeing his seven-year-old son, Edward Samuel Genesis, who they named after his first Centurion of Operations and confidant, Eduardo Sanchez. Eduardo died in the great battle of the First Universal War with the Kulusks nine universal years ago, and both Michael and Michelle thought naming their son after him was the greatest way to honor his memory.

Michael and Michelle entered their quarters just in time to see Eddie race across the room. Eddie was heading to his grandfather, but the door opening caught his attention and he stopped in mid-stride. He whipped his head around to see who had entered. He sported hazel eyes and dark auburn hair like all of the Osguards. His face was a miniature copy of his grandfather's, Michael's father, Parker Genesis. Michael always felt a pinch of jealousy that his son did not come out like a carbon copy of him, but in reality, his oldest daughter Sharyla did favor him the most, which lessen the sting a bit.

Eddie's eyes widened and a huge smile flashed on his face. With a wide receivers speed and timing, Eddie turned on a dime and ran straight to them screaming, "Mommy…Daddy, you're home!" With ape like agility he leaped up between them, falling into the warmth of their arms, followed by kisses and tears of a joyous reunion.

***

Sharyla Genesis, Michael's oldest daughter, sat at her desk onboard Searcy Capitol Station. She had grown into a beautiful young woman with the slim physique of a model. Her shoulder length curly auburn hair was almost crimson in color. She wore it loosely over her forehead, which brilliantly accented her hazel eyes and slender eyebrows. Her copper tone skin was radiant. She projected an air of regal authority.

She took a deep breath and thought she could smell the paint drying. The station was so new. Recently built as part of her father's expansion plan, Searcy Capitol Station was now the seat of power of the newly admitted Searcy Galaxy, some two point two million light years from Millmum Capitol Station…a place she considered home for the first eighteen years of her life. Now Sharyla was the twenty-three-year-old Osguard of Searcy Galaxy, Osguard One Hundred and Twenty-One. She was the first second generation Osguard to be installed, her sister Kashara was the second.

As Michael's daughters, much was expected of them, especially from her as the oldest. This was a mantle she did not want, but proudly accepted. Since her graduation from USSTAP Academy and her internship with her Uncle Shawn, she had grown into the reality of being an Osguard. Now she was responsible for over sixty-five thousand light years of space, containing two hundred inhabitant planets. Constant diplomacy and attention was the order of the day to keep the new members of USSTAP happy.

As she blew out a mighty cleansing huff, her door chime rang. "Right on time," she murmured. She straightened her uniform jacket; tussled with the ARIT flimsies on her desk and then responded, "Enter."

The diamond shaped door swooshed open revealing the large frame of the Chief Ambassador of Searcy Galactic Congress, Rotarian from Ogeaca. The Ogeacans were hairless and dark in coloring. Rotarian was no exception. The missing eyebrows were a little disconcerting to Sharyla, but after two months she was adjusting.

"Madam Osguard," Rotarian said in his best Chaktun.

"Just Osguard, Chief Ambassador Rotarian," she responded in the politest tone she could muster, hiding her irritation of constantly correcting him on this subject every time they met.

"Of course," Rotarian squealed back as he entered her office.

"What can I do for you, Chief Ambassador Rotarian," she pushed.

Rotarian moved to the seat opposite Sharyla and sat down with force.

Sharyla imagined the chair screaming underneath the enormous weight, and cracked a small smile.

"Madam Osguard," he roared, "I thought it my duty to bring to your attention the ramblings of the Congress."

Sharyla cringed, but kept her diplomatic smile.

After a pregnant pause, Rotarian continued, "Several planets want to leave the association."

"Oh! Sharyla whispered. "How many is several?"

"Eight, I believe at last count."

"Did the representatives give a reason?"

"Yes, Madam Osguard they did."

His tone told Sharyla he was proud of this information knife he was twisting in her gut.

"They feel they have been duped," he explained.

Sharyla remained quiet, not showing that he had hit a nerve.

"They feel like they have fallen prey to your father's empire building."

Sharyla wanted to scream. *Empire building...what the hell do you mean by empire building?* But she elected to remain silent and let Rotarian play all his cards.

Rotarian cleared his throat; showing annoyance that hadn't gotten a reaction from Sharyla. After another uncomfortable pause, he continued, "When USSTAP invited us into the association; it seemed like a stroke of luck. USSTAP offered this great pact, sharing information, technology and mutual defense, giving our governments the much needed opportunity to concentrate on its people; giving our governments the economic freedom to develop and grow...all for a measly ten percent of the trading profits that transverse the gate portal system."

"That's right," Sharyla responded. "It was an offer...one that the worlds of your galaxy gladly accepted and one that they can freely walk away from with no obligation from either party for the next five universal years. But how is this related to empire building?"

"After the war with the Tuits, your father began his quest for expansion in this galactic cluster. Prior to that, USSTAP had sixty galaxies under their sphere of influence, thirty that were indoctrinated under your father's watch. Since then, seventy-five new galaxies and dozens of satellite galaxies have joined USSTAP in the last eight universal years, including the

Searcy galaxy, bringing USSTAP's strength to over one hundred and thirty five galaxies."

He leaned over and resumed speaking, this time with a more diplomatic tone. "Additionally, the Osguard family expanded to over one hundred and twenty-six with the finding of the Ancestral Matriarchs' adopted lineage and lost lineage of Earth. And the First Osguard, like a dictator, has placed each and every one of the Osguards as the leader of each of the galaxies instead of appointing citizens from those galaxies."

"All which was part of the package," Sharyla insisted.

"Yes, it was understood that way," he testified. "But now you are in negotiations with the former galactic star clusters of the Tuit Empire and others who what to shamefully model their new regime after USSTAP."

"That's right…model, not join," Sharyla reminded Rotarian.

"What do you call the Guardian Supreme Council?" he quipped.

Sharyla paused for a second, realizing she wasn't going to win this debate, but knew she had to engage in it anyway. "The Guardian Supreme Council is the organizational body where all the Osguards and our counterparts in the five other galactic clusters meet to discuss the events and issues common to all, including trade agreements between the clusters." She leaned back in her chair, watching for Rotarian's facial expression as she spoke. "Besides, every galaxy, including this one has four representatives in the Universal Conclave."

"That's not the point," Rotarian countered. "The point is…the Guardian Supreme Council gives the appearance that USSTAP is running things, especially if your father is appointed as the head of the Guardian Supreme Council." Rotarian leaned back and shifted in his seat, crossed his legs and clasped his hands together in front of him. "What will that make it, seven hundred…eight hundred some odd galaxies he will have influence over? I call that empire building!"

Sharyla smiled and shook her head with the polite tone of a diplomat, "First of all, Chief Ambassador Rotarian, I don't see what that has to do with planets in this galaxy requesting to severe with the association. Second, my father is not interested in the office. Third, being a member of the association does not delete a government's sovereignty. And finally, there are some eight hundred planetary and ten galactic governments in Rojam Os, our own galactic cluster, that aren't a member of the association and we seem to coexist with no trouble. If planets from this galaxy, or if the entire galaxy, wants to secede from our pact, I will not stand in the way. I just hope it is for a real reason and not some imaginary excuse in which I dare say you may have given life to."

A frown appeared on Rotarian's face, "What do you mean by that?"

Sharyla stood, slipped from behind her desk and moved toward the door, "It is no secret that the Ogeacan government is upset that their nominee wasn't selected to be one of the four representatives to the Universal Conclave. And I suspect the planets discussing secession are members or former members of the Ogeacan Republic."

Rotarian huffed in disgust as he stood. His eyes betrayed his culpability in her statement. "You're very perceptive, Osguard," he admitted.

"If the Ogeacan government wants to leave, then so be it," she snapped.

After a few seconds of contemplation, Rotarian formed the words Sharyla knew he wanted to say when he first came in. "If the Ogeacan government doesn't have a voice in the new organization of galactic clusters, we will leave USSTAP."

"That's too bad, Chief Ambassador," I wish you the best of luck. I will not hesitate to sign your requests for secession when you present them. Just remember, the trading and economic ties you have formed with other galaxies and the two you have formed with governments in the Tuit and Gigantur Galactic Star Clusters will be hard to execute without gate portal travel. But, the Ogeacans are an ingenious bunch, I'm sure you will figure out a way." Sharyla moved to open the door. "Good day, Chief Ambassador."

Rotarian paused for a moment, staring into her eyes. She knew he was looking for a sign...something to signify she was bluffing. But she stood strong and resolved, because she wasn't bluffing.

Rotarian grunted, shook his head in disgust and as he walked past her and out the door, he murmured, "You'll be sorry, Madam Osguard. You'll be sorry."

***

One point three million light years away, on McNor Capitol Station, Kashara Genesis was sparing with Chief Ambassador of McNor, Castille Ettuma in the training room. Both ladies exhibited the grace and speed of gazelles, while maintaining the ferocity of lions on the prowl. Kashara was half a shade darker than her sister, Sharyla. She had broad shoulders, muscular arms and the toned legs of a swimmer's physique. She sported her short cropped auburn hair and hazel eyes like a badge identifying her as an Osguard. Ettuma had bluish gray skin. Her silky black hair was tied back in a pony tail and her eyes were like black coal which matched her black lips. She was slinky, but toned with long arms and long legs.

They were practicing the fighting technique from Ettuma's home planet of Shellamna called Kiruta. Kashara fell in love with the fighting skill when she took over as the Osguard for McNor Galaxy two months ago from Vanguard Husoma. Ettuma, who was a ninth degree master at the form agreed to teach her. Although, they were still at level one, Kashara was advancing through the lessons at a very fast clip. Kashara had already mastered Sixana fighting form from Chaktun, which allowed her to meld and fold her abilities into Kiruta.

Sweat glistened on her face as Kashara pushed and swiped her blows toward Ettuma. Ettuma slipped, ducked and blocked Kashara's attack, accept for one blow. A backhand slap caught Ettuma in the throat, knocking her off balance. She quickly screamed, "Halt!"

Kashara stopped in midstream of delivering an elbow to the jaw and backed away. "Are you okay," she asked.

"Yes, I'm quite okay," Ettuma winced. "That was a pretty good shot…unexpected I might add. It isn't a move I taught you."

"No, it isn't."

"It isn't Sixana either, is it?"

"No, it isn't," Kashara admitted. "It is something I picked up from a movie I saw on Earth some years back. It is a move from a fighting form called Krav Maga. It's an Israeli Self-Defense technique. It is quite effective.

"Do you know this Krav Maga?"

"I know some moves, but I wasn't trained in it. I just picked some of the moves up watching movies."

"I see," Ettuma pushed with some uneasiness. "Do you think I could see some of these movies? I would like to judge this form for myself."

Kashara glanced at the time piece on the wall. "Sure, I have some movies and a DVD player in my room. Just let me know when. But for now, I have to end our session and get ready for Unity."

"Fine, I will call you when you are back. But before you leave, can I speak to you about something."

"Sure Castille, what can I do for you?" Kashara offered as she walked to the side chair. She picked up a towel and wiped the sweat off her face. Ettuma followed, grabbing the other towel.

"McNor is relatively new to the association," Ettuma started. "As you know, we've only been part USSTAP for four universal years."

Kashara nodded.

"Well this unification with the former Tuit Consortium is quite exciting to us, but also a little bit frightening."

"To me too," Kashara interjected.

"Well anyway, word is coming to us that some of the association members are against this and are threatening to leave the association."

"Yeah, there are a few planets that feel this unification is an error in judgment," Kashara acknowledged. "But they are wrong. This unification is needed to keep peace among the stars."

"I couldn't agree with you more. That's why I just want to assure you that all the members from this Galaxy are behind this endeavor. However…" The pause was deafening. "…we are worried about exactly what type of vision USSTAP is building."

"What do you mean?" Kashara threw her towel back on the chair and started walking towards the locker room.

Ettuma threw her towel down and began walking with Kashara. "Others, outside our galaxy, are pushing rumors that your father is in the midst of empire building. That he is trying to become the King of the Universe."

"Not so," Kashara defended. "My father, the other Osguards and I are only trying to build peace through mutual support. The Tuit war was a nasty war, billions of lives were lost and the entire Eierre race was wiped out in the Siryman galaxy. That kind of devastation is mind blowing." She stopped at the locker room doorway. "We are trying to make sure this doesn't happen again."

"I know," Ettuma continued. "But how can you assure peace in six galactic clusters when your own home world is filled with war, famine, pain, suffering and diseases...all which the Osguards profess as things they are here to wipe out; and the main reason for the unification efforts."

"I don't get your point."

"If you Osguards were truly interested in universal peace and not empire building, then you would start at home...wouldn't you?"

"Earth is a complicated matter," Kashara expressed, lowering her head to hide her eyes.

"Osguard, you don't believe that for a moment," Ettuma pushed. "I can hear it in your voice, even though you shield your eyes from me." Ettuma took a deep breath and let out a loud sigh. "Look, I don't know what the reason is for you Osguards to keep your own home world in the dark ages, but my advice to you is if you want this unification with the former Tuit Consortium to work you're going to have to do something about this complicated matter called Earth."

"What do you mean?" Kashara raised her head and shot a challenging look at Ettuma.

"Look, I am not your enemy," Ettuma assured her. "We of the McNor Congress believe in what you say USSTAP stands for. I'm just saying, until you take care of Earth, you will have the accusation that your father is Empire building for his own devilish purposes rather than for the mutual support and peace. It just looks funny that he works so hard for peace in the universe while he stands idle and lets his home world go down the toilet. I implore you to talk to your father and the other Osguards. Let them know that good intentions start at home first."

"Why do you care on how we are dealing with Earth?"

"I don't care how you deal with Earth." Ettuma entered the locker room and looked around the place to make sure they were alone. "If you want governments of all these different planets, which are as different as the sands on a beach, to follow you, then you have to lead by example with your own planet."

"Like I said, Earth is a complicated matter," Kashara tried to explain. "First it is the home planet of the original sixty Osguards, but it is only a protectorate of USSTAP, not a member. The governments of Earth do not know of USSTAP's existence."

"Why?"

"It's complicated."

"Keep telling yourself that Osguard…keep telling yourself that. Then tell me how that's working for you," Ettuma preached as she stepped over to her locker. The words died in the air as silence consumed the conversation.

Moments later, as they stepped towards the showers, Kashara admitted with some trepidation, "There is wisdom in your words, Ettuma. I will broach the subject with my father. But I have to let Unity play out some before I do," Kashara delivered as a peace offering.

"Don't wait too long my friend. Unity may play out the wrong way if you do."

"I won't," Kashara pledged. "I will broach the subject as soon as I can. I promise."

Chapter 2—Report on USSTAP

"This is Janine Lenex reporting from Millmum Capitol Station for Rojam News Service," the reporter said into the holovidcam (HVC) from the reception hall. Her image and voice were being beamed through gate portal technology into trillions of homes and offices in the Rojam Os galactic cluster—over a hundred galaxies. Janine had sparkling eyes and a dazzling smile, which made her the perfect pitch person for the galactic cluster news service. "This is the eve of the special meeting of Unity to vote on the Collective USSTAP Charter. After nearly one hundred and twenty-five universal years since its inception, USSTAP is about to spread its influence outside our own galactic cluster unto five other galactic clusters; making USSTAP quantifiably the closest economic and security utopia known to man. USSTAP will regulate the peaceful trade amongst the planets in its sphere of influence while maintaining the mutual security pact of all signatories."

"For our new viewers out there, who don't know much about USSTAP, can you explain a little bit more on what you mean?" Karuno, the commentator in the studio office, requested as scripted.

"Of course Karuno," Janine beamed into the HVC. "But first, let me assure the citizens of the new signatories to USSTAP that each planet maintains its sovereignty. USSTAP does not police or occupy any land, their domain is open space."

"That's good to know, but what about the trade you mentioned earlier?" Karuno pushed, trying to get Janine back on script.

"Yes...yes...of course Karuno. Trade is based on one planet's abundant waste being another planet's rare commodity. For instance, on the planet Katolo in the Axer galaxy gold and silver are considered waste products and diamonds are deemed a rare expensive commodity. On Sraku in the Navain galaxy the opposite is true, gold and silver are rare commodities, and diamonds are the abundant commodity. Therefore, these planets trade using USSTAP as the honest broker. In return USSTAP receives a cut of the trade. This type of trade helps retrieve the necessary goods for production and upkeep of USSTAP personnel, ships and stations. Since USSTAP owns the technology and operates the galactic gate portal, which we all know makes travel between galaxies and travel from one part of a galaxy to another through inner space possible, they own the trigger to the galactic stock market. All signatories are briefed on all transactions, scientific discoveries; and are allowed to have their citizens join the ranks of USSTAP. In fact the citizens of their own galaxy man and command each star precinct, star station and all ships, except the capitol stations and Osguardian flagships. Hopefully the charter will bring this sort of arrangement to our cousins in the other galactic clusters abroad, which will increase the trade, ensure economic stability and strengthen our mutual resolve for peaceful coexistence."

"What about USSTAP's economic structure?" Karuno asked according to the script.

"The inner working of USSTAP's economic structure is also intriguing. It is a true blend of a militaristic organization and civilian freedom. Through various methods and options, USSTAP provides food, shelter, clothes, medical care, dental care, education, training, and free transportation to its members and their families, according to their family size, rank and position within USSTAP. However, some complain the system reeks of socialism, which would not sit well with the capitalist barons in our universe. Congruent to a true socialist system, USSTAP personnel receive pay, in the form of USSTAP credit, again according to their position or rank in USSTAP.

"Can you explain more about this credit? Is it hard currency or just an I.O.U.?"

"USSTAP credit, UC for short, is not hard currency, but is a valuable commodity that can be traded for goods and services within USSTAP shops and stores. When outside the USSTAP sphere, the UC can be exchanged for hard currency of different governments based on that planet's exchange rate, enabling USSTAP personnel to purchase goods and services outside

USSTAP. Then that government would use the UC to pay for taxes, goods and services when dealing with USSTAP."

"To some, the system is too sterile. Critics say it inhibits creativity and competition, because everything, all inventions and all technical discoveries, spring from USSTAP," Karuno questioned, going off script to provide some competitive dialogue.

"Of course, the thousands of signatory planets in USSTAP operate their own economic system, which in most cases encouraged creativity and corporate competition and give rise to new inventions and technical discoveries, which they gladly share with USSTAP—for a price." Janine was now winging it from her notes, while keeping her perky professional smile. "The targeted result of this arrangement is that with USSTAP providing universal security, the signatory planets concentrate more of their resources on their people, infrastructure and economy, allowing them to grow and thrive at a faster pace. Thus there is an uncanny balance in the universe, an unexplained harmony in which USSTAP is the catalyst."

"How does Michael Genesis fit into all this?" Karuno asked, getting back on script.

"Under the leadership of First Osguard Michael David Genesis, USSTAP has gone from a strong economic power to one of almost sovereign proportions. After Lt Osguard Ortho Chting's death, the Osguard Michael Genesis pushed the Mosleck solution, protected the universe against incursions from radicals, saved his home planet Earth, defended USSTAP against the Kulusk Empire and fought off the Tuit Empire, making invaluable allies of all his adversaries in the end.

"You mentioned USSTAP as almost a sovereign entity. What about it? Do the Osguards see USSTAP as a government?" Karuno pushed seeding the waves with controversy.

Janine had to drop her notes and go on memory from her crash course on USSTAP politics she received two months ago. "Remember, USSTAP has no land, planet or territory. However, they do patrol opens area of space as if it is their territory. So, I can see why some may think of USSTAP as a government. But no, the Osguards don't think of USSTAP as a government, but as an organization with a mission. The Osguards are the executive branch of the organization in charge of overseeing the seven primary corps of that organization; operations, security, engineering, diplomatic, economic, science and medical. Each galaxy has a policy branch, called a galactic congress, containing ambassadors from every planet in that galaxy, which is led by a chief ambassador. The Osguard Senate, which is made up of all the Osguards, is one of the policy branches for USSTAP as a whole. Osguard Michael Genesis as the First Osguard chairs the Osguard Senate. The Star Parliament, formally known as the Universal Parliament is the other USSTAP policy branch. It contains ambassadors from each of the planets in all one-hundred and thirty-five galaxies. It is controlled by a Prime Ambassador. The Senate and the Parliament act as checks and balances; ensuring the mission of USSTAP is not inadvertently or purposely corrupted by any single person or agenda."

"Janine, can you tell us about the Collective USSTAP Charter?" Karuno returned to the script as suggested by her producer.

"Now the question is can Osguard Michael Genesis and the other Osguards do it again? Can they make invaluable allies of what's left of the once treacherous and evil Tuit Consortium? The Collective USSTAP Charter is an agreement that will model the remnants of the Tuit Consortium after USSTAP. Several details need to be worked out and that is why this historic event will occur tomorrow, where all of the Osguards and four select ambassadors from each galaxy will meet in a virtual setting projected by ARIT sensors and gate portal technology, called Unity. Unity is the creation of Chaktun scientist Mezhak Zyder. The objective of tomorrow's meeting is to discuss and possibly vote on a trade agreement and a mutual security pact between the galactic clusters. This is very ambitious and I must say unbelievable."

"I'll say," Karuno added in a huff. "I know you will keep us informed during this historic event."

"Yes, I will, and let me say what a pleasure it is to be here and witnessing this live…well almost live. The virtual meeting will be streamed to us and we will present it as we get it to our viewers. Reporting live from Millmum Capitol Station, I am Janine Lenex for Rojam News Service."

***

Michael turned off his holovidpic projector in his office after hearing Janine Lenex describe thirty years of his life and what USSTAP stood for in a thirty-second sound bite. He shook his head knowing that what she just said will cause more debate than he was ready to engage in. The entire episode with the Collective USSTAP Charter was growing into a monster he didn't know if he could control. Thinking about it caused his head to hurt.

He grabbed two aspirin from a bottle in his desk drawer, popped them in his mouth and washed them down with a sip from a cold cup of coffee that had occupied his desk for the last three hours. Then he leaned back in his chair and closed his eyes. He needed to push tomorrow's events from his mind and get on with what he needed to do today.

After a few seconds relaxing he popped up in a sitting position and picked up the ARIT flimsy on his desk. It was the personnel file on the new Earth General of the World, also known as the GOW. General Lo had retired to Beijing and the Galactic Congress appointed General Ahmad Yousef, the first Iranian recruited into USSTAP as his replacement. Ironically, his first day as the Earth GOW was tomorrow, when Michael was schedule to be in the Unity Chamber; so he would be unable to preside over Ahmad's 'Take Command' ceremony as protocol dictated. Therefore, he needed to record a message for Ahmad to hear on his first day as GOW.

The misguided slight of the appointment was not lost on Michael. Michael knew the Congress was testing the governments of Earth by appointing Ahmad, but he had a feeling they were also testing him, knowing the political relationship between Iran and the United States was tenuous at best. Congress was testing whether his loyalty was with USSTAP or the United States. The funny thing was that Michael was so removed from Earth's politics that his loyalty should have never been in question. Michael applauded the appointment, because he too wanted Earth governments tested.

After a few minutes of contemplation, Michael combed his hair, straightened his uniform jacket and clicked his ARIT recorder.

"Begin recording.
To: General Ahmad Yousef, Earth General of the World.
From: Michael D. Genesis, Osguard; Millmum Galaxy
Reference: Governing expectations
Universal Date: 11.10.48264

Dear General Yousef,
Congratulations on your appointment as World General of Earth. It is a great honor, which is well deserved. As it is my tradition for any command activation, I would like to share my governing expectations for you.

Following the Tuit War, USSTAP established covert economic, technological and medical support to Earth, through the auspices of the planet's United Nations. At the insistence of the Osguard Senate, I arranged for this special support to be regulated by a unique group whose members included the former leaders of the United States, Russia, China and England. The former president of the United States, Frederick Walter Peters led this clandestine group through a non-profit organization called Guardian's Gate. Peters' office is in the Cochran Building, in Richmond VA, the same building that houses the main offices of Unlimited Associations. As you well know, Unlimited Associations is the cover for USSTAP on Earth.

However, to my disappointment, Guardian's Gate has failed to bolster the economic infrastructure of the 'so-called' third world nations of Latin America, Africa and Indonesia, as they agreed. Guardian's Gate has facilitated fourteen medical facilities in the U.S.; three in England; twenty in Russia; and twelve in China. There are none anywhere else.

Because of this, I asked Anthony Musoto, who is the FBI Director, thanks to the present president, George Willis, to investigate and question why Guardian's Gate failed to bolster infrastructure parity in the third world nations.

Musoto reported Peters gave several reasons for the inconsistency. First, Peters claims that anytime Guardian's Gate moves to push USSTAP technology in medicine by building hospitals or hospices; the local politicians, leaders or whoever is in charge want the construction to go to the local workers and the jobs to go to the local community. Peters blames USSTAP for tying their hands, by requiring only USSTAP personnel to do the construction, and to operate the hospitals and hospices. The Millmum Galactic Congress placed this requirement in affect because of security. The nature of our technology needs to remain secret.

Peters claims that pushing USSTAP technology would take more than political favors; it would take bribes and kickbacks. Guardian's Gate doesn't have the finances or the permission from USSTAP to do so. Also Guardian's Gate doesn't have permission to reveal USSTAP's existence outside the U.N. Security Council. Peters concludes that having USSTAP technology to dispense without the world knowing where it comes from is impossible. He claims the situation makes Guardian's Gate's effort all a cloak and dagger game that USSTAP doesn't understand.

Peters' second excuse is that the Middle East is too unstable, North Korea is too crazy, South America is too corrupt and Africa is too needy. They all wanted something other than what was being offered to them. They didn't jump at the chance to field medical care and feed their poverty-stricken population, even when Guardian's Gate tried to push it under the auspices of the U.N. Security Council. Because of this, according to Peters, Guardian's Gate's efforts just became a political quagmire and a public affairs' nightmare.

Peters' final excuse is that even in the areas where they were able to do business; they had to deal with organized crime, street gangs, drug cartels and terrorists. These entities sabotaged, blackmailed, blocked and even stole from Guardian's Gate.

Overall, I consider the initial agreement with Guardian's Gate as a small test to see if Earth was ready for inclusion into the universal family. It was a chance for Earth to become a trading partner with other worlds. It was a chance for Earth to experience new sources of energy and unheard of natural resources; to use new technology to improve living and provide renaissance education to improve their minds...all they had to do was clean up their act. This was the best opportunity USSTAP could have given Earth to prove that their people were worthy to be included into USSTAP.

With that said, my governmental expectation for you is to evaluate Peters' claims. If there is truth to his claims, I need you to work with Guardian's Gate to overcome these issues. If there is no validity to the claims, I want you to prepare a report for the Galactic Congress with a recommendation on how to proceed. Even though I have my own thoughts on how to proceed, this is your command and I will abide by your recommendation. Your job is tough. You are a diplomat to a world that doesn't even know we exist. Stealth is your shield and secrecy is your only weapon.

Good luck general and once again congratulations on your appointment.

Michael D. Genesis
Osguard, Millmum Galaxy
End recording."

Chapter 3 — Unity Room

Millmum Capitol Station's newest room lay at the core of the station. It was the diamond shaped unity room, where ARIT-Gate Portal technology allowed its occupants to commune and interact in a virtual world called Unity. Unlike the old conference chamber, which looked like a gas chamber, each unity room contained five pressure point beds that inserted into a tubular white ARIT-Gate Portal sleeve. Each ARIT-Gate Portal sleeve looked like a transparent Magnetic Resonance Imaging (MRI) machine.

Four of the five stations were for the galactic ambassadors. The fifth was for the galactic Osguard. The ambassadors, whether elected by popular vote or appointed by key governments, represented the four corners of the galaxy. There was a unity room in each galactic capitol station throughout the six galactic star clusters.

Inside the room, the familiar white-light of inner-space washed the area. Soon, a tall shadow formed within the light. The light faded as the invisible door slammed shut leaving Michael standing on the small platform. For security reasons, gate portal transfer was the only way in or out of the room.

"Good morning, Osguard," the gate portal operator greeted.

"Good morning, Riley," Michael responded, priding himself on the fact he knew almost everyone stationed at Millmum.

By the large smile on Riley's face, Michael knew this little interaction made the lieutenant's day. With a head nod, Michael stepped off the gate portal platform, and moved toward the round conference table in the center of the room. Besides the five chambers and conference table in the giant room, the room housed ten technicians sitting at various monitoring stations…two for each chamber. Riley's station doubled as the chief monitor's station. He greeted his technicians with a smile.

He stood in front of the smoky brown table, made of special polished polymers, with a feeling of dread resonating in his soul. Suddenly the gate portal light illuminated the room again. First Ambassador Byal Vren, a

Mosleck, stepped out of innerspace. Byal was one of Misul Rafinel's protégés, and when Michael killed Rafinel in that first battle after the awakening, Byal became Ralinget's right hand man. For years Michael and Byal stared each other down across the void of war, engulfed in a political quagmire, which left a stain of hatred in his heart, that now he fought with all his might to control. Byal was the last of the Mosleck Reclamation Order leaders left to sign the Mosleck Reformation Act, which resettled the entire Mosleck population to the Hustain moon after USSTAP terraformed it for human life.

Michael gave Byal a stern look of disgust and swallowed hard as he stepped off the gate portal platform. In all his life, he never thought he would be in the same room with Byal again. One of the stipulations of the reformation act was that no Mosleck Reclamation Order leader would ever hold elective or appointed office in the USSTAP organization or a position in the new Mosleck government. No one ever expected a need for an ambassador outside the USSTAP organization. Furthermore, Michael never thought the people would elect Byal as that ambassador.

Byal walked to his designated spot at the conference table and sat down, without acknowledging Michael.

The gate portal illuminated again, and the second ambassador to arrive entered the room. It was the ambassador from Kulusk, Finizackul Systik. Michael didn't know him personally, but he did know that Systik was a member of Kie Ritchen's Tonja. And since the Osguards were instrumental in the civil war that brought down Kie's regime, he knew there was no love lost between them.

Systik moved to his position at the table, with a smile that Michael deciphered as phonier than a used car salesman's pitch.

Once more the illumination swallowed up the room. The third ambassador stepped out of the light. It was the ambassador from Hustain, Jeiop Jeiopa. He was a mystery to Michael. Jeiopa had never crossed Michael's radar, no political affiliation to any government or domain within the galaxy, no business ties with USSTAP, and certainly no connection to the scientific or technological community. He was a true enigma that frightened Michael. At least with the others, he had some background to base his distrust, but with Jeiopa he had none. However, he still distrusted Jeiopa.

Michael plastered his most diplomatic smile as he watched Jeiopa move into position. Before Jeiopa could sit down, the light once more illuminated.

The final ambassador to arrive was Rillon Osguard, the younger brother of the Chaktun Maxum, Reppus Osguard. Michael first met him during the awakening, when Rillon was a seven year-old brat still playing with his toys. But even then, there was something still a bit unsettling about him. Michael thought it had something to do with Rillon's mother, then the

Chaktun Maxim, now the Grand Maxim. She doted over Rillon with sickly motherly love, which in turned made Rillon a weird little boy. Now that weird little boy was an even weirder grown man, wearing the mantle of Millmum Ambassador to the USSTAP Conclave.

As Rillon moved to his position, at the conference table, Michael wondered, *what the hell did I do to deserve this?*

Michael sat down, and after a few moments of false platitude to his fellow unity chamber occupants, pressed a series of pressure plate buttons and listened for a chime.

"Millmum Osguard checking in," he announced.

"Voice identification verified," the ARIT responded, "good morning Osguard.

One by one, the ambassadors checked in and received the same verification check from the ARIT. Then the ARIT informed them, "Please standby for conference."

Before long, miniature holographic images of Osguards Angela Santos and Stelana Rican, sitting behind their respective desks appeared in front of them in the middle of the table. The image rotated allowing each person to achieve momentary eye contact with the holographic figures.

Angela was the first to speak, "Good day Osguards and ambassadors, I am Angela Santos, Osguard for the Zincamin Galaxy."

"And I am Stelana Rican, Osguard for the Barrylum Galaxy," Stelana added.

"In about ten minutes," Angela continued, "we will use the unity chambers, which will connect our consciousness to the new Osguards and ambassadors of Tuit, Gigantur, Neant au Zar, Vergani Ur Fadin and Provello Galactic Clusters into the virtual ARIT world known as Unity. Stelana and I, along with the Diplomatic Corps, have worked diligently for the last four universal years to draft the Collective USSTAP Constitution, the CUC."

"And we believe," Stelana began, "that the CUC is the best comprehensive document that ties our USSTAP, with the former galactic star clusters of the Tuit Consortium. All of you have had ample opportunity to review the document and hopefully, we have answered all your questions and have faithfully represented your interests as leaders of the original USSTAP."

Michael studied each ambassador's face. He was searching for a sign…a sign that would betray their true intentions. But all he saw were attentive and almost enthusiastic faces. This should have quelled the uneasiness that clouded his stomach, but it didn't.

"Our job," Stelana continued, "is to ratify the CUC. The ambassadors of the conclave will vote first. And if the CUC passes with a three-fourths majority vote in the conclave, it will then go to the Guardian

Supreme Council for the final vote. There it needs another three fourths majority vote for ratification."

"Afterwards," Angela began, switching dialogue like a well oiled news team, "all the Osguards from Rojam Os, Tuit, Gigantur, Neant au Zar, Vergani Ur Fadin and Provello will appoint a president for the Guardian Supreme Council from amongst the members."

Michael noticed a mischievous smug look on Rillon's face as Angela was speaking about the president's position. It was like Angela hit a cord, which he was keeping a secret about. Michael's intuition kicked into high gear, wondering about what Rillon was up to. He knew that Rillon, and by default, Reppus, didn't agree that the council needed a president. They insisted that the council be subjugated to the conclave or better yet, vote a special panel of ambassadors from the conclave to oversee the supreme council. However, the guardians of all six galactic clusters rejected this objection. It almost became the point of contention that kept the CUC as an inspiring idea instead of the exciting reality that was knocking on the door today.

However, if he had enough votes to kill the CUC and recommend an amendment in favor of either of his ideas, then there would be a stalemate in the new organization before it even breathed life.

"Now," Angela said with glee, "it is time for us to make history. Please change into your chamber suits and enter your unity chambers and I will see you in person...well sort of."

***

Chaktun Science Academy sat on the southern most edge of the planet's main continent. A lush rainforest and the smooth aqua blue waters of the Merrimack Ocean surrounded it. The octagonal building was five acres of polished stone, smooth metal and lustrous glass that reached into the heavens, twenty-five stories high. White polished stone pillars that spanned the full height of the building engulfed all eight sides, dominating the exterior like gods holding open the gates to paradise. The building housed the best minds the planet had to offer. Multiple laboratories sprinkled each floor and each section testing technological, medical and scientific theories.

In unity lab fifteen, on the fifth floor facing the Merrimack Ocean the shadow of a lone figure lurked in the dim light. The shadow was confined to a Medical Artificial Intelligence (MARIT) wheelchair and wore a red metal mask that covered the left side of his face. The eye, nose and mouth slits were jagged, giving the impression of the devil's spawn. The uncovered side gave way to a dark man with no eyebrow, which framed the craziness in his eye. The hair on top of his head had grown out in two patches, leaving seas of bald spots.

As the lone figure wheeled his chair to the unity bed, the communications ARIT rang. The figure shook his head and raised his arm in disgust, upset that someone dare interrupt him while he worked. At first, the lone figure wanted to ignore the beckoning call, but the second ring grated at his stubbornness, and he succumbed.

"Mezhak Zyder," he yelled.

"Mezhak, this is the Grand Maxim Tishya," the voice sailed over the room intercom system.

"Yes, Grand Maxim, what can I do for you?" Mezhak responded, keeping his temper in check.

"Rillon contacted me and said the first unity connection will be at fifteen–sixty-seven, point zero-five hours. That will be in ten universal minutes. Are you ready?"

"Yes, Grand Maxim," Mezhak sighed, "I will be ready."

"Will be ready?" she shouted. "What do you mean…will be ready? Are you ready or not?"

"For the last time, Grand Maxim," Mezhak started to scold in exasperation, "I am ready. Now if you will stop bothering me." Then he wheeled over to the station monitor, activated several controls, and read the schematics on the four monitor screens.

"I've been waiting for this day for such a long time," she continued. "Now it is finally here."

"Yeah…yeah…yeah," Mezhak pushed, putting her voice in the white noise of the room. "I've heard the story a dozen times on how your son Reppus should be the First Osguard, how USSTAP should be run by Akaher's blood line, not Vedar's. That is why you aided and abided Misul Rafinel all those years ago." He grabbed the PARIT connector from the station and activated more switches, again reading the new schematics that appeared on the monitor screens.

"Don't scoff at me Mezhak," she said with the air of dignity worthy of a Grand Maxim, "remember I know who and what you are."

"That goes two ways," he warned.

"Is that a threat?"

"No," Mezhak responded while searching for the right words. "Just a gentle reminder of both our vulnerabilities in this endeavor," he pushed as he wheeled himself back to the bed area.

The click that followed the several seconds of deafening silence told Mezhak that the discussion did not bode well for his future. He shrugged, "Oh well!" he exclaimed aloud. He then pulled himself from the chair up onto the bed, opened the PARIT and hooked it into the bed station. The PARIT had a timing device synchronized to USSTAP's universal time clock.

After straightening his non-functional legs into place on the unity bed, he laid down. The bed slid into the notch in the wall and the transparent sleeve engulfed him. He covered his face with the chamber suit hood, closed his eyes and waited.

***

In Millmum Capitol Unity Room, Michael lay in the unity bed, the transparent sleeve covering his body. He felt like the beef in a big burrito, totally surrounded and enclosed. The chamber suit he was wearing was made of black ARIT cloth, with millions of microscopic nano-transceivers to receive and transmit energy from the unity stream. It was so tight; it grabbed him in every crease of his skin, leaving nothing to the imagination. He felt like it was a second skin, covering him from head to toe. A new feeling burned in him, he now started to feel the tinge of claustrophobia. His breathing was labored and he knew his pulse rate was rising, as he flipped the hood over his face.

He never liked the conference chair, and even though he had limited testing with the unity system, he had no love for it either. It reminded him of the out-of-body experience he had as a teenager, when Billy Red had stabbed him. It had been years since he had thought of that moment. In fact, he had almost forgotten the entire episode through the years.

"You are to embrace a new world and design a new universe. The Beginning and the End has chosen you to lay out a path so humanity can begin its journey to the next level."

The words in that same voice from years ago rolled in his head once again. Those words formerly gave him comfort as he forged new alliances and expanded USSTAP. But in recent years, those words no longer took root in his drive. It was curious why the words suddenly punctured his consciousness today...at this very moment.

"You are to embrace a new world and design a new universe. The Beginning and the End has chosen you to lay out a path so humanity can begin its journey to the next level."

The words rolled in his head once more. This time the comfort it once brought came with it. His tinge of claustrophobia now softened. He closed his eyes and took a deep breath. Outside he could hear his controller count down.

"Five–four–three–two–one...Activate!"

Red, white and blue lights spiraled in a candy cane effect. He felt his consciousness fly into the lights. It was an out-of-body experience, but more surreal than his near-death experience. The lights bent right and left, they curved up and down. Outside the cone of twisted colored light was pitch-black darkness. His soul told him that was the epitome of nothingness...the true void of the universe...the vacuum of life. It was literally the theoretical black hole. He was nervous that if his consciousness left the light and entered the black hole, he would die the most horrible insane death imaginable to man. This was just his paranoia, not backed up by any scientific fact, but he wasn't going to test his theory.

In actuality, Michael's body and mind was safely nested in the unity chamber. According to Dr. Mezhak Zyder of the Chaktun Science Academy the lights were energy connecting his consciousness with the virtual stream, called Unity. With advanced ARIT and gate portal technology, these lights traveled through the heaven, reaching out for and combining with other energy with the same configuration.

After a few more seconds of the disorienting light show, the lights faded and in front of Michael stood Rillon, Byal, Systik and Jeiop. Wearing the long stately robes of their position, tan for the ambassadors and crimson for Osguards, they stood in the Millmum Room, one of several hundred-conference rooms representing each of the galaxies. The room was pentagon shaped with four walls and bay windows in place of the fifth wall. The walls were angelic white, radiating light as they reflected the sun's rays shinning through the windows on the south side. In each corner stood a large gold pillar with strange alien symbols curved from top to bottom. The gigantic double door was opposite the bay windows, reaching from the vaulted ceiling to the brown stone floor.

It was amazing, brilliant and vibrant. It gave Michael a warm feeling, one he hadn't felt in a long time, since the birth of his last child. It was almost euphoric, and somewhat intoxicating. A slight smile broke through on Michael's face.

Systik let out a belly laugh, "This is something else!"

The others giggled, even Michael. Then after a few seconds the laughter subsided as the effects of the conscious connection to the Unity stream evaporated. That is why when the individuals appeared in Unity, they appeared in the galaxy rooms. It was a holding pen for them to wait until the euphoria of the stream dissipated. But the effects of the stream just didn't simply dissipate, they disappeared in a flash and the real emotions came crashing in like a bulldozer.

Taking a deep breath and shaking his head, Michael gained his composure, "I think you guys are supposed to go to the conclave chamber and I need to get to the main garden."

Without a word the five men flowed out the room and disappeared into the mammoth virtual structure called...Unity!

Chapter 4 — In the Conclave

Rillon Osguard walked into the conclave chamber. It was a large room that seemed endless. The room was divided into ten sections. Each section had several parallel, elevated rows of leather-like recliner chairs. Each chair had an ARIT control panel attached for voting and communications. The ceiling was a glass dome. The sun shone through it, brilliantly illuminating the various flowers that decorated the chamber. Like the Millmum room, the walls were white, the floors were made of fine polished stone and the rich golden pillars stood guard at each corner, reaching twenty stories high to the top of the dome.

The other ambassadors had already started filtering into the chamber. There were several hundred people congregating in the chamber. Soon there will be thousands. The voices had already begun to mix together giving the character of confusion to the room.

In Rojam Os, Chaktun was the first language of USSTAP, and English was second. All members of USSTAP had to speak one or the other. Rillon never liked or understood why English was the agreed upon second language, but he guessed it was because of Nausona and Laurona's affiliation with the English speaking people of Earth. However, now the table had been reversed. Tuit was the official language of this body; due to the fact most of the members were former members of the Tuit Consortium.

"Hello," a voice said in Tuit from behind him.

Rillon turned around. The voice came from the Tandorian Ambassador from the Gigantur Cluster. She was very lovely, an enchanting mix of Tuit and Gigantur DNA.

"Hello Ambassador Tou," Rillon responded in his best Tuit. "It is so nice to see you."

"As it is nice to see you...even if it is virtual reality," she bantered back, as she stepped closer. Her smile became even more electrifying as she spoke. "Ambassador, I must inform you that I've read your dissenting brief. Tell me...do your fellow ambassadors feel the same way?"

"I can't say," he said. "But I fully believe there are more that believe like me than not. USSTAP was never meant to become a governmental body, but an organization to supervise and regulate technology and trade amongst the planets and assure mutual security for that technology and trade. However, these Osguards seemed to have lost sight of the original concept. And frankly, Ambassador Tou, that worries me."

"I know," she interrupted. "It's all in your brief. I just want to know if you are alone in your beliefs."

Rillon paused trying to figure out if she was just curious or looking for allies. His gut was telling him to trust her as an ally. He turned to his side, as if to see if anyone was within hearing distance. He placed his hand on her arm, pointed with his chin in a direction off to her side and courteously ushered her away from the area, which he thought was too crowded to continue the conversation. They stepped a few yards to a more sparse area of the conclave, all the while Rillon scanned the area like a drug dealer on the corner watching for cops.

"There are enough of us that feel that way and we plan to push the issue during the CUC vote," he confessed. "But we need more support. Can we count on you?"

Tou gave him a blank look. Suddenly, Rillon felt like he may have made a mistake. He searched his mind for an escape statement that would soften his confession. He plastered his best diplomatic grin on his face and let go of her arm.

"I do have some doubts on the CUC, as it is written now, but I'm not sure your proposal is any better," she admitted.

Seeing he wasn't completely mistaken and that there was a crack in her armor on this subject, he inwardly gave a sigh of relief. "I assure you Ambassador Tou, it is the best alternative. Otherwise, we will hand the entire universe to egomaniacs bent on empire building." He paused to catch his breath and studied her face for any emotions his words may have elicited. "In our star cluster," he continued, "the Osguards rule. In your piece of heaven another set of Osguards will rule. Didn't you have enough of that when the Tuits ruled? Didn't you just fight a war to win your independence from such rule? Why would you turn around and give your hard fought freedom away to these Osguards...to these Guardians of the Universe?"

"It was your Osguards that instigated our fight for freedom," she protested. "Without them, their words...their support, I wouldn't be standing here."

Rillon felt he was losing the argument once again, and he was fighting the sinking feeling of despair from showing on his face. He wanted to debate this point, but knew he would be debating emotion, and that never worked.

"But," she continued, giving Rillon some measure of hope, "I am not too thrilled with the prospect of having another class of people ruling over us again."

"That is exactly what I'm talking about." Rillon said, controlling his urge to shout. Then with newfound confidence he continued to widen the crack, "I'm sure you aren't the only one to feel that way. It may behoove you to float this to others and let them know that today will provide an opportunity for us to voice our concerns and maybe amend the CUC to allow a more self-governing USSTAP and not this empire that it appears to be building now."

"I may just do that," she said still smiling. "Thank you Ambassador Osguard."

"Please, call me Rillon. Ever since the Osguard name has been tied to the power hungry people of USSTAP, I am almost ashamed to call myself Osguard."

"Oh, I see...Rillon," she agreed, and with a head nod, "If you will excuse me, I have other ambassadors to visit before we convene the conclave."

"No problem," he said with satisfaction.

***

On the far side of the conclave a small group of ambassadors gathered. In the center of this crowd, a tall gray-headed figure was speaking with eyes blazed in passion, captivating the crowd with every word. His voice was strong and confident, and his posture emanated authority. Amierwat B'Kailine was offering his views on the CUC, USSTAP and his hope for the new United USSTAP, which he called mankind's greatest step to everlasting peace.

Amierwat B'Kailine was a charismatic figure, who started his career in the D'Ardin military, in the Siryman Galaxy, just like his father and his father's father. He had become the top military man in the empire when the Osguards arrived. When the planets of the Siryman Galaxy joined USSTAP, he became an admiral in the alien organization, and the sire of Siryman Capital Station, under Jarod Stone, Osguard Eleven.

During the Tuit conflict, B'Kailine discovered the D'Ardin head of state, the Kinsile, had covertly aided the Tuits' incursion into his galaxy in hopes of driving the Osguards out and transferring their power to the D'Ardin Empire. Within six months of his discovery, all those involved, including the Kinsile and the USSTAP Parliament Prime Ambassador, mysteriously died. Soon afterward, B'Kailine was appointed to Parliament, where he served three years before being elected prime ambassador of the Parliament.

Now as one of the ambassadors to the conclave, he was in the running for conclave chancellor, and was now using his political savvy to build up his personal collateral with the other members of the conclave.

"I was skeptical of USSTAP at first," he told the crowd in Tuit. "I thought we were giving up our freedom and our sovereignty. But actually, the opposite was true. Our economy blossomed with the advent of new trade. Additionally, with the reduction in military costs, more resources became available for other things; like education, infrastructure and housing. The sharing of technology allowed us to save years in medical and scientific advancements."

As he spoke, his voice rose and fell, emphasizing certain ideas with thunderous punctuation. "And USSTAP never interfered in the internal running of the government, even when our laws were in direct contradiction to USSTAP rules."

A few whispers sprung from the crowd as several dozen private remarks were uttered in response.

"It is true," he pleaded. "Even though there were precincts, like mini embassies, spread on planets throughout my galaxy, USSTAP never interfered with the enforcement of our laws on our lands. Conversely," he warned, "in space…in USSTAP controlled domain, their law is paramount, and must be adhered to from everyone." He paused to let the words sink in. B'Kailine studied the faces surrounding him and knew he had hit an issue of debate. "But personally," he continued, "I find their laws less restrictive than ours. So adhering to them isn't a problem."

Glancing around the crowd and trying to make momentary eye contact with all, even if it was for a split second, he paused to gather his thoughts before pushing them forward. With outstretched hands and palms up, he pressed his thoughts even further. "The CUC is almost a mirror image of the constitution I have lived with for over twenty universal years…and my life is better for it…my planet is better for it…my galaxy is better for it…and I dare say my part of the universe is better for it."

"But what about the Osguards," a voice sputtered from the crowd.

B'Kailine twisted his head to the side and raised a finger to his chin as if in thought. He remained in this position for a few seconds, which to the crowd seemed like minutes.

"Let me be careful on how I phrase this, so I won't be accused of being offensive to anyone," B'Kailine began. "What about the Osguards?" A polite smile graced his face. "I don't mean to be crass, but the Osguards aren't gods. There are enough checks and balances to ensure they don't act like gods. Each galaxy has a congress and each star cluster has a parliament…all with elected or appointed representatives. The Osguards have to answer to these bodies. And before they make a move out of the ordinary, they must consult and get the approval of one or both of these bodies."

"What about the senate?" the same voice contested.

"The senate is our watchdog. The Osguards make sure all the galactic congresses and the parliament rule and govern by the intent of the constitution…the same way the Guardian Supreme Council will with the conclave."

"Why should the conclave answer to the council?" a different voice inquired.

B'Kailine let the question linger in the air for a moment, increasing the anticipation. Then he spoke, "The conclave is in session three times a year, the council will only meet, once every five universal years…or in cases of emergency…or when called upon by the conclave. How is that answering to the council?" He shifted his weight and stretched his arms out once more. "It's just checks and balances; the conclave will govern the united USSTAP, each parliament will govern their respective galactic star cluster and finally, each galactic congress will govern its respective galaxy."

Some heads nodded in acceptance, while others remained shaken and perplexed.

The buzzer sounded twice, signaling five minutes before the opening of the first conclave meeting.

"My fellow ambassadors," B'Kailine addressed, "I see it is time to begin the session. In accordance with the rules of the conclave, I will be speaking today in front of the conclave where I will be happy to entertain any more questions you may have."

Then like school children in homeroom, the ambassadors scrambled to their seats. By the time the buzzer sounded again, all the seats were occupied and the making of history was ready to begin.

Chapter 5 — Deliberations

"What is Rillon doing?" Reppus shouted.

ARIT gate portal technology was piping the deliberations from the unity conclave to view screens throughout the known universe. All known news agencies banded together and solicited their respective governments to broadcast the historic proceedings. At first, it seemed impossible to do, but the technology did allow for outside viewing of the unity stream, which bounced off repeater stations on a special band. Reppus Osguard, the Chaktun Maxum was watching the proceedings in his residence in the Steeple, along with his mother, Tishya, and his wife, Lequel.

"What is he doing?" he repeated in disgust.

Rillon was addressing the conclave espousing a negative tone to the CUC. He wanted several amendments, granting more power to the chancellor and the immediate dissolution of the Guardian Supreme Council. He painted a picture of the Osguards, and by association, the newly appointed guardians of the other galactic star clusters, as power hungry mongers, gutting the universe of resources in a desperate attempt to feed a dynasty.

His words were more poisonous than his original dissenting response, which had already garnered unwanted controversy. His words were spiteful and very undiplomatic for an ambassador, and definitely embarrassing to Reppus.

"Shut up," he screamed at the view screen, letting his temper erupt like a volcano. "I thought we had an understanding," he reflected as he turned to his mother.

Tishya sat in her plush leather red chair. The chair seemed to swallow her, but she somehow maintained her regal stature as she sat in it. A smile creased her lips and her eyes sparkled with mischief. "About time one of you showed some backbone," she commented.

"What?" Reppus demanded.

"You heard me. It's about time one of my sons showed some backbone and stood up to these...these...these zechas," referring to the Chaktun bug similar to an Earth cockroach. "These zechas used our name like a badge of honor and created the dynasty that you should be leading...not them." She stood and walked over to the seventy-inch view screen and stared at her son's virtual image. Then she turned back to Reppus and Lequel, who remained dumbfounded in their chairs. "Ever since Ortho brought those zechas to this planet and placed them as the leaders of USSTAP...an organization that should be yours...you have been kissing their ass at every turn. They tell you to jump...you jump. They tell you to run...you run. By Jus' law, if they told you to run through the square naked...you would."

Rage boiled inside Reppus, his eyes flamed with fury as he fought to control his temper. Mentally, he counted to ten, all the while staring at his mother—looking but not seeing her. The woman in front of him all of a sudden was a stranger, not his mother, but an enemy to his rule. "Lequel, can you please leave us alone, I need to talk to the Grand Maxim," he bellowed.

Lequel hesitated for a minute, her face rooted in confusion, and then like the dutiful Maxim she was, she stood and exited the room.

As soon as she was gone the Grand Maxim continued her berating. "You are just as weak as your father was." She moved toward the window overlooking the East Garden. "Those zechas have their memorial wall here. They entertain dignitaries here and they come and go as they please. This is their house, not ours. The main USSTAP Academy is here on Chaktun...thousands of aliens are educated and trained right here on our soil." She turned back to her son with tears in her eyes. "You aren't the Chaktun Maxum...you're the Osguardian caretaker. And you are too stupid to be embarrassed." She turned back toward the window, her voice cracking as she spoke. "I'm ashamed to call you son. Thank Jus I have Rillon. He is strong...confident and a worthier leader than you. Birthright keeps him from being Maxum, but genes will make him an excellent chancellor."

Her words cut him deeper than anything or anyone had ever done before. His anger was flushed away with the hurt her words brought. He held his breath to fight his body's urge to hyperventilate, while inwardly screaming prayers for his mother's love once more.

"Hopefully this time..." her words choked in her throat.

"This time...what do you mean this time?" Reppus demanded, as he stood and walked to her.

His demand was met with defiant silence.

He grabbed his mother by her shoulders, spun her around so he could see her face and dug his fingers deep into her arms. "Tell me now woman, what do you mean this time?"

"Nothing!"

"You're lying," he yelled shaking her in his grasp. "Tell me what you meant by this time, or so help me..."

"So help you what? You'll kill me! You would kill your own mother to protect them?" With her face scrunched up in disgust, she spit in her son's face.

In surprise he let her go, wiping the spit from his eyes and nose.

She stepped around him, moving back away from him, smiling. "Okay! I guess it won't hurt to tell you. You're too gutless to do anything about it now anyway." She moved back several more steps, giggling aloud. "The attack on the *Justice* after the 'Awakening,'...I ordered that attack! That's not all...the massacre at Talion...that was my doing to!" she gloated.

Reppus looked at his mother in shock. She had just admitted to two of the most mystifying events in USSTAP history, involving countless deaths that he personally knew weighed heavily on Michael's heart. And he didn't know how to take it. In his face the turmoil of torture reigned supreme. He bit his lip and shook his head as tears formed in his eyes. In the midst of his pain, he watched his mother walk from the room, and with her walked any love he ever had for her.

***

Many religions of the universe had an axiom that humans were created in the Creator's own image; however, humans in Rojam Os came in all shapes, sizes and colors. Now to add to the confusion, the humans from the other galactic clusters added more variety to the mix. The humans from Tuit had cat like yellow eyes, the humans from Vergani Ur Fadin had elf-like ears, the humans from Gigantur had small vampire teeth, the humans from Neant au Zar had one eighth inch devil-like horns protruding from their foreheads, and the humans from Provello had forked tongues, like snakes. The only constant is that they came in all shapes, sizes and colors as well, as evident by the eclectic mixture of Osguards in front of Michael mingling, talking and fellowshipping in Unity Garden now.

Unity Garden was so beautiful. It was a maze of hedges with flowers salting them from almost every planet represented at Unity. The center of the maze was as large as a football field. Michael had almost forgotten this wasn't real and that he was in a unity chamber deep inside Millmum Capitol Station having ARIT energy pumped into his brain. He was feeling every handshake, hug and kiss as he met his brother, sister, daughters and the rest of the Osguard family. He even smelled the fragrance emanating from the flowers in the garden. Somehow the experience was hypnotic, alluring and at the same time, somewhat frightening. He kept searching for something that would tell him this wasn't real...a glitch in the programming of some sort—

missing pixels—hiccups—fadeouts—something. But there was nothing. This unity stream was too much like reality.

Just as he thought he would go crazy looking for a flaw, he heard someone calling his name.

"Michael...Michael Genesis?"

He turned toward the voice and saw another guardian, not an Osguard from Rojam Os. He looked familiar, very familiar. He was a tall Tuit, with aerobic muscular tone. His yellow catlike eyes were friendly and warm...different from the first time they met.

"Adam?" Michael guessed.

"Yes, you remember!" the Tuit said, grabbing Michael for a hug.

Michael hugged him back, "Adam! Oh my God! It's so good to see you." He released him, "What are you doing here?"

"I'm the First Osguard of Tuit," he announced.

"Wow!"

"Yup, after you broke me out of that prison, I led the resistance in the Tuit Galaxy."

"You led the Freemans? You're Adam Freeman?" Michael asked in surprise.

"Yes, the one and only," he shrugged. "And of course, you know the rest."

"For the life of me, I never knew that the famous Adam Freeman, leading the fight here was you. Why didn't you tell Stelana or Angela?"

"Well," he began to whisper, "I thought it wiser not to mention my history with your USSTAP."

Michael didn't know how to take that, so all he said was "Oh!"

"I know you don't understand, but it all worked out in the end," Adam confided.

"Listening to Ambassador Rillon Osguard's remarks in the conclave, I'm not too sure it has worked out yet," Michael observed, wanting to change the subject. Michael always thought his intervention as the instigator of the Tuit revolt may be a detriment to the peace treaty and the forming of the CUC. Now Adam had just confirmed his suspicions.

"Yeah, I know what you mean," Adam remarked, looking around at the guardians. "It has caused some consternation with the other Osguards of Tuit, and I dare say with the other guardians."

"Sorry to hear that," Michael offered.

"It doesn't help that Ambassador Tou's convoy was attacked on her way to her Capitol Station."

"What?" Michael croaked.

"Yes, my friend...Ambassador Tou's convoy was attacked, but fortunately—thanks to you—she had a couple of galaxy cruisers escorting her in stealth mode. They provided adequate protection."

"I see," was all Michael could manage to say.

"Yes, the ambassadors are asking now more than ever for their own fleet of ships and a complement of guards…that answer to them and not the Osguards…for protection while they travel."

"Yes, I guess I've been thinking about that," Michael admitted. "There is a proposal in the CUC to assign firestars to the parliament ambassadors with a full squadron of firefighters and to assign fireships to the congressional ambassadors. Of course they would lack stealth capability and would run on dialairtic power instead of tribolemincic power, and most importantly, they would be rhetonic cannon neutered. There weaponry would be conventional only." He lowered his head and kicked at the ground. "On the surface, it is an option that I am no longer opposed to. Tuit space isn't completely safe yet, as evident by this attack on Tou. Besides, we are picking up some message traffic in Rojam Os that indicates our ambassadors may become targets to those who oppose our vision." Michael huffed. "If we do this, I would want to beef up the operational side of the other galactic clusters with a full range of ships; the same ratio of galaxy protectors, galaxy cruisers, star protector and star cruisers that I have in Rojam Os. I want the CUC to record a full partnership. But it appears the political pinheads hear don't want that. They don't believe in the USSTAP vision that guides my philosophy."

"I understand," Adam admitted, "But don't let the opposition dampened your spirit. We are better off because of you and USSTAP's vision, and we will stand with you for as long as it takes to bring USSTAP's vision to our galactic clusters."

"Are you sure?"

"Yes, I'm sure," he reinforced. "We have worked hard for these last years, trying to bring peace and order to our part of space. And we did, by using your association as a model. And now we have this idiot shooting holes in our new way of life." Adam placed his hand on Michael's shoulder, "I think we should meet with the other first guardians and talk this out."

"If you think it will help," Michael gave in, wondering what good it would do. He had kept a respectful distance from the other guardians during the last three years of negotiations, and he knew his input now would be unwarranted.

"Yes, it would help," insisted Adam. "Please come with me, I have something I need to show you."

Adam stepped aside and motion for Michael to follow him. The two men walked through the maze and back into Unity Hall. Michael wondered where they were going, but kept his mouth shut. They traveled through the wide corridor of the hall, up the marble stairs and around to a chamber in the west end of the hall—opposite the conclave chamber.

Inside the chamber, a catacomb of several hundred stations filled the area. In the front of the stations were six stations, five at floor level and one five feet above them. In front of them were four people, two men and two women.

"Michael, this is the council chamber," Adam announced. "And these are the other first guardians."

Michael was uncomfortable, but followed Adam to the bottom of the chamber.

"Michael Genesis, First Osguard of Rojam Os, this is Te Felkick, First Osguard of Vergani Ur Fadin; Kang Sario, First Osguard of Gigantur; Kollyna Senard, First Osguard of Neant au Zar; and Ree au Foulana, First Osguard of Provello.

"Hello," Michael managed to squeak like a shy boy on a date.

Each first guardian greeted him with a hardy handshake.

"What's this all about?" Michael wanted to know.

"Well there was a little something we asked Angela and Stelana not to tell you about the council chamber," Ree answered.

"Oh yeah...what was that?"

"These stations in the center are reserved for the first guardians," Kang informed him. "And that top one is for the council president."

Michael looked at the arrangement. His mind started to race and he started to feel that sinking feeling in his gut. Instantly, he knew that the council president would have to be a first guardian, which made his chances of being elected the president change from one in seven hundred and fifty to one in six.

"That wasn't what I signed up for," Michael protested.

"We know and we're sorry for the deception," Kollyna said. "But according to Angela and Stelana, if we didn't do it this way, you would object."

Michael felt a pinch of guilt run down his spine. He didn't want his feelings to be so well publicized, but they were. He needed an exit line to lessen the damage that his reluctance caused. "It's not that I would have objected, it's just since the majority of the new union comes from the old Tuit Consortium, I thought the council president should come from there as well."

"That's not it," Adam pushed. "Even though we only met for a few minutes that day you freed me, it was the beginning of my life. You didn't only give me a name, you gave me a purpose, and you spread that purpose throughout the former consortium like wildfire." He placed his arm around Michael's shoulders. "You are afraid that we harbor some ill will to you because your actions that day started a five year revolt, and many lives were lost during that time. Well, we are here to tell you that there is no ill will, only gratitude for your vision and the aid you rendered once peace was achieved. If it weren't for you as the First Osguard, we would still be struggling to pick ourselves out of the ashes of destruction instead of being the self sufficient organizations we are today."

"We are so grateful," Kang interrupted. "When we asked for your help, you sent aid and transport ships. You cured our sick, housed our homeless and fed our hungry, throughout five galactic star clusters. You not only did that, you showed us how to do it for ourselves. Then, so we could provide our own security, you provided us with star cruisers and star protectors," Kang continued referring to the newest additions to the USSTAP fleet.

The star cruisers were modeled after the ships commanded by Nausona and Laurona over one hundred universal years ago, which also played an instrumental part in pushing the Tuit fleet out of Rojam Os. The star protector was a larger version of the star cruiser with an aft launch and landing bay that housed one squadron of defenders. Michael and the other Osguards debated for months on whether to supply the starships or not. But at last they agreed to do so because compared to allowing them to regenerate the Tuit shipyards again and build fireships, firestars and firefighters; supplying them with USSTAP starships was a better alternative. It was a better alternative because, Tuit starships were a formidable adversary to the USSTAP fleet and none of the Osguards wanted to chance a rematch with the white devil ships that caused so much havoc eight universal years ago.

Besides, Michael had the industrial complex working overtime producing fleets of ships for the expansion plan that he conceived on the eve of his return from the Tuit owned space where he provided the spark that ignited the five-year conflict. So producing more ships was not a problem. Although, USSTAP suffered a three-year resource deficit for the first time in its history during this time, the capital gained in trade from the new areas restored USSTAP's financial stability in a short amount of time.

"There's so much we have done, but there is so much we still have to learn from you," Kang offered.

"With that in mind, we have voted you as the council president…the Chief Executive Osguard," Ree announced.

"What?" Michael asked in disbelief. This was the one thing he did not want. "Isn't that vote up to the full council? And the council hasn't even had its first meeting."

"That's academic," Kollyna insisted. "The president comes from the first guardians, and we took ourselves out of the running. So when the council does convene, there will only be one choice to vote for. And unlike the ratification rules, majority wins, so if you only get one vote and everyone else abstains, you win."

"Isn't that usurping the rules of the CUC, even before the CUC becomes official? The conclave may change that rule as well. Listen to Rillon speak. He's still going on about how bad a leader I am."

"Yeah, that may present a problem," Ree admitted. "But I think we can control the damage, especially if we act fast. That is why we are telling you this now, instead of during session, like we wanted to."

"So this is a done deal?"

"For now, yes it is," Adam asserted.

"But…but…but…" Michael stuttered

"First Osguard…this is Osguard one–two–one," Sharyla's rang in his ear from his CC.

Michael tapped his CC, "Osguard zero–one, go!"

"Dad, I need to talk to you ASAP, can you meet me in conference room sixty-six–F?"

Michael looked at his fellow guardians as he answered, "Tiah!"

He disconnected the communications and addressed the group. "I'll be back as soon as I can." Then with the urgency of a father answering a daughter's cry for help, he left the chamber.

Once outside the chamber, he pulled his PARIT and requested directions to conference room sixty-six–F. Unity Hall had several-hundred conference rooms designated for each galaxy and designed for private meetings where conversations were not recorded by the ARIT, but he wasn't aware of additional conference rooms. With that in mind, he wished the conversation he just had with the others had been in one of these additional conference rooms. He didn't want to imagine what would happen if Rillon got his hands on a recording of that conversation. Michael cringed at the thought of Rillon twisting it in his favor. Michael whispered curses as he moved through the cavernous halls.

He climbed the marble stairs to the sixth floor, amazed that he felt a little winded. The virtual exertion he was executing brought a realistic physical effect. He made a mental note of that. They said that food; drink and bodily functions would not be experienced while in the unity stream. However, they warned physical pain would be, something about the energy stimulating the proper part of the brain eliciting physical responses through the chamber suit that he was wearing in the real world.

In extreme cases, if someone experienced a death-causing event in Unity, they would die in the real world. Thus the program would not create weapons in Unity. However falling down the stairs or tripping and cracking your head open was a real possibility.

Thinking about all the precautions and dangers associated with this virtual world caused Michael to wonder if it was worth it. He was always dubious of virtual technology and the unity stream wasn't making him feel any less doubtful.

Finally he reached the conference room. The characteristic diamond shaped USSTAP door marked the entranceway. He stepped in front and the familiar swoosh hissed through the air as the door split in the middle and slid into the wall. The room was dark, but Michael was sure his presence would turn on the light as soon as he stepped in. In the back of his mind, he concluded his daughter had not yet arrived. He contemplated waiting outside for her for a split second, but he thought that would be awkward, especially if Sharyla meant for this to be a clandestine meeting.

He stepped in and the door swooshed closed behind him. The lights did not come on. "Sharyla," Michael called out, wondering if she wanted the lights to remain off.

A thunderous right cross connecting to his jaw was his only response. Michael fell back; his head hit the wall where the door used to be. The double tap of the fist and the wall weaken Michael. Then another right cross smashed into his jaw, crumbling Michael to the floor.

Chapter 6 — Disaster

Space was a cold dark vacuum, devoid of anything, except radiation surging from stars, black holes and other phenomena. One theory was that radiation in space was life in its truest form, and that the zeshion radiation contained the beginning spark of the big bang theory, or at least the left over residue of the beginning of the universe.

A zeshion storm could not be predicted. It would suddenly appear as if by magic. Then it would disappear just as mysteriously. The storms would last from five galactic minutes to thirty galactic days. For some unknown reason, the storm never occurred within a solar system, but usually light years away from a solar system. Unfortunately, Millmum station was fifty light years away from the nearest solar system and not excluded by nature in experiencing a zeshion storm.

As luck would have it, there was one, five kilomarks wide, bearing down on the station. The characteristic black mass with red, white and blue lightening flashes cracking through it, dangerously lumbered within Millmum Capitol Station sensor and scanner range. The last time the station saw a zeshion storm, over one hundred universal years ago; it gave birth to the Tuit quarrel, which the ambassadors and guardians in Unity were presently trying to resolve.

"Admiral Ritchen," the command observer, Commander Pam Stafford, called from her station on the observation deck. The observation deck sat on top of the diamond with a majestic three hundred and sixty degree view of the heavens and other stations in the capitol patch.

Tirana stood from her chair in the center of the observation deck, recognizing the stress in Stafford's voice, "What is it?"

"I'm picking up some strange reading in quadrant four...alpha...two."

Tirana stepped closer to her and looked over Stafford's shoulders to take a look at the reading. She saw a mix of activity – benion, trachion and restion radiation particles striking and swirling in random fluctuations. The radiation particles caused fissures into the ultra space and inner space inside a gravity well, known as a black mass. She recognized it as a zeshion storm.

Protocol called for her to shut down all operation of gate portals and fire radiation dampeners into the storm as soon as detected. It was a theory advanced by Admiral Vid Son soon after the first storm attacked Millmum Station. The theory had never been tested, because the five recorded storms since then had not threatened a USSTAP station.

"Terminate all gate portal activity," she ordered. "Load radiation dampener torpedoes into five starguards and launch."

"Admiral, unity transmission is going on. It uses gate portal technology," Stafford reminded her.

"Call the chamber room," she requested, "order the immediate recovery of our people, then cut the connection."

"Tiah!" Stafford responded.

***

"What do you mean...RECALL?" Rillon shouted into his CC.

His monitor was back in the unity chamber on Millmum Capitol Station pleading with his charge once more through the communications link, "There is a zeshion storm threatening the station. We have to close the connection while they neutralize it."

"How convenient," Rillon remarked. "You want to stop my speech. You want to stop me from telling the conclave the truth," he ranted, while standing behind the speaker's podium, looking out among the thousands of members in the conclave. Additionally, the entire universe was hearing his side of the conversation...him arguing with his unity monitor...being accusatory and not trusting his own handpicked observer over the universal news broadcast.

"Ambassador, just say the exit phrase, so we can shut this thing down," his monitor pushed back. "There's a zeshion storm bearing down on our position...that's right, our position. Your mind may be there, but your body is here. And if the zeshion storm hits here..." he stopped to gain his composure. "Come back now or I'll pull the plug," he said.

Rillon was taken aback by his monitor's words and tone of voice. But this made him believe, if this was a trick to shut him up, his monitor was not involved. He did see Byal, Systik and Jeiopa vanish some minutes ago when they received the call. He shook the doubt that was creeping into his mind from his head. He had more to say and he wanted to say it. He opened his mouth to address the conclave, but was cut off by a voice blazing over Unity's loud speaker system.

"Ladies and gentlemen of the conclave, this is Admiral Tirana Ritchen of Millmum Capitol Station. There is a zeshion storm one thousand kilomarks from the station. We will use anti-radiation torpedoes per the Son Theory. But to do that we must shut down all radiation producing devices, including gate portals. I must cut our connection to Unity. With that in mind, I'm sorry that we are interrupting your conclave, but I need our ambassadors and Osguard to severe their connection."

Rillon smiled in embarrassment. Admiral Ritchen had just given him a diplomatic punch in the nose. "I'm sorry fellow members of the conclave, but I must go." Then he turned around, away from the conclave members and spoke his exit phrase, "I am Osguard!"

Rillon's image faded as his consciousness disconnected from the unity stream.

***

"We have a problem," Michael's monitor announced.

"What?" Tirana demanded. She had decided she needed to be in the unity chamber after they told her Ambassador Rillon refused to comply with the evacuation order. But in all the confusion she had not noticed that Michael had failed to return. "Where's the Osguard?"

"Well his readings have been erratic for the last couple of minutes, and he has failed to answer our calls," the monitor reported.

"And you are just telling me this now?"

"The Osguard went into private mode when he went into the garden," he answered.

Even though the ARIT recorded everything outside the conference rooms, the monitors could hear every conversation conducted by their charges, unless they operated in private mode. Michael had requested private mode when he entered the garden, so he could have private personal conversations with the other Osguards. The monitors complied and just observed their position in Unity and body vitals.

"We lost his position just before you requested the emergency evacuation," the first monitor added.

"His vitals have been erratic ever since," the second monitor added.

Tirana huffed in disgust. "Get him out of there!"

Rillon stepped behind Tirana, still a little dazed from his recovery, "You're going to have to shut his connection because of the storm," he chimed.

Tirana shot a stern look at him. She had no time to deal with this egotistical maniac. She knew if she shut down the Osguard's connection, he would die. She also knew that was what Rillon wanted. She had to think fast. She didn't want to shut down the connection and kill the Osguard. But if she kept the connection open, the radiation from the storm may find route in Unity and spread out to the other stations, causing miniature zeshion storms at every station connected.

She tapped her CC, "Observation deck this is Admiral Ritchen...how long to starguards in place?"

"Two minutes," Stafford's voice echoed in her ear.

"Fine," Tirana sighed. "Continue."

Then she went to the main station and connected to Unity's intercom system. The system was connected to every room and every corridor in Unity. It also sounded in the gardens surrounding Unity. "All ambassadors...all guardians...this is Admiral Tirana Ritchen," she said in Tuit. "We have a critical condition at Millmum Station. A zeshion storm is about to hit us and we are unable to retrieve our Osguard. I request all of you to activate the emergency evacuation. I will be keeping the connection in which Osguard Michael Genesis is on, open. With that in mind, when the storm hits, it may find energy in the connection and move through Unity and eventually to your individual stations. Please...please...please, I implore you to evacuate Unity...Now. I repeat...please...please, evacuate Unity...Now!"

She closed the connection, hoping that her actions would not be the beginning to further calamity elsewhere in the universe. She closed her eyes and begged that the Osguard heard her words and was activating his emergency evacuation as well.

"What good will that do?" Rillon asked. "Keeping the connection open will kill the First Osguard just as sure as disconnecting it will," he reveled as he spoke. "You are murdering the First Osguard. I knew it would be only a matter of time before you would act. This is the first opportune moment you've had to kill him and make it look like an accident. How long have you Kulusks been planning this?"

"Ambassador," she screeched, "you either shut up, or I will shut you up."

"Are you forgetting who you are talking to...I am an ambassador to the Universal Conclave. You will treat me with the respect due my office."

"Until the CUC is ratified, you are simply a guest on my station. And as a guest, I expect you to treat everyone on this station, including me, with the same respect we give you." She moved closer to Rillon, to the point where their noses almost touched. "And that's what I just did; I gave you the same respect you gave me...now sit down and shut up."

"Once the CUC is ratified, you will be sorry you have treated me with such distain," he challenged.

Tirana sucked in her breath and blew out hard, "After your little speech, I doubt the CUC will be ratified any time soon."

Rillon lowered his eyes, signaling to Tirana she had hit a cord. Rillon turned away and moved over to the chair near his chamber like a beat puppy.

***

In Unity, Tirana's words were immediately adhered to and bodies faded away in rapid succession. There were no objections, no defiance and no attitudes given. Escape words were uttered without question. And once they were uttered, consciousnesses were disconnected from the stream. Within thirty seconds, every ambassador and every guardian was safely back at their stations…except for Michael Genesis

***

"No consciousnesses links in the stream," the head monitor reported to Tirana.

"What…what about the First Osguard," Tirana asked.

"Negative, the head monitor responded.

Tirana looked at Michael's monitors, "Where is Genesis?"

"Still no position, but his consciousness stream is still active."

"Where is it active…where is it going?" Tirana yelled.

"I don't know, but it isn't in the unity stream."

"The stream is shutting down," the chamber chief, Riley screamed in horror.

"The Osguard?" yelled Tirana, afraid that whatever glitch was keeping them from reading Michael's position also kept the stream from recognizing Michael's consciousness.

"Steady conscious connection, but his vitals are still erratic."

"Good," Tirana offered. Keep his connection up…no matter what happens…keep his consciousness connected.

"Connected to what?" the first monitor asked with confusion.

"Connected to whatever it is connected to," Tirana said with even more confusion. Then with a heavy heart, she tapped her CC, "This is Admiral Ritchen…fire torpedoes when ready."

***

Relying on his fighting training, Michael switched modes. He was on his knees in the dark, against a wall in which he could have sworn was a door a second ago. Furthermore, his assailant had the advantage of knowing where he was. Sight was no longer an input to his fighting form. He needed to use his other senses. His ears caught the sound of air swishing in front of him. He crossed his hands in front of his face just in time to catch his assailant's foot. Michael twisted the foot counter clockwise, feeling the weight of his assailant twisting with it, keeping Michael from breaking the ankle. The hard thud told Michael his prey had fallen.

Keeping a tight hold on the foot, Michael stood and fired a wicked kick that connected to his prey's kneecap. Then Michael heard a swishing sound from below as the other foot slashed up. Michael used the captured foot to block the kick and then jumped, twisted, and came down hard on the back of his prey with an elbow between the shoulder blades. The sound of air rushing out of the stranger's lungs gave Michael instant gratification. Then with lightening quick agility, Michael straddled his attacker's back, grabbed his head and banged it three times on the hard stone floor with enough force to crack the person's skull.

Suddenly the lights illuminated the room. Michael looked around, still holding the back of his attacker's head. Blood leaked from the attacker's head, splashing into its own red pool on the floor below them. It was an empty ten feet by ten feet boxed room. The walls were white, with no distinguishable windows and door.

Michael let the head go and let it plop onto the floor with a hollow thud. He stood confused and still a bit dazed. He checked each wall, pressing at various points, hoping to activate a hidden switch or something that would open a door. When he was satisfied there was no switch, at least not one he could find, curiosity took over.

He went to the motionless body, which he could tell was still alive, because his stomach rose and fell with each breath he took, and kicked it over. Below the blood spots and under the large gash on the forehead, Michael recognized him. Michael stepped back in shock.

"It can't be," he whispered, as he continued to study the face. But it was. Under the blood, cuts and bruises lay Billy Red—a little older and thicker, but it was Billy Red.

Or was it? Michael asked himself. Michael realized he was in a virtual reality and whoever this was, could have manipulated the program to present the image of Billy to shock him into making a mistake or some other psychological reason. Michael pressed his back against the wall, where he thought the door was and shook his head in disbelief. "This is why I don't like this shit!" Michael screamed, voicing his opinion of virtual technology. "The ARIT is playing with my fucking mind," he said aloud. "I hate this shit…I hate it…I hate it…I hate it!"

Michael made up his mind it was time to get out of here, closed his eyes and said his escape phrase. Then he opened his eyes.

Nothing…nothing happened. He was still in the room. "Oh shit, don't tell me I forgot my own escape phrase?" Panic started to take root. "Privacy mode off," he commanded. "Lieutenant Jack…Lieutenant Velemon…can you hear me? It's Osguard zero–one!"

No answer.

"Lieutenant Jack...Lieutenant Velemon...can you hear me? It's Osguard Michael Genesis." he reiterated.

Again, no answer came.

Michael then repeated his escape-phrase several more times, and every time, he opened his eyes and saw he was still in the same room.

Finally, Michael went to Billy, picked his head off the floor and started slapping his face. "Wake up...Billy. Wake up now!"

Billy's eyes cracked opened. Michael could tell he wasn't fully aware yet, but it didn't matter. He had to know where he was, or at least how to get out of this room.

"Billy...wake up...you dumb fuck. Wake up!"

"Yeah," Billy slurred as blood flowed from his mouth. "How do you like my world," he whispered and then slipped back into unconsciousness.

***

Near Millmum Capitol Station, in the cold vacuum of space, the zeshion storm was encroaching on the darkness. Five starguards were slowly approaching. The unmanned platforms, controlled by personnel on the observation deck of Millmum Capitol Station, parked five kilomarks in front of the storm, awaiting orders to fire their anti-radiation torpedoes.

The storm was eating up space at a faster pace now than when it first appeared, and now was threatening to engulf the gate portal diamonds. The main gates were deactivated, but the smaller gate, used for unity connection was still alive beaming Michael's consciousness through ultra space to parts of the universe...unknown.

Then suddenly, the starguards fired their torpedoes. Ten torpedoes left a trail of fire and smoke, slicing through space like arrows heading straight for their mark. The black mass swallowed the twenty-foot torpedoes. Then several flashes of white, then red, and then, barely seen by the naked eye, blue flashes popped inside the black mass. Afterwards, the edges of the black mass began to shrink. Like burning paper in a fireplace, the edges crumbled, cracked and folded inwards, dwindling in size and power.

The starguards fired another salvo of torpedoes, and then retreated back to the safety of the station's area. The torpedoes sailed into the heart of the black mass. Several seconds later, large explosions sparked the area, creating, pushing and then dousing bright orange fireballs. Blue, red and white twisted energy bolts cracked the heavens, shooting wildly in all different directions, searching for any radiation to feed it. Most of the red and white energy bolts dissipated, losing energy and life while the blue energy bolts, filled with trachion radiation spread themselves amongst the radiation of normal space.

All the thunderbolts seemed to die, except for one very large and ominous-looking, white energy bolt that found its way to the one active gate portal—the one controlling Michael's consciousness stream.

That energy bolt slid into the gate portal and spiraled around Michael's invisible consciousness stream, blazing a path in ultra space. The path led past where the circular unity stream once burned, to another stream being projected from Chaktun. Mezhak Zyder had attached his stream on a tangent to the station's original unity stream. Zyder's stream was one hundred times smaller than the unity stream and unperceivable to any USSTAP sensor or scanner system.

But now the unity stream was gone and the Zyder stream was the sole target left for the energy bolt. The bolt slammed into the invisible Zyder stream, opening another fissure of glowing green radiation. A new form of radiation never recorded by human, spewed etion particles and enveloped the Zyder stream.

***

"Clear!" the voice bellowed inside his head.

Michael looked up and saw the room walls dissolve into a green mist. He was getting hot, dizzy and nauseous.

"Again…clear!" the voice roared once more.

Michael started to fade, as if he was disconnecting from the stream. His dizziness quickened, sweat permeated his skin, and the taste of bile gurgled in the back of his throat. The walls, glowing in green radiation, started closing in on him. Michael was too confused to even register that fact.

"One more time…clear!" the voice yelled.

Michael fell on top of Billy, unconscious, barely visible, almost transparent as his body faded in and out. Deep inside the Zyder stream resided a holovidpic (HVP) program that Mezhak put together from USSTAP, Kulusk and Mosleck records. He intended to play it for Michael inside the small room after subduing him. However, the program found no root to project onto, so it fused onto Michael's neural net path. As Michael consciousness stream floated, his mind captured and comprehended eighteen terabytes of information clusters within a half a second. Then a split second later, the wall closed in swallowing him and Billy into the green glowing radiation, activating the HVP to play like a dream inside Michael's neural net path. The HVP began and it was the summer of 1983, the deciding moment in the making of Michael Genesis as the First Osguard.

Chapter 7—Stabbing

The knife appeared out of nowhere. One moment Billy Red had Michael by the throat, squeezing with all his might, the next moment the knife appeared in Billy's hand. It was a hunting knife…maybe a survival knife, one with a serrated ten-inch blade and a rubber handle form fitted for easy grip. The pucker factor now raised several factors in Michael's heart. He already feared for his life when Billy first attacked him from behind.

He had just been talking to Jackie in the middle of the park, playing it cool, trying to lay his latest lines on the girl and impress her enough to get some play. It was his first week back from college. He had completed his first year at Rutgers University and now felt he had something to offer the ladies in the area…something other than the drugged out punks with one foot in the grave and the other foot in prison – the lifestyle, which seemed to saturate the hood, like dirty water to a sponge.

Oh, she seemed pleasant enough…receptive enough, but that was all a game. She was using him to make her man jealous…to get him to pay more attention to her, a tactic Michael had been the victim of all too many times. A tactic Michael didn't recognize until the screeching pain popped in his head courtesy of a two-by-four wood beam that Billy swung like a baseball bat, using his head for the baseball.

His vision became blurred as he hit the ground. The world spun and his perception of reality escaped his consciousness for a fleeting second. Blood streamed from an open gash at the back of his skull, but he didn't feel it. He hardly felt anything…at first. It was like a hard slumber as he closed his eyes, welcoming the darkness. Then a sharp pain racked his ribs as Billy kicked him in the side. All of a sudden the sweet blackness of slumber vanished as the pain in his head and the pain in his side fought for his attention. Michael let out a low moan, while his other senses tried to jump-start his consciousness. A scream pierced the fogginess of his mind.

It was Jackie. He recognized her voice. Not so much from the scream but from the words, "Don't Billy…Stop Billy…You're going to kill him Billy. The words splashed him like cold water spraying in his face. *Kill him…she's talking about me…oh shit!* Michael struggled to get to his knees, barely feeling the blood soaked grass beneath his hands.

Billy kicked him again, this time in the stomach, like he was punting a football. Michael's body popped in the air and he twisted and landed hard on his back. Adrenaline flowed through his blood acting like a stimulant to his muscles. But he was still unable to command his body to do what his mind was ordering. He wanted to get up and run. The pain was in full blast; but, his faculty was in full awareness. *No girl is worth this shit!*

Blood spurted from his mouth. He coughed it out, struggling to his knees once more. This time Billy grabbed him by his neck and pulled him to his feet. Michael managed to open his eyes, and through the blood he saw Billy. Anger ruled his face, evil lived in his eyes, and a strange perverse pleasure hovered around him as Billy squeezed his fingers tighter around Michael's neck. Again the darkness narrowed Michael's vision and the pain seemed to dull. Coherent thoughts disintegrated as his lungs began to burn, searching for oxygen. Michael heard his own throat strain, pushing to open for air. In the background he could hear the crowd gathering and shouting, "Kill that motherfucker!"

Then suddenly Billy let go of Michael's throat and grabbed him by the collar. Air flooded into his lungs, once again pushing the darkness away. The pain rushed in like a thunderstorm from his stomach, side and head. Michael coughed, purging his lungs of the stale air.

In the background, he heard the faint sounds of a police siren. In the back of his mind he prayed the sirens were responding to his situation, but he could not be sure. Sirens whaled throughout the day in New Haven; many times passing by spots they needed to respond to only to arrive where they weren't needed. It was like some unseen hand of evil always ensured the police were where they weren't supposed to be. He just hoped that hand of evil had taken a break at this moment and some Good Samaritan had called the police for him.

But the sounds of the idiots in the crowd screaming for more blood, doused any hope of that happening. His neighborhood was filled with moral rejects and bloodthirsty morons. The good people had either moved away or they stayed indoors to avoid thugs like these. Something he should have done...stayed inside. But this was his neighborhood; he never had trouble dealing with people here before. Those he knew were trouble he gave a wide berth to...Billy being the number one person he always tried not to piss off.

Now Billy had him by the collar with his face so close, his bad breath was acting like smelling salt, waking him up even more. Michael now noticed the scar under Billy's right eye, his broken and missing teeth, from a fight that Michael imagined he was on the wrong end of, and finally the killer persona that Michael always knew was there, but didn't want to ever experience.

Michael reached over and around with his right hand, finding Billy's hand on his collar and twisted up and over, pulling Billy's hand, wrist and his arm in an unnatural turn, breaking his hold on him. Then without thinking, Michael kicked his knee up into Billy's crotch as hard as he could, bringing Billy to his knees and grabbing for his family jewels. Michael then took a deep breath, summoning his body to respond to his commands and feeding his boxer built body with the much-needed oxygen it required.

What Billy didn't realize, was that Michael wasn't the scared kid he used to be prior to going away to college. Michael had joined the boxing team and had trained in the ring. If Billy had taken the time to examine Michael, he would have noted the 'V' cut of his torso and the muscle tone of his arms. Michael was a heavyweight boxer and did pretty well as a freshman. But this wasn't the ring, and there weren't any referees to control the bout.

Michael picked Billy up by his collar and let loose with a vicious right hook. Billy, who was an inch taller and had about forty pounds on Michael, collapsed to the ground like a rag doll. The crowd fell silent, either in surprise or shock. Michael imagined it was both. He had never had a street fight in his life. The neighborhood thought him a punk for not getting involved in the daily one-on-one riots that took place in the hood. But Michael saw no purpose in dealing with fights. Even though he knew he could hold his own with half the thugs in the hood, he had nothing to prove to them. But now, he was fighting for his life.

Billy rolled over on his back, looking up at Michael in defeat, or so Michael thought. Michael patted the back of his head and for the first time noticed the blood and the open gash that crowned it. Michael continued staring at Billy, watching for his next move. Several seconds passed as the two gladiators sized each other up. Michael decided Billy was too surprised to continue. He spit more blood from his mouth and turned toward the crowd. He stared at the fifteen to twenty people who offered no help and wanted to see him die just a few minutes ago. "What the fuck are you looking at?" he yelled. "You all ain't shit, just a bunch of sad little fucks. Ain't nobody dying today. So go home...get the hell out of here...get out of my way!"

Suddenly Jackie screamed. Her eyes were fixed behind Michael, causing Michael to turn around, just in time to see it—the knife. Billy lunged toward him with the knife. Michael sidestepped the first stab, but Billy swung wide behind him as he passed. The knife caught Michael in the side, splitting his shirt and giving a path for more of his blood to spill. The burn was intense. Michael grabbed his side. Then two of Billy's friends rushed out of the crowd and grabbed Michael by his arms. He pulled against the bullies, but his wounds had drained what little energy he had left.

He looked up and saw the crowd part as two police officers fought their way through. *Thank God!* Michael prayed. But it wasn't enough. A slicing, piercing pain pushed through his side. The pain was so awful, so hot, so terrifying that he prayed for it to stop. He looked at his right side and saw the knife sticking out. He looked up and saw Billy's black face laughing in triumph, displaying his crooked, broken and missing-tooth smile. That was the last thing Michael saw before the warmth of unconsciousness, which he had fought off so bravely thus far, took him into a peaceful slumber. The pain was gone.

Chapter 8—Mosleck Threat

One thousand light years from Earth, in sector four, the Universal Security, Science and Trade Association of Planets' (USSTAP's) Galaxy Cruiser, *Uno* sailed the heavens in search of her pray. She was the flagship of the fleet. Her black hull and her side engines made her look like a gliding bat pushing her will through the night. On board, her crew of one thousand personnel stood ready for conflict with the enemy. Amongst them was the Lt Osguard, Ortho Chting, the keeper of the USSTAP constitution and the acting CEO of the largest nongovernmental organization known to man.

In his ready room, off the port side of the bridge, Ortho contemplated his fifty-two years of leading USSTAP. Even though he was from Chaktun, his bronze glow had left him in his youth and his skin now contained wrinkles made of years of space travel and of command. His blue eyes still burned with youthful exuberance, but his bald head showed the age of a man nearing the end of his life's journey. He sat stooped over his desk, entering into his Artificial Intelligence (ARIT) terminal the notes of today's journey.

***

From the Desk of the Lt Osguard
Universal Date: 05.06.48235.
Today marks the fifth week the USSTAP Uno has been tracking the Mosleck pirate ship Rojam. As noted, several weeks ago the Mosleck pirates ventured from governmental protected domains into the realm of USSTAP. The Rojam led an attack on USSTAP trading station Aruda, killing 2,000 USSTAP warriors and disrupting trade for at least three galaxies, making the Mosleck ship the number one threat to USSTAP. I have notice that the Mosleck problem has worsened in the last several years, and should have suspected the Mosleck would attack USSTAP interests.

The Moslecks were once a proud and fierce empire that subjugated a race of people called the Hustains, the original inhabitants of the disputed planet now called Hustaindom—one of the association members. Of course, under Mosleck rule, the planet was known as Mosleckite. Several hundred years ago, the Kulusks, the sworn enemy of USSTAP and the civilized universe had dominated Mosleckite and its people. However, in the last war Chaktun had with Kulusk, during my grandfather's time, Chaktun liberated Mosleckite and gave the domain back to the Hustains. Immediately upon garnering self-government, the Hustains renamed Mosleckite, Hustaindom and displaced their former masters, making the Moslecks the new nomadic tribe of the galaxy.

For over a century the Moslecks have reverted to terrorist actions on Hustaindom, bombing transportations hubs, assassination, and piracy. As long as the threat was localized inside Hustaindom's borders, USSTAP did not have a constitutional issue in the fight. USSTAP's charter stood firm on the premise of shared scientific knowledge, even commercial trade and common defense of universal trade routes for the self-governing domains in the association. But as a non-state domain, USSTAP had no authority to dictate how the planets within the association conducted their local affairs. However, on many occasions I've exercised my influence on governmental domains, to keep them within the charter.

Yet Hustaindom is a different animal. Chaktun made it out of war, just before the inception of USSTAP. Therefore the problem bore from war reparations in which neither Chaktun nor USSTAP could renegotiate. In some ways, I had empathy for the Mosleck cause. They are a people with no land and a vanishing heritage. But in no way do I condone their methods. In a report, I received from the Hustaindom government today, it is noted that the Moslecks are responsible for over fifty-nine thousand civilian deaths including women and children in the hundred years of conflict.

Upon reading this, I have lost any shred of empathy I once held for the Mosleck cause and now am committed in capturing the Rojam and its captain, Misul Rafinel, the unofficial leader of the Mosleck pirates.

But once again, the trail grows cold as our sensors and scanners lost the dialairtic discharge stream from their Mass Object Projection engines. We are backtracking to the point we first detected the dialairtic stream. I believe we have been chasing a ghost stream and that the real stream will now be evident and traceable.

However, this is one of many universal issues taking me away from my true duty of finding the rightful heir or heirs to the Osguard seat. I promised Laurona and Nausona Osguard on their deathbeds that I would find their lost descendants on Earth so they could lead USSTAP into the glorious organization that they both envisioned. I made that promise fifty-two years ago, with the hope that I would be able to fulfill the promise quickly. However, the business of the universe has continually pulled me from honoring that promise, and now I fear with old age knocking at my door, I will soon become too old to fulfill that promise. Now once again, the business of the universe, the Mosleck issue, has put my earnest attempts to honor a promise on the back burner.

As a man that has lived a comfortable, albeit dangerous life, I cannot imagine what it was like for the Osguard mothers in their youth. To flee from their home world after seeing their parents butchered to death, only to be mistaken as slave in a barbaric, cruel and backwards world, such as Earth.

Then to be whipped, beaten and raped by an enemy—all at the tender age of 16 galactic years of age. My grandfather rescued them, but at what price. Their children were left on Earth to fend for themselves in a world that treated them less than human, less than a dog and pushed onto them the self-esteem of a beetle. The Osguard mothers spent their entire life in search of their children, but died before they could pass the mantle on to them.

Now that task falls on my shoulders—a burden I proudly carried all these years. But after fifty-two years of faithful duty, I feel that the same fate may befall me, to die without finding an Osguard descendant. I must look to see who may carry on the tasking. After I capture and convict Misul, I will begin my new journey, and find a sincere successor to the Osguard seat.

"Close Entry"

***

Ortho peered up from reading his entry, rubbing the back of his neck, massaging the strain of command from his body. The massage turned into a big yawn and a body stretch as he continued to bend backwards and snapped the tightness from his soul. On his black uniform collar, he wore the four lightning bolts—three gold and one silver—signifying his ultimate authority and leadership of USSTAP.

The vidcon chimed and Ortho engaged it. On his monitor, his second in command, Centurion Albatio Yaw's face appeared. His bronze tint, black pupils and curly blonde hair were in stark contrast to Ortho. He was a product of a USSTAP marriage between a Chaktun man and a Kersch woman. His parents, who served USSTAP early in Ortho's career, have since retired to Kerschnee, where they enjoy the double dawn and the two sunsets afforded the planet by its unique binary solar system.

"Sire," Albatio began, "We are picking up the *Rojam* trail. It leads to the third moon of Calvara, about forty light years from here."

Ortho grinned, feeling that his luck was changing for the better, "Good, set a course…MOP fifty."

"Tiah!" Albatio responded and the screen went blank.

Moments later the batwing galaxy cruiser melded into the fabric of space, disappearing from sight as it manipulated the space and time continuum and accelerated through the speed schedule to travel fifty light years per hour.

***

The *USSTAP Galaxy Cruiser Uno* snapped back into normal space as her engines jumped from MOP, to hyperlight, and then to hypersonic speed, decelerating through the speed schedule with the precision of a neural surgeon. Ahead of the *Uno*, lay the Cal Solar System, containing five planets, Caldish, Calmet, Calvara, Calson and Calmar. The *Uno* adjusted its coordinates and entered the solar system, heading for the third planet, Calvara.

On the bridge, Ortho sat in the middle console, the command chair, flanked by Albatio, his Centurion of Operations, on his right, and Sylvia Marquez, his Centurion of Engineering, on his left. In front of him sat the double view screen, the left side was the window to the outside. On the right side, their route of flight over a star chart was displayed. The pilot station was in front of the left screen, and the navigator station was in front of the right screen. Along the port side of the horseshoe shaped bridge sat the science and life support stations. On the starboard side sat security and communications. Behind him were the defensive and offensive stations, manned and ready for battle.

Soon the left view screen in front of the bridge, filled with the sight of Calvara, a misty brown planet, whose surface was covered by only thirty percent water, barely inhabitable by any form of human life.

Several colonies from the neighboring Serine Solar System attempted to mine the planet for its duricatilite, a substance they needed to enrich their farming soil. But the venture proved too costly, and they abandoned the solar system fifty years ago and joined USSTAP, who now through trade negotiations, provide the duricatilite to the Serine population for their neolythium rocks, a commodity needed throughout the third galaxy. USSTAP's trade was based on one planet's abundant waste being another planet's rare commodity. Duricatilite was a waste product in about fifteen percent of the association, but a needed asset in ten percent of the association, while neolythium was an alternative fuel source in one galaxy and a biohazard in another. USSTAP bartered the trade with association members. And since USSTAP was the sole owner of gate portal technology that could whisk ships from one end of the galaxy to another or even to another galaxy in the blink of an eye, it arranged transport and delivery of all trade in the known universe. This cut cost for the governmental domains, spurred economic growth and lessened the strains of war over goods and services between domains.

It was supposed to be a utopia, except greed and power always harbored in the minds and hearts of small pockets of individuals. These pockets have challenged the status quo and lost for over a hundred years, and now another group was trying to flex their muscle—the Moslecks.

Calvara, a sign of years past, proved to be an ample haven for the Moslecks. The old buildings and supplies that the Serine government left aided the Moslecks in expanding their sphere of terror—a sphere that now enveloped the heart of USSTAP and garnered the attention of its leader.

Ortho gazed upon the planet, spying the third moon about to rise over the northern polar cap. "All sensors...all scans," Ortho ordered. "I want that ship."

Beeps, tones and other electronic sounds wafted through the air, as the bridge crew executed his commands. Invisible fingers reached from the ship, feeling space and the heavens for an unnatural body. Strings of imperceptible fibers swam, pounding and penetrating all in its path and echoed readings back to the *Uno*, like a bat's sonar. In fact the *Uno*, perched in orbit over Calvara was reminiscent of a bat hovering over its prey, lying perfectly still and screeching out inaudible energy waves.

Suddenly, one of the masked waves of sensors picked up an object on the far side of the third moon. Within a nanosecond, the ship's scanners slewed to the sensor reading and began running a database search of the parameters. Ten nanoseconds later, the scanner beeped with a ninety-four percent probability.

"Class One Mosleck Attack Ship...five–eight–nine decimal two–five–six, mark negative point zero–two–four...solar generator array is energized," the defensive officer yelled.

"Pilot, come twenty-five to port," Ortho said, after a brief second of doing the calculations in his head to turn the *Uno* toward the target. "Pagenay...full charge, Asher Torpedoes to ready ... Chromerion Field up!" He took a deep breath, cleansing his mind and preparing his body for battle. He held it for a few seconds, and then let it out, along with the tension of combat and the uncertainty of decision. "Hail them," he ordered.

"Hailing frequencies opened," the communications officer responded, after stabbing her control panel into operate.

"This is Lieutenant Osguard Chting, sire of the Universal Science, Security and Trade Association of Planets Galaxy Cruiser *Uno*. You are hereby under arrest for the flagrant attack of USSTAP Trading Station Aruda. Surrender and prepared to be boarded."

Several seconds ticked by as Ortho waited for a response. Then as if the gates of hell opened up, a fiery voice, soaked in evil and energized by the dead, crashed through the communications speaker, "Never!"

Ortho turned to Albatio; surprise ruled his expression and disbelief cornered his feelings. He clicked his communications button at his console, "This is not a request. It is an order, given to you by the Supreme Leader of USSTAP. Surrender now, or bear the consequences." Ortho punched the button off to emphasize his determination.

The ghastly voice, representing the avatar of evil, again responded, "Never!"

Ortho turned again to Albatio, "I knew Misul was crazy, but I didn't think he was stupid as well. Doesn't he know that the galaxy cruiser is the deadliest ship in the heavens? We have twelve particle generator array guns and six Asher Torpedo bays with a complement large enough to destroy a large moon—more than enough to blast his butt out of the sky.

"There is a thin line between crazy and stupid," Sylvia noted, pushing her way into the conversation. "Maybe Misul needs to be reminded of the line."

As if cued by her powerful but angelic voice, a spider looking spacecraft sailed from beyond the third moon on an intercept course toward the *Uno*. The ship grew larger and larger, approaching at hypersonic speed.

"Their weapons are charged," the Defensive Officer reminded Ortho.

Ortho shot a glance to the young officer, reminding him he was well aware of the enemy's status. The captain continued to stare into Ortho's eyes, standing firm on his readings and not allowing the shame that punctured his pride to show in his face.

Ortho smiled and nodded, giving the Defensive Officer the dignity of his post in front of his peers, "Thank you Captain Thorling." Then he turned to the Offensive Officer, "Now, Major Forthwright."

Forthwright, a brash but competent officer from New Zealand, responded with a heavily accented "Tiah!"

Ortho loved his accent. Forthwright turned the Chaktun language from a romantic, rhythmic language into a brawling, harsh street fighter's linguistic tool. He had an uncanny ability to make a compliment sound like a curse when he spoke Chaktun. Deep inside, just a small amount of tension was released as Ortho thought about Forthwright's accent.

Forthwright manipulated his controls, "Signal sent to fleet."

Ortho turned back to the view screen and saw the *Rojam* come to a complete stop. Surrounding her and coming into visual range were five more galaxy cruisers. They had shadowed the *Uno* in Stealth Mode ten, hiding in the recess of space. The galaxy cruiser, the mainstay of the security force, was coated with a special black substance called slitanium that absorbed refracted and bent light. This coupled with lights out and port windows blackened gave the ship a unique stealth quality, virtually invisible to radar, sensors, scanners and especially the naked eye.

Ortho clicked his vidcon once more, "Misul Rafinel, this is Lieutenant Osguard Ortho Chting. You and your people are under arrest for crimes committed against USSTAP Charter one–two–three–three…two thousand counts, and the attack of USSTAP Trading Post Aruda. Surrender and prepare to be boarded. This is your last warning."

Without hesitation, the devilish voice of evil rang through the communications network. "This is Misul Ralinget, the son of Misul Rafinel. I do not recognize your authority over the Mosleck people and refuse to surrender. If you want me, come and get me."

"Target pagenay guns to their chromerion field generators and weapons," Ortho ordered.

"Tiah!" Forthwright responded.

"All ships…fire!"

The heavens lit up with the flashes of searing blue sun heat fire—pure and efficient energy flew from all six, galaxy cruisers—piercing, slicing and tearing away at the *Rojam*. Parts of the *Rojam's* chromerion field, glowed yellow and then orange. Her chromerion field generator only afforded several seconds of protection, before collapsing. Then her weapons ports caved in, spewing red hot metal like an erupting volcano.

The attack was relentlessly deadly and accurate, surgically manipulating non-vital sections of the ship, while neutering her with precision. After thirty seconds, the *Rojam* listed to her port, like a dying fish in a river. Life support pods blasted from her like teenage zits.

Forthwright delivered each event with sportscaster precision. Again, his accent overshadowed the deadliness of the situation with a jovial street catharsis. "Sire, "Forty-five life-pods just ejected from the *Rojam*," he announced. "I'm reading a large energy feedback in their weapons system." She's building up! She's about to rupture."

"Cease fire," Ortho ordered, hoping his actions would somehow reverse the process.

But it didn't. Fire and energy cracks spider webbed outward from the weapons ports, ripping cracks into the hull and breaking giant size pieces off. The jigsaw puzzle flaked as the *Rojam* shed her skin. Pressure sucked her crew into space, crushing their lungs, collapsing and then imploding their hearts in the most gruesome death imaginable for a space weary soldier.

"How many crew?" Ortho asked.

"Counting over seven hundred bodies sire," the Defensive Officer confirmed.

Ortho lowered his head in a silent prayer and sighed. He wanted to capture the ship, not kill it. He wanted to arrest the people, not murder them. He thought his actions would be reviewed by every domain in the association, as either an act of revenge or an act of justice. With over seven hundred dead, he knew now his actions would be considered an act of revenge.

Six galaxy cruisers for one pirate ship, was it too much force? Would it be consider an ambush? Was it an execution? Did he subconsciously know his actions would result in this, and he just blotted it out of his mind? These questions and many more questions, concerning his motives and worthiness flashed in his mind in a split second of silence.

He raised his head and looked out onto the carnage. The strewn bodies littered the landscape of the battlefield like dandelions blemishing a lawn--beautiful in sight, but grotesque in nature. He was gazing upon his legacy—fifty-two years leading the universe as a peacekeeper, ruined by thirty seconds of combat. He had stepped from the platform of statesman to one of warrior. And he didn't even know he was moving.

"Collect the remains and pick up the survivors," he ordered.

Albatio nodded and with that one word, "Tiah!"

Ortho's world pretended to sink back into the normal routine. But there was nothing normal about this day. This day brought with it a new dawn, and Ortho knew he was too old to see dusk. The Mosleck issue had taken a new twist.

Chapter 9—Marked For Greatness

The darkness was disconcerting. It was as if he was asleep, but somehow still aware of his existence. The voices were distant and faint. Michael had to concentrate to hear them.

"Blood pressure is dropping!"

"We need more blood!"

"Two bags O-positive stat!"

"Doctor we're losing him!"

"Stand back. Clear!"

Then nothing, the voices were gone. It was like someone turned off the T.V. set in the middle of a medical drama, right as the doctors were about to pull off a miracle and snatch someone back from the jaws of death.

Then as soon as the thought struck Michael, it was gone. He no longer had a care in the world. A tidal wave of bliss surrounded him...a euphoria of completeness enveloped him and the darkness began to fade. A pinpoint of white light appeared to him, rapidly growing ... filling his world like someone had turned on the light and he was able to watch it push the darkness away. Then he felt himself floating. But it wasn't his body and it wasn't his mind, it was his soul.

Michael's soul floated toward the light giving him a sense of wonderment he had never known before. Then as he was about to enter the light, his soul stopped and hovered in front of it, suspended by an unknown invisible force.

"Michael David Genesis," a nondescript voice called.

Michael answered, "Yes."

"Michael," the voice called again. "It is not your time yet."

"Is this heaven?" Michael asked.

"It is what you believe heaven to be, but it has many names and many functions as dictated by the Beginning and the End." The voice paused to give Michael time to understand. "However, it is not your time yet!"

"Then why am I here?"

"This had to pass in order for you to become."

"Become...become what?" he asked.

"To become what the Beginning and the End has destined you to become."

"I don't understand."

"You are not supposed to understand. You are only to do."

"Do what?" The blissfulness began to recede in Michael's soul, only to be overcome by confusion and doubt.

"You are to embrace a new world and design a new universe. The Beginning and the End has chosen you to lay out a path so humanity can begin its journey to the next level."

"What? I don't understand. What are you talking about?" The light began to shrink, even faster than it grew. Panic filtered into Michael's soul as he felt himself move backwards away from the light and deeper into darkness. "Why am I here? What's my destiny? I'm no prophet." His voice changed from ruminative to desperate. "Please, I don't want to go back...I want to stay."

Soon Michael felt the presence had left him and he once again was all alone. The darkness swept over him like a blanket and he no longer had a sense of awareness. He lost his sense of self, mind, body and soul.

***

In a private room on the third floor of Yale-New Haven Hospital, Michael's eyes shot open. He was attached to several I-V bags and hospital equipment to monitor his heart rate, blood pressure and other vital signs. The machine monitoring his heartbeat beeped in the rhythmic dance of his heart like African Drums in the night. It was so early in the morning the sun had yet to greet the day. His family occupied the room with him, but they were asleep, from exhaustion, fatigue and fright.

His mother, Elizabeth Genesis slept in the chair next to his bed, holding his hand as only a mother could. His Father, Parker, was in another chair closer to the door, with his head down looking like a security guard who had fallen asleep at his post. His older brother, Shawn, found a patch of floor as his sleeping quarters. He sat with his back against the wall, cradling his knees to his chest with his arms, while resting his head on his knees. His younger sister, Patricia, lay across his chest with her arms wrapped around him as if she were pulling him out of bed or holding on for dear life. She was sixteen years old, and he was eighteen, and they fought like siblings always fought. However, they always protected each other no matter what. So it was no surprise she took point during the vigil. She probably drove the doctors crazy with her demanding nature. But that was his sister.

The entire fight stormed into his head in a second, but everything else after that was a blank, including his experience with the white light. All he knew was that he was alive because it wasn't his time yet. He also knew he was alive because there was something left for him to do. But what, he had no clue.

He gently patted his sister's head with his free hand. She stirred for a second and then snuggled up to his chin. Then like a lightning bolt, she shot up. Her hazel eyes were wide open and her auburn hair that she usually kept neatly combed tight to her scalp was a mess. But to Michael, she was a sweet vision of loveliness, a goddess in human form.

He smiled and said, "What are you doing here? Don't you have some boy you should be driving crazy?"

Her eyes started to water as tears formed. She smiled at him with a smile that could melt the polar caps. "Yeah, I do…you. What took you so long? Did you stop to check up on St. Peter?" Then she leaned over and planted a big kiss on his cheek and hugged him as tightly as she could.

Michael hugged her too with his free arm, fighting the tears he felt swelled in his own eyes. With his other hand he squeezed his mother's hand, enjoying the warmth of the two women in his life that he knew he could count on to be there when he needed them the most.

His mother woke from the pressure he put on her hand, and she screamed for joy, as if she was in church and had just received the Holy Ghost. Parker and Shawn jumped up, scared – not knowing if Elizabeth screamed because Michael had come to, or if he had passed away. After a few seconds they realized it was a scream for joy and soon they were in a dog pile type family hug, with Michael on the bottom.

***

Later that morning, after being moved out of intensive care, Michael lay in bed counting his blessings for being alive. He had been unconscious for five days. He fought to remember anything about what happened after the fight. But the last thing he remembered was Billy's ugly face triumphantly smiling at him and then darkness. His mother told him that they almost lost him. He was clinically dead for a few seconds. The doctors had to use a defibrillator to shock him back to life.

The phone rang, breaking him out of his contemplation.

"Hello," Michael said into the phone.

"Don't tell the cops shit, or your little sister is dead." The line went dead.

***

G.C. Uno slowed to subsonic speed as it entered the approach to Capitol Station. The Station was an amalgamation of seventy self-contained gray stations. They graced the area like shining stars. Each station was diamond shaped. They were of different sizes and positioned throughout the space line in some type of unseen mathematical array. The bigger stations had rings around them. A five-story ring, horizontally attached at the base, encased the biggest station, called Millmum Capitol Station. This station was eight miles wide at the base and two hundred decks long from point to point. Around its ring several galaxy cruisers were docked. The *Uno* maneuvered through the corridor of smaller stations, beaconed by the approach signal from Millmum Capitol Station. Soon the station filled the entire view screen. In the background, the Chaktun solar system gave the scene a golden picturesque view. The station had a multitude of window ports of different sizes, shaped like ovals, squares, rectangles and other shapes reminiscent of alien cultures from other worlds.

Ortho sighed watching the docking procedures as if he was about to meet his doom. The USSTAP Parliament, the governmental body made up of ambassadors from all of USSTAP's signatory planets had called him into a special session, to explain his actions against the Mosleck ship.

The Prime Ambassador, Ets Shaymirh was from NGC-7793 galaxy in the Sculptor Star Group of the Virgo Cluster, better known on the USSTAP Map as Galaxy ten, the Netalee Galaxy. Shaymirh lead the two thousand seven hundred-member-parliament, representing planets in thirty galaxies through the legal, political and judicial business of USSTAP, trying in every way to usurp his authority as the acting leader of USSTAP. Today's summoning was just another attempt, in a long line of actions by Shaymirh, to consolidate USSTAP's ultimate power under the prime ambassador's position. Unfortunately, the loss of six hundred and fifty Mosleck souls in an apparent USSTAP ambush versus any justification Ortho had for his actions gave weight to Shaymirh's cause. In Shaymirh's eyes, justice was too swift and too harsh and dealt out by the inappropriate party—Ortho.

When the docking procedure was complete, Ortho stood and made his way to the docking port. He pushed through the crowds, not stopping to observe the mastery of the many murals decorating the corridors like he usually did. He loved the stories each one told and admired the history each one represented. But, today he did not feel like loving or admiring the murals. He felt alone, tired and anxious to get this over with.

His one job in life was to watch over the burgeoning association created by the Osguards, until their offspring could be found to reclaim their rightful spot. But now he was in the sunset of his years, tagged with actions that may have inaugurated a guerilla war with space pirates and the sharks in the parliament smelled blood—his blood.

He was on autopilot, not watching where he was going, but letting his mind work his body without conscious management, pushing him toward the parliamentary chamber, where Shaymirh said they would be waiting for him. The guards posted at the chamber doors, recognized him and motioned for him to pass without challenge. The gigantic ten-foot wooden doors framed in granite slid open with an uneasy quietness. The chamber always reminded Ortho of one of those Roman Coliseums he visited on Earth when he was younger. And presently, he felt like a slave walking into that coliseum to do battle.

The floor was not dirt of course, but made of finely polished marble. The ministers however did sit above the center area, as did the spectators in the ancient coliseums, giving the majestic appearance of nobility and the mental appearance of superiority.

Ortho walked to the middle of the floor, which took quite some time, since the chamber floor was approximately fifty yards long. A spotlight highlighted him in the dimly lit area, ensuring all eyes were on him. He could not see up into the stands to make eye contact with members of parliament.

Ortho always hated how parliament was shaped and made. He knew it was only made in this fashion to satisfy the power hungriness of its members. Even though the immediate power rested in his authority, parliament wanted to feel and give the appearance that they had the real power.

After several seconds that seemed like an eternity for Ortho of standing in the light, Shaymirh's voice boomed, "Lieutenant Osguard Ortho Chting," he began. "The parliament has reviewed your report on the Mosleck tragedy at Calvara."

Ortho noticed the word *'tragedy'* and recognized at once the use of that word indicated siding, if not empathy, with the murderous Moslecks. He knew the parliament had already forgotten that these very Moslecks that Shaymirh was referring to were the same Moslecks that killed two thousand USSTAP warriors at the Aruda Trading Station and disrupted valuable trade for at least three galaxies.

"And we find your report," Shaymirh continued, not noticing the reticent look upon Ortho's face, "sorely lacking in details and very impassionate to the Moslecks who lost their lives under your guns." Shaymirh paused as if he was about to make a regal proclamation. "Furthermore, the use of six galaxy cruisers against one Mosleck pirate ship seems a bit much—don't you think?"

"Prime Ambassador Shaymirh," Ortho responded after a pregnant pause, "We had been chasing that ship for over five universal weeks after they killed two thousand of USSTAP's finest warriors at Aruda Trading Post. And let's not forget, how many other lost lives are attributed to this one ship. Just during our pursuit, this one Mosleck ship wreaked havoc in three solar systems, killing at least a hundred more women and children. So if you are asking me if I think the firepower I brought upon them was too much, the answer is no!"

A symphony of whispers bellowed from the crowd as his words drummed the air inside the chamber. Ortho didn't know if the whispers were whispers of agreement or whispers of condemnation.

"I offered Misul Ralinget plenty of opportunity to give up. He chose not to," Ortho added.

"Yes," Shaymirh admitted. "But Misul Ralinget didn't know the other galaxy cruisers were there, now did he?"

Ortho shook his head in disbelief, "You have my report. I explicitly recorded that the other five cruisers came out of stealth mode ten prior to my final warning. Misul Ralinget, who up until then, I thought was Misul Rafinel, refused to surrender."

"We only have your word for that," Shaymirh responded.

"Yes, my word as the leader of USSTAP. But if that isn't good enough for you, I also have the records from the ships."

"Which you may have ordered doctored to protect your skin," Shaymirh pushed back.

"You accuse me without proof?"

"I accuse you because of the lack of proof," Shaymirh voice rang.

"Oh…I see! I'm guilty because of the lack of proof to say that I'm guilty. What kind of insane logic is that?"

"It is the logic of the parliament."

The voices in the audience started to rise, no longer attempting to maintain the civility of a whisper.

Ortho rolled his eyes and pointed to where he knew Shaymirh should have been sitting, "Prime Ambassador, you are stepping on dangerous territory."

"USSTAP is not a dictatorship and if it was, you are surely not its dictator. USSTAP is an association of planets, and we at the parliament represent the planets. Therefore, you my friend are the one stepping on dangerous territory."

"Members of the Parliament," Ortho addressed, pulling the conversation away from Shaymirh. "We rescued one hundred and fifty crewmembers from the Mosleck ship, as noted in my report," he reminded them. At the same time, he activated the communication device on his collar, also known as the CC. "Bring in the prisoner," he commanded.

The doors once again opened. Through the archways, two black clothed USSTAP guards escorted a prisoner. They marched the prisoner into the light with Ortho, surrounded by the cacophony of voices belonging to the amazed parliamentary leaders. One of the guards handed Ortho an ARIT note pad.

Somewhat frustrated at the impromptu note, Ortho read it with a frown. His eyes widened and a devilish smile creased his face. The note seemed to give him hope. It gave him a newfound power to continue his participation in this inquisition. He coughed to clear his throat and regain his composure. Then he looked up in the command presence he was known for.

"Members of Parliament, this is Misul Ralinget."

The crowd hushed.

"Shaymirh," Ortho summoned, leaving out the title of Prime Ambassador. "Ask him your question."

"How do we know this is Misul Ralinget?" Shaymirh hollered.

"Check your own intelligence report, scan the prisoner, compare, ask the ARIT, or trust me as the leader of USSTAP that this is who I say it is."

"I am Misul Ralinget," the prisoner yelled. "And when my father finds out what you have done to me and my ship, USSTAP will pay dearly."

"Shut up and tell the parliament the events at Calvara."

"What events?" Ralinget barked. "You tracked me down, I wouldn't surrender, and you fired upon my ship and killed six hundred and fifty patriots of the Mosleck cause."

"Why didn't you surrender?" Shaymirh asked, "Didn't you see you were outnumbered?" he added.

"Six of your attack ships against a mighty Mosleck gunship, isn't being outnumbered. The *Rojam* would have blasted all of your ships out of existence if it wasn't for one of your ships getting in a lucky shot. The Mosleck Gunship is the most powerful ship in the heavens."

"That's enough," Ortho shouted. "Get him out of here," he commanded the guards.

Misul Ralinget kept up his tirade as the guards escorted him back out the chamber, his voice echoed like a madman in a cave. After several seconds of quiet, Ortho sighed.

"Are we done here?" Ortho pushed.

"No," Shaymirh responded.

"I think we are," Ortho replied. "And if you continue this mess, the Osguardian privilege to disband this parliament for just cause and push for a new election of ambassadors will be invoked. Jus knows you have given more than ample cause to do so."

"Under USSTAP Charter, Article One," Shaymirh interrupted, "the association is a binding agreement between the leaders of the planetary governments and the leaders of USSTAP, the Osguards. You're not an Osguard. You are a Lt. Osguard. You can't do that, Lt Osguard," Shaymirh laughed. "Only a true descendant of the Osguards can do that. And...oh my! There hasn't been a true Osguard running USSTAP in fifty-two universal years. And I doubt if we will see another Osguard heading USSTAP ever again. That is one of the reasons we called you here. This parliament plans on executing an election for an Osguard Senate. In other words we are going to elect a full-fledged Osguard and only members from the parliament will be able to run."

"Wrong again, Shaymirh...wrong again," Ortho yelled. "The missing Osguard line has been found on Earth and I'm on my way to pick up the first Osguard now. So an Osguard senate is a great idea; however, according to USSTAP Charter, only Laurona and Nausona's descendants will sit on it as true Osguards. That leaves you or anyone else in the parliament who thinks they can snatch USSTAP up for their own glory out of consideration. Now if you'll excuse me, I have to pick up the first Osguard.

Chapter 10—Revenge of One

A month had passed. It was now the 4th of July and Michael was sitting on his porch enjoying the shade from the tree and watching the Beaver Hill neighborhood sights pass by him like a parade. Mrs. Johnson walked past his house, toting her groceries from the corner store. She nodded to him. In the street, several of the neighborhood kids were playing tag football, moving out of the way every time a car wanted to claim its right to the street. When the car passed, the boys swarmed back into the street like water. Across the street, several young girls sat on a porch, listening to music streaming out of the window and comparing clothes, shoes and other accessories.

The sounds and sights of Beaver Hill seemed to flow in rhythmic harmony to the world. Kids still played, mothers still shouted out the windows to their kids to keep them safe, and the cars still rode by at a slow pace so everyone could admire the driver for either driving or for what he or she was driving. Yes, the parade still existed, except for the occasional gunfire that somehow forced its way as part of 1982 urban life.

New Haven, situated ninety miles outside New York, had always been a training camp for the Mob. But lately, a new crop of animal seeped out of the gutters. This creature was more violent, more aggressive and more psychotic than the Mob. The gangbanger had come of age and had become the *threat de jour*.

Most of the houses in the neighborhood were built prior to the turn of the century, old two and three family houses, once occupied proudly by upscale whites. Of course when the first black family moved in, around 1935, white flight occurred, sending the upscale Whites to the suburbs and leaving the neighborhood for the blacks to buy up. For years the Beaver Hill neighborhood around Whalley Avenue maintained its dignity and beauty. But something happened in the 70's that changed that. Drugs! And along with the drugs, came the gangbangers like Billy.

Michael tried to forget about Billy, but he couldn't. He felt like his old self. The physical scars were healing, but unfortunately the psychological scars remained open. Besides being the brunt of the neighborhood gossip as '*That nigger who got his ass whooped*', he also had to live with the shame of lying to the police. When they asked if he knew who had stabbed him, he pretended he could not remember anything about the fight. The doctors told him this was consistent with near death experiences. So the cops had to believe him. At least this way he left himself an out if he ever decided to rat them out later. He could always say his memory had returned. But for now, feigning he could not remember was all he could do to save his sister's life.

But the more he thought about it, the more he thought about how the neighborhood had changed because of people like Billy, the more he became enraged. *Something had to be done about Billy and his thugs.* The police let him go after his vicious attack on him, because no one in the crowd who witnessed the spectacle would speak up. But how could he blame them, he didn't speak up and he was the one attacked. People like Billy Red had the run of Beaver Hill, because people like him were too scared to say anything. *Well that stops...that stops now!*

***

That night, New Haven planned to celebrate the Fourth of July with a fireworks display at the New Haven Green. The Green was a central area used in colonial days as a community meeting place, something common to most New England towns. The modern day Green was the centerpiece in which the city displayed its colonial and American history. There was no better place to celebrate the country's independence than the New Haven Green. And there was no better place for Michael to declare his independence from fear.

It was 7:00 PM when Michael walked into the Green from the north end. City Hall and a police substation were across the street to the east. He felt funny and scared at the same time. He knew Billy and his thugs would be here tonight, and he knew Billy would try something with him if they met. He counted on that. That's why under his shirt he had his father's three-fifty-seven Magnum-revolver in his belt. Feeling the bulge against his hip gave him a feeling of power and control. It made him feel alive. He now felt like he was someone and not just another drop in the bucket. But it also frightened him, because in his power was an instrument of death, and if he wasn't strong enough to use it, it could be the very instrument of his death. Nonetheless, a little voice in him told him it didn't matter. One way or another his fright would end tonight, and his sister's life would be safe.

He strolled deeper into the Green, searching for Billy or any of his people. He didn't know what he would do when he found them. All he knew was that he wanted to spot him first, because if Billy saw Michael first, the evening would be worse than he could ever imagine. He felt his heart beat inside his chest, louder and harder with every step he took into the Green. His breath became labored, as if he were running. Anxiety was stealing his calm, pushing coherent thought from his mind. He stopped and took a deep breath, held it and blew it out hard after several seconds. He felt his body calm as his heart returned to beating at a normal rate.

Pop!

The first of the fireworks exploded in the air, shaking him back into a state of panic for a split second. He sucked in another deep breath, cleansing his lungs and forcing his body to calm down once again. At that moment, he realized he needed to leave, that he wasn't ready to partake in what he wanted to do. But another voice inside of him pushed for him to continue, because if he stopped now, he would never get his dignity back and more importantly, Patricia's life would always be in danger.

He was confused. He didn't know what to do. But as fate would have it, destiny had already chosen him, or so it seemed to him, because at that moment, Billy and the two thugs that held him passed no more than fifty feet in front of him.

Before he knew it, he was already moving toward them, with his hand on the gun. Whatever nervousness he felt earlier was long gone. The sight of the three that almost killed him, and threatened to kill his sister ignited a rage so animalistic; he did not feel like himself anymore. He was a spectator, watching the show on some type of cosmic television. It was him, but it wasn't him. He was aware, but not aware. Some internal, innate, instinct now controlled his every move. Michael was just along for the ride.

He streamed by several people in his quest to reach his targets. That is how he started thinking of Billy and the others, as targets. He had already dehumanized them, making it easier for him to do what he had to do. Originally, he wanted to use his weapon in self-defense; allow Billy to start the fight, let Billy pull out the knife, and then shoot him. But something snapped and that plan no longer had merit. Now it was just shoot the target and take whatever consequences the law had to give. At least his sister would be safe.

Billy and the other two had their backs turned toward Michael, as he approached within ten feet. His fingers gripped the gun underneath his shirt and he began to pull it out.

"Michael," a voice called to him.

Michael stopped and turned around, but no one was speaking to him. He shook his head and turned back to his targets.

"It is not your time yet," the voice continued. But this time Michael knew he didn't hear it. The voice was inside his head. The same non-descript voice he had heard some place else before.

"This had to pass in order for you to become."

Michael shook his head again and closed his eyes. Firework explosions banged the dark sky shredding brilliant red yellow and orange colors through the night. Everyone seemed to be preoccupied with the display. The sounds were somewhat deafening...deafening to the point people had to yell to be heard. But this voice was faint...almost a whisper in his head, and he heard it loud and clear over the fireworks in the sky.

"To become what the Beginning and the End has destined you to become. You are to embrace a new world and design a new universe. The Beginning and the End has chosen you to lay out a path so humanity can begin its journey to the next level."

A heavy hand clasped Michael's shoulder. He jumped, frightened that his paranoid distraction had allowed Billy to catch him off guard. He turned, still with his hand on the revolver, ready to use it if necessary.

"Michael," a tall firmly built man called. "Michael Genesis. My name is Ortho...Ortho Chting." Ortho was rugged with Middle Eastern features. He sported a clean-shaven head, making him look like Mr. Clean from the floor soap commercials. The wrinkles around his face told Michael the man was up in his years, but his body disagreed with that perception.

Michael regarded the man; about to rebuff this stranger's approach, but something told him not to. He released the grip on the gun, stood straight and with his best manners answered. "Yes, I'm Michael...Michael Genesis. What can I do for you?"

"I've been looking for you for quite some time," Ortho beamed. "I tell you, I'm damned glad to have caught up to you."

"Yeah...why?"

"Is there some place we can talk?"

"Look mister, I don't know what your game is, but I have something to do," Michael said, losing some of the politeness in his voice.

"If it has anything to do with that gun in your belt, I wish you would change your mind."

The two men looked at each other for a while, trying to figure what to say next. Michael knew the very fact he had the gun was enough to get him arrested, and this man had just shouted he knew he had one, but no one around them heard or no one around them cared. He shot a quick glance toward Billy and the other two. They remained engrossed in the fireworks display. He thought he would never get another opportunity like this. The explosions in the sky would conceal the weapons fire and he could get away with murder.

Murder? he thought. That is what he was here to do, wasn't it? *Murder?* If he continued with what he was doing, he would become the very thing he despised...a gangbanger...a street thug. Everything he had worked for, everything his mother and father had prepared him for would go down the drain, never to be reclaimed again. He lowered his head in shame.

"You are to embrace a new world and design a new universe. The Beginning and the End has chosen you to lay out a path so humanity can begin its journey to the next level," the voice reassured him.

Veiled fragments of the white light popped into his memory. The entire episode did not present itself, but enough of it did to remind him of how blissful it was to be in the presence of the light, and how the words meant something. What? He didn't know.

"Tell me something Mr. Chting, if I go with you, will I have a chance to embrace a new world, design a new universe and lay out a path so humanity can begin its journey to the next level?"

Ortho's eyes widened. Shock ruled his expression, and then he squinted, regarding Michael for several seconds before he spoke.

"How'd you know?"

Michael started to tell him he heard voices, but decided against it. He already thought he was going mad; there was no reason letting someone else know it. "An educated guess," he said.

"If you come with me, I will show you your destiny."

Michael didn't know what to believe, but he had the gun, so if this guy were a freak, he would be a dead freak! "Okay, let's walk over by the police station. We can talk there."

"As you wish," Ortho conceded.

Chapter 11—Recruitment of an Osguard

The two followed the path toward the police station on the other side of Church Street. They were like salmon swimming upstream, as they fought the crowd of people going deeper into the Green. Soon they found themselves on the steps of City Hall, next to the police station, watching the fireworks display

"I've practiced for this day my entire life and now that it is here, I don't know how to begin," Ortho complained.

"My mother always said start at the beginning," Michael deadpanned.

"Very well, I will start at the beginning," he relented. "Okay, here it goes. Two years before your Civil War, two young sisters; Laurona and Nausona Osguard, fraternal twins actually, fled from another planet, called Chaktun, to Earth."

The disbelief on Michael's face was priceless. "Bullshit, man. I'm out of here."

"You are to embrace a new world and design a new universe. The Beginning and the End has chosen you to lay out a path so humanity can begin its journey to the next level," the voice in his head pushed with more force, as Ortho reached his hand out to hold Michael from getting up.

Michael sat back down, "Okay, I ain't got anything else to do tonight. Go ahead man; peddle your shit. Why did they flee their planet…Chaktun is it?

"For years, perhaps centuries, the people of Chaktun have had an on again, off again war with the people of Kulusk. At this particular time, Chaktun was losing the war. They killed Nausona and Laurona's father and mother, the Maxum and Maxim of Chaktun. They were next, so they fled with the help of my grandfather."

"Ah, so you are from Chaktun?"

"That's correct."

Michael looked Ortho up and down. Michael didn't know who was crazier; Ortho for telling the story or him for listening to it. However, the bulge his gun made against his waist made him feel a little more secure than he would have felt without it. "Go on," he encouraged.

"To make a long story short, they ended up in Virginia and made friends with a conductor of the Underground Railroad, named Elizabeth Gentry. But there was a plantation owner that lived close, by the name of Pathgo...a Phillip Pathgo. Well anyway his sons raped and beat the Osguard sisters, leaving each with child. When my grandfather rescued the Osguards, they were unconscious and dying. He had no idea the princesses had had children. So they were left behind. We found out later the children were left in the care of a slave family the sisters had helped through the Underground Railroad. For years, we have searched this planet for any sign of those children. And until now, we had no luck."

"Until now?"

"Yes, until now," Ortho answered. "See, the Chaktun blood is slightly unique from others of this planet, but there is enough similarity to confuse our scanning and sensor techniques. So we had to go low tech and actually test blood samples. One of our agents at Yale New Haven Hospital saw the likeness you have to Vedar Osguard, the Chaktun Maxum and ran a blood comparison on your DNA."

"Wait a minute," Michael almost screamed. "Are you telling me that I am some sort of alien prince or something?"

"Yes and no," Ortho stated. "You are a direct descendant of Nausona Osguard. However, the sisters abdicated the throne to form the Universal Science Security and Trade Association of Planets...a sort of United Nations of the stars. It is an alliance of planetary governments for common defense science and shared trade. Presently we have members from thirty galaxies participating in USSTAP."

"Yeah...right!" Michael cooed.

"I know this sounds fantastic to you. Now that I say it aloud it sounds even more impossible to me. But I speak the truth," Ortho pleaded. He then pulled an electronic gadget from his pocket. It looked similar to a scientific calculator, but different in size. It was bigger. The screen was approximately three inches by five inches, and the keys were not push button; they were what he later learned as touch screen. The writing on the keys was strange, not numbers or letters.

"What's that?"

"It's my portable artificial intelligence…PARIT for short."

The screen lit up with vibrant color, similar to a color T.V. Pictures flashed on the screen. It flashed a picture of a man, who looked almost like Michael, except the man was of lighter complexion and much older. But still the resemblance was uncanny.

"This is Maxum Vedar Osguard. Do you see the likeness?"

"Neat trick," Michael retorted.

Do you have this shape anywhere on your body?" Ortho asked as he flipped to the next picture that showed a black diamond birthmark on the side of Vedar's neck.

Michael lifted his right hand and displayed the birthmark on the back of his hand. It was the same. It was the same that his sister, brother and father had on them as well, just in different areas. Michael had always thought of the birthmark as the mark of the Genesis clan, because all his cousins had the mark as well.

"So what? That doesn't prove a thing," Michael rebuffed.

Ortho stood, replaced his PARIT and removed another device. "This is my personal gate portal…also called a PGP." If you don't mind taking a little walk with me, I will show you how this works and then I'm sure you will believe me then."

Michael looked around and saw the streets were still crowded with spectators watching the fireworks display. He surmised it was safe, and that nagging voice in his head made him think, whatever this man was selling, he had to at least listen. He stood and nodded. "Walk me to my car. I'm parked over on Orange St.

They headed up Church Street and turned right onto Elm Street. All the while, Michael eyed the instrument Ortho called a PGP.

"So what is that, some type of ray gun?" Michael joked.

"No, I'll show you that later…and it's called a pagenay."

"I thought you said that was called a PGP?" Michael countered, thinking he had cornered Ortho in a lie.

"This is a PGP. The ray gun you spoke of is called a pagenay," Ortho scolded.

"Ah…" was all Michael managed to say. He fell silent wondering what loony bin Ortho escaped from. Again, he found comfort in the gun tucked in his belt. Now, Michael was calculating how long it would take him to draw the gun if necessary. But that nagging voice interrupted his thoughts once more.

"You are to embrace a new world and design a new universe. The Beginning and the End has chosen you to lay out a path so humanity can begin its journey to the next level."

Traffic on Elm Street now was bumper to bumper as the last of the faithful fireworks watchers were executing their escape. Michael knew it would be awhile before he would get home, because he had to wait for the traffic to clear. They then turned north on Orange Street. Like a vacuum, the street seemed empty and almost unnaturally dark. Most of the people were behind them now, on Elm Street, busing their way to and from their cars.

"I'm just up here to the right," Michael pointed out. He had parked behind the Children's Museum one more block up. "Don't you think whatever you have to show me, you best do it quick, because, I'm not staying around here for long?"

Ortho grunted. It was the first sign of a changed demeanor. Michael became nervous and moved his hand toward his gun. The street was empty. He could see that his car was the only one in the parking lot, sitting alone under a streetlight.

"What is a PGP?" Michael asked, trying to hide his nervousness.

"It is a device that opens a doorway to inner space, the fourth dimension." He slowed his pace as they entered the parking lot, and raised the PGP for Michael to get a better look. "Space is folded on itself in many layers. These folds connect space and time to every point in a field. Therefore, allowing us to cover great distances in space as easily as walking through a doorway into the next room."

Michael rolled his eyes in disbelief, "Yeah…right man. Are you sure you're feeling okay? I mean, I can drive you to the hospital if you want."

"How sweet…punk!" came Billy's voice from behind them.

Michael and Ortho turned around to see Billy Red and his two faithful sidekicks. For a split second, their eyes met and their minds passed an unknown code between them, saying, prepare to fight.

"What do you want, Billy?" Michael said, mustering the sound of confidence from his soul into the words.

"I want to finish kicking your ass," Billy snarled, making his two cronies laugh on cue, reminding Michael of the monkeys in the zoo. "And when I finish kicking your ass, I think I will go have some fun with your pretty little sister," he threatened.

Billy slid a switchblade from his pocket and clicked it open with one smooth motion. The blade sailed out of its holder, sparkling against the street light like a silver star.

Immediately, and without thought, Michael drew his gun and pointed it at Billy. The hammer coiled back and he was already applying pressure on the trigger. The smug look on Billy's face washed off. His sidekicks recoiled, leaving Billy as the first target in the line of fire.

Michael walked up to Billy, gun held high, pointing it right at Billy's forehead. He saw the fright that bore in Billy's eyes…the fright just hours ago he planned to put there. Now fate had delivered the chance without his intervention. He pressed the gun against Billy's forehead, showing no sign of nervousness or hesitation.

Billy dropped the knife. The switchblade clanged on the cement parking lot ground, bouncing twice before coming to rest beside Michael's right foot. Michael kicked it behind him, out of the reach of Billy and his friends.

No words were said, just a tense moment as Michael's eyes narrowed. He was savoring the moment. There was nothing in the world but this moment. Michael had drowned out the city noise and the fireworks. He narrowed his focus onto one spot—Billy Red's forehead. His finger tingled as it rested on the trigger. No thought, no sound, no feelings entered his body, only the steadfast resolve to end the nightmare called Billy Red.

Behind him Ortho watched with intensity. He didn't interfere, he didn't preach, he just observed like a wild life documentary reporting on the animal rituals of African lions in the jungle. If the antelope dies it was just the circle of life…the strongest will survive, or the all-encompassing label…shit happens.

Meanwhile, Michael's subconscious overtook his conscious mind and played back blinding flashes of the fight and the stabbing that almost took his life. With every flashback, anger inflated in his heart and he no longer saw the difference between right and wrong.

Billy witnessed the transformation and knew he was no longer staring at Michael, but staring in the eyes of death. He slammed his eyes shut, wishing, almost praying for salvation, but the only release that came was from his bladder. Urine slid down his leg, wetting his pants and fouling the air like a lavatory.

"You son of a bitch!" Michael yelled. "You son of a bitch!" he repeated. Then he screamed at the top of his lungs, matching the howl of a coyote, scaring what was left of saneness from Billy.

Billy dropped to his knees, with his hands up pleading for mercy. His two partners turned and ran, running for their lives from the crazy man that they inadvertently created.

Calm washed over Michael. Pushing the anger out of his spirit and subduing the horrible memory of his stabbing. He took a deep cleansing breath and blew it out hard

"This had to pass in order for me to become," he whispered. "This had to pass in order for me to become," he repeated more forcefully. He then put the gun back in his belt and turned to Ortho. "This has been one fucked up night."

"Perhaps so, perhaps not!" Ortho ruminated.

Then, three invisible doors slid open, from bottom to top, slicing the night and letting out the most beautiful white light, reminding Michael of his near death experience. He stood awestruck as three men stepped out of the light, wearing black jumpsuits and jackets, similar to the flight suits he saw U.S. Air Force pilots wear. Militaristic patches adorned their sleeves and chest. The doors slid closed behind them with an electronic swoosh.

"That's the PGP at work," Ortho told Michael. Then he turned to the men. "This idiot has threatened members of the Osguard family...take him."

Without a word, the three men snatched Billy up, activated their PGP and dragged him kicking and screaming into the light. Then as suddenly as they appeared, they were gone.

"Do you believe now?"

Michael nodded. He walked over to the spot where the hidden doors opened and stretched out his arms trying to feel for something...anything to explain what he just saw. "Hell yeah...I believe!"

"Good," Ortho smiled. You are the first Osguard that I have found. I need your help in finding the others." Ortho shook his head in astonishment. "For a minute, I thought you were going to kill that fool."

"For a minute, so did I."

"Thank your God you didn't."

"Why?"

"It would be tough handing you the keys to the known universe knowing that you were a cold blooded killer."

"What are you talking about?" Michael questioned, now more confused than ever.

"USSTAP...Michael. I'm talking about USSTAP, your inheritance. There is an entire universe waiting for you."

"You are to embrace a new world and design a new universe. The Beginning and the End has chosen you to lay out a path so humanity can begin its journey to the next level," Michael repeated from memory.

"No...that is your job, yours and the other Osguard descendants," Ortho corrected. Then he activated his PGP, calling the great white light of inner space to open up before them. He motioned for Michael to enter the light.

With a deep breath, a leap of faith and a new respect for humanity, Michael entered the light with Ortho. The door closed and they were gone.

Chapter 12—Doing Time a New Way

Once inside the light, Billy cowered like a little boy, believing he had died and God had sent his soldiers to reclaim his soul. He pleaded with the man to let him go, but the black clad arm of God who held him just sneered at Billy. Then a door emerged and the light faded as he was pushed through. All of a sudden he was in a room, a large room, and surrounded by other black clad soldiers of God. They spoke in a strange language, one he had never heard before. The soldier that had him was tall, rugged with olive color skin. His eyes burnt with a sense of duty and his body was built to take on a Mack Truck.

The soldier slung him like a rag doll and forced Billy to his feet. Then he dragged Billy through some doors that wisped open, and then down a narrow corridor. The walk seemed to take forever, as Billy prepared to meet his Maker. Billy began to pray for the first time since he was ten years old. "Oh God…Oh God! Please don't let this be death."

Then Billy thought about his life. Flashes of his misdeeds ran through his mind, from the first pair of shoes he stole, the cars he stole, to the drugs he sold and the people he had murdered. Billy soon realized he did not deserve God's mercy and the prayers fell silent on his lips. He resigned to take his punishment like a man. With that resignation, Billy stood taller and stopped struggling with the man-mountain soldier that dragged him through the corridor. The soldier sensed the change in Billy's demeanor, and loosened his grip.

Billy now took in the scene. He watched other black clad soldiers, both men and women; Black, White, Hispanic, Asian and people of other races he could not quite make out, gawk at him as they passed. He leered back; with the devil's own grin.

They stopped. The soldier placed his hands over a computer screen against the wall, and the doors parted open with a faint whoosh. The soldier motioned for Billy to proceed forward. Billy looked the soldier in the eye in a testosterone battle of wills, but he soon saw the soldier's determination. Whoever the soldier was, or whatever he was, Billy soon realized he didn't have any room to play. The soldier was not a cop or a rival gang member. If the soldier was a cop, Billy knew he would have been read his rights by now. If the soldier were another gangbanger, he would be dead by now. No, the soldier was playing by another set of rules. And until he knew what the rules were, Billy decided that discretion would be the better part of valor. Billy broke his glance, took a deep breath and walked into the room on his own accord.

Inside the room, the soldier made Billy strip, and ran him through a battery of electronic scans and searches, mapping and categorizing his brainwave pattern, DNA, fingerprints and other indicators to his physical being. The process also sought out any hidden weapons and contraband Billy may have hidden. The purple light first moved horizontally up his body and then in a heartbeat it moved to a vertical beam sweeping from left to right. Billy turned ninety degrees to his right and the purple beam process began again. Then another turn and finally one last turn, then his entire physical essence was downloaded into an ARIT database.

The room he occupied was sterile, with earth tone metallic walls and a grated floor that clang with every step he made. The bed sat on a metallic slab against the far wall. The bathroom facilities were controlled by a funky computer screen, in which he could not read or operate until the soldier demonstrated.

If he wished the use the toilet, he had to tap the screen in a certain sequence and a toilet complete with cushion and armrest would spring from the floor in the far corner. He also used the same screen to flush the toilet, which used compressed air instead of water. Then to call the sink, he would press another sequence and a porcelain sink would spring from the wall near the toilet, complete with liquid soap, white face cloth and a white hand towel. If he wished to bath or shower, he would press another sequence and either a porcelain bathtub or shower would spring from the ceiling, covering the toilet's area.

Billy tried not to look amazed as the soldier displayed the gadgetry, but he was. A sense of dread and relief occupied him at the same time. Dread, because he realized he was here for the long run, but relief because he realized he wasn't dead. It was a strange sensation that he tried not to portray. When the soldier was finished with his demonstration, Billy shot him a 'Get out of My Face' look, in which the soldier accurately interpreted. The soldier retreated to the door, turned and glanced at Billy's soiled pants. The look of defiance washed from Billy's face as the soldier stepped through the doors. The doors closed, sealing a shamed Billy in the room wondering about his fate.

***

Four days had passed since his capture, and during that time, all Billy had done was eat and sleep. The soldiers fed him four meals and two snacks a day. They fed him some type of egg and meat with coffee or tea in the morning for breakfast, followed by a mid-morning power bar. Then he had some type of soup, or what he imagined was soup for lunch with milk and water, followed by a mid-afternoon fruit. For dinner he had a meat and vegetable entrée with a drink and a dessert. Then, for an evening meal, he had a sandwich and a strange drink he imagined was some type of soda.

On the morning of the fifth day Billy's head was ringing with a sharp headache. The headache came from a mixture of confusion, fright and anger. Confusion about where he was and how he got there; fright from whom he was dealing with; and lastly anger for the situation he was in. The solitary confinement was more than disturbing; it was feeding his paranoia. The entire episode was like a bad dream, and he didn't know why. All he knew was it had something to do with Michael. Michael was why he was locked up. Michael was why he was here. His anger, fright and confusion soon focused on one person, Michael Genesis. Sitting on his bed in a fetal position with his back against the wall, he clutched his head, trying to massage the pain away.

"What the fuck do you want with me?" he screamed, hoping they were watching and listening. His voice echoed, vibrating off the walls and floor. "What do you want with me? I didn't do anything."

The sudden release of anger, eased the throbbing in his head, but the pain was still ever present. His outburst was the first emotional freedom he exhibited since his capture. However as soon as he spoke he regretted it, for he showed a sign of weakness, a sign that he was breaking.

***

Back on Earth, the room was just like Michael imagined it would be like—small and cramp with a small metal table and two old wood chairs. The room smelled of old cigarette smoke and there it was, the two-way mirror sitting in front of him. He had watched many police dramas on television to know that there was a hub of people behind the mirror watching him, trying to come up with a psychological profile from his movements and demeanor.

Michael leaned back in his chair with one arm swung over the back and the other lazily resting on the table. At first he was nervous when the police rousted him out of bed and dragged him, handcuffed, to a patrol car in his underwear. The neighborhood busy bodies had already gathered around his house, summoned by the blinking red and blue lights. Embarrassment overshadowed his fear as he saw all the neighbors pointing and gawking at him, suggesting he was just another street thug, pretending to be good. This one incident, whether justified or not, and it certainly was not justified, had tarnished his reputation for life, a reputation he spent countless hours in the library and the church to build up. And with one fell swoop of the local police, his name no longer passed the lips of his neighbors as someone to look up to, but someone to be ashamed of.

The pain in his mother's eyes, stuck with him, more than the neighbors' wagging tongues. His father looked like he was about to hit one of the cops, as they dragged him out. The shouting and the confusion was a spectacle deserving of the devil. And Michael knew the devil was behind this, testing him…tempting him to cross over. He didn't and this was the devil's payback.

When he arrived at the jail, they gave him his one phone call. Luckily, he remembered the phone number Ortho gave him. He called it, identified himself as Michael Genesis and spurted out his situation. The voice on the other line told him to hold tight, and tell the police he wasn't going to answer any questions until his lawyer was present.

When he hung up, the police threw him in the room. Five minutes later, a burly, detective with foul breath rolled in. Before he could open his mouth, Michael told him, "I'm not talking until my lawyer gets here."

"We'll see about that kid," he huffed. Then he took a seat and leaned across the table, "Don't you want to know what you're in here for?"

Michael peered to the ceiling, trying to hide his fear. He knew if the detective looked into his eyes, the fear would be more than evident. He blew out, controlling his voice and said, "Please don't speak to me until my lawyer gets here. If you don't respect me," his voice started to quiver. He cleared his throat and peered back at the detective, "respect the law! I have a right to an attorney and I am invoking that right...now!"

The detective's smug look vanished from his face, replaced by one of frustration, "Listen kid, you don't want to lawyer up now...do you?"

The burn in his eyes told Michael, the detective was ready to spit nails. But Michael never let his gaze falter. He kept it steady and piercing, looking past the man, into his soul, swimming into his conscious being...almost in a hypnotic trance. And with a whisper, defiant of fear and worthy of the Greek god Zeus, he said, "Yes...yes I do."

Michael's stare was so intense, but without malice or impudence, the detective started to feel warm and uncomfortable. He hadn't felt this uncomfortable since his first interrogation, some sixteen years ago.

In order to save face, the detective pounded his fist on the table and shook his finger at Michael, "You'll be sorry kid. You're making a big mistake. We could have cleared this up, without involving the suits. But you had to play hardball. You had to call your lawyer."

Michael smiled, "I'm just leveling the playing field, since you have home court advantage already."

The detective stood and shook his head, "Wrong answer kid...wrong answer." Then he left, not knowing who had won that round, him or Michael. As he closed the door, the realization struck him like an alarm clock...he had lost.

That was an hour ago. Michael had been sitting in the cold, Spartan room since then, wondering what the police had on him and weighing his options. Then the door blew open. The detective followed by two other people, a silver-tongued well dressed Italian looking man in a pinstriped suit, and a slight pudgy man in a dark gray polyester suit and loosened black tie. The detective sat down across from Michael, still smarting from their earlier conversation.

The Italian looking gentleman moved behind Michael and placed his hand on his shoulder, "Ortho sent me. I'm Spencer Martelli, your attorney." With those words, the tension Michael was hiding floated away.

"This is Detective Louis Cunningham from homicide," Martelli continued, pointing to the bad breath cop across the table, "and this is

78

assistant district attorney Gary Ford," he said pointing to the slight pudgy man.

Michael nodded to the gentlemen as Martelli introduced them.

"Now gentlemen, let's get down to business," Martelli said with a deafening business tone. "You are charging my client with the disappearance of Billy Red, because of the statements of two questionable characters that saw Mr. Genesis point a gun to his head on July Fourth."

Ford nodded with interest.

"Well gentlemen," he continued, "here is a statement from Mr. Ortho Chting, the CEO of Unlimited Associates, a well respected individual in the business, political and social community. In the statement you will read the accounts of that night, because he was with Michael during the incident. You will read how Billy Red attacked them both, and Michael defended them with his father's gun, which I know is in your possession now, because I gave it to you. You can see Billy Red and his cohorts, who you are using as witnesses, are responsible for stabbing my client several weeks ago, and for threatening his sister if he fingered them. You can read Mr. Chting's statement on how those witnesses of yours ran away and how my client held the gun to Billy's head, until he was sure he was no longer a threat--in other words, until he dropped the knife."

"Now, I've given you the knife as well. So let me tell you what you are going to find on the knife." His voice rose as if he was speaking to a jury. "You will find Billy Red's fingerprints. Also you will find the gun hasn't been fired. Now we admit, my client shouldn't have had the gun, but think about it. You're almost killed. The person who stabbed you is still making threats against you and your family...wouldn't you want to carry protection. And thank God he did, or my client would be dead right now, along with Mr. Chting."

Martelli lowered his voice, but did not give Ford or Cunningham a chance to speak, "You have no body, you have no crime scene, you have no weapons. All you have is the word of two people who should be arrested for attempted murder and conspiracy to commit murder." Martelli was on a roll and he wasn't about to give up his soapbox now. "My client is a victim, not a perp. He is a scholarship award winning college student with no record, except the dean's list. He's a choir member. I can parade dozens of character witnesses that will make your witnesses look like the sons of the devil. Now if you don't charge those two for attacking my client, I will sue the city for..."

Ford raised his hand to squelch the rhetoric; "I've heard it all before counselor. Let's just see what the gun and knife reveal from our forensic lab."

"Fine!" Martelli agreed, "A smart move. Now let's see what other smart moves you can do. Release my client now!"

Ford looked down at the ground, searching his options.

"Now!" Martelli yelled, surprising both Ford and Cunningham.

"You're free to go," Ford said. "But don't leave town."

"Bull!" Martelli responded. "When your forensic lab confirms Mr. Chting's statements and my assertions, I expect you to resend that order and I also expect a written apology to my client and his parents for the rude and unnecessary way you dragged him down here. Your commando tactics may work for those who don't understand the law or who can't afford a competent attorney. But my client is neither."

"People like you don't make my job any easier!" Cunningham yelled, showing his disgust at the turn of events.

Martelli smiled, "On the contrary Detective Cunningham. People like me make your job much easier, by making sure you stick to the rule of law. Because if you don't, criminals go free and innocent victims suffer. You need to get your priorities straight. Where was the exuberance you are showing in pinning a fictitious murder on my client when it was time to find out who stabbed my client?" Martelli's eyes burned with ire as he stared at Cunningham. "Nowhere! I don't understand you Cunningham. I know justice is blind, but you made it deaf, dumb and crippled when it came to my client."

Cunningham lowered his head, feeling the pains of shame shatter his sense of professionalism. He had joined the force to make a difference. But lately, he felt like he wasn't making a difference, he was only taking out the trash, handling each person as if they were human waste, whether they were victims or perpetrators. Martelli's words stung him in a place he no longer thought he could feel, his conscience.

Satisfied his work was done, Martelli tapped Michael on the shoulder, motioning for him to get up. Then they both walked out of the room and the police station with their heads held high. Outside, Michael's mother, father, sister and brother were waiting. They swarmed him, shedding tears of joys.

Michael turned to Martelli with tears of joy, "Thank you, Mr. Martelli."

Martelli smiled and nodded, "Tiah!" he responded in Chaktun.

***

Later, in a USSTAP courtroom, Billy succumbed to the fact he couldn't beat the machine. The court proceeding, or whatever it was, was not rigged in his favor. With every question they asked the machine strapped to his head would let the judges know whether he was lying or telling the truth...most of the time he was lying.

The machine confirmed he had stabbed Michael. It confirmed he had threatened Patricia if Michael talked, and it confirmed he tried to kill Michael on July Fourth. Every explanation he invented, the machine identified as false. When he spoke the truth, the machine identified it as true. It was the ultimate lie detector. And unfortunately, it was admissible in this court.

He sat at the rich looking walnut table with his advocate, Major Nacsy, who he'd just met several minutes prior to the proceedings. Nacsy had the complexion of a Puerto Rican, but with uncharacteristic short red curly hair and bushy eyebrows. Billy thought of him as a reject from the clown factory, and did not offer him an ounce of respect. Nacsy told him he was a Wellian, which meant nothing to Billy, but only added to his perception of Nacsy's incompetence.

Opposite them sat the event seeker, recognized as the prosecutor to Billy. His name was Commander Lionel Gold, to Billy's surprise, a brother from Harlem New York. Gold looked like a running back for the New York Jets; strong, muscular and built like the Hulk. He wore his Afro short and neat with a smartly trimmed mustache.

Projected on a view screen to their right was a four-judge panel. On the panel sat four black men from the United States, Marshal Charles Mann, from Boston, Commodore Antoine Masters from Chicago, General Don Mitchell from Los Angeles, and Admiral Derrick Thomas from Atlanta. All four looked battle ridden and street tested. But they also had another look about them…a look not readily perceptible to Billy. It was a look of pride mixed with honor…two feelings that had eluded Billy all of his life.

The evidence included something he never heard of before, called deoxyribonucleic acid. His DNA, as they referred to it, was all over the knife. It also included the testimony of a Lieutenant Osguard Chting. Billy recognized him as the man Michael was with that night. But what scared Billy the most was the utmost respect everyone paid to the man, as if he was the President of the United States. His word was gospel, as indicated by the truth telling machine, Billy soon learned was called a MARIT, blinking solid blue. If it were red, it would be indicating a lie. It had blinked red with Billy.

Then Michael walked into the room. The reverence the people paid to Ortho now transferred over to Michael. Billy hung his head low, perplexed by Michael's treatment. They called him Osguard Michael Genesis. Billy sat in awe, his confused state hastened to the point of insanity. He still didn't know where he was. He still didn't know what was going on. No one bothered to explain what was going on. He didn't know what Michael had to do with it either. He was mesmerized, thinking it all a nightmare as Michael told his story. Again, the MARIT signaled all he said was the truth. And Billy knew Michael was telling the truth.

The entire proceeding took ninety minutes. When it was over, Admiral Thomas pronounced the panel's judgment, "Billy Red, you have been found guilty of the attempted assassination of an Osguard. Usually our jurisdiction does not extend to self-governing domains, except for this one provision. Paragraph twelve, subsection three of the Universal Science,

Security and Trade Association of Planets Charter states: 'Jurisdiction for prosecution for any attack, kidnapping, maiming or murder of an official representative of the Universal Science, Security and Trade Association of Planets, no matter place, time or area, will rest in the courts of the Universal Science, Security and Trade Association of Planets Judicial Corps.' Your advocate has argued that the domain governments of Earth are not signatories to USSTAP, but under special provision two–two–one of the charter, Earth is a protectorate of USSTAP. The reason for Earth being a protectorate is due to the lost children of Osguard.

Michael Genesis is a descendant of Nausona Osguard, and the heir to USSTAP. An attack so vicious and as heinous as yours against him is usually punishable by life on a prison planet. However, your advocate has effectively argued that without your intervention, we would not have found the lost children of Osguard. In fact, your attack was the precipitous act that put together a long line of coincidences that allowed Michael Genesis to be identified as an Osguard. So with that in mind, your sentence is hereby commuted to twenty-five years to be served on Prison Planet Zeta Claire." Four chimes rang out to punctuate the sentence rendered by the judges. "Let the ARIT reflect the sentence to be executed immediately. This judicial committee is closed." Five chimes rang out signaling the close of the proceedings.

The nightmare had just become worse for Billy. He closed his eyes, praying to wake up now. But there was no change. He still felt the presence of the sterile environment imprison his soul as the words rang in his head. He still smelled the filtered air fill his lungs and he still heard the electronic hum resonate through the air.

Then, his personal guard grabbed him by the arm, slapped a restraining device on his wrists and ushered him from the room. As he walked, he realized he would never live his life again. His body and soul belong to this organization called USSTAP. He knew as the door closed behind him that he would never see New Haven, Beaver Hill or any of his boys again. He would never see his mother, who must be worried to death about where he is. He looked at the guard, and for the first time felt lost. A tear rolled from his left eye as fright ate away at his self-control.

Then without thought and without hope, he screamed, "No! No! Please stop…give me another chance…I'll change…I swear I'll change! I'm sorry! I'm so, so sorry! Please don't!"

His screams fell on deaf ears as they echoed throughout the facility. Soon the vastness of the hall swallowed his voice and no one in the room could hear him. But Ortho, Michael, Nacsy and Gold still could see him in their minds, pleading for his life. They stood silent for a few moments, staring at the closed doors, letting the image fade from them.

Then with a deep breath, Ortho asked Michael, "Are you ready?"

"Ready for what?"

"To get the other Osguards."

"Tiah!" Michael acknowledged, speaking his first Chaktun word.

Ortho smiled, "Good…real good…Because I've been waiting for this day all of my life."

Chapter 13—The Osguard Plan

From the Desk of the Lt Osguard

Universal Time: 07.01.48235. With Michael Genesis' help, record searches and family interviews, the Historical Department was able to trace the majority of the lost children of Osguard.

Laurona's Daughter, Kashara, was named Lilly by her adopted family. She married a man named Glenn Nightman, and they had two daughters and a son. We were able to trace the lineage of one daughter and one son, but as I feared, due to the Tuit Incident 79 universal years ago that claimed my father's life, there are no signs of their daughter, Betty Nightman, or any children she may have had.

Nausona's Daughter, Sharyla, was named Amanda and was raised as Kashara's sister. She married a man named Neil Grace, and they had two sons and a daughter. I am afraid their daughter, Shirley, met the same fate as Betty.

However, we have found 153 Osguard family members and spouses still living on Earth. The majority of them are old and in my opinion unable to make the transition to the demands of running USSTAP. With the Mosleck issue brewing, now is not the time to indoctrinate the elder Osguard descendants into the fold. So with congressional and parliamentary approval, the prime members of the Osguard family, ages seventeen to twenty-five will be indoctrinated into the USSTAP fold and ultimately ordained to lead the association. Of these, only sixty remain viable candidates after eliminating those with drug and alcohol addiction. Unfortunately, the elimination was necessary, for the induction ceremony would cause adverse and potentially fatal effects, when given the drug to awaken their Chaktun Omega two-four-four DNA sequence. I have numbered the remaining candidates for easier grouping, in the order in which I contacted them.

Of course those not contacted will be afforded the comfortable life in which their status deserves. However, as discussed and approved by the congress and the parliament, this will have to be done covertly, without their knowledge. Presently, this will be done through the generosity of the inducted Osguards.

The sixty Osguards slated for induction, include mostly students in various phases of education. However, a few had embarked on successful careers. One Osguard candidate, Debra Black, is a popular and successful singer. She had to cancel her summer concert tour for the Awakening. Another candidate, Jarod Stone, just finished his first season as a professional basketball player, earning a multi-million dollar contract. Candidate, Rachael Stone, had begun a budding acting career and had to give up a regular appearance on a television series to attend the Awakening.

Approaching and convincing the candidates was a hard venture and an even harder sell. However, Michael Genesis was with me during each contact, paving the way for open dialogue. He understood their apprehension and was able to speak to them in terms, I still can't quite grasp. But the ease and readiness each of the candidates finally accepted their calling let me know that they were aware that they were meant for something greater than what they were doing. They understood that destiny had chosen them to lead and that destiny had prepared them for that moment of acceptance. It was like a religious arousing, seeing the expression wash over their faces as the realization of the truth pierced their reality. They knew they were different, they just didn't know how. They knew that they had something more to offer mankind, they just didn't know what. That was until I contacted them and gave them the chance to embrace a new world, design a new universe, and to lay out a path so humanity can begin its journey to the next level...as Michael so eloquently put it.

Now the question is how to organize the Osguard candidates. If I follow the Chaktun rule of succession of following the lineage of the first born, Candidate Daryl Gaines would be the leader of the Osguard candidates. But I feel following the Chaktun rule of succession is not the appropriate thing to do. For one, USSTAP is an apolitical association, following the rules of no particular domain, but the eclectic laws of just governments. With that in mind, following a traditional rule of succession would invalidate the legitimacy of the association, giving cause for unfavorable elements in the association to energize opposition in a time where unity is needed.

I cannot give the unfavorable elements a reason to oppose USSTAP's authority while the Mosleck issue looms over our heads. Therefore, I have decided the Osguards will share power as a senate governing body. No one Osguard will have authority over another. However, I have decided to make Michael Genesis the Chairman of the Osguard Senate, the First Osguard.

I feel his resemblance to Vedar Osguard, the father of Nausona and Laurona, will help legitimize the senate and hopefully speed up the Osguards acceptance to take over governing USSTAP. As the First Osguard, Michael's responsibility will be to call the senate together to oversee the dealings of the galactic congresses and universal parliament and mediate any issues of discourse.

After the Awakening, I have decided to introduce the Osguards into the association over phases in the next six years. The Osguards who have not finished college, and do not intend to go to college, will enter the USSTAP Academy on Chaktun for the full three-year training and education period. Upon graduation, they will be assigned areas of responsibility throughout the thirty galaxies associated with USSTAP. They will replace the command ranks of nolvar, solvar and vanguard, as these ranks will retire from the association. Thereafter, every ten universal months, an abbreviated eighteen-month training and education period will commence at the USSTAP Academy for those Osguards who have finished formal education on Earth. Upon their graduation, they will join their fellow Osguards in commanding and protecting the known universe by replacing the diminishing ranks of nolvar, solvar and vanguard as well.

The Universal Parliament is now reviewing my decisions for implementation. My sources have informed me several heated debates have occurred in reference to my decision. However, my usual opposition is in favor of the decisions. I think it is because they feel; they will be able to manipulate the new Osguards, once they are in power, because of their naivety in universal politics. I also fear this. So it is my job to educate them and provide them with my experience, in order to eliminate any chance of manipulation. These Osguards will be my living legacy and the reason for my life.

I must honor Laurona and Nausona by executing their dying wish. Their blood must lead USSTAP once again. It has been my pleasure to hold the mantle of peace during these last fifty-two years, but I'm becoming too frail and too old to continue the fight. The mission of maintaining the peace is for younger blood and more enthusiastic hearts than mine. Running USSTAP belongs squarely on the shoulders of the young Osguards. And I will do everything in my power to see that the young Osguards are ready for USSTAP. In order to do that, I must forge the highest quality steel in their beings that I can, starting with Michael Genesis—the First Osguard.

End Entry

Chapter 14—Going to Jail

Reality was setting in for Billy; especially, as his soldier guard was pulling him once again through the corridors. He understood he had been arrested, by some secret organization, one that didn't play by the rules of any law enforcement agency he had run up against in the past. Therefore, he realized he had no rights…no right to remain silent…no right to an attorney—at least one that could help him. Meaning, there were not tricks or technicalities to the law he could use to gain his freedom. The feeling of doom and despair hovered inside of him and he no longer cared where the soldier was taking him.

Along with this despair came the first ever character change…compliance. The soldier didn't have to struggle with Billy as he had done before. Billy knew he was beaten and there was no sense in struggling with this behemoth. He had thought several times before and for a fleeting second now that he could overpower the soldier…maybe a quick jab followed by a right cross…Maybe a quick crack across the head with some opportune piece of equipment in the hall…Maybe a hard kick to the groin and then knock the hell out of him? But every time these things flashed in his mind, the power of the soldier's grip wiped the thought from his consciousness.

The soldier tossed Billy through a set of open doors into a small room. Billy fell to the floor on his knees, surprised how easy the soldier handled him, but not surprised after mulling over what he had gone through in the last couple of weeks. That look of surprise that occupied Billy's face was slowly replaced by the look of shame.

The soldier picked up his charge and pushed a PARIT in Billy's face. With a timid hand, Billy took it.

"Your instructions," the soldier bellowed.

"Instructions?" Billy whispered.

"Instructions!"

"For what?" Billy almost shouted, but pushed the anger back into his throat.

The soldier took the PARIT and punched a couple of keys. The screen came alive and he pushed it back to Billy.

Billy took the PARIT and began reading the screen. He read the first page and then flipped to the next, as the soldier had shown him earlier. He read some more and flipped to another page. Blood drained from his dark colored skin, giving him the ashy whiteness of a dead man. And that is how he was feeling, like a dead man. The PARIT was an instruction book of rules and regulations on how to survive on a prison planet.

He looked up at the soldier, "You can't be serious?"

The soldier smiled. It was a sinister smile; one that would have made the devil proud…at least Billy thought so. This made Billy more fearful…*A prison planet?* After the so-called trial he was struggling with his situation. They told him he was on Lilly Station, which meant nothing to him. But in the back of his mind he thought Lilly Station was some type of space station. However, he tried to dismiss this as a trick of his imagination, borne of some boyhood fantasy of all those science fiction television shows he loved to watch. There was no way he was in a space station…so he tried to convince himself. Now this soldier was confirming what the trial judges had told him. He was about to be imprisoned on a planet reserved for criminals. And he was powerless to stop what was happening to him.

At first he thought this was all an elaborate trick to get him to confess to something he'd done that was more serious than stabbing a street punk. Lord knows, he had committed more dastardly crimes. Also, he had connections to some of the most influential lieutenants in one of New York's more treacherous crime families. He just knew it had something to do with that. But they hadn't asked any questions concerning that or anything else. The only questions they posed to him were about Michael. Now he was about to journey to a prison planet. *What did the judge call it, Zeta Claire?*

The soldier signaled to the man behind an operating station. The man manipulated some controls that Billy couldn't see and then the white light of a gate portal opened.

Billy shot back, which made the soldier giggle. Billy shrank with embarrassment. He was no longer the bad ass that had murdered, stole from and battered the people of Beaver Hill in New Haven. He was no longer the protégé of the New York crime family lieutenant who wanted him to begin a drug trade in New Haven. He was now the scared punk he thought Michael was. He was scared of every person he met in this new world. He was scared of every sound made, every shadow encountered and every movement made that was not his own. All because he went after a stupid punk named Michael Genesis. He wouldn't be in this mess if it weren't for Michael. *What the fuck is an Osguard anyway?*

With a shove from the soldier, Billy stumbled into the light, and emerged on the other side in a mirror image of the same room. Except in this room, a woman stood behind the control station and the guard awaiting his arrival was different. This guard was light blue colored; his skin was blue like a summer sky over New Haven. And the pupils of his eyes were essentially red, and his hair was jet black, almost Asian in texture, but not quite like an Asian. He stood about six feet, five inches tall with a slim but definite muscular build. And on his face he wore that same sinister smile as the olive colored man-mountain soldier he had just left.

"Welcome, William Red, to the USSTAP Prison Transport Four," boomed the prison guard.

Chapter 15 — The Awakening

"How are you doing?" Ortho asked.

Michael looked up, eyes widened with fear and face drawn with anxiety. He didn't know how to answer the question. It was a simple question, but for some reason, this time it needed deep contemplation and forethought. How did he feel? What did he feel? He looked at his older brother, Shawn, sitting across from him, holding his sister's hand. Patricia had just turned seventeen years old and it took a lot of convincing, and creative imagination for Shawn and him to persuade their parents for Patricia to join them on a summer vacation away from home. With her two big brothers watching her, there were no better chaperons. Besides, she was about to enter her senior year of high school, she needed an adult excursion; at least that is what their mother thought. Then he looked around the cabin, recognizing most as his cousins and not recognizing some. It was a hodgepodge of sixty young people; all related to him through ancestral lines, running through Nausona or Laurona Osguard, the matriarchs of USSTAP. It was a contrast he couldn't quite get his head around.

He looked up at Ortho, after what may have seemed an eternity of thought and found his lips parting, "Tell me, how am I suppose to feel? I'm in a starship cargo bay, hundreds of light years away from my home. Surrounded by the last remaining seeds of my family about to step to a strange planet that you tell me is my home planet, and take part in a ritual that you say will bring clarity to my confused mind." Michael stopped and saw the perplexed expression on the elder gentleman's face. It was almost comical, making Michael smile for the first time in two weeks. He reached out and grabbed Ortho's hand, an action that seemed to calm his fear and anxiety. He looked into Ortho's deep brown eyes, searching for more information, but just ran into the same mysterious wave he had run into since he met Ortho. "I feel fine," he responded. "I feel like a million bucks."

He let go of his hand and breathed a sigh of relief, "Now are you sure you aren't an alien satanic cult leading us to some ritual where we will all end up dead?"

"Yes," Ortho quipped.

"Yes, you're not an alien satanic cult, or yes you're not leading us to a ritual where we all will end up dead?"

"Yes and yes...satisfied?"

"Yup...I'm cool!"

"Michael, you know you were the first Osguard I found and inducted into the association. You helped me find the others. You didn't have any doubts then, why do you have doubts now?"

"Perhaps it's because you whisked me to all parts of the world, including Lilly Station at the bottom of the Atlantic Ocean and Moon Station Set, I felt I was close to home. Now I'm about to set foot on another planet, meeting other aliens like yourself, hundreds of light years from home. It's a little daunting, don't you think?"

"First," Ortho said with exasperation, "you are of Chaktun blood, as well as the others we have assembled. Therefore, we aren't aliens, unless you put yourself in that category. Second, I agree it is a little daunting, but compared to accepting your inherited right to manage the association, this is small potatoes."

Michael giggled, giving a rare smile to Ortho, "Small potatoes…I like that. You must've spent quite a few years on Earth searching for us."

"If you only knew…if you only knew," Ortho said, and then moved on to speak with the next Osguard, Roger Genesis, Michael's cousin and running partner, the second Osguard Ortho contacted with Michael's help. "Hello Roger! How are you doing?"

Michael sunk back into his chair, appreciating the soft but sturdy nature of the material. It felt like Corinthian leather, but it was made out of eberg plant skin. Ortho told him that eberg plants grew three times as tall as a man and that the skin was cultivated after the plant died to make furniture. Michael didn't know what to believe, whether a plant grew three times as tall as a man, or a plant had skin. For now it didn't matter. He just snuggled into the recliner chair, lifted the leg support and closed his eyes. Soon his anxiety and fear subsided, overtaken by a much-needed sleep.

***

Two hours later, the USSTAP Galaxy Cruiser *Justice*, with her black hull, long concave engines attached to her side and her pointy bow, sailed high above the atmosphere of Chaktun, like a giant black bat gliding over its prey. The red power seams that stretched across her hull glowed like neon lights. She was almost a mile in length, and with her engines, she was a half a mile wide. Inside, she was made up of seven decks of intricate passageways. Her concaved engines on both port and starboard side were like wings, spread for flight. They melded into a sharp edge point at the bow and stern, and were attached by triangular spars to the midpoint of the ship. The main ship was shaped similar to a submarine, but had an arrowhead form at the front, which sat a pear shape bridge.

Michael looked out the side port to view his adopted mother planet. Chaktun was twice the size of Earth, orbiting a large orange sun that made the planet seem more alive. Yellowish whispers of clouds danced in the sky, celebrating their arrival. Several landmasses dotted the surface, but like Earth, the planet was mainly composed of water. However the water was a crisper blue than what Michael observed on Earth from Moon Station Set.

Michael tried to memorize the landmasses' contours. He made a game of it, similar to comparing the shapes of clouds in the sky to animals.

On the largest landmass to the north, he saw an eagle; with its wings spread soaring over the planet. In its claws he saw a snake, dangling lifeless. The head and tail of the snake crossed the equator. There he saw nothing but ocean to about a third past the equator, another landmass appeared. It looked like a giant bear on its hind legs, stretching for the snake above it. Directly east of these landmasses lay another ocean, but beyond that ocean a much larger landmass developed. It appeared to take on the shape of a wolf's head, more like a werewolf, Michael imagined. The long nose seemed to be pointing directly toward the eagle's beak. A large lake took on what Michael thought of as an eye. The rest of the landmass connected to the back of the wolf's head spread up and down toward and engulfed the polar caps. The rivers flowing through the landmass looked like veins supplying blood to the area.

Near the wolf's eye sat the capital city of the Chaktun Republic, Kraal. In the center of Kraal lay the Steeple, the main resident and palace of the Chaktun Maxum, Igna Osguard. Inside the Steeple's East Garden, a large crowd of dignitaries, politicians, military personnel and USSTAP representatives gathered to witness the Awakening. All in all, a crowd of five hundred packed the garden.

"Okay Osguards," Ortho called. "It's time! Now remember what I told you and this will go by quickly."

Somehow, Michael knew Ortho was stretching the truth about this going by quickly. He knew anytime you endure a speaker, time goes by slowly, and according to Ortho, several were scheduled to speak at the Awakening. Michael feared it would be worse than high school graduation, but he also knew it would be just as exhilarating.

Next, the cargo bay's gate portal system activated. An invisible wall opened up to the energy of inner space and white light flooded the bay. Michael could not get over the beauty of the light. It was a pure energy, manifested by God and harnessed by man. And each time Michael stepped through the light, he felt a touch of guilt as if he was intruding on heaven without God's permission. Yet that guilt always gave way to sheer pleasure just as he stepped through it, as if he had just talked with God. It was hard to explain, but he knew his heart beat and blood pressure probably rose each time he used the gate portal.

He was the first up. He looked around to his brother, who stood third in line behind him and gave a thumb up. Shawn smiled and winked, giving Michael the tacit approval to move on. Michael stepped into the light and emerged on the other side in the East Garden, followed by the other Osguards in line.

The crowd that had gathered cheered and clapped as they approached. They wore the red tunic embroidered with the black diamond of the house of Vedar Osguard. The ceremonial hood was attached to the tunic. It covered them like a shroud of darkness, not allowing any of the cheering crowd to get a clear glimpse at them.

They lined up in six rows of ten. Michael was the first one in the first row, signifying him as the First Osguard. Unbeknownst to any of them, Ortho had already assigned them their Osguardian number as represented with their position in line.

They exited the light, marching in the Chaktun style up to the palace steps, where Igna, stood in his red regal attire, similar to the Osguards. However the diamond on his chest was royal blue. They stopped in front of the railing separating them from the Maxum. Then Igna said several words accepting them into the family in Chaktun, which Michael and the others could not translate without the help of a Medical Artificial Intelligence (MARIT) device hooked behind their right ear.

"You are of my blood, and I am of your blood. Even though time and distance have kept us apart, you are home now, and I am home now. I am happy to call you cousins in the House of Osguard. Although your lineage is different, we are the same. This is your home; this is your planet...welcome."

When Igna was finished, the Osguards, pulled their golden rods of power, pushed a button and the tops flipped down into a seat. They planted the end of the rod into the grass as Ortho trained them, and took their seats. The seats were metal, hard and very uncomfortable, but it was better than standing. Because after that, it seemed like every government leader in the universe gave an acceptance speech, welcoming the Osguards as the leaders of USSTAP. Even though each statesman was limited to a five-minute segment, the entire proceeding took over four hours – most of the speeches took more than five minutes.

When the last speaker finished, Ortho approached the railing and gave the final signal of acceptance. In unison, the young Osguards stood, removed their hoods, reassembled their golden rods, and clipped the end that exposed a chalice. Inside the chalice was a sparkling purple liquid. They placed the golden chalice to their lips and saluted Ortho. Then they drank the ceremonial drink, which Ortho told the young Osguards, would awaken their Chaktun DNA, giving them clarity of thought, and greater strength, endurance and agility.

It was an immediate reaction. Michael's blood warmed, his muscles tingled and his mind became clear. It was an intoxicating buzz, but also an enlightening encounter. It was exhilarating like an out of body experience. His vision dimmed and then exploded in bright colors. His hearing faded and then sharpened to the point where he could hear the bugs walk on the grass blades. He could now separate the different fragrances of flowers in the garden, where before they were a hodgepodge of smells. Now he had a discerning pallet and was able to taste the difference between different ingredients in the liquid, where before it was a collage of taste exploding in his mouth.

He turned to his right, Jarod Stone, Osguard eleven, was smiling ear to ear. He knew at once, Jarod was feeling the same sensations. He looked down the front row past Jarod and watched Osguard twenty-one, Kendall Steele, Osguard thirty-one, Clay Trent, Osguard forty-one, Peter Grace IV, and Osguard fifty-one, Brian Nightman Jr. beam the same euphoric grin. He turned around to look for his brother, Shawn, who smiled as if he was in the spirit. He couldn't completely see his sister, but he could see her head sway as if she were in the spirit as well. Michael then nodded his head and slapped Jarod's hand, giving him a soulful welcome into the experience.

Chapter 16—Prison Planet Zeta Claire

Zeta Claire was about the size of Earth's moon, with several fresh water lakes reflecting the most sparkling aqua green images that could be seen from space with the naked eye. The lakes were framed with the whitest sandy beaches known to man. The forest ran the entire width and length of the planet, untouched by technology except for a few patchy spots that were cleared to house small cubicles of isolation.

Zeta Claire, the fourth planet in the Zeta solar system, housed eight thousand USSTAP prisoners who were detained for violation of USSTAP laws. Most were former members of USSTAP who had committed breaches deemed deserving of incarceration and the minority of the population contained civilian citizens who committed the most severe atrocities against USSTAP or their personnel.

In one of these cleared patches of land, the alarm rang out, waking Billy from his slumber. He had thirty seconds before his bed would de-materialized, no matter if he was in it or not. The first several days, Billy remained in the bed not heeding the warning of the alarm and soon became familiar with the cold metallic floor. This morning he didn't want to find himself three feet off the floor testing gravity in a no win situation. So he hopped from his bed and slinked to the far corner. As he stepped back the shiny black magic cloud of vapor and mist enveloped the bed and appeared to eat it into thin air.

This was Billy's sixth day on this prison planet and he already felt his sanity fade. He slowly moved toward the bathroom area of his ten feet by ten feet green camouflaged metal cubed room. He operated the facility fixtures in the same manner as he did in his cell on Lilly Station. He completed the call to Mother Nature and then showered. His body fell into the ritual fairly easy, but his mind still reeled with unbelief.

He dressed and moved toward the one door. He took a deep breath and blew out what he knew was the cleanest air his lungs ever tasted. He peered outside searching his surroundings; scanning each patch of land inside the twenty feet by twenty feet force field keeping him prisoner. In front of him was another prison box. In the doorway of that box was his cellmate of sort. He was his cellmate, because they shared the potion of death.

The potion of death was an ARIT transmitter and receiver implanted in his neck and tuned to the one implanted in his cellmates neck. They shared a constant connection as long as the two prisoners stayed within one hundred yards of each other. If that connection was broken, the ARIT would release a poisonous chemical into their blood streams. Once that was done, they had two hours to get immediate medical attention or they would both parish. This was an extra security measure to ensure compliance with USSTAP prison rules, one that Billy thought was frighteningly inhuman, but hellishly effectual. With the potion of death residing in his neck he hadn't thought once about escaping. Then again, if he did find a way to escape, there was nowhere to escape to.

Misul Ralinget was already in his yard, pumping out his two hundred push-ups, a part of his morning exercise ritual. Billy was impressed watching Ralinget rip out push-ups, sit-ups and various other exercises. It just reminded him of the first time they met. Ralinget stood tall and proud, his dark golden skin glistened with strength and his deep voice thundered with authority, which made the guards speak with a tone of civility he had not received. From that moment he knew Ralinget was a man he wanted to get to know. It was just perfect fate that they paired the two of them together. Billy never thought of fate as being perfect. Like luck, Billy had experienced the darker side of fate since he was born.

Billy's mother was fifteen when she gave birth to him. His father was not around. Billy always knew he was a product of one night of teenage lust, but he also felt his mother's heart was broken by his father, a nameless and faceless entity not to ever be spoken of. He often wondered about the men that hung around his mother, and they were many. He wondered if one of them was his father. He would often search their faces, check out their physique, watch their mannerisms and compare them to him; searching for any trace of them in him in hopes of eying his father just once. But he never saw anyone he could say was his father.

His grandmother helped raise him. In actuality, his grandmother was still raising his mother, which made his relationship with his mother seem more like brother and sister, than mother and child. He called his mother by her first name, Dee, and he called his grandmother, mamma. Dee introduced him to his first beer when he was seven years old and his first joint when he was eight. He used to enjoy getting high with Dee. She treated him like an adult.

Of course, this played havoc with his grades in school. Billy became unruly and an incorrigible delinquent, always getting into fights. Billy's first fight happened when he was eight, soon after he started getting high with his mother. From the earliest time he could remember, the older boys teased him about being fatherless, calling his mother a whore. One fateful morning, Scooter MacPherson, a twelve year old, tore into Billy with horrific taunts, calling Billy a bastard and Dee a worn out bitch. Well Billy had just had enough of the teasing and something in him finally snapped. Before, he would run away in tears, something Scooter was counting on, but this time Billy didn't run.

Fueled by the aftermath of smoking and drinking with his mother the night before, and ignited by years of uncontrollable rage, Billy picked up an empty soda bottle and smashed it against the school wall. Scooter froze for a second, wondering why Billy did that. The crowd of boys, who were standing behind Scooter, egging him on, now disappeared, leaving Billy and Scooter facing each other as if they were two gunfighters ready to draw on each other, except Billy already had his weapon out.

Scooter stood about a foot and a half over Billy and had ten pounds on Billy, but fear still found its way into Scooter's spirit, placing an occupancy sign on his face. Billy read Scooter's fear and somehow became elated that he now had control over the situation. The first sick smile of torturous delight, which Billy became infamous for, bore on his face.

Scooter somehow mustered up the will to ask Billy what the hell he thought he was doing. Billy just squinted and leaped with such blinding agility at Scooter, that Scooter didn't even have time to get his arms up in a defensive posture. Billy sliced his left cheek from ear to lip, drawing bright red oozing blood. Billy didn't even think before he swung again; slicing Scooter's left sleeve and again drawing blood. Billy saw the damage he had done and became delirious with happiness. Madness had now taken over and Billy obeyed every one of its commands, thrusting, slicing, cutting and shredding the object of his torment.

The melee lasted about thirty seconds, before two teachers were able to pull Billy off the older boy, but it was too late. Scooter had sustained several deep, gashing cuts, requiring over thirty stitches and permanently disfiguring him. From then on, Billy never endured another word against him or his mother. The suspension from school, the court proceedings and the transfer to an alternative school for troubled youths fed his street credit as someone not to mess with. The legend of Billy Red was born.

Billy lived up to the hype that came with the legend. Bullying was not the name for what he did. He was a young criminal in the making. He committed several crimes he was caught for and some he was not caught for including breaking and entering, and assault and battery and last but not least murder.

Billy committed his first murder at the tender age of sixteen. He was playing dice at the park with Gene Caldwell, a local low rent pimp one night in September of 1979. The dice were flowing well for Billy, which made Gene more upset. Gene was cursing up a storm, but somehow managed to keep his cursing away from any insult to Billy. Billy smiled with that ugly crooked smile that seemed to enhance his reputation as a crazy son-of-a-bitch, which made Gene curse even more. Then Dee strolled up to Billy, catching him by surprise.

She wanted Billy to go home now, which was out of character for Dee. Billy was amazed at Dee's sudden boldness. Dee reminded Billy that she was his mother, which confused Billy more. The crooked smile faded from Billy's face as he shot Dee a stern look. Then he just whispered "No." Dee became frantic and begged him to leave, he didn't have to go home, but she wanted him to leave and get away from Gene.

Gene began to laugh, with a deep bellowing laugh, at the events unfolding in front of him. Billy turned his attention to Gene. He shot him an 'I'll kick your ass' look. Gene shrugged the look off and started shaking his head in disbelief.

Billy wanted to know what was so funny. Gene kept laughing. Dee started pulling Billy away from Gene, but Billy took a step back, still demanding to know what was so funny. The more Billy demanded an answer the harder Dee tried to pull him away, saying let's go, and the harder Gene continued to laugh.

Then with a deep cleansing breath, Gene calmed down and the tension appeared to subside between Billy and Gene. But Dee continued to pull at Billy. Billy shook Dee loose from his arm and demanded once more in his most authoritative voice, "What's so funny?"

Gene looked at Dee and said it was she who was so damned funny. Billy asked why, seething with anger. The next words out of Gene's mouth began with 'This bitch'. He didn't get to finish his sentence, because Billy had heard enough. As soon as Billy recognized Gene was calling Dee a bitch, he pulled out his knife and gutted Gene, twisting and churning the knife in Gene's belly before ripping it out, creating a gashing hole and bringing with it parts of Gene's intestines.

Gene's face was expressionless as he fell to the ground. Dee screamed, and then covered her mouth silencing her own scream from echoing in the night. Billy grabbed her and turned her around so she would no longer gaze on Gene as he lay gasping for air while clutching his belly. Gene started to yell, but Billy swung around, leaned over, grabbed Gene's shirt collar and sliced his neck from side to side. The gurgling sound of the blood rushing into his windpipe and out his neck rewarded Billy with the pleasure that he had done the job right.

Dee did not turn around to see the end result, but by her body language she knew that her son had just committed murder. She shook with dread as she looked skyward, and with a calm, almost angelic voice, she moaned to Billy, "He was your father."

The words echoed in Billy's head for a split second before he replied, "He should have said something," as he wiped the knife on Gene's pants' leg. "I may have shown him some mercy and slit his throat first."

That memory of how he felt that warm September night, elated and avenged, now flooded his thoughts as he watched his cellmate continue with his workout.

He knew little about Ralinget. The guard on the transport told him that Ralinget was the son of the Mosleck leader, and was one of the most fearsome Moslecks in the known universe, a terrorist born on a spaceship, who never knew the pleasure of a home world and bred for one thing, killing anyone not Mosleck. Rumor had it that Ralinget's mother was a Hustain prisoner who Ralinget's father took as his concubine, raping her mentally as well as physically on a daily basis. Ralinget was the product of that illicit situation. It is also rumored that Ralinget's mother died in childbirth and his father responded that Ralinget had saved him the trouble of killing the Hussy, before throwing her body out of the airlock. Billy gathered that Hussy was a derogatory term for a Hustain...a term that somehow made its way into English slang.

Ralinget was sentenced to life on the prison planet because he was responsible for the death of over two thousand USSTAP personnel and countless Hustains. Billy didn't know what or who a Hustain or a Mosleck was, but the fact that Ralinget had killed so many USSTAP personnel, his new enemy, and so many Hustains made him someone to admire...a role model to emulate.

Another alarm rang out, signaling the beginning of the breakfast period. Behind him he could hear the familiar buzz of the black cloud that took his bed. He turned around and witnessed the materialization of a plastic table, chair and a plate of food and a pitcher of a green liquid that he surmised was milk from some space beast he never heard of or wanted to know of. He tried to ask Ralinget, but Ralinget did not speak English...a factor he had not considered before.

He huffed and went to the table. He knew he had about ten minutes to gobble down the breakfast, if that is what it could be called. The meat was white and the eggs, or what he thought were eggs, were prepared sunny side up, looking more like human eyes looking straight at him from the plate. The only thing that looked and tasted like it should was the toast. For the first three days, that was all that he ate from the breakfast plate, the toast...dried without butter or jelly. The lunch and dinner menus were just as unappealing. But hunger won out over discretion and he ate the white meat and eyeball eggs. To his surprise, the meal was somewhat satisfying. It awakened different taste buds he never noticed before, making it palatable enough to finish. The green milk was frothy and also satisfying.

When he finished he peered out the door wondering if his cellmate was finished as well. The alarm rang out again; making him shoot out of the chair for fear that the setup would dematerialize, leaving him to test the gravity of this planet once more. Five seconds later, the setup did disappear, swallowed up by the black sparkling cloud he now no longer feared, but accepted as a part of his life from now on.

This routine played out again for lunch and dinner. The alarm rang, he had ten minutes to eat, the alarm rang again and he shot from his chair. With nothing to do between the meals but to sit on the ground and watch his cellmate do endless pushups, sit-ups and infinite other strength conditioning exercises, including an eloquent but frightening display of a fighting forms and movements. There was no chair, nor bed or any type of furniture in his prison box on which to sit. There were no materials to read, puzzles to solve or utensils to write with. There was just the alarms, meals and the bed that appeared for a few hours during the night for him to sleep on.

On the fifteenth day of fighting the solitude, Billy decided to join his cellmate in his venue. When he woke up, he went outside and attempted to copy all that Ralinget did. Of course he could not do as many repetitions of the exercises as Ralinget, but he gave it a hundred percent. That first day he was sore by lunch time, sweating from head to toe, making the lunch of purple meat and yellow vegetables satisfying, especially washed down by the sweet nectar of the red juice. The juice reminded him of Kool-Aid he drank as a kid.

After lunch he joined Ralinget again. This time he copied the striking movements of a fluid, exciting and energetic fighting form. The intensity that Ralinget possessed in his technique continued to impress Billy. He watched, and then copied each movement.

Ten days later, Ralinget slowed down his pace and began barking instructions through the force field separating the two. Billy strained his intellect to understand the instructions flowing from Ralinget's lips in a language he never heard on Earth before. Eventually, through gestures, body language and sporadic movements, Billy Red overcame the language barrier and began to understand Ralinget. A kinship, branded in a morning alien ritual, blossomed.

Chapter 17—Unspoken Challenge

"So how do you like our little planet?" Reppus asked with a contrived smile.

Michael looked out of the oversized oval window onto the baking orange rays of the Chaktun sun. The sun was one third larger than Earth's sun, giving the appearance of a giant eye in the sky watching and studying the small humans that occupied the planet. The eye spewed hot on hundred plus degree temperature days, baking his skin into rawhide.

But for now he was inside the cool comfort of the Steeple, the home of the ruler of all of Chaktun, and the very room where his heritage began. Here, inside the Maxum's office his forefather, Vedar Osguard, once ruled and spread his wisdom and authority over thirty light years of space. The Maxum's office chamber sat in the middle of the six-story, one hundred room palace, surrounded by forty acres of lush green rolling hills bounded by forest laden bushes and trees.

Michael took a deep breath and continued to admire the beauty of the landscape. It was magical and mystical at the same time. In its form the landscape was a soothing hypnotist, calling for inner peace without making a sound. The flowers were vibrant with color, the grass was a rich dark green, and the birds sang happy songs. There were no car horns, loud music, street jackhammers or crashing bottles on the street to be heard, nothing but the birds pushing their tranquility to anyone who would listen. And Michael had been listening to the call of peace for several weeks now.

Without turning away from the picturesque scene, Michael said, "Very impressive, Reppus...very impressive indeed."

"Someday this will all be mine," Reppus announced.

"So I'm told," Michael responded, turning toward Reppus. I'm glad for you...I think."

"What do you mean, you think?"

"Well for this to be all yours, doesn't your father have to die? I mean Maxum Igna is the current ruler of the land, not you. That seems so unfeeling, to look upon your inheritance in such a manner." Michael moved to the velvet chair opposite the desk and plopped down with a solid thud. Reppus was sitting in his father's office chair, like a kid playing grown-up. "I know I would never think of my inheritance...if I had one," he began to preach. "Because that would mean my father had died. And no amount of inheritance, even the chance to rule an entire planet, would compare to the grief I would feel over my father's death." The sternness of his last words matured his face beyond his nineteen years. "Why are you so anxious for your father to die?"

Reppus was caught off guard with the question. In his eyes, Michael could tell he was searching for a proper response, whether it was the truth or not was irrelevant. He had just entered the first diplomatic battle of his stay. One that Ortho warned him and his relatives from Earth about so many times during the past several weeks of indoctrination and training.

"I'm not anxious for my father's death," Reppus answered. "I'm only stating the inevitable…that's all!"

"You know Reppus," Michael said, catching his frustration in his own words. "I'm new at this, but it seems to me the inevitable need not be spoken."

Reppus bristled at the words, seeing a gauntlet, not laid down, but fired at him. "You may be a distant cousin or something, but do not forget who you are talking to!" he warned.

Michael stood up, straightened his pants crease and walked back to the window, peering once again at the serenity of the palace grounds. "Look, Reppus," he responded, "A few weeks ago, I was just a kid home on vacation from college, in New Haven Connecticut." Michael turned and noticed the confused look on Reppus' face. "On Earth," he added. Reppus' confusion dissipated, and Michael gazed once again out of the six-foot oval shaped window.

In that instant, Michael's mind flashed back to the events, starting with Billy Red stabbing and leaving him for dead, his near death experience that prepared him for his destiny, Billy's threat against his sister and his subsequent quest for revenge with a loaded three-fifty-seven Magnum. But he intentionally left out these juicy tidbits of information in accordance with Ortho's plea.

"Anyhow," he continued, "Ortho catches me at a Fourth of July celebration and lays this entire weird ass story on me about leading USSTAP." Michael turned around and leaned against the sill, staring at Reppus, so his words would not be misunderstood. "Your inheritance is this planet and the others in the solar system. But if I'm not mistaken, my inheritance is USSTAP, an alliance of planetary governments, including yours, in a mutual support pact to share scientific knowledge, to provide defense and to oversee the peaceful trade of goods in about thirty galaxies." *So who should be careful about what he says to whom?* Michael wanted to add, but knew his implication came across loud and clear. As he had already said, the inevitable need not be spoken.

Reppus looked away, collecting his thoughts so he could put the emphasis on his agenda more emphatically. "We are both direct descendants of Garriss Osguard," he opened, "Vedar Osguard, died and his children spawned bastard offspring on Earth, in which you and the fifty-nine other impure descendants sprang from."

"Nausona and Laurona were mistaken for slaves, beaten and raped by a plantation owner," Michael interrupted, trying to overlook the term *'impure'*. "Don't you sit there and throw around disparaging remarks about my ancestors, as if they are dirt. They braved a strange world and survived. You don't know what my country was like for a black woman or man before the Civil War. Shit, it wasn't a picnic after it either. I can't imagine the horror they went through, but they returned with honor and led the revolt that ended your war with the Kulusk. Where was your ancestor, where was Akaher?" he asked in a seething rage. "I hear nothing of his exploits during this time. The first I ever hear of him is after Laurona and Nausona returned to Chaktun."

Michael walked over to the desk and leaned over, placing his face within spitting distance to Reppus. "I know...I know," I've heard the story a million times, just in the past few weeks. Akaher Osguard, Vedar's younger brother assumed the duties of Maxum after his nieces, abdicated the throne in pursuit of creating the Universal Science, Security and Trade Association of Planets. From that moment the family split. That is why your family crest is a royal blue diamond and mine is a black diamond. But what did he do for Chaktun, while my great-great grandmother was in hell on Earth?"

Reppus remained silent.

"Not a damned thing, I suppose." Michael retorted, pushing back from the desk.

After several agonizing seconds in which, the two engaged in a testosterone stare down, Reppus stood. "Why so hostile, Michael?" he asked. "I only meant to state the facts...did I offend you with my choice of words? Remember, I do not speak your language on a regular basis. Please tell me what did I say to offend you?"

Michael took a deep breath and blew it out as if to find his center once more. He sat again, waving the insult away, "Nothing...just forget it. Maybe it is me. You're right. I read something in your words that I'm sure you didn't mean to convey."

"Well for that, I'm truly sorry. I mean no disrespect. I just wanted you to know, I understand the overwhelming task, you and your people have. I don't envy you. And even though law separates our families, we are still joined by blood. Therefore I offer my assistance anytime you need it. I know running such a big organization must be frightening."

"Thank you Reppus." Ortho had warned him that the Chaktun government was anxious to get their hands on USSTAP and had made covert moves in the USSTAP parliament and congress to procure USSTAP's reign on the occasion of Ortho's death, if he did not find the rightful heirs. Now that the rightful heirs have been located, Reppus had to execute another plan to take over USSTAP. "Ortho has been running USSTAP just fine since Nausona's death. I'm sure he is the only mentor we would need."

"Still, there are sixty of you and only one of him. Plus he is an old man, pushing eighty in earth years," he pressed. "I just want you to know I am here for you."

Seeing no graceful way to say no, Michael just shook his head, "I'll remember that. I will certainly remember that you will be behind me in all my decisions." *With a knife!* He mentally added.

"I only offer my services because of the enormity of the task you are about to take on. After all, you have no training in such matters, except the few weeks Ortho has afforded you. But USSTAP, like you suggested, is a large organization, with many governments, worlds that stretch over thirty galaxies. You are a kid from the streets, as you so aptly pronounced several times before. Only the most experienced veteran could hope to manage such a tasking. Admittedly, there are sixty of you, but that could only add to the confusion."

"What are you getting at?" Michael asked.

"Let's say during a show of force against the Kulusks, a USSTAP science vessel crashed on Biago. What would you do as the First Osguard?"

"I would send the closest ship on a rescue mission," Michael said.

"What about the Biago government?"

"Of course I would request their assistance," Michael added, not sure what Reppus was getting at.

"Wrong answer on both counts," Reppus gloated. "You led with your heart and not with your head. There is no Biago government. Biago is a category X planet, no life; no water…nothing but fiery lava bathing a molten rock core. If a science vessel crashed on the planet it would have been immediately engulfed and destroyed. There would be no reason to send a ship and weaken your show of force. Such a move would demonstrate a weakened resolve to the Kulusks, and thus risking another war. You must know any sign of weakness would invite the Kulusks to attack again."

"That was a trick question," Michael defended.

"No it was a legitimate question. In fact it was a situation Vedar Osguard ran against during his reign."

"What did Vedar do?"

Reppus sighed and stared at him, making Michael feel more naïve than he did when he came to Chaktun. "It doesn't matter what he did. The fact still remains; it's a waste of time to do so. Leading with your heart will get people killed and waste valuable time and resources. It's also a sign of a weak leader."

Michael continued to stare, seeing past Reppus and looking into his own inner thoughts. The fear he had harbored in a small place in his mind burst out. *How could a few weeks of training and education prepare him with a universe of knowledge he needed to make simple decisions, let alone the complex decisions of life and death?* He began to shiver with doubt.

Reppus noticed the change wash over his prey. *Mission complete!* He thought. "Don't worry, dear cousin," he pushed. "I won't let you or any of my earthly relatives make such a wicked mistake."

"How's that?"

"Well," Reppus began, knowing he had Michael hooked. "I know, as well as my father and other leaders in USSTAP, that you and your kind are ill-equipped to handle the business of the universe."

"They do?" Michael questioned. "That's not what they said during the Awakening."

"That was political expediency," Reppus explained. "No, in reality, they are just waiting for you or the others to falter, giving them the excuse and opportunity to bank USSTAP into their own power. They figure Ortho will die soon, and when he does, they are betting you and your people will be so overwhelmed, and will gladly relinquish power to the strongest government in the association. And that dear cousin, will be the seed that causes war. USSTAP will splinter and finally cease to exist. You don't want that to happen, do you?"

Michael shook his head, "No," he whispered, showing the doubt creeping into his soul. "So what do you propose we do?"

"Do what you are doing, and until you feel comfortable in your newfound position as leaders of the known universe, I will be your covert consul. This way the others will see your strong leadership and will subsequently abandon their hopes of procuring USSTAP for themselves. Ultimately, together we will secure USSTAP for future generations and protect the universe from itself."

Noticing he was shaking, Michael stood, turned, retrieved his personal gate portal from his belt and activated it. The room hummed as the invisible door slid open, releasing the beautiful white light from inner space. He looked over his shoulder and repeated what he said before, "I'll remember that." Then he stepped into the light. The door slid down, returning the spot to the laws of normal space.

Reppus leaned back in his chair and silently patted himself on the back. *Good job,* he told himself. *Soon USSTAP will fall under Chaktun rule.*

Chapter 18—Prison Escape

In the black slitanium watchtower hovering twenty miles above Zeta Claire, five squads from USSTAP Security Division and one squad from USSTAP Medical Division watched the prisoners of Zeta Claire. They regulated the magic machines that delivered the meals and bedding to all eight thousand prisoners. Marshal Lam Gala led this detail, one of eight prison planets in the Millmum Galaxy, making up USSTAP's five hundred- prison-planet system. Zeta Claire, like the rest of the prison-planet system, considered the probability of an outside threat low; therefore, the watchtower merely contained a regiment of pagenay guns.

Gala sat in the command chair on the observation deck contemplating the wonders of the universe, while staring at the majestic beauty of God's hand. It was different from his home world of Gantor. There the filth and smog obscured the sun in the day and the stars at night, like shutters. Gala left that world and entered the USSTAP Academy on Chaktun, never to look back again. Now he was about to retire from a thirty-five-year career with USSTAP, and return to civilian life. The question is, will he return to the bleak world of Gantor, or to another majestic world.

He had been a security specialist all his adult life, traveling from ship to ship, planet to planet, and station to station, moving up the ranks in a wonderful life that he could have never found if he had stayed on Gantor. He had all the joys of life, except a wife or family. Now he felt since his career was about to end, so was his life. A clinical psychologist would diagnose the feeling that Gala was going through as the beginning stages of depression.

A beep from the ARIT interrupted Gala's concentration. He turned his attention to his chief controller in front of him, noticing him adjust his station's controls.

"Sire, Hustain class-nine transport entering normal space, sector Four–J," Commander Sineh Filahman reported.

"Hail them," Gala ordered.

"Registry is X–T–forty-five–J–eight–nine and he is responding," Sineh reported a second later.

"Visual," Gala requested as he stood to face the space shield in front of Sineh

Like clockwork, the majestic view of God's yard disappeared from the space shield; only to be replaced by another vision of God's grace…a head and shoulders shot of a beautiful young woman. She was a shiny brunette with sparkling green eyes, a dazzling smile and golden honeysuckle skin. Her hair draped over her bare shoulders, adding to the sensuality she was oozing through the screen.

The five men, including Gala, on the observation deck straightened up. Gala's receding gray hair seemed darker, the laugh lines around his eyes seemed lighter and his square jaw seemed more pronounced.

"Hustain Registry X–T–forty-five–J–eight–nine, this is Marshal Lam Gala, sire of the USSTAP Zeta Clair Watchtower. You are entering restricted space. Please stop and retreat."

"Marshall Gala, this is Kimna Tre of the Hustain Transport X–T–forty-five–J–eight–nine," she announced with a sexy but husky voice, "my navigation system has failed and I'm in need of repair before I attempt faster than light travel again. It was pure luck; I was able to find a USSTAP station. Please don't turn me away."

Her eyes danced with every word and she seemed to keep her dazzling smile even as she spoke, which promoted an air of familiarity, breeding a sense of comfort.

Gala smiled, "Standby, we will assist as we can."

Sineh closed the connection.

"Commander, direct her to docking station one. Have a maintenance crew meet her and give her a hand in fixing her navigation system." Then Gala went back to his seat and before sitting down, he gave way to his intuition. "Commander, execute security protocol one and have a security detail meet her as well. She is not to board the station."

"Sire?" Sineh questioned.

"Just do it," Gala sighed as he flopped down into the command chair.

"Tiah!" Sineh responded, activating Gala's commands from his console.

The forward pagenays came alive and centered on the pillbox shaped smoky gray transport. All the watchtowers' sensors and scanners beeped and chirped as they swept through and read all energies from the small five-passenger transport.

"X–T–forty-five–J–eight–nine, slow to subsonic, turn port four–five decimal eight, mark zero–zero–one," Sineh commanded, watching his controller screen to ensure the ship complied with his instructions. "Beam away...Call intercept."

"Beam intercept," Kimna's voice rang through his interphone.

"Slow to mark speed...three hundred miles per hour...six thousand kilomarks from touch."

"Slowing...seven hundred...five hundred...three hundred miles per hour," she announced.

But the blip on Sineh's screen disagreed with the voice. It displayed the transport increasing to hypersonic speeds. "Check speed," he demanded in an urgent tone.

Silence, not even a whisper came in response. Then his warning tone echoed in his earpiece. He checked the sensor and scanner report...Torko Bombs.

"Sire!" Sineh called in desperation.

"I see," Gala responded. "Trigger pagenays, blow her out of my space!" he said feeling betrayed by his initial sense of trust.

Four blue beams of destruction sprang from the diamond shape watchtower and pierced space in a fraction of a second from the time Gala uttered the command. However, at the same time he uttered the command, the Hustain transport X–T–forty-five–J–eight–nine entered the speed schedule and slipped into hyperlight speed, causing the pagenay blasts to miss its intended target. Less than six thousand kilomarks away, the distance the transport ship had to travel took less time than a split second.

***

On the planet's surface, the night sky that covered Billy's prison patch, lit up with a bright white flash followed by flashes of light covering the colors of the rainbow. He jumped from his bed and ran outside. He was confused and somewhat frightened at the spectacle playing out over his head. He watched head high, eyes staring toward the horizon, cursing his plight. Then with one phrase that seemed to sum up his life so far he screamed, "What the fuck?"

Across from him, Ralinget was watching the same display of dazzling colors. As the last of the flashes faded from sight, Billy could see a devilish grin occupying Ralinget's face. Somehow, Billy recognized that Ralinget knew what was going on and it pleased him. If it pleased Ralinget, Billy decided whatever was happening would please him as well. So he began to laugh.

As if cued from his laughing, the force field separating the prison buildings came down as evident from the extinguished red lights that traversed the length of the twenty-five-foot poles in each corner. Billy stopped laughing and snapped his head around eying each corner like a caged animal deciphering his getaway. Confusion occupied his eyes and uneasiness rocked his soul. He turned to Ralinget, who had crossed into his part of the yard. The grin Ralinget wore just seconds ago had faded, only to be replaced with the staunch look of a warrior on the prowl.

At first, Billy thought of running, but his street blood kicked in and told him to stand his ground. "What do you want?" he growled.

Ralinget didn't respond. He continued to walk toward Billy, until he was face to face with him. He then looked Billy up and down, as if he was sizing him up for a fight.

Billy's uneasiness turned to an adrenaline rush, as he stood tall ready to pounce on Ralinget at the slightest wrong move. His breath became deep, steady and very audible, like a bull snorting at danger. The two men stood inches from each other. Billy could smell Ralinget's breath, which smelled like the bottom of a trashcan on a hot summer's day. But Billy knew he couldn't let that bother him. Any movement now would be considered a sign of weakness, and weakness wasn't what he wanted to show.

Billy knew Ralinget could kill him with one well-placed hit. And he knew that Ralinget was too quick and too swift for him to counter or even avoid such a hit, but he wasn't going to back down.

Slowly, but deliberately as if he knew what Billy was thinking, Ralinget raised his hand and placed it on Billy's shoulder and smiled. Billy reciprocated with his ragged-tooth smile as well. Deep inside, Billy relaxed, but still was somewhat guarded.

Then a gate portal opening appeared behind Ralinget. Ralinget turned toward the light, not releasing his gentle grip on Billy's shoulder. After a split second, Ralinget readjusted his grip on Billy and ushered him into the light with him. In the background, before the gate portal door slid close, Billy could hear the yell and screams of the other unseen residents of Zeta Clair. The sounds were a mixture of pain, joy and evil encompassing the night, making Billy happy he was leaving USSTAP's hellhole.

***

On the other side of the light, Billy and Ralinget stepped out onto a small platform in a dimly lit, smoke filled room that was no bigger than his cell on the planet's surface. Ralinget rushed toward a tall, smiling, burly bearded man and gave him such a bear hug that Billy thought the man's eyes would pop out. The gate portal door exit vanished behind him, giving Billy a sense of claustrophobia. The two men spoke in low voices, which was unnecessary because he couldn't understand their language anyway.

Then the bearded burly man approached Billy. For an instance, Billy thought he may have made the wrong decision by coming with Ralinget. He took a step backward, hoping to somehow activate the gate portal.

"Billy Red?" the elderly man asked in a weird accent, stepping in front of him.

Billy stopped moving backwards, surprised the man spoke English, and mustered his streetwise attitude, "Who wants to know?"

"Misul Rafinel, leader of the Mosleck Reclamation Order," the man responded with pride, while looking Billy up and down.

"So what's that mean to me," Billy snarled, clenching his fist.

"It means I have the power to save your life, or let you die. Or did you forget about that potion of death in your neck?" he said pointing his finger to the exact spot where Billy received the injection.

"What?" Billy yelled, showing the first sign of being scared, fighting the feeling to snatch Rafinel's finger and bending it back...a move he learned on the streets that always forced his opponents to their knees.

"Forgive me, Mr. Red," Rafinel pushed, lowering his hand back to his side. "But when I remove the potion of death from my son's neck, your potion will be released and then you will only have two universal hours to live."

"Yeah...yeah...yeah...I almost forgot about that shit in my neck," Billy said. Then realizing his fate, Billy looked Rafinel in the eye and asked, "You mean you can take this thing out of my neck?"

Rafinel nodded.

"Then what?"

"Then, Mr. Red, if I decide to help you, I can arrange your passage back to Earth."

"How?" Billy said with actual curiosity and leaning forward.

"One of my benefactors is the Kulusk Maxum, Kie Ritchen. He has a way of getting you back to Earth."

"Why? I mean, what's in it for you to help me get back to Earth?" Billy inquired in a whisper.

"My son tells me, we may have a common enemy...Osguard Michael Genesis."

"Michael Genesis...hell yeah," Billy almost screamed, bouncing back a step. "I owe that punk motherfucker a date with God."

"Good, Mr. Red," Rafinel smiled. "You see, him and the other Osguards are pretty much untouchable to us. But to you, back on Earth, he will be easily accessible."

"What?"

"There's too much security for us to kill him, but there will be no security on Earth, so you can kill him."

"Why do you want to kill Genesis?"

Rafinel took Billy by the arm and ushered him along as they talked. "Come with us to the med lab so we can get the USSTAP poison from your neck."

A smiling Ralinget joined them as they left the room through an open doorway.

"Mr. Red, the finding of the lost family of Osguards has started a terrible chain of events that I fear will lead to the imperialistic conquering of the known universe," Rafinel began to lecture, still holding a tight grip on Billy's arm. "And believe me; my people know the greed of the imperialist. We are still in the final throws of war against the Hustain Empire, but when I found out that the mythical lost family of Osguard was not a myth and that they had actually been found, I knew the war we have against the Hustain Empire must widen to include USSTAP."

"Oh, I see!" Billy managed to utter, not quite understanding what the hell Rafinel was saying.

"I don't think you do, Mr. Red," Rafinel corrected. "Just like the Hustain Empire, USSTAP threatens the freedom of all men in the universe, especially now that they found their messiah...actually sixty messiahs."

"Listen Misul Rafinel," Billy broke in with, "I don't know, or care what your problem is with Genesis. But if you give me a chance to take care of him, I promise you won't have that problem anymore."

Rafinel stopped in his tracks, and released his grip on Billy, "Fine, Mr. Red, I will give you that opportunity. But first, we have to get those things out of you and my son. The defense parameter is down and in approximately twenty minutes, those chemical time bombs will go off. And once that happens, I can't save you, no matter what my agent on Chaktun can give me to help."

Chapter 19—Mentoring of an Osguard

On the western continent, known as Agoya, sat the USSTAP Academy (USSTAPA) where USSTAP officers train for three universal years before entering the ranks of USSTAP. For the past six weeks, the academy had been closed to the normal parade of cadets to allow sixty individuals to take a crash-training course.

In one of the many lecture halls on the campus grounds, Michael sat in the first seat as always, according to his Osguardian number as assigned by Ortho. They had just finished running their physical fitness test, in which Michael had scored twenty points less than he did the day before, and the others had improved their scores by thirty points.

After six weeks of climbing hills in desert high temperatures, completing ten mile treks over frozen tundra, living off the jungle land for six days, and playing prisoner in a mock Kulusk prison for another six days, it was understandable the body began to deteriorate. But Michael's score was well within acceptable parameters. Therefore the low score did not set off any alarms for Ortho.

Ortho stepped onto the platform and turned to face his students. Pride beamed through his entire body as he watched his protégés prepare for today's lesson. He had found the lost children of Osguard. A tear began to form in his eye as he gazed upon the fruit of three generations of labor.

"Osguards," he called, signaling the lecture had begun. "Today's simulation is quite simple. In fact it isn't a simulation at all. I will put forth a scenario, and on the ARIT pads in front of you, I want you to write how you would handle the situation." He watched the young Osguards and saw the look of excitement in some eyes, and the look of concern in others.

He then clicked a remote sensor in his hand, and a holographic screen displayed a red planet in a system, Michael did not recognize. Orbiting the planet was a USSTAP ship, smaller than a galaxy cruiser, but shaped similar, like a black bat. The slitanium hull, when energized, worked like a chameleon skin, fading the ship into the darkness of space, by reflecting and bending light, making it almost invisible to visual and radar detection. But with the hull not energized and against the backdrop of a red planet, it stood out like a sore thumb.

After the first orbit, the ship arched down and forward and plunged to the surface. The animated holograph, pushed the sequence of events faster than real time, but the outcome was still the same. The ship disappeared amongst the clouds and atmosphere of the planet, allowing the imagination to fill in the blanks.

"You are the Osguard of this sector. What is your next move? You have just lost all contact with the *USSTAP Science Vessel Rosary* as it was surveying the planet Biago. Biago is lava laden with a volcanic rock as its core. Temperatures reach four thousand chimes at its polar caps. What you saw is an ARIT simulation of what scanners and sensors report from the area." He looked around and witnessed the attentive faces asking for more information. "That's all the information I have. What would you do? Oh…by the way, the Kulusk space fleet is poised for an attack and your advisors tell you that you need every ship to protect the borders. Now, what would you do?"

Michael lowered his head in despair. He knew the right answer. Reppus just gave him this same question two days ago. But he still didn't like it. He picked up his ARIT Pad and began to write.

'I must excuse myself from this situational test, for I had discussed this very situation with Reppus two days ago. When he asked me what would I do, I did not know of the impossible survivability of the planet and chose to send a cruiser to lead a rescue mission. I also requested coordination with the planet's government…both which Reppus joyously told me were in error.'

Michael put his writing instrument down for he was finished with his answer, so he thought. After a few seconds of thought, he picked up the ARIT once more and began a second paragraph.

'No human should die alone without hope of rescue or survival. And as long as I am Osguard, no one will ever have that despair while performing a mission for USSTAP. So even though the prospect of finding any survivors is unlikely, I stand by my original decision to send a rescue mission. As for a government inclusion, someone must own that piece of rock. Whether it is private, commercial or governmental, I would send the diplomatic corps' representative to establish connectivity with them and let them know what is happening and offer for them to join us.

As for the Kulusk poised to attack, I'd rather have one ship searching for the lost crew, which will raise the morale of my troops, than leaving the crew out there to die. Once the rescue ship establishes whether the crew is alive or dead, I will proceed from there.'

Michael put down the ARIT, looked around and noticed the others were complete and staring at him, waiting for him to finish so the class could continue.

"Okay, it appears all of you are complete," Ortho announced, giving one last check around to see that all were done. "Now, I want you to transfer this assignment to your private log. I need not see the answer. I just wanted you to think about this situation."

"Why?" Michael found himself asking.

"Because, my young Osguard, this is a situation your ancestor, Vedar found himself in, two years after his father, Garriss' death and he became Maxum at twenty-nine. He sent out a battle cruiser to investigate and launch a rescue mission if necessary, even though he was on the eve of another war with Kulusk."

"What happened?" Patricia asked from the third row.

"All of you happened."

"What?" Michael jumped in.

"My grandfather, Mitiah Chting was on that ship that was lost over Biago. The same Mitiah Chting who later saved your ancestors from the Kulusks ten galactic years later, and who rescued them from Earth two years after that. The act of compassion, saved his life in which he vowed his allegiance as a Sandson Guard ever since. If Vedar didn't send the rescue ship, my grandmother and several other family members would have lost love ones. You see the ship managed to sustain minimum flight in the planet's atmosphere. The rescue ship reached the planet and rescued the crew with no time to spare by stepping them through the gate portals. As the last person stepped off the ship, it plunged into the lava laden ocean."

The young Osguards eyes widened with a spirit of disbelief.

"So Vedar's one decision to risk sending a ship to rescue what all had said was a doomed mission actually started a chain of events which produced you."

Michael's confidence rose as the lesson sunk into his head. *Sometimes a leader has to follow his instincts more than the facts. A leader's decision is based on a mixture of the two, not solely on one over the other.*

"I see," Michael said without noticing he spoke aloud.

"You see what?" Ortho inquired.

"I see your point. There is a balance between a gut feeling and facts, and a great leader like Vedar exercised that even in the midst of uncertain odds."

"I guess so," Ortho admitted, looking at Michael like they shared some eternal secret to leadership. "I guess that is exactly what this incident illustrates, but to tell the truth I just wanted to introduce to you a turning point in history in which our families are inextricably intertwined. Leave it to Michael to find a nobler objective to the lesson."

"Kiss ass," Shawn whispered to Michael.

"I can teach you, if you want to learn," Michael whispered back.

"Well that's it," Ortho concluded. "Tomorrow you will be paired up and assigned a galaxy cruiser to observe for the next two weeks. Afterwards those who are under twenty-one years of age will go back to Earth and continue their training under their local precinct advisor. Those who are twenty-one and older will travel back to Millmum Capitol Station to start their advanced training." He looked around beaming with pride once more. "Excellent job people! You've accomplished more in these six weeks than I would have ever expected. I know I am looking at the future leaders of the universe. I'm looking at the Osguards. Dismissed!"

Chapter 20 — Strategy

Sitting alone in his ready room, aboard the *USSTAP Galaxy Cruiser Uno*, the news seemed grave indeed to Ortho. The details were sketchy, but there was enough for Ortho to paint a vivid picture. The Moslecks used their patent 'komrockfa' attack, similar to the Japanese kamikaze attacks of Earth's World War II, to obliterate the Zeta Claire Prison Watchtower. The komrockfa was a cowardly attack usually reserved by the Moslecks for assassinations of Hustain political or influential dignitaries. The Moslecks have never used this type of attack outside their dispute with the Hustains. But then again, the Moslecks did attack the USSTAP trading station Aruda, killing two thousand people. That was also out of character for the Moslecks.

Now add five hundred more personnel and approximately eight thousand prisoners to the Mosleck scorecard. In total, he had lost more people under his watch in the last two Mosleck attacks than in his entire time as Lieutenant Osguard. When the watchtower exploded, the homing beacon that kept the poison of death from releasing also was destroyed. When the switch inside their necks did not get the homing signal's hourly update, it decided the prisoner had escaped the field of view and initiated the chemical protocol, and two hours later, every prisoner was dead, except one—he was sure of it. Ralinget must have survived. The entire operation was to free him from the prison…*but how? How did the Moslecks get that close to initiate komrockfa? How did they neutralize the poison of death?*

Ortho had no idea. All he knew was the Mosleck problem he had feared was on the horizon had now crossed the horizon. Fortunately, this problem was isolated to only one sector of the Millmum Galaxy. Therefore, he would allow Vanguard Shyira Kyoi, the operational commander of that sector to devise the strategy in which to handle this problem.

Ortho gathered his command writing ARIT and began jotting down thoughts he wanted to share with Kyoi. The voice of revenge was hard to hide in his writing, as he commented *'containment was no longer an option'*. Ortho instructed Kyoi that she was authorized to use whatever force she deemed necessary to engage the enemy in decisive operations, *'to break their spirit', 'reduce their assets'* and *'diminish their support infrastructure'*. In short, Ortho gave permission for Kyoi to wage war…war against a non-government actor, with no home world, nor known staging area. The Mosleck pirates were ghosts, whispering about the cosmos, echoing from star to star as galactic nomads who stole life and liberty from one people…the Hustains. But now they have expanded their shopping objective against USSTAP, which was surely a harbinger of bitter days to come. He ended his communiqué warning Kyoi the Mosleck pirate ruthlessness knew no bounds, but that did not give her the right to deviate from USSTAP accepted rules of conflict.

Ortho closed his communiqué with a heavy sigh, realizing he was about to open USSTAP to a conflict that if not dealt with could spread into a treacherous protracted galactic war…one he may not see the end to before his god reclaimed his soul. With a heavy heart he concluded that the importance of training the Osguards as the leaders of USSTAP was more imperative now than ever before.

Chapter 21—Osguard Forged By Fire

The information seemed legitimate thus far, which made Rafinel smile. His agent on Chaktun had pinpointed the exact whereabouts of Michael Genesis, the so-called First Osguard. Rafinel rubbed his hands together, savoring the future expected moment when he would wipe the ship carrying Michael out of existence. His four-man bridge crew scurried about, checking weapons, navigation and defense protocols. They knew today would be a brilliant day for the movement, a truly inspiring scene to watch.

The bridge was dimly lit, due to the fact that the Moslecks were sensitive to light, an effect of the galactic nomadic way of life, forced upon them from having their home world stolen from them. The atmosphere on the bridge was hazy and smoky from the poor life support ventilation system pouring in metallic oxygen. Metallic oxygen was the cheapest form of life support that the Moslecks could acquire. Metallic oxygen did sufficiently sustain life, but at a price. The Moslecks on board would suffer continuous headaches as well as suffer from poor circulation. Some believed this was the root to their paranoia and surprisingly violent character.

Pure oxygen was hard to obtain on the black market. USSTAP had a strangle hold on all exports and imports using the gate portal technology to traverse the known universe. USSTAP charged a ten percent tax on all goods for each ladle of travel, making the black market entrepreneur almost extinct. However, this gave life to the burgeoning pirate lifestyle, which the Moslecks were just becoming proficient at.

On the computer display view screen, a dot representing the USSTAP galaxy cruiser carrying Michael was now coming into view. The sight excited Rafinel; eagerness now filled his entire being.

"Is that Michael," Billy asked stepping from the shadows behind Rafinel. Billy's trip to Kulusk had been interrupted by this new development, and he was more than happy to delay his passage back home in order to see Rafinel kill Michael. His sole regret was that it wasn't him.

Rafinel grunted and nodded acknowledging Michael was on the ship. "Silent run," he pushed with authority. "Pull in behind them, get into their MOP echo and shadow their movements, increase closure by two thousand marks per universal second."

The crew moved with purpose, adhering to the command orders still rumbling in the bridge chamber. The crew knew at faster than light speed, this maneuver would make them appear to the target ship as a harmonic feedback. This phenomenon would mask their slow approach.

The spider-shaped Mosleck Cruiser fell directly behind the galaxy cruiser, trailing her at one hundred thousand kilomarks. The Mosleck pilot was very skilled, matching each course correction the USSTAP starship made within a fraction of an instant, while maintaining the prescribed closure rate, bouncing off the waves of trachion particles, which made up the medium of outer space. His delicate talents made the Mosleck ship look like a sensor echo, caused by the rare occurrence of a USSTAP MOP engine in need of a system calibration. The Mosleck pilot conducted thirteen universal hours of intricate piloting, closing to within weapons range without a note of detection, before another pilot of equal proficiency relieved him.

Rafinel could not be more proud of his crew. He had ordered the most impossible task from them, and they delivered. Even though he wore the obvious scowl of a warrior on his face, his heart was smiling with delight. Now it was time for the hardest part of his plan to execute...patience. The attack could not start until the USSTAP ship dropped out of faster than light speed.

His patience soon paid off. The USSTAP ship dropped out of MOP and executed the downshift through the speed schedule until they came to a complete stop, in the middle of nowhere. The new Mosleck pilot followed suite, without being ordered, which made the need for a decision most urgent.

"Ready the pulsar cannons," Rafinel barked. "Chromerion field activate!" he continued, standing and moving to the screen.

"Switching to real-time view," the navigator informed the bridge.

The USSTAP galaxy cruiser came into view, sending chills through Rafinel's spine. "Lock on and fire!" he growled like a dog with a bone.

A quick succession of red fiery balls leaped from the ship's bow, darting through the dark cold space honing in on their target like arrows of death on a buffalo hunt.

***

The blast rocked Michael to the floor. He fell hard to his knees. It was the twentieth blast the ship had encountered in less than four minutes. He tried to lift his head from the floor, but the G-force from the coaster's upward movement pushed it back down. After several seconds, his body adjusted to the upward push of the coaster and he regained his equilibrium. Then another blast rocked him against the seat. He tripped over Roger who was having the same difficulty gathering his balance. Michael shook his head to gain awareness. This was a dream…no a nightmare. One he could have never fathomed in a million years. But he was here, in the heat of battle.

Michael snapped to his feet and sat in the seat that ran along the tubular coaster. He grabbed onto the railing for support, as did Roger. The high pitched wavering sound of the Alert One buzzer rang through the air, cutting at his eardrums and grating on his nerves.

"Are you alright?" he asked.

"Yeah, I'm okay," Roger coughed.

Just then the coaster doors whisked open. Another blast rocked him and Roger, throwing them into the corridor like rag dolls. They fell on their backs, reaching for the walls for support. He hopped to his feet and peered left over his shoulder and down the corridor. His hazel eyes gleamed with steadfast concentration. He had to get to the bridge. He had to know what was happening. He grabbed Roger and helped him to his feet. Then, without speaking a word, they both sprinted to the end of the corridor. He placed his hand in the DNA lock reader. A red light scanned his hand and the door slid open to the right.

In front of him lay the bridge of the Universal Science, Security and Trade Association of Planets Galaxy Cruiser *Justice*. Broken bulkheads, fallen supports and cracked panels littered the 'U' shaped room. Bodies carpeted the floor and dangled from control stations. The ship's sire, the commander of the ship, Centurion Qlee Traxel, lay in front of the command chair in the center of the carnage, dead—blood dripping from his head, mouth and nose. His arm was unnaturally bent backwards underneath him and he had the look of death frozen in his blue eyes. Colonel Tamara Lightfoot, his second in command lay next to him. She was dead as well. Her long silky dark hair had shaken loose and covered her chest like a blanket. Death forever marred her beautiful golden Native American skin's luster. And the same death stare occupied her dark and lifeless eyes.

The sight frightened him at first, and then it sickened him. His stomach cramped as he struggled to breathe. But his mind chased the feeling from his body. He blinked several times in an effort to wish the carnage away. But it didn't disappear. Reality smacked him. He was eighteen years old. He was to enter his sophomore year of college in less than a month. But he was seven thousand light years away from Earth on a galaxy cruiser in the middle of what? What the hell was going on?

Michael and Roger stepped onto the bridge. Michael glanced at the double screen in the front of the bridge. The right screen projected a star chart and the left screen displayed space, in its infinite wonder and splendor. But the left screen also contained an object he had never seen before. It contained another space ship. It looked like a spider of some type, with eight long spars connecting to an engine pod on the starboard and port sides. The image was almost grotesque. A red ball of energy sprang from the ship's bow. The spider had spit, and it was heading toward them. He grabbed the railing in front of him.

"Brace for impact!" shouted the young ensign at the piloting controls.

The red ball hit with such fury, it pushed the ship back several hundred marks. The impact caused Michael to jerk back and then fall forward over the railing. Pain shot up his spine as his back met what he once considered a soft, rubber like floor. Michael shot up straight and looked around, somewhat embarrassed he had lost his balance, but consoled in the fact that everyone else had also lost their balance and were fighting to regain control as well.

"Report!" he commanded.

The ensign turned to him and shook his head. "Get off the bridge kid; this is not a training exercise."

"I said...report!" he repeated.

"Look kid," the ensign started, trying to control his anger. "I said get the hell off the bridge."

"ARIT," he called to no one in particular. "This is the First Osguard, authorization.... five–six–five–eight–Mike–Delta–Sierra–Papa. I hereby take command of the Universal Science, Security and Trade Association of Planets Galaxy Cruiser *Justice*."

"Confirmed...The First Osguard is in command," floated a sensuous female voice from the overhead intercom.

"Transfer all codes associated with command to my authority," Michael commanded.

"Completed," the voice sang.

"ARIT," Roger called. "This is Osguard zero–two, authorization ...one–zero–zero–two–Kilo–Mike–Mike–Papa. I hereby take second in command of the Universal Science, Security and Trade Association of Planets Galaxy Cruiser *Justice*."

"Confirmed...Osguard zero–two is second in command," the voice reported.

"Transfer all codes associated with second in command duties to my authority," Roger ordered.

Outside in the midst of space, the attacking ship spat another blast. The red ball of energy flew toward the ship with seemingly marked determination. Michael saw the impending doom through the left screen and reached for something to sturdy him. "Brace for impact," he called.

The hit knocked the bridge crew about. They tumbled, twisted and crashed to the floor. Michael cracked his side against a railing, bruising his ribs and crushing air from his lungs. He pulled himself up, and stumbled toward the tactical station, just left of the pilot station the young ensign occupied. Roger moved to the right, next to the empty navigator station, toward the defensive station, being careful as he stepped over the body of the station's former occupant.

Michael looked at the ensign with displeasing eyes, "Look," *you shithead,* he wanted to add. "I am the First Osguard, ordained by Ortho, sanctioned by the Congress and approved by the Parliament. Stop giving me shit and report for God's sake!"

The ensign looked into Michael's eyes and saw the steel of an unwavering commander and the tenacity of a leader. He shook his head in disbelief, and then he looked at the bodies on the bridge. The navigator, the defense officer, the tactics officer, the centurion and the colonel were dead. He, the communications, the life support and the science officers were the only ones left from the original bridge crew. And at that moment he was at a loss for words and too scared to act.

"Chromerion field down, weapons down, Asher torpedo bay one operative...all others are down...engine drive down...all we have left is thrusters." The ensign nodded to the screen. "Mosleck pirates! They came out of nowhere...blind side hit. They took out our Chromerion field generators on the first shots."

Roger turned in frustration. "How the hell did you not see them coming?"

"Don't know, but when we get out of here, that will be the first question I'll look up."

"Fine!" Michael pushed. "Damage to the ship?"

"Decks four through ten report hull breeches...unable to contain...heavy casualties throughout, and we are leaking dialairtic gas from the stern," said Roger.

"Great...just fucking great!" Michael complained. Then his eyes brightened. "Do we still have stealth capability?"

Roger checked his station, "Yes!"

"How about decoys?"

Roger touched several pressure points at his station, "Yes!"

"Stealth mode ten...come about...heading two–nine–eight, decimal nine–seven–four, mark twenty," he commanded.

"But the dialairtic gas...it is a neon sign pointing straight to us," the ensign complained. "We need to shut it down. It's explosive. Those energy balls could ignite the gas and we will be dead in seconds."

"Just do as I say," Michael commanded. "I know what I'm doing." Then Michael turned to the remaining bridge crew. "Comm...send a distress call, all channels, to the nearest USSTAP base. Life Support...direct personnel in outer decks to cargo bay one and then divert all power from those decks to engineering. Engineering...I want speed. I don't care if it's the hypersonic, hyperlight, or MOP engines; just get me some speed in the next two minutes. Understand?" The nods and the flurry of activity that followed his orders, assured him they understood.

The USSTAP Galaxy Cruiser *Justice* glowed for an instant as energy charged her black hull. Then the ship defied the laws of light as it faded into blackness, matching the blanket of space surrounding her. The orange glow of the venting dialairtic gas swirled in a circle as the large ship swung about to the new heading. The ensign swallowed hard as he kept the left screen fixed on the pirate ship throughout the turn.

Going to stealth mode ten confused the pirate ship, causing the Moslecks to lose their lock on the *Justice*. The pirate ship worked to reacquire its prey. But the newly energized hull of the USSTAP Galaxy Cruiser *Justice*, bent, reflected and distorted energy as well as light, making it impossible for the Mosleck sensors to find the *Justice*. They had to move in closer to achieve burn-through and gain proper weapons lock. The Mosleck captain ordered the ship to move forward, two thousand kilomarks.

The pirate ship moved at one-third hypersonic speed to the new position. The dialairtic gas, which was venting from the *Justice*, now attached to the Mosleck's chromerion field, taking on the oval shape of the field surrounding the ship. However, unbeknownst to the Moslecks, the dialairtic gas not only adhered to the outside of the field, it had permeated the field and began adhering to the inside of the field as well.

"We have hyperlight drive, sire," the *Justice*'s engineer announced. "But I can only guarantee five minutes."

"That's enough," Michael replied. "Decoys away!"

Roger engaged his decoy sensor, and several circular two-mark diameter energy balls, wrapped in fine polished glass, pounced from the stern ejector pods. The glass amplified the energy balls and gave the faint signature of a full size ship in quiet mode.

"They are firing!" Roger acknowledged. "They are firing at the decoys."

"Fire torpedoes...hyperlight engines engage now!" Michael yelled.

Then the USSTAP *Galaxy Cruiser Justice* flashed for a second, adhering to the laws of light and reappearing in space several hundred kilomarks from the decoys. Two torpedoes, ten marks in length, sailed from the torpedo bay, hooked left and flew under the port engine nacelle toward the Mosleck ship. Then as soon as the missiles were launched, the ship disappeared again, defying the laws of physics, crossing space at speeds faster than light.

Behind them, the Mosleck's energy balls, smashed into the dialairtic gas filled chromerion field, igniting the gas and sending waves of energy blasts, ripping the field open and dancing toward the pirate ship. The ship rocked backwards, thrashing its occupants back and forth with such force the hull breached, buckled and ripped at several locations. In the midst of the explosions, *Justice*'s two Asher missiles flew through the clouds of yellow, orange and red smoke, and blue fire, booming into the bridge of the Mosleck ship. The resulting detonation equaled a thousand kiloton nuclear blast, as evident by the characteristic mushroom cloud that engulfed the ship. When the smoke dissipated, all that remained of the Mosleck ship that once housed Misul Rafinel and eight hundred other personnel were small penny-sized embers of brittle metal.

However, clustered in the fireball floated a lone smoldering, damaged life pod, ejected from the Mosleck ship's bridge, without purpose or direction or chance of survival.

Michael breathed a sigh of relief as he gazed at the screen. He was too far away to see the carnage, but his mind knew it was there. His actions had resulted in multiple deaths in a short span of two minutes. And his conscience was amazingly clear. Any doubts he had of his ability to be the First Osguard had melted in the heat of battle. What he didn't know was his actions today had solidified his position for life with the members of USSTAP.

Chapter 22 — Transition

"Are you okay?" Shawn asked Michael. It was the first words said between them since they returned from Chaktun. Michael, Shawn and Patricia were on their parents' front porch, enjoying the last days of summer. The two men sat on the top porch step facing the street, while their sister sat on a step below them resting her body against her big brothers' legs, using Michael's right leg and Shawn's left leg as a back support. The lazy September afternoon was full of mugginess, the type that zapped all the energy from an average soul. But after the time they had spent on Chaktun, working under that blazing sun, Earth's summer heat felt like winter breeze.

"Yeah, I'm okay," Michael answered.

Michael hadn't spoken about his ordeal aboard the *USSTAP G.C. Justice* since they returned to Earth two days ago. In fact none of the three spoke about any part of their secret adventure. However, Patricia wore a keen smile throughout the day, which made her mother suspicious.

Shawn looked to see if anyone else was around and then moved closer to his brother, "I can't imagine what you are going through," he continued. "Man, I never realized what the hell we were getting ourselves into, until they told me about you and what happen on the *Justice*. I mean I could have lost you forever...and for what...some bullshit galactic political crap. Shit, I don't give a damned about the political crap in this country, why should I get involved over that crap."

Michael took a deep breath and looked skyward, collecting his thoughts and forming his words in his mind before they passed his lips. He huffed and lowered his head. "Shawn, I don't understand everything about this either, but I do understand one thing, USSTAP has been looking for the Osguard children for a long time. And that faith that the Osguard children would be found is what kept the peace in the known universe for all this time. Now that they found us, people are counting on us to christen that peace. If any one of us decides not to accept our fate... our destiny if you will...that peace will erupt into full blown war that may just envelope Earth."

"That sounds like Ortho talking...not you Michael," Shawn interrupted. "What about Patricia?"

"What do you mean what about me?" Patricia shouted back, turning to face Shawn.

"What if that was you that the Moslecks attacked? What if you had gotten hurt or worse...killed?"

"First of all Shawn, I'm not that little baby sister that started out the summer," she retorted. Her face glowed with passion and her voice thundered with confidence. "I went through the same training you did. I was right next to you and received the same enlightenment as you. My Chaktun blood is awakened and now burning through my veins as much as it is through yours. Being an Osguard isn't political crap, it's a calling." She stood, towering over her brothers, "I would have done the same damned thing Michael did," she growled in a low tone.

Shawn placed his hand on her arm and guided her to sit. The pain was evident on Patricia's face. She was losing her temper, and he knew he had to calm her down. "Cool down sis," he pleaded.

"Can't you feel it in your blood, can't you feel the calling beating in your heart?" she preached. "You are an Osguard! Just when you thought you were no one of any consequence...just when you thought being a black man in America would be your only legacy, Ortho comes along and tells you that you are more important than that. I always knew there was something better for us."

Shawn shook his head, "You are starting to sound like Ortho. Did he brainwash you as well?"

"Ortho didn't brainwash anyone," Michael pushed. "You went with us and you know that you feel exactly what Patricia is talking about. No one could put it into words, but you know damned well this is who we are and what happened to me on the *Justice* is what we do."

"That's just fine," Shawn shouted. "Tell that to Pepi, across the street there," he continued, nodding his head to the vagrant across the street. "Look at him," he ordered. "Pepi has been running these streets since I can remember…homeless and dirty…kids teasing him, people spitting on him and no one really caring that he is another human being. Look at him! No job, no family and worst of all no shame. He eats out of garbage cans. He wears clothes that stink and probably never saw water other than the rain that God sees fit to share with him. Where is our precious USSTAP when it comes to Pepi?"

Shawn's voice cracked a little as he continued, "What about Lois down the street. What is she…seventeen years old and already a mother of three? Living off the state during the day and living off the street at night…whoring just to make ends meet and feed those kids. Where is our precious USSTAP when it comes to her?

Or how about Cooter…the drugged out coke head kid who lives around the corner. He dropped out of school to support his sick mother and three brothers and sister, and got involved with Billy Red, selling drugs to the high school idiots on the corner. He used too much of his own product and fried his brain. And now that Billy is gone, he's at the mercy of the new punk asshole drug pusher, Tony Corda. It didn't take long for Corda to claim Billy's turf, and he's crazier than Billy ever was. Where is our precious USSTAP when it comes to Cooter's mother, brothers or sister?"

Silence was his only answer.

"For every noble galactic reason you can give me for continuing with USSTAP, I can point out a dozen souls in New Haven that need that resource more," he continued to preach.

Again silence was his only answer, as Michael and Patricia lowered their heads. Then with a low voice of reason, Patricia spoke, with her head still lowered and her eyes on her feet. "Every city in this country has thousands of sad stories, in which USSTAP can use their resources to alleviate. But for every story in this country, there are hundreds of stories in Africa, South America or even Central America. Listened to the news! New Haven doesn't have the market cornered on pain. And for every story you can find on this planet, there are millions of stories on Seteth, Pamasira or even Chaktun. So where do we start Shawn?" Her voice rose as she turned to her big brother and stared into his eyes. "Where do we start, huh Shawn? Tell me where do we start pushing our USSTAP resources? Who do we help first? What planet? What government? What person? Shawn, suffering is all around us." Her voice now morphed into a plea. "We start where we can, that's where we start. We start by ensuring the safety of those governments responsible for those people. We start by ensuring thriving economic growth for those governments. We start by ensuring the common sharing of ideas and technology for those governments. Then we pray to God to give the leaders of those countries the wisdom to use what we gave them to help those people."

Shawn let the words sink in and saw some wisdom in her words, but still had a fire inside of him to deny the logic. "Okay, what about Earth? What about here…right here…right now? Earth has no real part in USSTAP. Damned, the governments of Earth don't even know USSTAP exist."

"For now," Michael interrupted. "For now, but later…things can change," he charged. "But it won't happen if you divide us."

Shawn started to argue, his lips parted, his eyes narrowed and his heart pumped harder. But then calm enveloped him and he knew any argument he presented could be rebuffed by that simple logic… *It won't happen if the Osguards did not lead as one.* He huffed, and waved off the conversation, giving his siblings a reason to smile. "I still don't like it," he conceded.

In back of them the screen door opened and Elizabeth, their mother, stepped onto the porch. A hush fell over them and they turned toward the street as if they were watching a baseball game.

"What you kids talking about?" Elizabeth asked.

"Oh, nothing much," Patricia cooed, "just talking about the people in the neighborhood."

"Like who? Who are you all talking about?" she asked, taking the seat next to the window. Her flower print dress blended in with the flowers adorning the porches edges.

"Shawn was just talking about Pepi over there," Michael pitched in, never letting a dig on his brother go by without his input.

"Oh, poor Pepi," Elizabeth empathized, "you know he wasn't always like that. He used to be so handsome and so smart."

The three Osguards realized they had opened the door allowing their mother to begin her diatribe of gossip. With no avenue of escape immediately available, they settled in and prepared for the tongue torture only a mother could give.

***

The cloudiness lifted and the darkness faded. Billy opened his eyes and slammed them shut, trying to block the searing pain caused by sudden light pouring into the eye accustomed to darkness.

"Are you okay Mr. Red," a voice said with a heavy accent, he could not recognize.

Billy squinted while blocking the light from his eyes with his hand, trying to see who was talking to him. "I've been better," he admitted. Then after several seconds of allowing his eyes to adjust to the light, he asked, "Where am I?"

The owner of the voice stepped forward. "You're in a hospital."

Billy then realized he was lying down in a bed…in a hospital bed, complete with guardrails. When his eyes adjusted to the light, he surveyed

121

the room. It wasn't like any hospital room he'd ever seen before. The room was a dreary metallic gray; the ten-foot bay window that seemed to magnify the radiance of a red sun was so large, took up the entire side of the room. It was the red glow his eyes had so much trouble adjusting to. On the other side of him, were several machines, registering his heartbeat, pulse, blood pressure and brainwave activity.

"How'd I get here? And who the hell are you?" Billy asked with a little bit of anger in his voice.

"First, I am Byal Vren, Misul Ralinget's second in command."

With those words, Billy's memory came flooding back, at least everything up to the ship ejecting him in a life pod.

"Second," Byal continued, "one of our ships found your life pod."

Byal was tall dark and very rugged looking. His eyes burned like black coals when he spoke. His hair was jet black and slicked back, held in place by some invisible gel. He wore a long sleeve brown shirt, opened to show his muscular, but hairless chest. In his left earlobe, he wore a diamond studded gold earring.

"When we lost contact with Misul Rafinel's ship, Misul Ralinget quickly sent out a scout ship to assist. On the way, we heard on the USSTAP comm link that a Mosleck ship was destroyed trying to attack the Galaxy Cruiser *Justice*. Ralinget knew right away it was his father. The scout ship picked up a faint emergency beacon. That beacon was you."

Byal turned and walked toward the window. The red glow emanating from the window seemed to swallow him in a red aura. His appearance was now ghostly, almost demonic, as he peered out the window. With his back toward Billy, Byal continued, "It was my scout ship that found you."

"Err...thanks," Billy whispered.

"Whatever," Byal responded. He took a deep breath and blew it out. "Anyway, Misul Ralinget instructed me to take you here. You were unconscious, hurt, bleeding and barely breathing. This was the closest medical facility we could safely take you to. You were unconscious for two weeks." He turned to face Billy, the glow of the red sun still surrounding him like a halo of evil, "USSTAP is out in force looking for anything Mosleck. We have to stay here and lay low for a while. Besides, we have access to gate portal technology here."

"Where is here?" Billy said, showing his confusion.

"Here is where we will train you, teach you and make you a soldier for the Mosleck Reclamation Order."

"What?" Billy was surprised to hear these words. "No...no...no, all I want to do is go home and forget all this crazy science fiction shit."

"In due time, Mr. Red, you will go home, but only after we train you to kill Michael Genesis, Misul Rafinel's assassin."

"Wait a minute. What do you mean Misul Rafinel's assassin?"

"USSTAP is proudly announcing that it was the First Osguard, this Michael Genesis that commanded the ship that killed Misul Ralinget's father. And Misul Ralinget wants justice for his father's death. He wants you to go to Earth and kill Michael Genesis and then kill the rest of the Osguards, before they can be fully trained and take over USSTAP."

"Why me?" asked Billy, knowing full well that killing Michael was always his intention anyway.

Byal moved away from the window, stepping closer to the bed, reducing the red sun's halo effect. "Because if anyone else hates Michael Genesis more than Misul Ralinget, it is you," he said with conviction.

"Maybe," Billy admitted, "but I don't have shit against the others. I just want Michael dead."

"Once you kill Michael, do you think the others will let you live."

The words had spirit. Billy realized there was always someone who wanted revenge when a loved one was murdered. Most people relied on the flawed justice system, which Billy knew how to manipulate. So, he rarely worried about revenge seekers. And for those few times, he did worry about revenge seekers, he simply killed them first. But the Osguards were a different story. He had firsthand knowledge of that from his stay on the prison planet. Justice in USSTAP was swift and flawless, unsusceptible to greed or fear. But most of all, it was merciless in its pursuit and exact in its execution. No, he didn't want another round with the USSTAP justice system, if he could help it.

"At least with the training you will receive here, you will be well prepared for the task. And you will have a better chance to live to talk about it," Byal told him.

"Again, where is here?"

"Kulusk…you are on Kulusk."

"Can we trust the people here?" Billy asked, letting Byal know he was interested in his proposal.

"Believe me," Byal said moving closer to Billy, "our hatred for Michael Genesis and the Osguards have just begun, but Maxum Ritchen and the Kulusk's hatred for the Osguards is legendary. If anyone can be trusted in this venture, it is the Kulusks."

With a Machiavellian smile, Billy spoke for the first time in a civil tone, "Oh, I see…tell me more."

Chapter 23 — To the Rescue

Rutgers University's Archibald Stevens Alexander Library was cavernous and cold, with the acoustics that would echo a whisper to the third floor. She sat across the table from him. Michael thought she looked like a Nubian goddess. She had perfect colored skin—the sunrise shade between light skin and dark skin. Thin black mascara lines accented her bright dark chocolate eyes, which were almond-shape, giving her exotic Asian Pacific beauty. Her lips were full, encasing a bright and friendly smile. Her body boasted of a dancer's training—a mixture of a ballerina, skater and tap dancer. She had full, firm, muscular and definitely sexy thighs with round hips and tight buttocks to match her nicely proportion breasts. The black jeans she wore—or the jeans that were wearing her—seemed to have been painted on by Michelangelo himself. The brown short-sleeve pullover knit sweater also hugged her and highlighted her shape, leaving no place for imperfection to hide. Her hair was short and curly, cropped into a magnificent shiny afro. When she smiled it seemed to make the room brighter for that instant. He didn't know what caught his attention first, her smile or her nervousness. Luckily, something drew him toward her. Later he would call it fate. For whatever reason, he was drawn to speak to her.

"Is there something wrong?" he whispered. At first she was shocked he approached her. Her nervousness grew.

She shook her head and whispered, "Nothing's wrong."

He nodded and continued reading his book. Every so often he would peek up from his book and study her. Each time he could tell something was agitating her.

Michael soon finished with his studies, but something told him to stay. He didn't know if it was curiosity or instinct. He just knew he had to stay. Therefore, he retrieved books on space and the universe. He wanted to know everything he could about it. Ortho had opened up a thirst he didn't know he had. So Michael figured there was no better time to explore his roots of space than now.

Now it was 10:45 P.M. and the library was about to close for the night. He looked up at the beautiful woman sitting across from him and noticed she was beginning to pack her belongings. Michael left to put his books back on the shelves. When he returned, the young lady was gone. He scanned the area and did not see her. He shrugged, gathered his belongings and left the library.

It was a cool October night, and he had to walk all the way across campus to his dorm room. He criticized his decision to play big brother to a girl he didn't even know. On the other hand, he had done that all his life. Now it was becoming more than annoying, it was a nuisance in his character. However, he still wondered why she was nervous. Then he thought it might have been him making her nervous. She could have been nervous because he was a strange man sitting so close to her. Or it could've been because of his height—he stood six feet, two inches.

'Well there is nothing I can do about it,' he thought as he pulled up the collar to his jacket and stepped onto the walkway leading to his dorm room. Then he heard it, muffled but still distinctive, especially to him with his new developed Chaktun senses. It was a scream, a woman's scream. It echoed from the parking lot. He turned.

In the back part of the parking deck, away from the lights, he saw four figures. One he estimated was a female, and the other three were dragging her deeper into the trees that bordered the parking deck. No one else appeared to be around. The area was vacant, devoid of any other student.

He ran toward them as fast as his new acquired Chaktun abilities would allow. He was eating the distance between him and his prey, two hundred yards away, at an amazing speed, but he didn't notice. He was on autopilot—adrenaline powered his every move. He jumped over the roof of a parked car, clearing it by two feet, and landed in the area where he last saw the people. He stopped and listened. The sounds of a scuffle were coming from his left. He set off toward the sounds.

He soon came upon the people, three men, two white and one black, and the young woman from the library. Two men held the woman down in the dirt by her wrists as the third man stood over her. Her red sweater was ripped. Michael knew what was going on. The woman was nervous because three female students had been abducted without a trace within a month. Her studies had taken her pass sundown, which made her vulnerable. Unfortunately, her fears rang true.

The black man looked at Michael, "Turn around…this ain't none of your business."

"I'm sorry man, but you just made it my business," Michael said. Then he stepped toward him. The black man had a knife and began waving it at him. Michael moved with bird like agility, kicked his wrist, causing him to drop the knife, then executed a perfect roundhouse kick, landing his left foot across his face with such force that it caused the black man to stumble against a tree with a broken limb, which impaled him through his ear.

Seeing their partner down, the other two men let the girl go and charged at Michael. He swung around and connected with a backhand against the one on the right's nose, breaking it under the force. Then he bent forward and let loose with a rear kick connecting to the left guy's groin. He turned to face his assailants and landed a left right combination to the throat of the one on the right side, crushing his windpipe. The gurgling sound indicated the blood and air mixture filled his throat, but not his lungs. His eyes bulged from the pain. Michael then grabbed the man's neck and snapped it like a twig. The sound of the break echoed through the night.

Michael turned to the other man, who remained bent over on his knees. He lifted his right leg and forced it down over the man's head, bringing the darkness of unconsciousness to the surviving attacker, who now lay flat on his face in the dirt.

Satisfied, he turned to the girl, who was now cowering in the fetal position against a tree, fright still controlling her emotions and motor abilities. He bent down and offered her his coat to cover herself. She took it around her shoulders. Then she looked into his eyes. He saw the fright commanding her soul, but he didn't know what to do. Then she burst into tears, and began shaking. Michael pulled her toward him and she buried her head into his chest. He hugged her, trying to give her comfort.

"Everything will be all right!" he whispered. Soon he could feel the tension release from her body as she cried.

In the distance three white lights slid up like invisible doors, revealing three black clad security corps soldiers. They were from USSTAP, wearing an impressive array of weapons on their belt, called a delta belt. The belt held a quick release holstered coronet side arm strapped low on the side of the thigh at hand level. The gun was a sleek sexy looking eight inch barrel black weapon with a curved handgrip conformed to fit in the owner's hand. The gun shot rapid coronet energy pellets at the speed of light. The impact of anything traveling at the speed of light especially a coronet energy pellet not only put a hole in its target, it ripped through its target cutting clean seared grapefruit size holes.

The belt also contained a palm-size three-button pagenay strapped to the right hindquarter. The blue button fired the blue beam that quickly and neatly burned its target with high unbearable heat. The red button corresponded to a red beam of energy, which overloaded the human axons and dendrites in the nerve cells with heat, rendering its victim unconscious. Then the yellow button corresponded with a yellow beam that disconnected its victim's axons and dendrites causing momentary sensory deprivation and momentarily disorienting its victims.

The belt housed another remote control weapon called a mation II. Upon the call of the owner, this weapon shape shifted a metal liquid polymer into any type blade. The operator pushed a button and audibly stated the blade desired and the weapon would conform into that blade. It could change from a knife to a saber to a sword or even to a machete.

The delta belt was the epitome of personal defensive weaponry for USSTAP. It was the top level of defensive equipment right below full combat gear. Due to DNA locking, each weapon on a belt could only be operated by its owner.

The girl looked up and saw the three men approach. He raised his hand and waved them off.

"Osguard?" one whispered, checking to see if Michael was injured.

"I'm fine," he replied. "This is something for the local police to handle, not us. Go back and have someone meet me at the police station. I think I have some explaining to do."

"Tiah!" the soldier replied. Then the white lights framing an invisible doorway slid open, the soldiers stepped through and the light slid down closed, enveloping the soldiers into the night.

Michael then reached for and clicked on his communications collar, trying not to disturb the girl, who still had her head buried into his chest. She was sobbing and oblivious to what was going on around her. All she knew was there was comfort in Michael's arms and she was safe.

"Control...this is First Osguard Genesis," he whispered into his thin black leather collar with silver studs on the sides.

Her sobbing began to subside as awareness of her situation crept into her consciousness. Now she was becoming attentive to her surroundings and realized her rescuer was speaking to someone. She grasped him even tighter, more afraid to let go than ever.

"Control here..." a female voice rang in his hidden earpiece.

"Dispatch New Brunswick police to this location," Michael demanded. "Tell them a woman has been attacked. The attackers are here...two dead...one unconscious. Tell them to bring an ambulance for the woman." Michael stroked Michelle's hair; feeling her tense up at his touch and then relax as if she recognized it was he. "Control...I need you to hurry," he added.

"Who are you talking to," she whimpered between sobs.

"No one," he lied, clicking off his collar. "No one..."

He raised her off his chest and looked into her eyes. She was despondent, gazing down at the ground. Her tears had smudged her mascara down her cheeks making her look like a Halloween zombie. Her hair was frazzled and her eyes bloodshot. He wiped her cheeks with his hand, trying to clear the smudged mascara. She had stopped crying, and just stared at him, seeing him for the first time.

"My name is Michael Genesis," he offered, trying to pat her hair back into shape.

She remained limp, like a pet in its master's arms, secure and safe, allowing him to clean her. "I'm Michelle...Michelle Murray," she said, bringing back the confidence and self-respect she had lost in the attack. She reached up and grabbed his hand and pulled it away from her hair. "Thank you!" she said, staring into his eyes.

Michael saw life crawl back in her expression. She tugged at the coat to ensure it covered her exposed bra. He caught the hint and released her, shuffling his body away to give her some space. "Are you all right?"

"I think so," she whispered, while checking for injuries. "How about you...are you okay?"

"Yeah, I'm fine," he said standing up. He moved over to the unconscious attacker and nudged him with his foot. "That's a lot more than I can say for him or his buddies."

She looked around and saw one man stuck to a tree with a tree limb sticking out of his ear, and the other laying on the ground with his head almost turned around. Then her eyes turned toward him, who seemed to be studying the devastation like an archeologist, interested but dispassionate.

"What happened?" she asked.

"You tell me," he responded

"You did this!" she said with wide eyes.

"Yeah, I guess I did," he acknowledged without remorse. "They looked like they were about to kill you or worse."

She closed her eyes, reliving for an instant the fear. "I know, and then you came. You saved me."

"Yeah, I guess I did."

"You were sitting next to me in the library, weren't you?"

"Guilty," Michael shrugged. "You seemed a little scared. I was curious to why. Now I know."

She started to get up. Michael moved over and helped her to her feet.

"What now?" she asked.

In the distance the wailing sounds of police sirens answered her question. They said nothing to each other for the next few minutes. The morbidness of their surrounding encased their feelings. Michael didn't know what his next move would be. In his head, he scolded himself for getting involved, but he also praised himself for saving Michelle's life. He just didn't know if he was prepared to face the consequences of his actions.

Soon afterwards, three police cars, containing six of New Brunswick's finest, along with a Rutgers University police car with two more want-to-be cops pulled up. The police, hopped from their cars, converged on the scene, pistols drawn and pointed toward Michael.

"Don't move…hands in the air…get down on the ground," the police shouted in a cacophony of yells.

"I'm unarmed!" Michael yelled. "I'm putting my hands in the air and getting on my knees. Don't shoot. I'm unarmed."

Michelle moved toward Michael as if to shield him from the cops.

"No," Michael ordered. "Step back. Just tell them the truth. They will eventually let me go. Just tell them the truth." His eyes were not full of fear, but they did plead to Michelle and she understood.

The cops ran up to Michael, pushed his face into the ground and handcuffed him. Before Michelle could get the attention of the lead cop, Michael was in the back of a patrol car being whisked away to the local jail.

***

The Kulusk sun was relentless, bearing down on Billy like a river of molten lava. His shirtless body glistened with sweat and his usual crooked smile was dampened with concentration. Billy was in the training pit, outside the capitol city of Renard practicing the first battle rhythm movement his instructor presented. His execution of the movement was mechanical and slow, full of hesitation and thought; not artful or graceful, not instinctive or automatic, but technically correct. He blocked, parried, swung and swiped at an invisible foe. It was a one-man dance, a movement of death blows, but in Billy's interpretation it was an awkward launch into a break dancer's routine.

His instructor, a solid wall of muscle and bone, stepped into the pit with an obvious pain of disappointment plastered on his face and stopped Billy in mid stride. "It looks like I must demonstrate again," he chided.

Then the instructor went into the same routine, precise and deliberate, but with grace and artfulness. His arm movements were so crisp and so sharp the air screamed and snapped when he moved.

Billy watched in awe, imagining the day when he would use this fighting technique on Michael. But for now, he had to learn it, breathe it and nurture it within his soul. Something, he was sure the instructor thought he didn't have the ability to do.

"Do you see now?" the instructor said, not stopping his demonstration. "It must be fluid, seamless, and most of all you must not think about it beforehand. You must see and do…bypass your brain. You see your enemy move…you don't think…you move to counter…then you move to attack. When you attack…you watch…you hear…you feel…you use all your senses."

"Right on, man!" Billy chuckled.

The instructor, Gic Esher, stopped, turned and with a blurring movement cracked Billy across the face. The force of the punch lifted Billy off his feet and whirled him around like a kite, sending him flying backwards several feet, and crashing into the ground.

"You will respect me, or I will kill you," Gic said with the thunder of a demon from hell. "I am your Toam and I have the power to end your pathetic worthless life with a flick of my finger."

The words echoed through the fog closing in on Billy, the pain that originated from his face was now streaking throughout his body like lightning. He fought to open his eyes, but his body failed to listen to him. Blood flowed from his mouth, mixing with the blood already gushing from his lip.

Gic strolled over to him, knelt down, grabbed his nappy hair and lifted his head up so he could study Billy's face. Billy had no resistance, no life…he was just a glob of human flesh. Gic shook his head in disgust, "I guess we are done for today. I will see you at the house tonight for dinner, and we will try again tomorrow morning." He dropped Billy's head, allowing it to bang back into the dirt like a rock. "And if you fail to show me the proper respect tomorrow, it will be the last day you will ever see."

Through the pain, Billy heard the dirt crunching under Gic's heavy load as he walked away. With each fading sound, Billy felt relief and happiness that he was still alive. It took another fifteen minutes before Billy could shake off the pain and sit up in the blood stained dirt. When he opened his eyes, sitting on the stone wall that circled the pit, was Vidia Esher, Gic's wife. Through his hazy vision he could see that she was smiling, almost laughing. Vidia was the opposite of Gic. First of all she had a smile that rivaled the sun, opposite of the stern pout that always occupied Gic's face. She had shiny dark hair with slight slivers of gray, compared to the shine that illuminated from Gic's baldhead. Lastly, she was slender and lean, contradictory to Gic's mammoth body builder physic. Vidia also was a professor of science and technology, a brain of large proportion, which was different than Gic's unassuming intelligence. The only thing they had in common was that they were both lily white, pale as snow; which was somewhat disturbing considering how hot the sun burned during the day.

"You shouldn't antagonize Gic like that," she yelled to him. My husband has killed people for less."

"What the hell did I do to antagonize him?" Billy croaked, not knowing what the word 'antagonize' meant. But he cracked his jaw back in place and guessed antagonizing him was another way of saying he pissed him off.

"He is your Toam," Vidia continued, as she hopped off the wall and walked towards him. She carried a bucket of water and a large cotton-like fiber cloth. She knelt down beside him and began to clean the blood from his face. "Gic sent me out here to make sure he hadn't killed you...yet."

"You know as well as I do, Gic can't kill me. I am here as a guest of your Maxum."

Vidia smirked, "If that were so, then you wouldn't be swimming in your own blood...would you? You are a guest because of the potential you have to rid our Maxum of a growing enemy, but don't be fooled for one minute that that fact is a golden shield giving you immunity from Gic's justice. If you continue to wrong him...if you continue to disrespect him, he will kill you and it will be acceptable to the Maxum. And even though I would be full of sorrow if that were to happen, I would be duty bound to accept your death as my husband's inevitable will."

A tinge of fright shivered down Billy's spine, as her words pounded home the strange truth. Then he grabbed her wrist, pulled it away from his face and with a huff blurted out, "What about me? What about respect for me?"

"There are two ways to get respect; you either earn it, or you take it," she answered shaking loose from his grasp. "My husband has earned the respect due him through serving the Kulusk Empire as a Toam and leader of the Kulusk military. And if he chooses to do so, he is strong enough to take it. I hope you think highly enough of my husband to freely give him the respect he has earned or he will surely take it over your dead body. The choice is yours." Her smile then brightened, as she wiped the last bit of blood from his lip. "Your chance to earn the respect you so richly desire is to kill the First Osguard. Until then you have no respect coming."

"On Earth, I was like your husband. People respected me…feared me even."

"Well Billy, this isn't Earth. This is Kulusk. And the sooner you understand that, the better chance you have of living through my husband's training." She threw the cloth in the bucket as if to punctuate her words.

"Tell me something," Billy pushed, "is Michael getting the same training on Chaktun.

"Yes and no," she answered. "I assume he is learning the same fighting skills, but not in the same way, not with the same hunger and rush my husband teaches. He is probably learning it as an art not as an ability to be nurtured and controlled. Besides, I suppose he is also going through academics that will take away from his training."

"Academics, do you mean he is going to school…for what?

"I guess to round him out as a leader."

"Round him out…what do you mean?"

"You know, to complete him. Fighting isn't the only thing to make a man. He must have knowledge and wisdom to be complete."

"What about me?" Billy questioned with evident confusion. "I've always felt I was not complete…that I was missing something. What do I need to be complete?" Tears formed that clashed with the blood pools in his eyes. He was bearing his soul…something he would have never done on Earth.

"What do you think you are missing?" Vidia bounced back.

"I don't know…maybe you can teach me something, so I can have knowledge and wisdom."

"Teach you…I fear that is out of the question. You are here to learn how to fight and kill, not to further your education."

"Further my education? Lady I have no education. I went to reform school at eight and dropped out of school at fourteen. The streets became my school and hard knocks became my teacher. So you wouldn't be furthering my education, you would be giving me an education."

Vidia's smile disappeared as Billy's words washed over her. Confusion soon became dominant in her demeanor. "Okay, I don't understand what you said exactly, but I understand you don't have an education. What do you want me to do?"

"Teach me science…teach me about your technology."

Still confused, Vidia replied, "How…when…and most of all, why?"

"How; with books, you do have books on this planet…don't you? When; at night…after dinner, and why; because I need to be complete. I need to be as complete as Michael Genesis in order for me to kill him." Billy pressed through clinched teeth.

The challenge brought back Vidia's smile. "Okay, we will try something tonight after dinner. But if it hampers what Gic is teaching you, we will stop. And if you continue disrespecting my husband, we will stop. Is that understood?"

"Yes ma'am, I understand."

"Now we must go, it is getting late," Vidia ordered, helping Billy to his feet.

"Toam Gic sure packs a punch," Billy joked, rubbing his cheek.

"That is good," Vidia commended. "You called my husband by his proper title. You're learning."

"Yes ma'am, I don't have to be hit on the head twice with a brick."

"What?"

"Forget it ma'am…forget it. You're right…I'm leaning," Billy concluded with a genuine smile. Then a moment of awkward silence fell upon them.

"Let's get you home and have a look at that head. I think my husband might have damaged your brain in some fashion," Vidia commented, as she stepped to exit the pit.

"No, he didn't," Billy admitted as he limped next to her. "He just knocked some sense into me."

"Again, I don't understand."

"It doesn't matter. I understand…that's all that matters…I understand." Again silence took command and stayed in command all the way to the Esher house and throughout dinner. After dinner, a different tone pushed its way through the air. That night Billy began his formal education.

***

"So you took on three men all by yourself?" Lt. Flowers asked again.

Michael looked skyward in unbelievable desperation to get this idiot off his back, "Yes…yes…yes, for the third time in as many hours yes. I saw them drag her to the back of the parking deck, I ran over and I fought with them."

"And you killed two men with knives and knocked the third unconscious?"

"Yes lieutenant, I did," Michael answered jerking his head back to stare Flowers in the eye.

"I just can't believe it," Flowers admitted. "You know what I think, Genesis?"

"No lieutenant, what do you think?"

"I think you were part of this all along," he began. "I think you picked Ms. Murray out at the library, signaled your friends when she left and then something went wrong. I think you guys fought over who got to do her. That's what I think."

Now the interrogation made sense to Michael. These idiots were after a confession, because he was a suspect, not a witness. Now he was frightened. The cops had taken his communications collar as well as his other USSTAP toys when they brought him in. He had no way of contacting Ortho or the Control Center at Lilly Station. He was on his own. Or was he? His street training kicked into high gear.

"Okay lieutenant, if you think that, the ground rules have just changed," he affirmed. He looked at the two-way mirror, knowing someone of authority was watching from behind it. "You had a cooperative witness that could have put the last remaining guy away, but now you don't. I want to be released immediately. If you don't, then you better damn well charge me with something and get my lawyer. I'm not saying another word. Understand?"

Flowers stood and banged the table with his fist. "That's not how the game is played kid," he threatened.

"Flowers," he said, purposely not calling him by his rank. "You get me my phone call or get me my lawyer. Because if you don't, I will have your badge and the badge of whoever is behind that mirror. You don't know who you're fucking with."

"Look kid. I don't know who you think you are, but you aren't the king of the universe. You can't have shit done to me."

"I may not be the king of the universe, but I'm the closest thing to it you will ever see," Michael said with a smirk.

"Let's talk about Billy Red," Flowers said changing the subject.

"Lawyer," Michael repeated.

"Okay, let me talk about Billy Red. You can listen," Flowers insisted. "Billy Red and his crew stabbed you last May; left you for dead. In fact you almost died. You had no memory of the attack when you woke up. Then you recover and Billy goes missing. His boys tell the New Haven police you had a gun to his head the last time they saw him."

"Lawyer…"

"All of a sudden your memory comes back and you testify against his boys for stabbing you. They're sent away for five to ten, and you're walking the streets. But where is Billy Red? Now later you're involved in a double homicide. The same sweet innocent college kid, who was fiercely attacked by street thugs now has the ability to thwart off three assailants with knives with his bare hands, when he couldn't do so five months earlier? I don't buy it."

The door swung open. A tall gentleman wearing an Italian suit strutted in and slammed his briefcase on the table. "You don't have to buy it, because we're not selling," he commented. "I'm Pierce Dale. I'm Mr. Genesis lawyer."

He was tall, slender and looked of money. His blonde hair had a specialty cut and his cologne smelled of fifth-avenue. His features were strong and tapered, signifying a confident man with skill. He was a high priced lawyer whose character said he meant business.

"This interview is over," he announced. "My client will be leaving now," he continued as he opened his leather briefcase. He pulled out a paper and slammed it on the table. "This is an affidavit from Ms. Michelle Murray, stating my client's innocence and the events that happened."

"How'd you get this?" Flowers asked in disgust.

"Never mind that...If you act without haste, I may forget how you denied my client his right to a telephone call or a lawyer."

"Your client wasn't under arrest," Flowers responded.

"Good, then we are going," he ordered, ushering Michael to stand.

"Listen Mr. Dale, if your client knows anything about the other three ladies who were kidnapped, he better speak up now."

Michael stopped in his tracks, turned and looked at the detective. "You mean to tell me that that is what all this is about?"

"Yup...The guy you knocked out says they are still alive and he's going to cut a deal rolling over on you. So whoever speaks up first gets the deal!"

Michael walked up to the detective, staring down on him. "You fucking idiot, you're being played and you don't even know it. I don't know that piece of shit from Adam, and I doubt he even knows my name, unless you assholes gave it to him. For the last time, I saw them attack Michelle and I stopped them. That's it. I know nothing about the three other kidnappings, and I never saw any of those jerks until tonight. Instead of sweating me, you should have been sweating that punk I left alive for you. If those girls are alive, he's the only one who knows where and you just wasted three hours on me." Michael huffed, turned and left the room with his lawyer, slamming the door to the interrogation room.

The slam echoed in the room and in Flowers' ears as if to accentuate the point he was following a bad lead. Flowers plopped down into the chair staring off into space, wondering what to do now.

Chapter 24 — Reflection

Lilly Station, the home of the Earth Forces of USSTAP, sat on the Atlantic floor of the continental shelf, once known as Atlantis. The old Kulusk station was the spherical hub, housing the command section and gate portal rooms. Several wings extended from the hub like spokes of a wheel, housing different corps. Extending at the end of the wings were concourses where the sea cruisers docked when in port, and where the startram catcher was also housed.

In the ready room, next to the command center Ortho sat behind the desk. Michael stood in front of the desk awaiting his scolding. Ortho looked up with his eighty year old eyes, the light beaming off his dark shinny bald head, and motioned for Michael to sit. "Michael," he began. I know this is all new to you, so I guess I have no one to blame but myself."

"…Blame?" Michael asked in surprise. "…Blame? There is no blame here. Someone was in trouble and I helped out. Isn't that my job? I mean isn't that what an Osguard does?"

"It's more complicated than that Michael," Ortho went on to explain. "USSTAP has no jurisdiction on any planet of the thirty some odd galaxies we administer to. We control the technology, security and trade between those planets. Civil law is not our concern. If it were, we would be placing our moral authority throughout the universe and overturning in some cases centuries of planetary customs."

"Sire, with all due respect, I'm not convinced that's true," Michael spoke up. "I wasn't placing my moral authority on anything…I was saving a life"

"By taking two others," Ortho interrupted, "That is law enforcement."

"Sire, that's a little hypocritical, don't you think? Just last month I was responsible for the death of an entire starship of Mosleck pirates. I fail to see the difference."

"That was in space, where USSTAP law reigns. Laws approved by the parliament represented by all the signatories. They signed up to abide by those laws we enforce. But on their planets—"

"—But on their planets," Michael interrupted, "we abide by theirs. And on Earth, a crime was committed in which a life was in danger. I stepped up and stopped the crime. Now my only shame is that I did not control these new Chaktun powers you gave me and it resulted in two of the three attackers' death. However, at that point it was justifiable. They attacked me."

"But—"

"—But nothing sire. I've lived on this planet all my life. Then you grab my cousins, sister and brother and me and tell us we are some long lost descendants to Chaktun heirs, and by the way you are now the ruler of this great organization called USSTAP. You whisk us eight hundred light years away; make us drink this liquid to return our Chaktun abilities, train us for six weeks in military, diplomatic and economic tactics. Then plop us back on Earth…plop me back to my life as a college student and expect me to act like you. Sire, I just turned nineteen last week. Don't you think you can cut me some slack and see it my way? The girl needed help. If it weren't for my Chaktun hearing, I wouldn't have known she was in trouble. I just can't walk away from that. Could you?"

Ortho looked perplex, searching for something to say. But elected to let the moment of silence be his answer.

"Besides," Michael continued. "I've watched the graphic holovidpics of my ancestors being raped on an antebellum farm. The same ancestors you say founded USSTAP. And even though I am a distant byproduct of that rape, I could not stand by and know another woman was going through that…not now, not ever!"

Ortho hung his head down in despair and whispered, "But the consequences. Now the cops think you are involved somehow. You drew attention to yourself and ultimately toward USSTAP. We cannot let the people of Earth know of our existence. It would be too devastating."

"I know…I know. You've drummed that into our heads a million times. That's why our parents and grandparents are still in the dark about all of this," Michael acknowledged. "The people aren't ready, the economy would fall, war would ensue, and the seven plagues would consume the Earth."

"You may be the First Osguard and the ultimate leader of USSTAP, but don't be flip," Ortho warned. "You know as well as I," Ortho began with a stern lecturing voice, "that the Artificial Intelligence model indicates, if we share our technology with Earth, the mortality rate would fall and the population would grow exponentially. This would cause worldwide famine in ten years. And to head that off, we would institute trade, which would increase the wealth of the third world nations. This in turn would threaten the economic stability of the other nations, causing the beginning of your World War III."

Michael leaned closer to the desk. "I tell you something, sire, I don't think I believe the ARIT model. But I do believe the people aren't ready yet. I know what you…I mean *we* have to offer them would only confuse and scare the leadership into doing something stupid. And I do believe our assistance will hurt the world economy. But I think it would only be temporary." Michael stopped and lowered his head in resignation. "However, I'm not willing to take that chance."

"Good!" Ortho praised. "At least you learned something."

"Yet," Michael warned.

Ortho shot a stern look at his protégé. Michael didn't flinch. The steeliness in his eyes projected an unwavering determination challenging Ortho and his words.

"Oh yeah…sire! I've learned a lot. And there's much more you can teach me. Yet there is much more you can learn as well."

"Like what?"

"Like everything isn't about USSTAP, there are things bigger than USSTAP."

"Yeah…like what?"

"People are needlessly dying on Earth. Drugs are taking my generation. Crime is running rampant. Where I come from, most kids my age have no hope, no dreams…nothing to look forward to. There are no role models for them, other than the pimp prostituting his sister or the drug dealer killing his brother." Michael's eyes began to tear up. He took a deep breath and looked away to regain his composure.

After several seconds he turned back to Ortho and continued. "College to most is a fantasy. What's real is the almighty dollar…how to make more of it, and how to make more of it fast. Those on the bottom just get stepped on, pushed aside or disappear in the noise. It's the eighties, almost thirty years since Martin Luther King spoke so eloquently for equality. And the only thing we seem to have become equal in is the amount of pain we can inflict on each other. We are killing each other for a pair of sneakers. Before, we were a proud race…a race that hung together, worked together and played together. Not anymore!

I always said if I had the power, I would stop the drugs, stop the violence and bring back the hope and the pride. Not just for the Black community, but for all of mankind. Four months ago, you gave us this power. My faith was renewed. But then you told me I couldn't use it. I couldn't use it to eradicate drugs. I couldn't use it to cure the terminally ill, and I couldn't use it to stop the violence in my neighborhood, let alone around the world. You told me, it wasn't our job, that it was theirs. I swallowed that hook, line, and sinker; and my faith was lost again…buried in a sea of despair, wants and wishes. But now sire, I'm telling you, there is something mightier than USSTAP…something better than you that guides my conscience."

Michael reached into his coat pocket and pulled out his copy of the Lonson, the religious book of the Chaktun god Jus. He threw it on top of the desk. "It's amazing how your Book of Lonson and my Bible seem to be in concert with each other. If you are looking for something bigger than USSTAP, look to Jus. I'm sure you will find the answer. As for me, I've looked to my God to lead me in the right direction. And helping Michelle was what God led me to do. See if Jus disagrees?"

Ortho placed his hand on the Lonson and his face lit up with understanding. "You are wise for someone so young, Michael."

"I have to be. I'm the First Osguard. And as the First Osguard, I make you this promise. I will find a way to make Earth as peaceful and pleasant as Chaktun. I'll regain my faith and bring back the hope and pride of humanity to Earth. That is why I've decided to study International Relations for now!"

"Before that," Ortho interrupted, "as the First Osguard, you need to get the cops off your back first."

"Yeah, I know, and I'm working on that," Michael responded noticing the preacher's tone in Ortho's voice. "But there is something else I have to do first."

"What's that?"

"Find those missing girls!"

"So USSTAP be damned?" Ortho challenged.

"No, Ortho, USSTAP won't be damned. USSTAP is too big, too powerful and too complicated; to let a small insignificant planet like Earth, cause its damnation. It's the damnation of Earth I'm trying to prevent," Michael conceded. "Finding those girls won't start or stop either from happening. But it will damn sure allow me to sleep at night knowing I tried."

Ortho huffed and remained quiet for a minute, lost in reflection, trying to find a response to Michael's logic. Finally, he gave up and turned to exit the room. "Michael…Make sure, whatever you do…it's the right thing for USSTAP, for Earth…and for those girls." Then he left, signaling to Michael tacit approval to begin his search for the missing women.

Chapter 25 — A Little Help

Eight hundred light years away, Billy Red woke at four in the morning and ran the equivalent of just over five miles in forty universal minutes. Then he showered and ate breakfast with Gic and Vidia. After breakfast, Gic marched him to the training pit and instructed him more in the fighting forms of Chaktun's Sixana, Mosleck's Restil and Kulusk's Nowan, including weaponry and tactics.

Billy enjoyed all three forms, but gravitated towards the Mosleck's Restil fighting form. Gic kept Billy in the pit for ten hours, running workouts, endurance drills and lifting weights. His only respite was a five minute water break every two hours and an hour for lunch.

It was late in the afternoon. The sun was making its final dive behind the horizon and the air was cooling off a bit with a slight breeze from the north. Billy was practicing the last movement of the Restil defensive maneuver. His arms were sore, his legs were cramping and his chest hurt, but he continued flowing through the movement with grace and speed. Every so often, a pop and slap echoing in the air from his movements rewarded him with the pleasing thought he was performing the drill correctly.

"Stop," Gic commanded. "I believe that is enough for the day."

Billy snapped to attention and bowed towards Gic, "Soli, my Toam."

A slight smile whipped across Gic's lips, "Billy, you are coming along fine today. I hope you can keep up this level of effort in the coming days and months."

"Yes, my Toam," Billy reported. "I will give it my best, and with your instruction, I know I will be a great warrior someday and bring honor to you, the Kulusk and my Mosleck sponsors by killing Michael Genesis."

"Indeed," Gic offered. "I believe you may actually fulfill your destiny in that regard. But for now, you need to cool down and then go home."

"Soli, my Toam." Billy raised his head and watched as Gic left the pit.

When Gic was outside the pit, Billy found a boulder near the outside wall to sit on and began his cool down breathing exercises. With each cleansing breath, he pushed his mind into a relaxing state, invoking a rule of meditation. Soon the aches and pains his body was housing, subsided. After ten minutes his body felt like it had just awoken from a good night's sleep. His eyes popped open and he felt refreshed and invigorated.

He hopped off the rock and began to gather his belongings, when he heard a voice call from behind him. He turned and saw three men at the pit entrance. He didn't recognize them, but for some reason at least one of them knew him by name.

"Billy Red," the man in the middle called.

Billy nodded, fighting the urge to revert back into his streetwise mantra. "Yes, I am Billy Red."

"Good Billy, I am Tinsic Yumphet and these are my sons, Brisca and Ebris," the man said walking towards Billy. "So you are the one that Misul Ralinget is training to take out this new Osguard."

Billy allowed the man to approach before answering, "Yes, this is true."

"Why?" Brisca huffed.

"Excuse me?" Billy questioned, trying to keep the state of peace he had just achieved through meditation from dissipating.

"Why you and not us," Ebris elaborated. "We're already trained. We speak the Earth language and we've been studying for this opportunity since we were children."

"I can't answer that," Billy responded with even measure. "That is something you will have to take up with the Maxum." Billy's eyes surveyed the three men for a moment, watching for sudden movement, but did not see any. "Now if you will excuse me, my Toam is waiting for me for dinner." Billy threw his backpack across his shoulders and side stepped the three men to pass.

But before he could pass, the father brandished a knife. Billy saw this and snapped his bag off his shoulders and threw it at the men. It blocked the knife, but didn't stop Ebris. Ebris, with the quickness of a cheetah blocked the bag and threw a left hook, which hammered into Billy's jaw. Billy fell to the ground, but bounced, spun and was back on his feet in a defensive stance.

"Quick learner," Brisca announced moving into an attack stance.

Tinsic stepped back allowing his two sons to continue the attack. Then the two brothers fired an onslaught of punches and kicks. Billy blocked, parried, ducked and spun from most of the onslaught, but several hard hits connected to his face, chest and side. Billy was unable to muster an offensive, he was stepping back, losing ground, falling and slipping when he was hit and desperately searching for an opening. A kick to the chest pushed Billy up against the wall, and with nowhere to retreat and no room to maneuver, the onslaught took on the character of a beat down. Soon Billy no longer resisted. His arms dropped and his face, chest and legs became a punching bag. Darkness consumed his vision as each hit hammered home more pain.

Then the pounding stop and Billy sank to his knees. Blood oozed from cuts around his eyes, cheeks and lips. But he refused to lie down. He staggered back to his feet and tried to lift his hands in a defensive position. But Brisca and Ebris had their back turned towards him. He wiped the blood from his eyes and looked past them to focus on the two figures standing in the middle of the pit. Gic had Tinsic in a headlock, and Tinsic's eyes were wide with fright.

"The house of Yumphet has attacked my house without cause," Billy heard Gic yell. "You ambush my student…my charge…in the house of Esher training pit." Anger ruled Gic's voice as it thundered in the pit. "This day, honor has left the house of Yumphet and the house no longer deserves a place in the Kulusk community."

"Let our father go," Ebris screamed.

"No," Gic yelled back.

Then two gate portals flashed open, revealing four Kulusk security guards with their weapons drawn. The guards stepped through the light and rushed towards the Yumphet brothers. The brothers fell to their knees with their hands grasped behind their heads.

"Let our father go," Ebris pleaded, "and allow us to face the Maxum's justice."

"Your treachery shall not go unpunished," Gic declared. Then with one quick movement, he snapped Tinsic's head around, breaking his neck. The pop was loud and echoed in the pit, letting all know that Gic just brought death to the House of Yumphet. Tinsic fell hitting the ground with his knees and then face. However, he felt no pain, because he was already dead before Gic let him go.

Ebris and Brisca howled like wolves. Their pain and agony reverberated off the stone walls and echoed into the air. Their shouts of disbelief turned into murderous curses of revenge against the House of Esher and Billy. Gic walked up to them as the guards lifted the brothers to their feet and handcuffed them. The howls died down to grunts and whispers through clenched teeth, but the words remain just as damning. Then Gic grabbed the brothers by the throat, one in each hand, choking them so hard that they could no longer speak and could just barely breathe.

"You will leave my House alone, and that includes Billy Red who is part of my House, or I promise your death will not be as quick and painless as your father's." The shocked brothers fell quiet, only the wheezing from their labored breathing could be heard. Gic saw the fright in their eyes and released them. "Take them," he ordered.

The guards then rushed them into the lights of the gate portals. When the gate portals closed, Billy crumbled to the ground, allowing the darkness to rush in and shut his brain down from the pain. His last thoughts before the blackness took over was, *'Gic came back for me…he came back for me…and he killed for me!'*

***

Chilled winds circulated throughout Rutgers' College Avenue Campus. The leaves sported brown and orange colors decorating the skyline and the lawns. A perfect setting for the three-day Halloween weekend celebrations planned at the Student Center. Michael walked out of the gym; fresh from his workout. He noticed Michelle leaving the College of Nursing Lab. He jogged and caught up to her at the corner of College Ave and Bartlett Street.

"Michelle," he called.

She turned; face expressionless as if she didn't know what feeling to have at the sight of him. His mind raced to find the words he wanted to say to her. It had been two days since their ordeal, the girls were still missing, and the police still suspected him. He had ordered a full search, all sensors and all scanners in the local area, but without specific DNA to compare the finding against, it was like looking for a needle in a haystack. For once, Michael understood why it was so difficult for USSTAP to isolate their DNA in their search for the missing Osguards.

Michelle tilted her head to the side and a smile graced her face. The sight of the smile erased Michael's hesitation.

"Michelle," he repeated. "I've wanted to talk to you."

"Oh!" she managed to say, and began walking again, signaling Michael to walk with her.

"Yeah, I wanted to see how you were doing."

"As well as can be expected...considering"

"I can only imagine," Michael responded, in his most empathetic tone. He didn't know what else to say. He just knew he had to check up on her. Also, he had to see if Michelle believed the cops about him or not. It shouldn't have mattered, but it did matter what she thought of him.

"First my roommate and then me," Michelle continued.

Michael stopped and grabbed onto Michelle's arm, "Your roommate? What about your roommate?"

"She was the first one taken, three weeks ago."

"You mean Susan Tillman was your roommate?" Michael questioned with astonishment. He was already thinking of ways he could get a DNA sample to use for comparison from her dorm.

"Yah, but I thought you already knew that."

"Why should I have known that? I didn't even know you until the other night. In fact, I really didn't pay attention to the missing women until I met you." Michael's emotions betrayed his thoughts. "You think I had something to do with—"

"No," Michelle interrupted. "I don't believe the police about you at all. Remember, I was there. I know what happened. They don't." She began walking again.

"Where are you going?"

"You're walking me to my dorm room, right?" she asked with a smile.

"I guess so...that's if you say so," he said. Michael began to wonder what Michelle was up to. He now became afraid he might have sparked a romantic attraction in her. But he had to play this out to gather further information.

He pushed forward and stepped alongside her, walking lost in thought. Michael needed to find an excuse to get into the dorm room, look around and find a hair sample or something to extract a good DNA code from, without encouraging any further romantic interest.

"I'm glad you don't believe the police about me," he said.

"Well, if you had never contacted me, I might have started to believe them."

Michael swallowed hard, wondering how to respond. Again, he remained silent. No class in Ortho's crash course in diplomacy had prepared him for this encounter. He looked over at Michelle and saw the same attractive woman with the same radiant smile he first saw in the library. The scared little girl he saved was not visible at all. He knew she felt comfortable with him and in some way he was beginning to feel comfortable with her.

After a brisk five-minute walk, they entered her dormitory. However male students weren't allowed beyond the lobby. He'd forgotten about that rule. Part of him, who was expecting this walk was a prelude to some type of romantic advance, began to relax. But the side of him that needed the DNA sample just went into overdrive. They stopped at the stairs leading to the rooms. Michelle turned to Michael. He saw her face transform from happy thoughts to one full of worry.

"Michael, I don't know who you are, or what you are. All I know is that I trust you. You saved my life. And if there is any chance Susan is alive I know you will find her. But I think you need help, Osguard!"

Michael's eyes popped. She had called him Osguard. He didn't know what to do now. A reactive cough lodged in his throat, almost choking him. He covered his mouth and turned away.

"What did you call me?" he countered.

"I called you what your friends from the light called you," she smiled.

"What friends?"

"Like I said Michael, I was there. I may have been scared out of my mind, but I wasn't out of my mind."

Michael shot a concerned look at her, "I'm pledging a fraternity and Osguard is my pledge name. Those were some of the big brothers checking on me. I suppose the lights you saw were their flashlights. I asked them to call the police. But other than that I didn't want to get them involved. So I didn't tell the cops. Did you?"

"Don't worry Michael, I didn't tell the police about them. And I don't want to know anything you're not ready to tell me. Just know you have a friend in me. But I need you to find Susan."

Michael saw the sincerity in her eyes, "What makes you think I can find her?"

Michelle continued staring into his eyes. Michael felt lost. She was ripping his secret right from his brain with her stare. After several seconds of silence, he nodded. "Okay Michelle, suppose I have resources that could find her, I would still need help."

"How can I help?"

"I have a friend with some pretty smart bloodhounds. I probably can use them to search the campus. But I need something I can use to track her scent with…hairbrush; sweatshirt; a sneaker; something the dogs can get a scent from."

Michelle smiled, like a great relief fell from her shoulders. She hugged Michael, kissed him on his cheek and whispered in his ear, "I'll be right back!"

She scurried up the stairs and two minutes later returned with a paper bag. She handed it to Michael. He looked inside and saw a hairbrush, several blouses, and other items he figured his scientific team could extract a good DNA sample from.

"I'll have these things back to you as soon as possible," he said closing the bag. Looking apologetic, he placed his hand on her arm, "I can't promise you what I can find, but you will be the first to know when I find it."

He recognized the search for comfort in her eyes, and tried to radiate the best hopeful gaze he could. This was one time Ortho's diplomatic courses came in handy. He ripped a piece of paper from the bag and jotted down a 1-800 number.

"This is a number you can reach me, night or day. Just ask for Osguard Zero–One."

He passed the paper to her and then turned to go outside. As he approached the door he noticed two men stepping out of an unmarked police car. One was Detective Flowers. Michelle looked up and saw them as well.

Michael knew if he were caught with Susan's stuff, it would make things worse for him. Michelle knew it too.

"Give me the bag!" she pleaded, turning Michael back to face her.

At that point, he knew Michelle didn't set him up, however for a brief second the thought found root in his mind.

"No," he said, "go out and stall them. I'll call you later."

He shook her hand and hurried to the downstairs bathroom area. Once inside he checked to see if anyone was around. When he was confident he was alone, he activated his personal gate portal, PGP. The earmark invisible door lifted, spewing the brilliant heavenly white light of inner space onto the bathroom walls. He stepped into it and the door closed behind him, swallowing him briefly into another dimension, only to step out on the other side onto Lilly Station.

***

"Where's Michael Genesis?" Detective Flowers demanded.

Michelle looked back and witnessed the white light flash from under the bathroom door and confidently answered, "He's not here. Why?"

Chapter 26 — Push comes to Shove

Billy looked in the mirror. The scars seemed to be healed and the swelling gone. He was amazed that only twenty-four hours ago he looked like he'd gone ten rounds with Mike Tyson. For a minute there he thought he was going to lose his right eye, a couple of teeth and be permanently disfigured. But thanks to the miracle of Kulusk science and technology, he was almost back to normal. The doctor said he just needed a few days rest, which meant a reprieve from the pit. Billy wanted to use this reprieve to better himself in other ways than becoming a robotic killing machine.

He went back to his desk and turned on the ARIT book. Vidia had assigned him reading on the mathematical equations behind gate portal technology while he was recuperating. Vidia had started Billy's education with math a few days ago. The years of playing cards, throwing dice and running numbers had sharpened Billy's mind with respect to numbers. He was able to comprehend and excel in every math problem Vidia presented. But there were some minor setbacks due to language translation; therefore, Vidia added Kulusk as part of the curriculum, and she thought reading up on the mathematical properties of gate portal technology, which was considered primary school math, in Kulusk would help bridge that gap.

Billy struggled with the language, but somehow, because numbers are universal, he was able to soak up the equations like a sponge. His eagerness was fuel and his curiosity was a black hole. The more he studied the more he questioned, and the more he questioned the more he studied. Soon Billy created his own theories, based on some of the science fiction shows and movies he saw on Earth. With the ARIT to help him, he played with the equations, maneuvered the numbers and adjusted his point of perception, but the desired outcome eluded him. Still he thought he was on to something, so he recorded all his work in a private log. He had just finished his last entry when Gic called for him to come downstairs.

When he reached the community area, a room in the Kulusk house used for entertaining guests, he saw Gic wasn't alone. Maxum Kie Ritchen, Misul Ralinget and a tall pale woman with cat like eyes were in the room with him. Gic motioned for Billy to join them.

"Well...well...well, Billy how are you feeling?" Kie asked.

Billy marched up to the foursome, strong and steady, "I'm feeling much better, sire. Thank you for asking." The words churned in Billy's stomach. The subservient attitude he was displaying was against his nature and he felt like a cancer was growing in him to continue this charade.

"Good...good...nice to hear that," Kie continued. "Misul Ralinget was worried that the little incident in the Pit had harmed you and that you would be unable to complete your task at hand."

Billy's eyes rolled to Ralinget, "Please inform Misul Ralinget that nothing will keep me from killing Michael, certainly not a fight with a couple of punks like Brisca and Ebris."

"I told them that," Gic interrupted, "But he had to see it for himself."

Billy took a deep breath and nodded to the woman, "Who's she?"

Kie cleared his throat then said, "An interested party from far away...far...far...away. Her name is Rina. She's just like Ralinget, she doesn't speak English. She barely speaks Kulusk."

"What does she want," Billy demanded and then in a softer tone added, "Sire."

"The same thing we all want and what you promised to deliver," Kie beamed, "Michael Genesis' head."

***

That night the Kulusk air was unusually cool. The quarter moon glowed with intensity, like a spotlight breaking through a sea of darkness. For the first time in ages, Billy tossed and turned in his bed. He couldn't sleep. He was on his back peering through his triangular shaped window, looking at the moon, but not seeing it. His mind was restless; wandering through a field of equations and theories. It was like Vidia had switched on a part of his brain that lay dormant since birth. And now that it was activated, it was running on a seemingly endless surge of energy. He sat up in bed and began recording his thoughts in his private log. The equations flowed from his lips into his log in a steady stream; no pauses, no stops and no hesitations.

After an hour of dictation, the numbers became jumbled in his brain, and he stopped. He knew he wasn't done, but he couldn't see what equations came next. The order was disrupted, the flow contaminated. He put his ARIT log back on the night stand and rubbed his hands over his face, trying to massage the thoughts back in order. He was wired, but confused. So he lay back down and closed his eyes. *'Maybe a good night's rest will help,'* he thought.

It was three in the morning. Luckily, Billy didn't have to get up to go to the pit this morning. Even though he was technically recuperating, he felt as strong as he did before the fight and wanted to go back to training in the pit; but not this morning. A quick yawn brought the first flakes of drowsiness. He knew he needed to get some sleep, so he turned to his side and tried to push the jumbled equations from his mind.

As he lay there he heard the faint squeak of the floor on the other side of his door. He thought either Vidia or Gic were up and checking on him. Since the fight, they tended to do that every so often. They had become like the parents he never had. Gic was strong, stern and mentoring; teaching Billy the ways of becoming a man, like a father would with a son. Vidia was sweet and nurturing; ensuring Billy ate right, completed his lessons, listened to him when he had something bothering him and reassured him of his place in life, like a mother should. A smile crept across his lips as he thought of one of them on the other side of the door, listening and checking to see if he was okay.

Then a loud blast broke through the silence. Vidia screamed. Her scream was like an electric shock to Billy. He shot up in bed, stunned and bewildered. Then the unmistakable sound of coronet gun firing four times froze him. The scream stopped, cutoff by the gunshots. Billy jumped out of bed and his door slid open. He rushed through with adrenalin pumping anger coursing through every muscle in his body.

Red emergency lights dazzled the corridor. Smoke fogged the area. And Vidia and Gic's door was blown from the wall. A shadow popped out from the blown door. It was thin, lanky and tall. Billy knew it wasn't Gic or Vidia. It was an intruder, someone who didn't belong in the house and apparently someone who had harmed his Toam and his wife. Then for a split second the red dazzle of the light caught the intruder's face. It was Ebris.

Ebris raised his coronet rifle and aimed it at Billy. The sight of Ebris in the house caused Billy to lose his mind and fly into a rage. In a split second, Billy covered the ten feet between him and Ebris disarmed him and use the rifle to beat him in the head. Billy sensed movement in the shadows to his right. He dropped the rifle and dove to the floor just as a coronet pellet whizzed by his shoulder. He sprang to his knees and with catlike agility pounced at the figure in the shadows. A second shot winged Billy's left shoulder, but it didn't alter his trajectory. Before a third shot could ring out, Billy had tackled the figure. The rifle flew in the air away from them, leaving Billy with free reign to bring down destruction on the figure's head. The red dazzle of the emergency light flashed on his assailant and illuminated his face. It was Brisca, which Billy had already assumed.

Billy straddled Brisca's chest and wailed on him with punches and elbows to the face. Billy could feel Brisca's jaw break under the thunderous power of one of his punches; then the nose crunched under the blow of his elbow. Now Billy was aiming for the eyes. But someone grabbed him and pulled him off Brisca. It was Ebris. Ebris had Billy in a Nowan hold similar to a Full Nelson. Ebris was behind Billy with both arms underneath Billy's armpits and his hands locked behind Billy's neck. He swung Billy around, back into Gic and Vidia's room.

As Billy struggled, he could see, through the haze of the red emergency light, Gic and Vidia's bodies in the bed, shredded to pieces by the coronet rifle blasts. Blood and guts were spewed all over the place; on the walls, the sheets and the furniture. Gic's eyes were frozen open in defiant anger, his body lying across Vidia, trying to shield her from certain death. Vidia's beauty was marred, frozen in fear; eyes seared in disbelief. The sight of their bodies released another shot of anger laden adrenalin. Billy's muscles flexed as his street fighting skills kicked in. He dropped to his knees, rocking Ebris off balance. Then he shot his fingers backwards into Ebris' eyes. Ebris let go of Billy and covered his eyes with his hands. This was all Billy needed. Now, in his mind he was back in the pit, working and perfecting Gic's eclectic fighting style of Sixana, Restil and Nowan. However, he fused his own style of street fighting with them and created a whirlwind of unbearable pain for Ebris and Brisca. Punches, kicks, knees, elbows and head butts cascaded into relentless explosive death blows. After five minutes, Billy was done, the anger abated. He stood in the middle of Vidia and Gic's bedroom covered in blood, his knuckles torn and raw, grinning at Brisca and Ebris' dead bodies—beaten to unrecognizable bloody pulps.

Chapter 27 — Search and Rescue

In a geosynchronous orbit over New Brunswick New Jersey, in stealth mode ten, invisible to conventional radar, Michael sat in the command chair of the *USSTAP Galaxy Cruiser Justice.* He was dressed in the black USSTAP uniform with four silver thunderbolts on his right collar, signifying his authority to the crew. Michael had adopted the ship as his official flagship, since the Mosleck battle, where he was so unceremoniously baptized the leader of USSTAP. But tonight, he had an unofficial use for the galaxy cruiser.

In front of him lay two screens. The right screen displayed a satellite view of the city, with a blinking signal south of the campus. The left screen delivered the picture of Earth from two hundred miles up. The borders of the northern continent discerned only by the lights of cities on the coast. Whispers of clouds stretched over the land and sea like tissue paper.

Usually, Michael would stare at this screen feeling the awesome power of God surrounding his aura. Nothing was as beautiful and mysterious as Earth. So simple, but complicated—A rock with water and atmosphere, floating in the middle of nowhere, attached to nothing—guided by unseen forces to spin on an imaginary axis and rotate around a fireball of energy and gases, without so much as detour of an inch from its intended path. Gravity, weight and other components of physics had no place here. But tonight, he was just interested in the right screen.

"Sire," the communications officer beaconed from his right. "We are getting a hit."

Michael stood and stepped to the viewing screens. "On screen...Maximum magnification," he ordered.

The right screen zoomed in on a red house in a residential area.

148

"Are you sure?" Michael asked.

"Tiah!"

"Life signs?"

"Three life signs."

"They're alive!" Michael said to no one in particular. It was a situation Michael hoped for, but did not prepare for. *What now?* "Where are they—in the house?"

"It looks like the basement," the communication officer answered, switching to a 3-D view and swinging it around on the screen.

"Signal the local police," Michael said, "anonymously of course," he added.

"Tiah!"

Michael sat back down in the chair keeping his eye on the right screen. A story was about to play out for him on the screen. One he hoped he would have a hand in writing. One he prayed would have a happy ending.

Several painful minutes crawled by, with no sign of anyone approaching the house. Michael was becoming agitated at the slow response of the police force. He didn't know if the police took the anonymous tip seriously or logged it under another prank call. Either way, Michael decided he would give the police five more minutes before he would act.

He stood once more and moved between the pilot and navigator stations. He put his hand on the navigator's shoulder, startling the young lieutenant.

"Sire?" the navigator asked.

Michael looked down and realized his hand was on his shoulder. He removed it.

"Why is it taking so long?" Michael asked him.

The navigator turned back to the screen and shrugged, "Don't know, sire."

Michael moved to his right, toward the security officer. "Prepare a security team to secure the area," he ordered.

"Tiah, sire!" she responded. Without hesitation she clicked her intercom. "S-Team Alpha–One, report to Gate Portal Room Five."

Her eyes were ablaze with intensity as she tapped out the situation and instructions on her control console. When she was finished, she reviewed her creation on her monitor, making small corrections.

Michael's eyes never left her face. He wanted to review the instructions, but decided against it. He knew Lieutenant Gail French understood the assignment and would promptly and accurately relay it to her people. Her businesslike demeanor accentuated the point for Michael.

When she was satisfied, she tapped her console and sent the instructions to the S-Team leader in GPR-Five.

"Osguard!" the pilot called. "It looks like the police have arrived.

Michael turned to see heat signatures of two people approaching the front door to the house. "Hold the S-Team," he commanded.

"Tiah, sire."

Michael went back to his seat, never looking away from the screen. On the screen he saw the heat signatures moving through the front door into the house. They seemed to be pushing through the house in a leapfrog fashion. Move and cover, he interpreted. In his mind, he saw two police officers, guns drawn, bearing down on every shadow that moved in the house. They searched the front room, staying close to the walls. Probably to ensure no one got the drop on them.

"Basement," Michael whispered. "Go to the basement, you fools."

The heat signatures then moved to the kitchen. It was too small for both of them to enter with guns drawn, so one stayed in the doorway, while the other slinked to every corner, probably moving boxes and opening cabinets.

"The basement," Michael told them through the screen.

After several agonizing moments in the kitchen, the heat signatures moved back through the front room, toward the bedroom area. This time the signatures separated and each took a room. The signatures crept, again hugging the walls.

The anticipation was getting unbearable for him. He bit his lower lip, mentally calling to the police to go in the basement. He wanted to tell them, *all was clear, move with due haste and get to the girls.*

"Sire," the communication officer called.

Michael turned to him, not wanting to take his attention from the action on the screen.

"Lilly Station is patching in a call for you," he continued. "It's a Michelle Murray."

"My station," Michael responded. He then clicked a pressure sensor on his chair's control arm. "Yeah Michelle, what's up?"

"Detective Flowers called," she responded. "David Parsons is out on bail."

"David Parsons? Who is David Parsons?"

"The third guy who attacked me," her voice cracked, showing strains of emotions. "I think I saw him outside my window a few seconds ago."

"Okay Michelle, did you call the police?"

"Yeah, they say they will send a patrol car by in about thirty minutes." The fear in her voice rose, telling Michael that thirty minutes might be too late.

"Stay calm. I'm on my way," he promised. He clicked the connection dead and turned to his communication officer. "Get Michelle's coordinates and pass them to GPR-One. I'm on my way down there now."

"Osguard, I'll divert S-Team Alpha One to secure the perimeter."

"Won't that be a little suspicious?"

"Gail gave a rare smile, "its Halloween."

"Oh yeah," Michael acknowledged. He then turned and stepped up to the exit door. "Bravo belt," he commanded the bridge guard.

The sentry handed him a bravo belt containing a pagenay and a mation II. Michael took the belt and disappeared through the door.

***

In the midst of the night, behind Michelle Murray's dormitory, three USSTAP security corps members emerged from the white light of inner space. In the distance a *Frankenstein's Monster* was chasing *Charlie's Angels* down the street. On the other side, members of the singing group, the *Village People* watched in glee. On the path between the dormitories, a vampire, equipped with bloody fangs and a black cape seemed to skulk. The two-men, one-woman team, looking like rejects from a recent Hollywood Science Fiction movie, appeared to fit right in with the dress of the night. All they needed was a large fury creature bellowing out lion-like roars next to them to make the scene complete.

Alpha-One leader pointed for the other two to fan out to the flanks. Each drew their pagenay and moved out. Alpha-One planted himself behind a pine tree at the rear of the building. The woman, Ann Fox went to the front lobby, found a chair and pretended to read a magazine that was sitting on the nearby table. The third security agent hid in the shrubbery outside of Michelle's second floor window. Their directions included David Parsons picture, but none in the group figured they would recognize him if he was in costume. So they eyed all who approached the dormitory with suspicion.

***

Several minutes later, Michael emerged out of the white light of inner space into the corridor outside Michelle's room. The corridor was empty, just like the GPR scanners and sensors indicated.

"He knocked on Michelle's door. "It's me," he called in a raised whisper. The door flung open, exposing a frightened Michelle. Michael stepped in, "Are you okay?"

She tossed her arms around him, hugging him like a stuffed bear and digging her head deep into his chest. He wrapped his arms around her allowing her fear to dissipate into his grasp.

"Michael, he's out there. I know it. I can feel it."

"Are you sure," he asked.

"Yes, I'm sure," she sobbed. "I'm so scared."

"There's nothing to be scared of, Michelle. I'm here now."

***

The door swung open to the lobby. Ann turned to see who it was. To her surprise, Parsons stood in the doorway, dressed in a black jogging suit and wearing a skullcap. She stood pressing the emergency call on her communications collar. The signal went to her partners.

Parsons stared at her for an evil minute before he brandished an eight-inch knife. "Bitch, why didn't you leave? You needed to go, so I could go upstairs and take care of my business. But no...you had to stay here like some guard dog and ruin my plan. Now I guess I have to kill you too."

Ann winced at the implication, fingering her pagenay, wanting to trigger the kill setting, but knowing she could only use the daze or stun setting. She moved toward Parsons, who now stood about fifteen feet away, showing no fear. He was shocked at Ann's audacity, and held the knife higher to assert his authority in the situation.

Then as easy as a wave, Ann pointed her pagenay at Parsons and clicked the yellow button. A yellow beam shot from her palm, hitting Parsons in the throat. A shock, much like electricity, jolted Parsons. His body convulsed and the knife fell from his hands. He hit the ground hard with his knees, almost like a giant hand slammed him down. He was aware, but unable to control his body. He was paralyzed, fighting for breath, fighting for his lungs to work again. Then, air magically rushed into his lungs and he could feel the floor beneath his knees and hands. However, he still didn't have command of his movements.

Ann stood over Parsons, enjoying the freak show she had just caused. To her, it was better than killing him, watching him squirm, like a cockroach avoiding poison. "David Parsons, I presume," she announced. As she watched him, shaking on all fours, slobbering and drooling with spittle leaking from his mouth, rage formed in her about what he had done to three women. The rage intensified, shaking her limbs. Seeing him, watching him bent over in perfect position exploded something in her head. Then without thinking she let go with a wicked kick, connecting to Parsons' jaw. He flipped backwards onto his back, staring at the ceiling, with blood gushing from his lips, still unable to command his body to move.

Her partners entered the lobby, pagenays drawn and wearing the intense look of battle on their faces. Her rage then subsided and once again the calmness of a USSTAP professional possessed her personality. The two men holstered their weapons and picked Parsons up. Without a word, the three USSTAP security agents dragged the dazed man outside.

***

The voice ringing from Michael's CC earpiece broke the moment of solitude in Michelle's room. "Osguard–Zero–One, this is S-Team Alpha–One leader."

Michael released Michelle, pulled the mation II from his belt, while activating the speaker on his CC. "Walkie-talkie," he announced to Michelle. "Go, Alpha–One leader," he pretended to say into the mation II.

"Look outside the window."

Michael stepped to the window, followed by Michelle. Below, handcuffed to a bike railing was David Parsons.

"Wrapped and sealed for your local police," the leader announced over the communication collar. "We're heading back."

"Good work Alpha–One," Michael praised. "I'll see you back at the barn." Then he turned to Michelle. "Fraternity brothers are great," he lied.

Michelle regarded him for a moment, but soon smiled as the fear faded. "Please stay until the cops come."

Michael nodded.

"Osguard Zero–One," the ship's communication officer's voice rang through his collar, "this is Williamson."

Michael pretended to speak into the mation II again, "Genesis here, go Williamson."

"The police have found the missing girls. They're safe…dehydrated, a little emaciated, but they will recover. They are taking them to the hospital now."

Michael smiled at Michelle, "Thanks Williamson, and Genesis out." He turned to Michelle, "I think Mr. Parsons will keep outside until the cops come. Let me take you to the hospital," Michelle nodded with life in her eyes like Michael had never seen before.

***

Two days had past when Ortho walked into Michael's ready room aboard the USSTAP Galaxy Cruiser Justice. Michael looked at Ortho, wondering how to broach the subject. Their eyes met and some secret message passed between them. "So why didn't you stop me," he started.

Ortho tilted his head and gave his most diplomatic smile. "You know Michael…I've seen the humans of your planet try to annihilate each other for over forty years. I stood by and watched the Germans almost exterminate the Jewish race in the holocaust. I sat still, knowing what was happening in the killing fields of Cambodia. I sat across from Idi Amin during the height of his reign. Right now, I am aware of unspeakable horrors the people of your planet are doing to one another."

Michael's eyes widened as the picture Ortho was painting took root in his imagination. The totality of the situation soaked his soul. For once he realized the world's problems were bigger than what he'd seen in his young life. Organized crime, drugs, street violence, poverty and illness, although large, paled in comparison to what Ortho was describing.

"Go on," he urged, thinking Ortho was about to begin a galactic civics lesson. How did the problems of Earth compare to the centuries of war between Chaktun and the Kulusk? How did the problems of Earth compare to the Mepson Galaxy? In reality, what he considered as Earth's problems, were miniscule to the problems of the known universe he must answer to as the First Osguard.

"Well, let's just say, I have lived my entire life with the consequences of doing nothing," Ortho continued, placing his hand on Michael's shoulder. "Now I'm ready to start living my life with the consequences of doing something."

Chapter 28 — Not This Time

Billy stepped through the light like an old pro. The feeling he should kiss the ground or something overwhelmed him, but his street nobility contained it for the moment. After three years, he had returned to Earth, wiser, tougher and more ruthless than he was before he left.

The light faded as the invisible door slammed closed with a whisper, leaving Billy in the pure darkness of the night. He was back in the parking lot, in the same spot the USSAP soldiers took him from. It was night and the quarter moon was barely visible. The lot was empty and the sounds of the city were conspicuously absent, indicating that it was either real late or real early.

Billy had lost track of time. He had no idea of how long he had been away, but now looking at his surroundings, he wasn't sure he really was away. *Could he have been hallucinating? Had he just gone through the most harrowing experience in his life?* He shook his head, wondering if he had just gone through the simple aftereffects of a cocaine-induced fantasy, and this was still that fateful Fourth of July night. But the PGP in his hand told him his plight was indeed reality. After spending several weeks on a Mosleck ship, he took pleasure in sucking in a deep cool breath of metal free oxygen. Even though he had that freedom while he was on Kulusk, it wasn't the same.

After Vidia and Gic's death, Kie Ritchen took him into the palace, where he trained with the palace guards. Kie treated him like an old ally; delicious food, fine women and all the wine he could drink. Kie even showed Billy a way to process cocaine into a solid crystal to smoke. Billy was amazed at the fact that the Kulusks were so knowledgeable in cocaine, until Kie told him that it was something his grandfather brought back with him from Earth when he was sent there to kill the Osguards. Since that time, the

Kulusk have cultivated the plant and perfected the drug to maximum potency, covertly bringing that knowledge to Earth.

Billy overheard Ralinget and Kie speaking one night, and found out that some special micro ingredient of cocaine neutralized the Omega two–four–four DNA sequence. Somehow this was an important part of their plan, because neutralizing this sequence would assure the eradication of the Chaktun blood and thus the eradication of any Osguards left on Earth. Unfortunately, that plan didn't work, but succeeded in creating hundreds of thousands of addicts and double that number in deaths throughout the years. Billy felt a slight twinge when he realized he, as a drug dealer, took part in this galactic political shell game; and that is when the oxygen on Kulusk started tasting stale in his lungs. However, he always knew he contributed to the spread of the drug culture in New Haven, and it never bothered him before. As long as he was getting paid, he didn't care.

This little flaw in Billy's character is what Kie recognized and played upon. Kie offered Billy the opportunity to become one of the biggest drug dealers on Earth. Kie had set up many connections in the drug world and had the invisible hand of control on the industry throughout Earth. In reality, the Kulusks were the mastermind behind every drug cartel and gang; making, shipping and selling cocaine on Earth. And all Billy had to do was kill the Osguards on Earth, starting with Michael—a proposition he gladly accepted.

Armed with a Mosleck fighting knife, a Kulusk pagenay and a T-Comm, Billy felt like a new man, almost invincible and ready to take on the challenge. He looked around with a newfound inner strength and confidence and then began walking toward New Haven train station, fading into the shadows of the night like a mystical demon on the prowl.

***

The score was nine to eight. The game was to eleven, and it was their ball. Michael took the ball behind the top of the key, surveying his opponents in this three-on-three game. It was his last summer of hanging with his friends. Michael had just graduated from Rutgers University, with a degree in International Relations, and was preparing for his eighteen-month stint at the USSTAP Academy on Chaktun. He knew his life would never be the same, and he doubted if he would ever see his friends again. He wished he could tell them about USSTAP. He wished he could take them with him.

These were his boys…his best friends. They grew up together, hung together. And for the past three years he had kept the most important secret in his life from them. When he looked into their eyes, he felt a touch of guilt, the salt of betrayal that clouded their friendship. At least he was able to tell one friend.

Michelle Katherine Murray sat in the bleachers watching her fiancée, Michael David Genesis play basketball. Michael had proposed to her on the eve of their graduation from Rutgers University in New Jersey. When she said yes, Michael took her on the abbreviate tour of his new world, thanks to his PGP and his adopted galaxy cruiser, the G.C. *Justice*.

Michael glanced over at his love, winked and got down to business. A few perimeter passes, and the ball was back in Michael's hands. He eyed Reggie, who was guarding him. Then he stepped right, back and then right again, testing Reggie's response to his movements. Then with lightening speed, he shifted left and barreled toward the rim. Reggie recovered and with help from Tony, collapsed in front of him. He spun and passed the ball back out. As soon as his man caught the ball, he passed it back to Michael. Michael caught it on the bounce, spun left past Reggie and jumped skyward to lay the ball in the hoop with his right hand. Tony rushed toward him. Michael switched hands, shifted his weight in mid-air, using his right hand to guard off Tony. Then with a mighty force, Michael dunked the ball with his left hand, rattling the rim and clanging the chains with his thunderous force. Michael hung on the rim ensuring Tony and Reggie were clear before he dropped down.

"Ten to eight, we're up," Michael yelled.

Daryl took the ball out this time. After checking the ball, he passed it to Ron to the right. Before, Joe could check him; Ron aimed, jumped and shot the ball. The sweet clang of the chains was like a dagger. The game was over; the last point was fast, effortless and very painful for the losing trio.

"Run it back!" Reggie yelled.

"No," someone interrupted from the sideline. "I have winners."

Michael thought the voice sounded familiar, but didn't want to believe his ears. The gasp of the people in the bleachers and on the sidelines fed into Michael's imagination. He turned around and looked for the source of the voice.

Three young men, against the fence became the focal point of his attention. The one on the right looked like a Puerto Rican, bald, wiry but tough looking. The one on the left, also looked like he was Puerto Rican, with a buzz cut, muscular with a prison attitude. But it was the one in the middle that made his heart jump. His eyes were brimming with hatred, and his body language stated he was ready to pounce.

Billy smiled like a lion looking at his next meal. His teeth were fixed and even white. And even though the scar under his right eye had softened, he still maintained that ugly thug look. Memories of the first time they tangled flooded his mind, putting him on the defensive.

Michael's demeanor changed, his senses were at a heightened alert. All this time he thought Billy was dead, and to see him now standing here in the middle of the park confused his world. Billy knew who he was and what he was. Billy knew about USSTAP and more. *Where had Billy been all these years? And who the hell are these guys he's with?*

Michael didn't have to wait long to formulate the answers to his questions. Billy pulled out a knife, and with a crazy laugh, told Michael he wasn't there to play basketball. The crowd dispersed, the players ran to the sidelines, leaving Michael alone on the court. At a glance, Michael recognized the knife as Mosleck. Instantly, Michael surmised the truth. Ralinget didn't kill Billy when he escaped the prison planet, but took him with him.

Then with a savage growl, Billy ran and lunged at Michael. Michael sidestepped, spun and cracked Billy in the back with a forearm. Billy's momentum carried him further forward before he spun around. Now face-to-face, Billy began thrusting, charging, punching and swinging. Michael countered each move, by blocking, parrying, shifting, and ducking. Michael recognized Billy's style as a mixture of several fighting arts but mostly as the more modern fighting Mosleck form, called Restil. Michael was losing ground, backing up with every defensive move. He couldn't see an opening. He was just reacting, instead of acting, working hand-to-eye coordination without the brain engaging in the foray.

The only thing his mind was engaged in was beating himself up over not having his communication collar on him. He had left it with his shirt near the fence. He never liked the collar. He thought it made him look queer. But now he would rather have looked queer and used it to call for backup than be fighting for his life.

In the background, he could hear Michelle screaming, which fueled his desperation to put an end to this madness. Then suddenly, he didn't see the knife any more. His mind had allowed his situational awareness to slip. His eyes widened, he blocked a punch, and then the pain. There was the knife, slicing a gash in his side; almost covering the scar Billy had given him three years earlier.

Michael slipped to his left and slung a backhand uppercut, connecting to Billy's jaw, his first offensive-move yet. It bought him time. Above him was the rim. He jumped and grabbed the rim with both hands, scissor kicked out. Fighting the pain, he snapped his legs around Billy's neck. But Billy still had the knife and was about to slice at Michael's leg. Michael let go of the rim, twisting in the air applying pressure on Billy's neck and whipped both of them to the ground, him on his side and Billy on his head. This action made Billy lose the knife. And the dimming darkness of unconsciousness was covering Billy, while Michael continued to choke him.

Then a boot struck him in the side, and another and another. Billy's associates had come to his rescue. Michael let go of Billy and began rolling away. With the swiftness of a gazelle, he picked up Billy's knife and popped to his feet. The baldheaded one tackled him. Michael rolled with the tackle, flipped and landed on top of him, the knife centered on his throat.

The second guy snuck up behind Michael and put him in a sleeper hold. Michael reached back with the knife and sliced his cheek from eye to lip. The second guy let go, stepping back holding his fresh wound with both hands. Michael then let loose with a crashing left hook on the baldheaded one he had on the ground, knocking him out cold.

Satisfied with the damage he had done to him, he sprang to his feet, searching for his main prey, Billy. He saw Billy pushing his way through the crowd, trying to make his escape.

"Michelle," he scream, "CC in my shirt, call for help!"

Michelle calmed down as she witnessed her fiancé beat down three assailants in mere minutes. She jumped off the bench and moved with a purpose toward Michael's shirt.

Michael then turned his attention to the remaining attacker. He was still holding his face, blood gushing from his wound. Michael moved toward him and with cheetah like quickness, whipped a high roundhouse kick, knocking him out before he hit the ground. Satisfied the job was done, Michael turned once again toward Michelle and saw her pick up his CC and pushed the emergency beacon as he had shown her before.

Michael ran into the crowd, which parted like the Red Sea because of the large white knife, dripping with blood, he held in his hand. The Mosleck knife was made out of Chinone bone, similar to ivory. Both edges were jagged bent at an angle making entry smooth, but making pulling the knife out just plain carnage.

Michael saw Jackie as he pushed through the crowd. She looked giddy, laughing like a maniac. Michael imagined she was laughing because she thought they were still fighting over her after all these years. Michael wanted to stop and slap the smile right off her face, but elected to continue on his present mission. In the back of his mind, Michael conceded that entire incident which allowed Ortho to find the Osguards was due to her. But he still wanted to wipe that smirk off her face. He just shook his head and ran off down the street.

***

Michelle watched Michael run through the crowd, still in shock. She saw a side of him, she didn't know existed, and she knew she had to be just as strong. She ran into the crowd, realizing Michael may need his CC.

But Jackie stepped in front of her, "Where do you think you're going, bitch?"

Michelle stopped in surprise, "What?"

"Where do you think you're going, bitch?" Jackie repeated.

158

"Oh, I don't have time for this," Michelle told no one in particular. Then with both hands, she grabbed Jackie by the head and shoved it into the fence, banging it into the fence four...five...six times, until she went limp. When Michelle let go, Jackie fell to the ground.

Several girls then surrounded her, trying to come to Jackie's defense, but stepped back. Two black clad mean looking men had forced their way through the crowd, throwing and shoving people from their path.

"Ms. Murray," the tall one said. "Are you alright? Where is the...um, where is Mr. Genesis?"

Michelle looked up and recognized the one speaking as the sentry on the bridge of the *G.C. Justice*. "Michael is in trouble. Three men attacked him. He's chasing one of them down that way," she responded pointing down the street.

***

Michael ran down the street, eyes wide and alert, searching for a trap. His cautiousness allowed him to lose sight of Billy for a split second. Michael stopped to get his bearings. The street traffic was light; however, the street was full of parked cars. The old three story wood-framed houses with chain-linked fences characterized the area. Most of them were rundown and dilapidated. Others were kept up with pristine love and care. However, there were a few that were abandoned and ready for the demolition team. Two doors down, there was such a house, but the front door was not boarded up. It was opened as if someone just kicked it in.

Michael had a hunch that Billy went into that house. He took a quick look around making sure there wasn't some other place that Billy could have run. Satisfied that this house was the only place Billy could have slipped away to in that critical split second, Michael rushed toward it, hopped up the five wooden stairs and slipped to the side of the open door.

He took a deep breath and turned his head to listen for any sounds coming from the house. Inside he heard footsteps echoing in the hall, near the second floor.

Michael entered the house and began creeping up the stairs, praying not to be heard. As he shifted his weight onto the third step, a loud haunting squeak vibrated throughout the stairwell.

"That must be the famous Osguard, Michael Genesis," Billy's voice echoed. "Obviously you flunked 'How to be Stealthy' class at the USSTAP Academy."

Embarrassment soaked Michael's pride.

"So you know how to fight now...ah punk," Billy continued to taunt.

"Yeah, always did," Michael responded, moving up the stairs with his back to the wall. "If it wasn't for the knife, I would have kicked your ass three years ago, just like I did three minutes ago."

"I don't need a knife to kick your ass,"

Michael clung to the wall closer, "Yeah, right. But I see you learned some moves since the last time we fought. Where did you learn to fight like that?"

"None of your damned business," Billy shouted.

"So I guess the Moslecks didn't kill you," Michael pushed, fighting for time while he climbed the stairs. He was almost to the second floor now. He stopped short of the second floor landing, trying to pinpoint Billy's voice.

"No, in fact they took me in as one of their own...until..." Billy's voice trailed off almost muffled out.

"Until what?" Michael yelled.

"Until you blew Rafinel's ship out of the sky."

"Yeah," Michael pushed for Billy to talk more.

"Yeah, I was on that ship," Billy confessed.

"No way, I was told everyone died in that ship," Michael said with surprise. He hadn't realized that Billy was on the Mosleck ship that attacked him on his maiden voyage.

"Everyone but me," Billy screamed.

Michael heard Billy's voice rumbling from the third floor. He jumped the second floor landing and moved to the stairs leading to the third floor. "How's that?" Michael questioned, hoping to get a clearer location on Billy.

"I was sitting in the command chair when it sensed what was going on, and grabbed me thinking I was Rafinel and activated the command escape pod," Billy explained.

Michael caught Billy's voice coming from the third floor, and realized Billy was moving. Michael gripped the knife in his hand, raised it to the ready position, and raced up the stairs, throwing caution to the wind.

Halfway up the stairs, Billy crashed through the wall and tackled Michael. Plaster and wood exploded, blinding Michael just before getting hit, by what felt to him like a Mack Truck. Michael dropped the knife as he fell, pain racking his side from his fresh knife wound. Up until now, Michael had ignored the pain and almost forgot he was wounded. They both tumble down the stairs and landed hard on the second floor landing.

Billy jumped to his feet and laid a powerful kick into Michael's side, causing the pain to shoot from his side, up his spine to his head. Michael rolled to his side and scissor kicked out, tripping Billy. Then mustering what little strength he had left, he flipped up and over onto Billy, grabbing him by the throat with both hands. Billy hit down onto Michael's arms, breaking his hold, then kicked up, pushing Michael up and over, through the apartment door and onto his back.

Michael coughed, as he moved to his knees. Before he could get his bearing, Billy kicked up and connected with Michael's jaw sending him flailing backwards. Michael, carried from the momentum of the kick, spun to his side and landed on one knee. He was now inside the kitchen area of the second floor apartment.

Billy rushed Michael. Michael slipped to the side, kicked his leg out and up. He kicked Billy in the stomach, pulled back and kicked Billy in the face after he keeled over. Michael swept his foot under Billy, tripping him once more, and then using his hand, flipped over to give himself the right angle to have his leg crash down on Billy's head.

Michael, using the stove for balance, struggled to get up, thinking he had knocked Billy out. However, Billy had recovered, lifting himself up from the dust and grime of the kitchen floor before Michael could get halfway up. With a crashing force, Billy tackled Michael against the stove. Michael's head hit the oven door, jolting the stove from its base. Billy then flung Michael across the kitchen table. Michael fell over the table to the other side of the kitchen.

Michael fought to clear his head, while he again struggled to get up on his feet. After a few seconds of pushing the pain from his mind, he was on his feet. He shook his head and wiped the blood from the fresh cut on his forehead. Through his fingers he saw Billy standing in front of him with a Mosleck pagenay. Michael inhaled, figuring this may be the last breath of life he will ever enjoy. But the breath brought a foul smell along with it.

"Billy," Michael called out. "Don't you smell that? It smells like gas."

Billy smiled, holding the pagenay on Michael and savoring the moment he would kill the center of his hate.

"Billy, I really think there's a gas leak," he huffed between breaths. "If you fire that thing we're both dead."

"I don't care," Billy said. "I've been dead for the past three years anyway."

Debris from the hole in the wall cracked and fell onto the stairs, banging on the steps as it fell. The noise startled Billy and he turned toward the stairs.

During that split second, the flight instinct took root in Michael. There was no escaping down the stairs, because he had to get past Billy and that pagenay. No, that wasn't going to happen. The only ray of light entering the room was shining through the half-boarded up window behind him. It was like the last beaconing ray of hope, tapping on his shoulder. He turned, darted and crashed through the window, breaking out the loose boards and glass from his path.

Billy fired his pagenay. The searing blue beam of death sliced the air next to Michael's left ear. But the heat from the pagenay blast was nothing compared to the fire ball that followed it. The blast had ignited the gas; as Michael suspected, and smashed into Michael's back, knocking him out of the body tuck in mid air. Michael twisted as the blast pushed him further out the window. After several seconds of flight, he crashed on the top of the flat roof of the detached two-car garage across the walkway from the house. Michael rolled twice and stopped on his side, with splinters of wood, metal and glass showering him.

Michael pushed the darkness away from his soul as he commanded his body to stand once more. He turned and saw the house become an inferno, engulfed in flames and smoke. The heat scorched his skin. He knew when the pagenay exploded, the resulting energy would probably vaporized everything within five feet of it...including Billy. But the knife was still in the house. If it wasn't within the path of the pagenay when it exploded, it could survive the fire.

He knew if someone found the knife, its unique design would incriminate him in the disappearance of Billy once again. He needed to call a clean-up crew, but he wasn't wearing his CC. He cursed under his breath. He vowed no matter how funny the CC made him look, he would always wear it from now on.

The sirens pierced the sound of the flames eating the house, signaling it was time for him to go. He climbed down from the garage roof, cut and bloody with his body darkened with soot and racked with smoke. He knew his best bet was to find Michelle and hoped she had called for back-up.

He turned and looked at the burning house once more. The reflection of the flames salted the burn in his eyes, which foretold his fate. Now he had nothing left to do, but drop his life in New Haven as Michael Genesis and pick up his life in USSTAP as the First Osguard.

Chapter 29—Birth of Pain

The *USSTAP Galaxy Cruiser Justice* patrolled sector seven of the Millmum Galaxy in search of Mosleck pirates. Inside, her one thousand person crew was on edge and her sire, Michael sat at his command chair contemplating his next move. After Ortho's death three universal years ago at the hands of a Misul Ralinget ambush, Michael took on USSTAP's full mantle of leadership as USSTAP's First Osguard. He took on this mantle with brash, bold exuberance, found in youth with no sense of mortality.

On his right flank sat Centurion Eduardo Sanchez, his Centurion of Operations. Sanchez, a Hispanic from Puerto Rican ancestry, was a former U.S. Air Force colonel and F-15 combat veteran from the Gulf War. His dark glistening eyes, graying temple and lined forehead reflected the military genius he'd garnered in his twenty-five year military career. He was the tutor and Michael the student—passing along military strategy he applied in the skies over Iraq that had proven foreign in the heavens of the galaxy—strategies that kept the Moslecks and others at bay until now.

On his left sat Sonya Bellevue, his Centurion of Engineering, a handsome, intelligent but shy woman, who treated the engines more as a lover than man-made technology. She was third generation French-American, with silky brunette hair, mechanical brown eyes and a haunting curt smile that faded like a shadow exposed to light.

In front of him sat the double view screen, the left side was the window to the outside. On the right side, their route of flight over a star chart was displayed. The pilot station was in front of the left screen, and the navigator station was in front of the right screen. Along the port side of the horseshoe shaped bridge sat the science and life support stations. On the starboard side sat security and communications. Behind him were the defensive and offensive stations, manned and ready for battle.

"Osguard, I'm getting a distress signal. It's a commercial cruise ship." Lieutenant Blake Fillmore, the communications officer, announced.

"Location?" Michael asked.

"Twenty light years away, heading three-zero-five, decimal nine-nine, plus eighteen on the plane."

"Set heading, MOP Sixty," Michael commanded.

"They're under attack," Fillmore added, "Moslecks!"

"Alert one...battle stations...Alert one...battle stations," Michael yelled, understanding he was going into battle. The ship lurched through the speed scale, disappearing from sight, defying the laws of physics as it reached a speed of sixty light years per universal hour.

Meanwhile, Michael's brain went into overdrive. The Moslecks had been a thorn in USSTAP's side well before Michael and the other Osguards were indoctrinated into USSTAP years ago. To Michael, the Mosleck problem felt eerily familiar to the Middle Eastern problem back home on Earth. Unfortunately like that problem the Mosleck problem had a wide and varied range of diplomatic solutions that all failed. Misul Ralinget, the apparent leader of the Mosleck Reclamation Order, was an insufferable ass with no redeeming diplomatic skills. He was still wanted by USSTAP for the attack on USSTAP trading station, *Aruda*, which killed two thousand USSTAP personnel and disrupted trade for at least three galaxies over two universal years ago. Additionally, Ralinget was wanted for the destruction of the prison on Zeta Claire, which killed five hundred USSTAP personnel and eight thousand prisoners. Besides, Michael wanted Ralinget to answer questions about Billy Red that had been nagging him for years.

As the First Osguard, he wanted to order the rules of engagement changed from criminal to military when dealing with the Mosleck Reclamation Order, essentially declaring war on the Order. But because the Moslecks loved to put their women and children in and around highly regarded military targets, even their starships, it was a change in tactic which would have been difficult to execute, so to his dismay, the parliament forbade this change.

Twenty minutes later, the *Justice* rolled up to the Vansonian cruise ship *Paqlo*, listing on its port side. The *Paqlo* was approximately the same size as the *Justice*; however her many decks, wide hull, and miniature engines suggested she was made for comfort and not speed. Her light gray hull was scorched from weapons fire and small flames venting from her skin sprinkled her stern. Life pods floated in the area like lily pads.

"All sensors...all scans," Michael ordered.

"Tiah," his second in command, Sanchez, acknowledged.

"Prepare for rescue operations," Michael said, rising from his chair to get a better look through the view screen.

"Sire, I think you need to see this," Sanchez interrupted

Michael went back to his seat and called up his holographic monitor. The data from the sensor and scan sweeps ran across it. His eyes widened as he interpreted it. "You've got to be bagging me," he said with surprise.

"No sire, I've double checked the data," Sanchez assured him.

"Fine, send this data to all bridge stations...Alert two...no verbal," he pushed.

"Tiah!"

"Communications officer," Michael bellowed, "Send location and request for transport to the nearest USSTAP station and have them notify the Vansonian government and the cruise line." Then a smirk pursed his lips. "I'm sending you a coded message to tack on in the header...Osguard priority four."

"Tiah," responded the communications officer.

***

Eighteen hours later, the Justice had rescued seven hundred of the twelve hundred passengers and crewmembers listed, and extinguished the fires on the *Paqlo*. Her cargo bays became makeshift morgues, housing the dead; men, women and children—sometimes entire families.

At the end of the rescue operations, Michael walked through one of the morgues and saw for himself the horror, which up to now he could only imagine. Bodies of innocent civilians, none of them associated with the Mosleck problem, lay burnt and scorched like charcoal, giving off a nauseating stench. He fell to his knees, sick with agony and despair, fighting back the bile forming in his throat. When he agreed to accept his inheritance and run USSTAP as an Osguard, he never believed his ancestors' legacy would contain such horror. USSTAP's mission, set forth by Laurona and Nausona rang in his soul as inspiration that he, his siblings and cousins were destined to lead humankind into a new age of peace and cooperation. But today, that inspiration was fading.

He got up, head reeling with rage, and exited the morgue. He made his way to the bridge and plopped into his command chair. He looked around and sensed a quiet storm brewing within the hearts of his crew. They were going through the motions, devoid of emotion. Except for the chirps and beeps of the bridge equipment, which he had tuned out in the past, the silence was deafening.

***

Twenty universal hours later, the survivors and the dead were transported unto three USSTAP transport ships. Also, four ships from the Vansonian cruise line arrived to begin salvage operations. The once quiet area of space was now bustling with activity, while the *Justice* provided protection.

Sanchez pulled him aside after the daily staff meeting in his ready room and requested privacy mode from the ship's ARIT. "Michael, what are you going to do about this?" he challenged.

Michael looked up from his seat and seemed to stare past him. The only thing he registered was that they were alone now. After a few seconds he answered, "What do you mean, what am I going to do about this?"

"Look Michael, all your attention has been on the rescue and recovery operations," Sanchez began, taking his seat once again. "I understand that. But the Vansonian ships are here, the survivors and the dead are on transport ships and we are sitting here with our thumbs up our ass."

"So, what else is there for us to do?"

"Get the bastards that did this, that's what."

"We will as soon as this operation is done."

"Do you think they will wait that long?"

Michael lowered his head, shuffling some ARIT flimsies, which were like computerized papers with holographic print, containing recent reports and ship status. He picked up the one he was looking for and scanned it. "I don't know what these assholes will do next, but whatever they try, we are ready," he said. Then he passed the flimsy to Sanchez.

Sanchez scanned the flimsy and then took a deep breath and blew it out with a heavy sigh. "I hope you're right," he said. "Because this is a big risk you are taking."

"I know," Michael whispered. "But," he began with more power in his voice, "if we can end this here, it's a risk I'm willing to take."

Chapter 30 — Sitting Duck

It was a grueling task, but the three USSTAP transport ships finished their last items on the checklist. The wounded were protected in medical stasis; the other survivors were made as comfortable as possible and the dead were secured with dignity inside traveling coffins. With that complete, the fleet captain in the first transport ship signaled the *Justice* for permission to leave.

"Permission granted," Michael pushed. "Tell them...safe travel."

With precision-like timing the three ships, eerily looking like black coffins with wings, maneuvered in unison and exited the area. Michael studied the view screen until the transport ships disappeared into the star sprinkled tapestry of space. The low harmonic hums, beeps and tones emanating from the ARIT ports at each station on the bridge melded into a musical fusion of sounds that seemed to serenade the transport ships' departure—a computerized playing of Taps bellowing its mournful good-bye to the dead. At least that's what it sounded like to Michael as he took his seat in the command chair.

Several minutes rolled by as he replayed in his mind his walk through the cargo bay of death. The smell of burnt flesh still stung his nostrils from that walk almost two days ago. He turned to his offense-officer behind his right shoulder. "Anything yet?" he asked.

"No, sire...no change as of yet."

"Fine, keep watching," Michael commanded.

"Tiah!"

"I guess we're not attractive enough for them," Sanchez commented as he took his seat next to him.

"I don't know what they are waiting for," Michael observed aloud. "We've been here for almost three days. We gave them a target rich environment; three transport ships and four Vansonian salvage ships. I don't know why they didn't take the bait."

"Maybe because they smelled a trap," Bellevue hypothesized from her seat.

Michael's eyes begged Bellevue to continue.

"Ralinget knows you are just as devious as you are smart. You killed his father in your first combat by employing unorthodox tactics...imaginative even for a Mosleck. No, I guess he is watching, weighing his options, playing out the scenario from every conceivable angle." Bellevue shifted her weight in her chair and gave a quick glance toward the view screen. "He's out there, wanting to attack again, but afraid to."

Michael gave a slight small giggle, "You mean to tell me, you think the meanest, evilest son-of-a-bitch that ever roamed this part of the galaxy is scared of little-ole-me?"

"I wouldn't say scared, sire." Sanchez cautioned, "I would say more guarded when it comes to you."

Michael leaned back in his chair with his hands behind his head chewing on Sanchez's words. "Scared…guarded…whatever, on the streets that means the same thing. He punked down, and diplomatically speaking, this gives us the upper hand."

"Sire, I wouldn't be so bold if I were you," Bellevue warned. This isn't the streets, and Ralinget isn't a street thug. He's the devil's son, born to do only one thing—kill. Just because he took a pause for a cause, doesn't mean we have the upper hand."

"You may be right, Bellevue," Michael reflected, "but the fact that I made him pause, even for a moment, gives us the upper hand. And I intend on taking advantage of that."

Sanchez pushing for action asked, "How?"

Michael's answer was an arrogant smile. However, the smile didn't last long.

"Contact zero-four-four, decimal two-nine, zero on the plane," yelled Major Liam, the defensive-officer.

"Confirmed," pushed Major Fitlow, the offensive-officer. "It's a new contact. It's a Mosleck pirate ship—labeling M-2."

"Where's M-1?" Michael asked.

"M-1 is still there."

"I'm receiving five more contacts—bearing zero-nine-nine, decimal five-six, zero on the plane," Liam announced with a raised voice.

"Confirmed," Fitlow added. "They're Mosleck pirate ships…labeling M-3 through M-7."

Michael had heard enough, "Alert one…battle stations. Alert one…battle stations. Chromerion field up. Send the bug-out message to the salvage ships. Get them the hell out of here!" His voice bellowed like a foghorn in the midst of the night, summoning his crew to follow his directions.

"Six more Mosleck contacts…bearing one-four-seven, decimal seven-nine, three above the plane," Liam announced.

"Confirmed," Fitlow said allowing fright to push into his voice. "Labeling them M-8 through M-13." He no longer saw it necessary to identify them as Mosleck.

Twelve Mosleck pirate ships, looking like spiders sliding on black-ice raced toward the *Justice*. Hatred and revenge lubricated their movement as the promise of Michael's destruction fueled their pace. Meanwhile, the four Vansonian salvage ships initiated an emergency dive below the apparent upcoming fray and ignited their speed schedule to MOP forty intersecting a pre-arranged escape route in the opposite direction of the Mosleck ships. The attack ships didn't alter course to challenge the escaping Vansonian salvage ships, but stayed steadfast toward the *Justice*.

"Signal the fleet," Michael ordered.

The communications officer pressed several areas on his smoky-brown glass counsel. Several lights flashed corresponding with electronic hums and beeps. Outside in the cold recess of space, six USSTAP galaxy cruisers emerged from stealth mode ten, adhering to the laws of physics and becoming visible to the naked eye. They had been lurking in the area under stealth mode ten, since the transport ships arrived.

"You'd think he would have learned by now," Michael whispered to no one in particular. "We've captured Ralinget once before, using this same technique of concealing the USSTAP fleet prior to confrontation."

"I know," Sanchez said with bewilderment. "Be careful sire. Ralinget is no fool. I can't believe he didn't account for this in his plans."

"Ralinget is a terrorist, not a military strategist," Michael said with condemnation. "He is a fool waging war against professionals. And as a fool, I expect nothing less of him than to be a creature of habit."

Sanchez began to speak, but thought better and kept his silence.

Bellevue looked at her monitor and blinked. "It's still almost two to one."

"Don't worry, our weapons and our training swing the odds in our favor," Sanchez added. He then rose and went to the offense station. "Prepare the fleet for attack option victor-four on my mark."

Fitlow sprang into action; his fingers flew across his counsel. He nodded signaling the fleet was in position. The six ships flanked the *Justice*, three on each side forming an arrow with the *Justice* as the point.

Sanchez looked at Michael, their eyes pushing pure thought between them.

"Hail them," Michael said.

"No answer," Fillmore said after a few minutes.

"Open all frequencies...all channels," Michael commanded.

"Opened..."

"Ralinget," Michael began. "This is the First Osguard, Michael Genesis. I need your ships to stand down. I know you are out there. We've been tracking you since we arrived. Your position is locked into our firing ARIT. If your ships continue to approach, we will be forced to fire on them." Michael turned toward Fillmore, questioning with his eyes if there was any sort of response.

"First contact, M-2, is ten thousand kilomarks and closing," Fitlow announced. "Nine-thousand...eight thousand..."

Michael nodded.

"Now," Sanchez yelled.

Together the seven USSTAP ships lurched into the speed scale, reaching hypersonic fighting speed.

M-2 thru M-7 joined up in a fighting formation about six thousand kilomarks in front of the USSTAP ships. The closure speed gave them about fifteen seconds before they were on top of each other. Michael thought the Moslecks were in a *'komrockfa'* attack, similar to the Japanese kamikaze attacks of World War II. But suddenly red fire balls spat from the spider-like Mosleck ships.

"All ships…lock onto target, full power, no dispersal and fire at will," Michael commanded.

Space lit up with twenty one blue beams of light, searing from the USSTAP ships, slicing the heavens with the energy of the sun. A split second later a Mosleck energy ball crashed into the chromerion field and rocked the *Justice*. The resulting jolt was similar to a car smashing into a brick wall going ten miles an hour. Luckily, the crew was in their seat harnesses, keeping them from falling and flailing about. Four-tenths of a second later the pagenay beams homed in on their targets. Several small explosions dotted the heavens. Debris scattered the area as pieces of the Mosleck ships ripped apart.

"Report," Michael demanded.

"Minor hull breaches on decks five and seven," the female ARIT voice responded. "Field is holding at ninety-five percent."

"What about the fleet?" Sanchez interrupted.

"Fleet reports Grade-A, minor damage…no casualties," the ARIT reported.

Michael turned to the view screen, "Mosleck fleet?"

"M-2, M-3 and M-5 weapons arrays are inoperative. M-4 engines are off-line and M-6 and M-7 chromerion fields are down to seventy-five percent and sixty percent respectively."

"Concentrate all weapons on M-6 and M-7 and fire…fifty percent yield…dispersal twenty-five," Michael ordered, calculating the power needed to cripple the ships without destroying them. "Maneuver the rest of the fleet to engage M-8 through M-13…weapons full power…no dispersal." Michael figured the other ships needed to be hit quick and hard, just like they had done with M-2 through M-7.

The light show again dazzled the darkness as three pagenay beams shot from the *Justice*. But the two Mosleck ships both spat red energy balls before the pagenay beams found their marks.

"Evasive maneuver delta-nine-mike," Michael ordered. As the *Justice's* pagenay beams hit M-6 and M-7 two red balls of energy barreled down upon her starboard side. "Increase energy to starboard chromerion generator."

Liam completed the transfer of energy just as the red balls hit. Again the field held, but the resulting blow rocked the ship like a five point zero earthquake. Shockwaves cause the seat harnesses to tighten, squeezing the air out of their occupants and causing some to almost lose consciousness. Dizzy eyes tried to focus on their equipment and fingers held so tight to the crash bars that blood circulation momentarily stopped.

"Report," Michael said while regarding the Mosleck ships on the view screen.

"Fire on deck nine...venting area in ten seconds," the ARIT replied. "No casualties, fifteen people injured...dispatching medical personnel."

Michael unstrapped and wiped the blood from his lip, where he bitten it during the last barrage. M-6 was cut in half, two pieces floated in space with debris and bodies circulating around it like pollen. Eight hundred Mosleck pirates—dead! M-7 was adrift, a derelict in space, with no lights or signs of life. He knew its life support was failing. His next move was to begin rescue operations, but before he could sound the command to do so, Fitlow interrupted him.

"Sire, M-1 has popped to life. It is bugging out on an intercept course with the Vansonian transport."

"Shit, I forgot about M-1. We just maneuvered the fleet away from M-1 and now he's behind us." Michael took a breath and exhaled in frustration. "Tell the fleet, we're going after M-1. We have to stop it before it catches those civilian ships."

"MOP engines are damaged," Bellevue chimed in. "The best I can give you is MOP thirty."

The news made Michael's eyes roll in disgust. "I guess I have to take it." Then he lowered his head and closed his eyes to grab some semblance of internal peace. With a mighty huff he commanded, "Set in a pursuit course...maximum MOP." He calculated the target ship, M-1 was traveling at MOP fifty, gaining separation of twenty light years every hour from the *Justice*. "How soon until M-1 catches the salvage ships?" he queried.

The navigator spoke up, "Nineteen minutes and fifty-four seconds...U.T." U.T. stood for universal-time, a commonly accepted standard measurement of time based on the average measurement of time on human-inhabitant planets. The universe in its infinite wisdom had created human-inhabitant planets alike in distance from their sun, rotation and tilt, making the standard of time nearly exact. Yet, on the average, U.T. measurement was slightly longer than earth-time measurement.

"How long before we get there?" Michael asked, showing despair in his voice.

"Thirty-three minutes," the navigator moaned with the same despair.

"That gives them over thirteen minutes," Michael commented, "more than enough time to destroy them." With the anger of an Olympian god, his voice then thundered, "Bellevue, I need more speed. Push the engines. I don't give a damn if they break—as long as I get to those salvage ships before that Mosleck bastard does."

"Tiah, I'll do what I can."

***

Thirty-three minutes later, the *Justice* dropped through the speed scale from MOP, through hyperlight and hypersonic to subsonic speed. Her full complement of weapons was charged and ready to fire. Besides the pagenay, her coronet guns, which shot invisible energy pulses at the speed of light and her Asher torpedoes, the ultimate nuclear weapon, were ready to rain hellfire in the black heavens.

However, the offensive officer only saw carnage through his monitor. All that was left of the Vansonian salvage ships were pint-size splinters of metal and debris. The monitors didn't register any life. Death embraced this corner of space with a sickening glee, while massaging the still eeriness with a warped sense of peace—like a graveyard at midnight.

In his office, flanked by Sanchez and Bellevue, the feeling of failure shrouded Michael as the different stations reported their findings. The words flying at him tried to soak into his consciousness, but were deflected by the rage growing in the pit of his stomach. No survivors and nothing to salvage—as the complete horror of the utter destruction grabbed a part of him that he never imagined existed. His eyes blazed with the devil's intent and his voice changed to personify the evil he had so richly subdued until now. Failure, hurt and shame stewed in him to make for the perfect recipe—revenge!

"Fix those damned engines, Bellevue or so help me God, I will have your fucking head for a foot stool," he blurted, throwing the ARIT flimsies that he held at her.

Bellevue sucked in her shock and picked up the flimsies. As she put them on his desk, she responded in an even tone, "Give me four hours and I will have the MOP engines back at one-hundred percent." Her stare beamed the hurt she felt and she needed to strike back. "Sire, you knew we couldn't catch them, why didn't you stay in the battle and send one of the other cruisers to chase M-1?"

"What?" he screamed.

Being more forceful and smelling blood, Bellevue continued, "You chased after target M-1, because you thought Ralinget was on-board her. And you want Ralinget for yourself. So because of your pride and your selfishness, four Vansonian salvage ships paid the price. You could have sent any of the other cruisers to chase after target M-1. Their engines were one-hundred percent and they would have caught up to M-1 a hell-of-a-lot faster than we could ever catch up to it. No the mighty First Osguard had to be the one to take down Ralinget, once and for all. No one else could do it but you. Well I hope you're happy. One-hundred and twenty Vansonians are dead. And it's not because I couldn't get you MOP sixty from the engines…it's because you couldn't spare the thought that someone else could take care of Ralinget but you."

His stare narrowed and then blossomed as her words stung him. He let out a heavy sigh as if to collect and bottle his anger. "Are you through, centurion?"

"She's right sire," Sanchez offered. "I too wanted Ralinget so bad, I could taste it. As your second-in-command, I could've offered you that sound advice, but I didn't."

Michael snapped his head toward Sanchez and then closed his eyes. He dropped into his seat, severely chastised and defeated. He began rubbing his forehead and eyes, pushing the tension of revenge from his body.

No longer smelling blood and with her thirst to strike back quenched, Bellevue placed her hand on Michael's shoulder. "Four hours and I'll have your engines ready, she whispered. "Until then, we can't go any faster than hyperlight."

"Sonya," he mumbled, "I'm…."

"I know, Michael. I am too." She patted his shoulder. "I should've spoken up before now."

"Lesson learned," Sanchez interrupted, "This can't ever happen again."

Michael opened his tear-swelled eyes and began to speak, but his words stuck in his throat. After a few seconds, he nodded in agreement, "Lesson learned."

***

Four hours later and after tempers cooled and feelings were somewhat eased; Michael, Sanchez and Bellevue sat in their respective seats on the bridge resolved that the MOP engines needed to be fixed soon. The additional hurt from today's tragedy was soothed a bit by the news that the USSTAP fleet captured the Mosleck ships and was beginning clean-up operations. Even though USSTAP casualties were light, Michael still cringed at the thought of more people under his protection and or command dying fighting a race of people who had no honor or shame in an undeclared war.

In an eerie déjà vu, Fillmore broke his concentration when he announced, "Osguard, I'm receiving a distress signal."

Moslecks…Misul Ralinget! Michael thought. He had to beat back the swelling of revenge and hate in his soul and focus on his professional training.

"The planet Talion, in sector six is under attack," Fillmore continued.

Ensuring the professional tone of an Osguard, "Distance?" he asked.

"Seventy-three light years—bearing...two-five-five, decimal three-three-five...negative point five on the plane," Fillmore responded.

"Are there any other ships around?" he queried, applying the hard lesson he had learned earlier in the day.

"Negative," Sanchez pushed, as he checked his instruments. "We're the closest ship. All other ships are involved in the clean-up or out of range."

"Do we have MOP engines?"

"Tiah, sire," Bellevue chimed in, "just came on line."

"Fillmore...relay the distress signal—all channels...all frequencies. Pull the *Starlight* and *Blackfire* from cleanup operations to rendezvous with us at Talion...maximum MOP and battle ready. Pilot and navigator...set course for Talion...MOP sixty...five minutes out, sound Alert one...battle stations," Michael ordered.

"Course set...E.T.A...seventy-three universal minutes," the young navigator announced.

"Seventy-three minutes—again, time and distance isn't on our side," Michael commented in disgust to no one in particular. He knew deep down inside they would be too late to affect any type of rescue.

***

Five minutes out, the Alert One horn warbled, breaking the tension and signaling battle was near. According to protocol, the ship's sensors and scanners flicked on. The scanners were active detection measures, which washed light years of space with invisible fingers, probing and pinging any solid matter in its way, while the sensors were the passive detection measures that sniffed, listened and searched the heavens for spurious signals and anomalies—things that are out of place. The multitude of gadgets, arrays and instruments charged, fed and correlated the signals through the ARIT to present the best intelligence picture possible from as far away as ten light years. The situational awareness this process presented was vital.

"No signs of any ships," Fitlow announced, "switching to the planet." His fingers glided over his console. Information popped onto his screen as silence captivated the others on the bridge. "I'm reading residual from multiple Mosleck weapons fire."

"How many ships do the Moslecks have?" Bellevue questioned aloud.

"Intelligence report said they only had ten operational ships, and they mostly stayed in within forty light years of the Hustain solar system," Sanchez responded. "But we've seen thirteen in the last couple of days."

"Obviously, our intelligence was wrong," Bellevue sniped back.

"I guess they had a couple of non-operational ships they put together for this little operation," Michael pushed, trying to quiet the small storm brewing between his senior officers. "The question is, how many did they pull out, and how many are we dealing with here?" With the question lingering in the air, Michael turned to Fillmore and commanded, "All points report...get this on the net...galaxy-wide posture one...I want every able-bodied USSTAP ship in this sector that can shoot a weapon here at top speed." Then he stood from his chair and walked to the view screen. "I don't like this. I don't like this at all. I smell a trap."

"Run all scanners...all sensors again," Sanchez ordered taking the cue from Michael. "I want every square inch of space within five light years of Talion touched."

Fitlow replied, "Tiah!"

Four minutes later, the *Justice* reversed the speed scale and faded into view as the laws of physics and light once again applied to the black slitanium coated bat-looking ship. She sailed into an orbit above the main populated city on Talion, searching for life on the surface. As the buzz circled around Michael, he sat in his command chair, berating himself for pulling the USSTAP cruisers *Starlight and Blackfire* from this sector to engage in the battle with the Moslecks. The *Starlight* and the *Blackfire's* main mission was to protect this sector and Talion from Mosleck attack, and if he had just pulled some other ships and left the *Starlight* and *Blackfire* alone, the catastrophe that he was just learning about wouldn't have happened. It was another arrogant, ill-conceived move—no, blunder was the right word—yes blunder that may have gotten hundreds if not thousands of innocent civilians killed.

Michael had underestimated Misul Ralinget—a flaw not becoming of First Osguard of USSTAP. Doubt began to eat at his self-esteem. Uncertainty began to plague his confidence. Neither mixture he could afford at this time. The bold, cocky loud-mouth leader of the greatest organization known to man was now reserved and challenged.

"I'm getting energy distortions," Liam announced. His fingers flew over his console as he tried to get a geo-location on the disturbance. Then his eyes widened in horror, "four Mosleck ships coming out of stealth!"

"How the hell did they get stealth technology?" Michael roared. Then he pushed the question to the back of his mind, because it wasn't important now. All that was important was that they had it and he had been duped again. Swallowing his pride, and centering his pain, he then barked out a hail of commands, pushing his people for battle.

His crew energized the chromerion field, charged all weapon banks, loaded Asher torpedoes and readied the coronet guns. The *Justice* was ready to fight.

"Liam, search for more stealth distortions?" Sanchez followed up.

"Should we run?" Bellevue questioned.

Michael stared into her big brown bright eyes. He searched her soul for the meaning behind her question. Was she scared? Did she think this was it? Was running a better option? But her eyes told another story. Her eyes conveyed that it was her duty to present the option to him, but she did not want him to accept the option.

"No," he said. "We end this shit here—one way or another."

Chapter 31— Genesis Maneuver

The heavens showed no more distortion as the *Justice* approached. These Mosleck ships were different. They were updated, modernized with sleek rounded curves and new black slitanium hulls. They sported the same red energy seams that were characteristic of USSTAP ships, but they still looked like ugly spiders with eight legs—its spars—stretched downward at sixty degrees. The spars, four on each side, connected to the ski-like engine pods, one on each side.

Two of the Mosleck ships fired. Six red energy balls—the size of large boulders—pushed toward the *Justice*. The *Justice* slipped into stealth mode five, depleting her chromerion field to sixty percent, but breaking the scanner locks directing the fires of death raging toward it. Then while engaging in evasive maneuvers she ejected decoy sensors—several circular two-mark diameter energy balls wrapped in fine polished glass that gave the faint signature of a full size ship in quiet mode.

The red fires of death smashed into the energy balls, exploding in a spectacular eruption of bright colors, synonymous with a direct hit. The other two ships fired several shots in the same direction, but their fire sailed through the area undisturbed. The smell of fear washed over the area as the Mosleck ships fired in all directions, groping the area with their sensors to get a fix on their prey. Visually they had a faint sense—a delayed echo—of the *Justice,* but could not get a solid fix to direct their weapons. They would have to move in closer, which they did.

The *Justice* continued evasive actions while spewing sensor decoys, which further complicated the Mosleck firing solutions. However, the Moslecks kept firing at every echo, every shadow their sensors seized on, peppering space with a dazzling light show. When a Mosleck weapon hit a sensor decoy, it was rewarded with stunning explosions, further complicating senor information. This caused the four Mosleck ships to move in closer with a tighter formation to share sensor information—four ships, one brain.

This is what the *Justice* was waiting for. Although her energy weapons were off-line in stealth mode, she still had her Asher torpedoes. A direct hit on one ship would cause a cascading effect on the other ships. With the precision and patients of a plastic surgeon, the *Justice* bided its time until the right opening. Then like Zeus, the *Justice* fired a hail of torpedoes at the second Mosleck ship, and then executed a very dangerous light-jump. This maneuver skipped the approved speed scale increase and jumped straight to light speed for a fraction of an instant to a direct stop at pre-determined coordinates. This was a onetime maneuver because the MOP engines needed a fifteen-minute recharge between use, and short distances overloaded the dialairtic converter. If the dialairtic converter ruptured the ship could implode.

This maneuver placed the *Justice* fifty kilomarks behind the Mosleck ships in time to watch the barrage of missiles home in on their target. The Mosleck ships attempted evasive maneuvers, but their close quarters caused them to bump and shift into each other's chromerion fields—essentially weakening them. As the torpedoes crashed into the second ship's field from the front, the *Justice* let loose with another barrage of torpedoes from the rear, accompanied by the rage of their pagenay fire and coronet gun blast. The assault on the Moslecks chromerion field caused it to collapse within seconds. Now she was a sitting duck.

No longer in stealth, the *Justice* took no mercy. With weapons free, she pounded the second ship, ripping and slicing her hull like a Thanksgiving turkey. Small explosions turned into big explosions as the cascading effect rippled through the spider—sparks of death, shot from her, and pushed their way onto the neighboring Mosleck ships—spreading destruction. The *Justice* switched firing solutions to serenade the destruction of the other ships—unleashing hell associated with revenge and anger. The fourth Mosleck ship, which remained untouched for the moment, raced from the carnage.

When the *Justice* stopped firing, the shell of three Mosleck ships lay in space, broken, battered and for most intents and purposes—dead—twenty-four hundred souls wiped out in a ten minute battle.

**

"All clear," Liam announced after surveying the area. "M-17 has bugged out…light speed," he added referring to the last Mosleck ship that escaped the battle.

"Alert two," Michael responded. He was standing in front of the viewer, processing the spectacle. Again, he was responsible for a large Mosleck body count. In his mind he heard the screaming of the ones he had killed in battle. He wondered if there were children on those ships—family of the warriors waging war against him.

"Sire," Bellevue interrupted, "We need to change out the dialairtic converter and inspect it for damage."

"How long will it take?"

"Ten, maybe fifteen minutes to change out…we can always inspect it later. In fact, I would rather just put in a new one—period."

"Okay!"

"We'll be running on auxiliary power," she added, "Chromerion field will be down, energy weapons down…all I can give you is thrusters for maneuvering ability and subsonic for engine speed."

"Does it have to be done now?" Sanchez questioned. "We just got through with the heaviest battle this ship has ever encountered and we aren't in friendly territory."

"It can wait," she acquiesced.

"Well then, I want this wreckage searched for survivors and any intelligence we can use," Michael ordered. Then he sat in his command chair, carrying the weight of the dead on his shoulders.

Without delay, the ship's systems hummed into life, people motored about and orders were delivered. Initial reports indicated no survivors and no tangible intelligence. The Mosleck computers were destroyed and all information lost in the fight. In fact there wasn't much left of the Mosleck ships to scavenge through. However, the crew was thorough and precise, meticulous in its pursuit and redundant in its review.

After waiting the requisite fifteen minutes and satisfied that his crew did all that could be done, his attention turned to Talion. He knew he had to begin rescue and recovery operations as quick as he could. He ordered to set a course back to the planet at light speed. Bellevue started to object, but kept her mouth shut. Preliminary status check indicated the dialairtic converter was running sufficiently.

Thirty seconds later the *Justice* entered into orbit above the Hustain encampment. Invisible energy from her scanners bathed the area, while her sensors scooped up the environment. As with the Mosleck wreckage, the scanners didn't find any life-forms to report. All in the encampment were dead. The *Justice* stretched her hand over a wider section, searching for life. Still the ARIT reported—no living soul. Bereaved and full of despair, Michael relented and authorized Bellevue to replace the dialairtic converter.

Four minutes into the process, Mosleck ships M-1 and M-17 snapped into the area from light speed, guns a blazing, spewing out long lines of red energy balls. They took a play out of Michael's playbook and executed a near perfection light jump. Their timing was impeccable, for the *Justice's* chromerion field was down, and her energy weapons inert.

The *Justice* took the hits like a punching bag. The characteristic sterile atmosphere of the *Justice's* bridge was now strewn with debris, smoke and venting gases from broken conduits behind the walls and ceiling. The bluish emergency light pushed the darkness away as power conduits strain to deliver their supply to critical functions. With the loss of artificial gravity, the eleven person bridge crew, who were flung from their seats, struggled against the laws of space to get back to their stations and lock themselves into place.

"Hull breaches...section three, decks four, five and six...venting atmosphere...fires section four, decks three, four, five and six...fatalities reported," yelled the life science officer over the sounds of battle blanketing the bridge.

Fatalities—a term Michael had yet to experience when it came to his crew. He had not lost a soul in battle in the years he had sired the *Justice*—until today. The feeling of loss punched him in the stomach, cut into his brain like a migraine and pierced his once invincible armor of pride that the galactic congress on one occasion labeled arrogance.

"Evasive maneuvers!" Sanchez ordered a split second before Michael.

"Port engines off-line," the pilot screamed. "Starboard engines venting energy...she's going to blow!"

"Eject the port engine," Bellevue ordered, following emergency procedures.

With that, Michael got an idea. "Reroute all power to the micro-portal generators. Load Asher torpedoes," he commanded.

Ten more brutal hits rocked the *Justice*, as the Moslecks unleashed another barrage of hatred. Four holes with visible fire spouting from them raged from two-thirds of her dorsal to her stern. Bodies spit from the fire like popcorn. She began to list to her left. The *Justice* was being mauled to death—bit by bit. As if to give up the ghost, her port engine blasted loose from her in a violent explosion from the spar and pushed away in a clockwise spinning motion. The venting orange glow of dialairtic gas swirled in a majestic way, spilling an ominous beauty in the midst of hell.

"Micro-portal generators lock on to port engine and transport to these coordinates," Michael pushed with confidence, as he punched the control panel at his command chair. The micro-portal disassembled things at a micro-cellular level and reconstructed it at pre-designated coordinates. But because the generators couldn't pass on the pulse that told a human's heart to beat or lungs to breathe, they were only used to transport solid goods, nothing living. "Offense...Lock on my coordinates and fire torpedoes on my mark," he continued as the plan formulated in his head.

Then a devilish voice sprang from the speakers. "Michael Genesis, I've been waiting six years for this day. You killed my father, now I will kill you."

Michael recognized the voice. It was Misul Ralinget, and he was commanding one of the ships attacking him. "Not today, Ralinget," Michael responded. Then he turned to Bellevue, who was manning the micro-portal generator sequence panel, "Execute!"

Outside in the stillness of space, the fifteen micro-portal generators' yellow energy beams engulfed the engine, mapped its micro-cellular structure, disassembled it into cellular pieces and shot them through the cold vastness of space. Within a second the micro-portals reconstructed it a half a mark below the first Mosleck ship.

"Fire all torpedoes now!" Michael ordered. Then he triggered the radio and in a moment of revenge said, "Say hello to your father for me, Ralinget."

Six Asher torpedoes shot from the *Justice* and sailed towards the engine on wings of hope and prayer. The Mosleck ships began evasive maneuvers. The lead ship, M-1, turned right sixty degrees, and the second ship turned left sixty degrees. But it was too late. The six torpedoes crashed into the engine, igniting the dialairtic gas and exploding in a rainbow of devastation, obliterating the first Mosleck ship, M-1, into coin-sized embers, and snapping the spine of the second ship with a concussion wave of pure energy.

***

Hours later, after the *Justice* was stabilized and the USSTAP Galaxy Cruisers *Starlight* and *Blackfire* arrived on scene; the taste of death rested on Michael's tongue, deposited by the grey black smoke floating over the camp. Mud mixed with blood caked on his boots as he stepped over the dead, whose skins were ripped, torn, burnt and peeled from their bodies, leaving bloody piles of raw muscle and bone draining into the soil. The buildings were bombed out shells, broken spires of architecture reaching through the smoke into the skies praying to be relieved of their straining burden. Michael choked back the mournful yell swelling in his throat.

Talion was a Hustain outpost filled with eight hundred civilian families, women and children who settled here to get away from the civil war plaguing their planet. Here they were supposed to be under USSTAP protection, political refugees granted asylum by the association. They were his responsibility. He was supposed to protect them. Not to mention his crew. He had lost over two hundred and fifty of his crew, in a battle he now knows he shouldn't have engaged in.

Michael continued his walk among the dead on Talion. Before he stepped to the planet, he had learned that Byal Vren, the new leader of the Moslecks, wanted to negotiate a peace accord. That knowledge brought some solace to him. For the madness he had gone through in the last five days needed a reason.

As he stood in the muck and mire, a tear rolled down his left cheek. He knew that the galaxy had paid a terrible price in the last couple of days to keep the peace. Now it was his job to maintain it. He pulled out his personal gate portal—PGP and activated it. An invisible door rose from the ground, about seven feet high and three feet wide. A heavenly white light shone from it, glowing majestically outwards. The white light of innerspace shone onto the land like a message from heaven. Even though he knew it was just a

179

gateway to his ship, the message he gathered from the majestic light seemed to convey that today the weight of the universe got a little bit heavier, and his shoulders bore more than he bargained for, but it was the price of being an Osguard—the price of being the First Osguard.

With a prayer and a slight smile of acceptance, he walked into the light and disappeared—back to his ship—back to his job—back to laying out a path so humanity could begin its journey to the next level.

***

Then all went pitch black. The HVP ended and Michael neither felt nor heard anything—no sight, no sound, no feeling, no smell and no taste. Even the sense of existence no longer lingered in his soul. His mind was dormant, swimming in a sea of darkness, the epitome of nothing, drenched in the true meaning of death.

Chapter 32 — Breaking News

Every news agency that was connected to the unity stream buzzed with activity. Instantly, the entire known universe…six galactic star clusters…seven hundred and fifty galaxies…three hundred thousand planets, knew of Michael's disappearance from Unity. The news agencies broadcasted the news, giving the impression that Michael was actually missing, instead of lying in the unity chamber on Millmum Capitol Station.

"The First Osguard of Rojam Os is lost," the beautiful newscaster from Letep announced, trying to muster the sound of sincerity. Her olive colored skin, bedroom purple eyes and curly dark brunette hair that draped over her shoulders was a strange combination, but exotic and electrifying. Her essence exuded from the holographic video picture (HVP), which added to the unsettling feeling in the pit of Sharyla's stomach.

She hit the mute button, tired of hearing the news about her father from unconfirmed sources. Deep down inside, she was fighting to maintain control of her feelings. She wanted to cry, she wanted to scream…she wanted to hit something. Sitting in her office, trembling in angst, she attributed her emotional swirl to the aftereffects of being connected to the unity stream for so long. She and the others were connected for almost five hours, longer than tested, but well below the recommended maximum time of seventy-two hours. However, was the recommended time limit wrong? Did the length of connection have something to do with her father's disappearance?

By impulse she activated her communication panel, "This is Osguard one–two–one…contact Admiral Tirana Ritchen, Millmum Capitol Station."

"Tiah," the voice on the other side of the communication link responded.

Sharyla tapped her fingers on her smoked glass desk, while waiting for her communication link to clear. Her mind raced to the conversation she had with her father in the unity stream; it seemed so real, hugging and kissing her father...holding his hands. The thought that her last moments with her father were nothing but a fabrication of computer magic and not real, now sickened her. She wrapped her arms around her stomach, clasping it hard, trying to squeeze the hurt out.

"Osguard one–two–one, Admiral Ritchen here," Tirana's voice cracked the silence.

Sharyla cleared her throat and took a second to regain her composure, "Osguard one–two–one, admiral. Do you have anything to tell me about what's going on with my father?"

"Not much Osguard," Tirana admitted. "We dissipated the storm, but an energy bolt hit the gate portal transporting your father's consciousness. It attached itself to it and rode the stream into ultra space."

Sharyla inhaled in fright. This was the first she'd heard about the zeshion storm energy bolt riding her father's consciousness. The thought of what that meant was mind-boggling. She wanted to interrupt Tirana, but she realized it was better to allow her to keep speaking.

"Our sensors were able to track the event, and for a split second, we picked up the signature of a virtual stream. We believe the First Osguard's consciousness was in this stream."

"Was?" Sharyla questioned. "What do you mean was?"

"We lost contact with the stream after the energy bolt struck it." Tirana added.

"And my father, what about his consciousness?" The sound of a daughter's love and worry mixed in her voice.

"It's still connected to something, I think?" Tirana offered.

"You think...?"

"It's still flowing somewhere, so that means it's connected," Tirana explained. "The bottom line is your father is still alive and we are still getting readings that his mind is active, so he's connected somewhere. Where, we don't know."

"What about this other virtual stream?" Sharyla wanted to know.

"It could be a subset of the unity stream; I suppose," Tirana surmised, "a part that broke off or something."

"Well, where would its programming come from?" Sharyla protested. "I mean the unity stream is a program projected by all of the stations."

"Well since we didn't shut down our part of the program, maybe a residual of the program is being transmitted with your father's consciousness," Tirana remarked as a guess. "I don't know; we have to talk to the Chaktun Science Academy to see if that's possible."

"Okay, but until you do, let's connect Unity one more time," she pushed. "Get all the stations on line, but his time, I go in alone. If this is a subset of Unity, maybe if we connect Unity again, the subset will connect to us again, and I can find my father."

The silence was deafening, as her last words seemed to drift in the air for a while. Then Tirana spoke, "Your call Osguard, I will get in touch with the other stations' admirals in Rojam Os, but you will have to negotiate for the stations in the other galactic clusters to play along."

"No problem," Sharyla said with glee, "Osguard one–two–one, out!"

She disconnected the link and contacted her communications officer, "This is the Osguard…get me Osguard one–zero–seven, Angela Santos and Osguard seven–one, Stelana Rican."

***

Tishya had heard that your entire life flashed before your eyes before you died, but did not put much stock in it—until now! Her left arm went numb and the pain in her chest was like a building had fallen on it. She grasped for air, opening her mouth, but her lungs decided not to work.

She was on the floor of her quarters in the Steeple, banished there by her son after her jubilant display in the courtyard when the news of Michael's disappearance was announced on the local news broadcast. She had let her personal aspirations overshadow her public persona of a supporter of USSTAP. Her dreadful display with her son in the privacy of the Steeple was one thing, but to demonstrate that same behavior in the courtyard, amongst the duly elected officials of the planet, their wives and other dignitaries was appalling and politically damning.

She clutched at her heart with one hand, while pounding her fist into her chest with the other. But the pain worsened. She tried to scream, but just managed to gurgle out spit from her lips. Finally, with her last ounce of strength she kicked at the table near her feet.

The three-legged thin four-foot table held the Camarian Vase. The Camarian Vase was a gift to the third Osguard Maxim over nine hundred universal years ago, after the signing of the first Chaktun Alliance. It was a beautiful powder blue vase with flowers and animals similar to earth Siamese cats painted on it.

When the table rocked, the vase wobbled and spun, almost fighting gravity not to fall. It precariously balanced on its circular edge, shifting from side to side, dancing with the rocking of the table. After that, the vase slipped from the coordinated dance and leaned too far to one side. Gravity then took over, calling on the invisible laws of God and pushed the vase down, cracking it on the table as it bounce. Then gravity vengefully crashed the vase onto the polished wood floor, punishing it for existing for so long as a work of beauty and a symbol of peace.

When the vase crashed, Tishya closed her eyes and her life began to flash before her eyes. Segments of her life that were once foggy rang it with bell-like clarity. She saw her parents doting over her as a child. She saw every fight she ever had with her brother and sister. She saw her years in school, she saw when she met her husband, Igna, and she relived the birth of her two sons, Reppus and Rillon.

During these flashbacks, a warm cleansing feeling came over her. It was like sunshine wrapping around her. Then in the midst, pain wracked her once more, shooting from her arm, through her chest and into her lungs. And with that pain, came the clarity of the most telling moment in her life.

***

It was soon after the birth of Rillon. She was in her fourth day of recovery in her room in the Steeple, contemplating how wonderful her life was and how wonderful it would be for her children.

USSTAP was growing in leaps and bounds. The association had just signed its twentieth galaxy into the fold, under the brilliant leadership of Ortho Chting. All the while, she considered USSTAP an extension of the Chaktun Republic; therefore, the more the association grew the more she figured the Chaktun Republic grew.

In her mind, the association needed an Osguard to lead it, and since Laurona and Nausona left no legitimate heirs, it was a matter of time before the association would tap one of her sons to lead the organization. One son would be the Maxum and the other would be the head of USSTAP...the Osguard, as the office became to be known. Who would be better to sit as Osguard other than an Osguard? She smiled at her fortune, and thanked Jus for giving her two sons...future leaders of the known universe.

The door chime rang, signifying an unannounced visitor. A little irritation tinged her, wondering who would dare interrupt her rest.

"Who is it?" she managed to say, hiding her irritation.

"Ortho Chting," the voice came from the other side of the door.

She was somewhat bewildered at how Ortho managed to be in the Steeple unannounced to her, or why he wanted to see her. There was only one way to find out. "Come in," she called to him.

The door opened and Ortho Chting walked in. He was young and handsome with a smooth and shiny bald head. His face was rugged, carrying the mantle of leadership. He wore the dark black USSTAP jacket with one silver and three gold lightning bolts, on each side of his collar, signifying his chosen rank of Lt. Osguard. He had rejected the title of Vice Osguard several years ago, because it denoted the need for someone to be called Osguard. Lt.

Osguard seemed more palatable, especially during diplomacy with governments of other galaxies.

"Tishya," he greeted. "How are you doing?"

Tishya bristled at the familiarity in his tone, after all she was the Chaktun Maxim, the wife of what was once the most powerful government in the galaxy. She sat up in bed, a little more than just a little irritated. "I'm doing fine, Lt Osguard," she huffed with pomp.

"Tishya, I'm not here as Lt. Osguard. I'm here as a family friend."

Tishya turned away, looking at the sunshine piercing through her window. "Whose family, the Osguard family or the Wtong Family?" she punched back.

"The Wtong family," Ortho announced. "I promised your brother and sister I would stop by and check up on you and their brand new nephew."

"Oh!" she dredged up, turning back to Ortho. "How are the Vanguards?"

"Your brother has his hands full with marauders in the Axer galaxy, and your sister is in the middle of some touchy negotiations in the Telo Galaxy. Running USSTAP in other galaxies is hard work. They said they wished they could be here for you, but they knew you were in good hands with Igna."

"I'm sure they do, like they wanted to be there for our father's funeral," she responded, letting her anger run free.

"That wasn't fair," Ortho admonished her.

"No I guess not," she continued. "Just like it wasn't fair that Laurona handed over the reins of command to you instead of my grandfather or my father?"

"Come on," Ortho said raising his voice. Then after a brief second of regaining his composure he commanded a civil tone back into his voice. "That was over twenty-five universal years ago."

"I know it and it still hurts today," she admitted. "The Wtong family helped build USSTAP just as much as the Chting family," she began to explain. "But when it was time for the great matriarchs of USSTAP to will their baby out, they willed it to only one family...yours, the Chting family. In doing so, they left the Wtong family out in the cold and left us to work our way up the food chain again. I wasn't going to play that, but my stupid sister and brother chased after the great USSTAP dream and came crying to you for the few crumbs of respect you could give them. I guess the rank of Vanguard is better than nothing."

She paused for a second, wondering how to continue with the conversation. "Tell me Ortho," she started, "why didn't Laurona make my grandfather Ecned Wtong the Vice Osguard instead of you, or at least along with you? He was the oldest member, more experienced and more knowledgeable about USSTAP's dealings in the universe at the time. Besides he helped the sisters run USSTAP between the time your father died and when you became old enough to join them."

Ortho stood still and shrugged, "I don't know, sometimes I wonder why myself."

"Then why didn't you offer to step aside and let my grandfather assume the duties of Vice Osguard? Or better yet, why didn't you offer the rank of Lt. Osguard to Taman or Loial? My brother and sister would have gladly accepted."

This time Ortho remained silent, but behind his eyes she saw the signs of a guilty man. Did he not think of it, or was he so drunk with power, he didn't want to share it?

She adjusted her position in bed, to give a more regal appearance. "USSTAP belongs to the Wtong family...belongs to me and my children as much as it belongs to you. And now that my kids have the Osguard name, I will make sure they get what is theirs."

"USSTAP belongs to no one," Ortho tried to correct her, "not me, not you and it sure doesn't belong to your kids."

"We'll see about that," Tishya warned.

***

The last words she ever said to Ortho that day were her last thoughts in life. The sound of the crashing vase caught the attention of the Sandson guards outside Tishya's room. They rushed in and saw the maxim lying motionless on the floor. One of the guards called for medical help, while the second one rushed to check her pulse.

The second Sandson guard couldn't feel a pulse and began chest compressions. The first Sandson guard propped her neck up and began mouth-to-mouth resuscitation. They administered cardiopulmonary resuscitation (CPR) until medical help arrived.

The medical team applied MARITs trying to stimulate her heart and lungs into working again. They introduced nanobots into her bloodstream and into her heart to repair any damage the heart attack may have caused.

But it was too late. When Reppus arrived at the room the doctor had the sad duty of telling him that the Grand Maxim Tishya Wtong Osguard was dead.

Chapter 33 — Waking Up From A Coma

The doctor was feverishly working. Two nurses in pink and red flowered blouses watched in horror. They crowded the tiny one-bed room. The eggshell colored walls framed the energy vibrating in the room.

"Pump it up to three hundred," the doctor said. His pale face glistened with sweat, traversing the lines around his eyes like racecars on a track. His eyes beamed with intensity and his hands were steady with confidence as he applied the paddles of the electric defibrillator on the patient's chest for the fourth time. "Clear," he shouted.

He activated the paddles and a brief surge of electricity flowed through the paddles into the chest and into the heart, shocking it and the rest of the body. In that same split second a green current pushed through the room and slammed into the patient, pulsating throughout the body, burning and tingling at the same time with the intensity of blue fire. The muscles expanded and contracted, giving the patient the appearance of involuntary movement. As soon as the pain from the electric current dissipated, Michael jolted up in bed, with a deep-throated gurgling scream that could have come from the devil himself. His eyes were inhumanly wide with pain, which added to the fright of the emergency team working on him.

The doctor and nurses jerked back in fear, frightened by what they were seeing. Their fear increased as they listened to the ghastly scream howling from Michael's lungs and watched the ghostly distortion of his face as he reclaimed life from the final force that man always knew about but didn't quite understand—death.

One nurse was so frightened her entire body shook. She grasped the doctor's arm squeezing it so tight that the doctor started to lose feelings in his fingers.

Michael's scream flattened as he now gasped for air to fill his lungs. The tingling pain still resonated in his body, but his mind was beginning to gain control of his body. His eyes loosened into a normal glance as he moaned to wash the rest of the pain from his body. As relief began to wash over him, he laid his head back and closed his eyes, thanking God for his deliverance.

"Mr. Genesis?" the doctor managed to say.

Michael lifted his head, opened his eyes and turned toward the doctor. The pounding in his head made his movement so slow and methodical that it added to the eeriness that seemed to hover in the room.

"Yes," Michael croaked out, coughing the dryness from his throat. Somewhere inside Michael in the midst of the grogginess he was feeling a tiny voice wondered why the doctor addressed him as mister, instead of Osguard, but his conscious mind dismissed the voice. However through the haze of his vision, the strangeness of the room grabbed his immediate attention. The sunlight streaming through the small window behind the doctor and the others suggested he was on a planet and not on Millmum Station. But his mind did not grab the significance of that small observation. Fighting the double vision that seemed to be clearing up, he scanned the room, especially the medical equipment on the crash cart at the side of his bed. It wasn't USSTAP's, in fact it was archaic compared to what he was used to. Caution, became his alarm…something wasn't right. "Where am I? Who are you?" Michael asked, coughing again to clear his throat as he spoke. Soreness enveloped his throat as he spoke and burned his throat when he coughed. He began massaging his throat as he waited for someone to speak.

After a few nervous seconds, the old man in front spoke. "I'm Dr. Stephan Pierson. I'm your doctor."

Michael looked the doctor over, beaming at the inconsistencies that stood out like a sore thumb. First of all he didn't recognize the doctor, who spoke to him in English, not Chaktun. Second, the doctor was wearing a white lab coat, instead of the dark brown smock of the USSTAP medical corps. Lastly, the white-hair doctor was wearing glasses. No one in USSTAP wore glasses, all vision problems were easily corrected with minor surgery and a MARIT implant. His own nearsightedness was corrected several years ago by a vision MARIT implanted in his pupils, which now seemed to be damaged. His concern registered on his face.

"Now calm down, Mr. Genesis," the doctor warned.

The tiny voice in the back his head became louder.

"I'm calm," Michael assured the doctor in a broken whisper, rubbing his throat more. "Where am I?" he asked once more, showing his agitation.

Dr. Pierson stepped forward, putting the defibrillator paddles onto the crash cart.

When Michael saw the paddles weren't MARIT devices, he sighed and attempted to move into a defensive position, but his body was slow to respond, almost sluggish to the point of paralysis. The strain brought back the dizziness.

"Mr. Genesis," the doctor said more calmly than before, "you are in New Hope Convalescent Home, outside New Haven."

"Where?" Michael demanded, closing his eyes to steady the woozy feeling washing over him.

"You're in New Hope Convalescent Home," Pierson repeated with compassion. "We almost lost you a minute ago," he continued, leaning closer to Michael. "How do you feel?"

Michael took a mental survey of his body, calculating how and what he felt in a genuine effort to answer the doctor's question. He lay back down in the bed, staring at the ceiling, "I feel like shit."

The doctor pulled the blanket back onto Michael, "Well, you look like shit too."

Michael chuckled, causing him to cough, which reminded him of his sore throat. "Oh, you got jokes," Michael whispered. His mind was starting to drift and he was feeling more lightheaded. "How did I get back to Earth?" he whispered, closing his eyes once more.

Pierson looked at him at first with shock, but then his shock turned into a sympathetic smile. "You rest now, and I will explain everything to you when you're ready."

Michael had no strength to argue or resist Pierson's directions. He coughed once more and drifted off to sleep.

Pierson looked at the four nurses cowering in the corner, shrugged his shoulders in confusion and then barked orders for the nurses to clean the room and then clear out and get back to their stations. Before the last nurse left, he requested she draw blood from Michael for testing.

She looked back at Michael as if she was staring at Frankenstein's Monster. "Can't you get some other nurse to do it?"

"No," Pierson roared. "You draw the blood."

The fire in his eyes told the nurse that any further objection may end in her termination as a nurse. She looked back at Michael, who was now sleeping, and back to Pierson. "Right away," she huffed. "But you know what we just witnessed isn't right...it isn't natural."

"What's wrong Nurse Callahan? You never saw a miracle before?"

"I've seen what some people may call a miracle...several times. But this isn't a miracle. I think it is just the opposite. If you ask me, we need to get a priest in here, along with some crosses to put over the door and windows."

"Nurse Callahan!"

"Fine," she relented, leaving the room in a fiery hurry, her words still echoing in Dr. Pierson's ears, *it isn't natural.*

***

In the reconstructed Unity, "Are you sure we are in the right spot?" Kashara asked.

Sharyla looked around. She had been feeling uneasy ever since she found out a call from someone pretending to be her had lured her father away. She had spoke to Osguard Adam Freeman before entering the unity stream again, and heard it was her who supposedly requested a meeting with her father. She then checked the unity records, which confirmed the call. Fortunately, the unity records also showed she had not made that call and was in the East Garden speaking with Kashara at the time. Which meant her father's disappearance was not a fluke, but a planned kidnapping. With that in mind, she asked her sister to join her in tracing their father's last steps in

188

the unity stream. According to the unity records, their father entered a room at this point. But there was no door, only a solid wall.

"Yes, this is the right spot," she answered, allowing her frustration to slip out in her tone. "According to the record, there should be a door here," she said with a raised voice, pointing to the wall.

"Well, there ain't no door there now," Kashara observed. And as if an afterthought just hit her, she pressed up against the wall with her hands, pushing with all her might. "Maybe it is a hidden door," she wished aloud.

"Kashara," her sister called, "you know that the plans for Unity didn't have a room here in the first place. It was a wild shot to see if the door still existed."

Kashara stopped pushing against the wall; despair began to wash over her face. She turned, fighting back the tears in her eyes. "What do we do now?" she mumbled.

Sharyla turned to the side, pushing away the feeling of grief that was trying to grip her soul. She knew her father was alive; at least he was alive in the unity chamber at Millmum Station. That meant wherever his consciousness was, it was in good shape. So this was not the time to give up hope.

She turned back to Kashara, with the confidence of an Osguard, just like Michael taught her and said, "We find our father, that's what we are going to do now!"

Kashara's face broke from the look of despair to the look of an Osguard, commanding and determined. "Fine," she said, "there's nothing more we can do here. But let's keep the unity stream going, just in case Dad can find his way back here. However, until then, you and I should plan to meet up on Millmum Station. There are a couple of ambassadors I would like to speak to."

"I know I would like to speak to one ambassador in particular," Sharyla pushed.

The two sisters looked into each other's eyes, as if they were reading each other's mind, and with eerie timing, they both simultaneously said, "Rillon!"

Chapter 34 — Somewhere Else

Michael looked in the mirror, and what he saw staring back at him was unrecognizable. The face in the mirror was drawn, his body emaciated. He could see the bones through his winkled leathery skin. He guessed his weight at no more than one hundred and forty pounds, a far cry from his normal two hundred and twenty pounds of lean muscle. He was darker, his eyes bulged out and he had bedsores everywhere, on his arms, legs, sides, buttocks, back and stomach. He was a walking festering wound. He could smell the puss oozing from the sores. His hair was a mangled mess, an Afro gone awry. And his teeth were stained and yellow from lack of care. With his tongue he felt several of his back teeth missing, an uneasy sensation for him.

He didn't understand what was going on, but what he was looking at was the beginning of a nightmare he didn't want to finish. The hospital gown he wore, opened in the back, but it didn't matter, because he was so skinny, the gown wrapped twice around him.

He thought this was another virtual reality stream he was stuck in. However, he was confused about why his appearance was so altered. The body suit he wore back on Capitol Station should be projecting his true appearance no matter what reality he was in. Maybe the reflection was the altered piece in this reality and not him. But his momentary epiphany was washed away as he gazed upon his arms, legs and body without the mirror. The same ghastly sores, the same bony figure and the same awful smell permeated his senses and butchered his awareness.

He fought to control the panic that was climbing from his gut. In every situation he had encountered since becoming an Osguard, he had some tool to use in a course of action. But now, he was lost. He wasn't really here. It was all in his mind, and there was no physical tool to use. His fate was in the hands of energy streams running rampant, spiraling continuously in space. He never liked the idea of the unity stream. All his fears of the stream were coming true, loss of control; confusion of perception; and his most dreaded fear, being stuck with no way out.

Remnants of the HVP flashed in his mind, like a bad memory trying to break through into his consciousness. His tried to grasp its meaning…its purpose. The recording of him was accurate in every detail. So did that mean the recording of Billy Red was accurate? If so, that would explain a lot. But why did the HVP fuse into his mind? And most of all, who was behind it? And finally, what was happening to him now? These questions plagued him with no mercy.

He closed his eyes and took a deep breath, as if to shut the questions out. Then he edged his way out of the bathroom, for walking was painful. He felt like he hadn't used his legs in years. Besides screaming in pain with each step, his legs were wobbly and unsteady. He had to balance himself against the wall and furniture in the room in order to maneuver. In addition to the pain and the weakness, he felt light headed and dizzy, and his throat was dry and scratchy, almost like having a hangover without the pleasure of the drink.

He balanced his weight against the doorframe of the bathroom, then the chair next to his bed, and then against the headboard to his bed. He pivoted to his side and fell into bed. The additional pain that shot through his body reminded him he had bedsores on that side. He felt like he just busted some open and he could feel the wet sticky liquid squirt out of the sores. His first instinct was to yell, but he clinched his jaw tight, muffling the gurgling sound of pain deep inside his dry throat.

Swallowing the pain, with slow, methodical, but deliberate movements, Michael managed to push himself up into bed and onto his back. When he was finished, Michael was gasping for air, huffing hard as if he just finished running a marathon. Michael couldn't explain the pain, or his overexertion, other than to say the program that put him here was too close to perfect. Living in this stream was like being in prison, trapped in a body and a world that you were free to move in, but impossible to maneuver in. The irony was almost poetic. Eventually, Michael decided that virtual streams did have one good purpose…they could take the place of the prison planets. That thought brought a simple smile to his face.

However his personal reflection was interrupted by Dr. Pierson standing in the doorway to his room.

"Michael," the doctor called, "do you feel like a visitor?"

"What?" Michael berated the doctor.

"A visitor, do you feel like having a visitor?"

Michael eyes narrowed as he tried to anticipate what the program had next in mind for him. It had already conjured up the worst enemy ever from his past in Billy. And now it was about to lay another surprise on him. Whoever was behind this program knew enough about him to create a Billy Red persona, which was scary enough. But he wasn't sure he was ready for whatever the program had in mind now. However, he knew he couldn't stop it. He had to play along in order to collect some information about what was going on, or at least who was behind it. And finally, he had to find a way out of this mind trap and get back to reality.

"What if I say, I don't feel up to it?" Michael snarled.

"Well, I think this person who wants to visit you can cheer you right up," Pierson pushed, giving the impression that 'no' was an unacceptable answer.

"Well I don't feel like having any visitors," Michael pushed back.

The doctor lowered his head in defeat and began to leave when he was pushed to the side; in his place stood Shawn Genesis. Well at least someone who reminded Michael of his brother.

This Shawn was wiry, dirty and unshaven. He wore blue jeans with holes in the knees and a Blue New York Giants football jersey with the number eighty-two on it. His hair looked almost as bad as Michael's did, uncombed and knotty. The smile he was sporting was missing a few teeth, but it didn't keep him from grinning from ear to ear.

"Hi bro, glad to see you're up," he said with a deep hoarse voice.

"Shawn?" Michael questioned, pushing pass the unkempt aura surrounding the figure in the doorway.

"In the flesh," he replied, creeping inside the room. "How are you feeling?" he asked, taking a seat at the foot of the bed.

The doctor reappeared in the doorway, gesturing to Michael in a questioning manner if it was all right for Shawn to visit. Michael nodded that it was fine, and the doctor disappeared again.

Then Michael sighed, reflecting on how he should play this. He knew this wasn't really his brother, but for some reason the master of this program wanted him to believe that. Immersed in this reality only a short time after leaving his was all very confusing. "Like shit!" Michael responded.

"I bet," Shawn offered with some empathy. "Shit bro, you've been in this damned coma for almost thirty years. If I were you I would have stayed asleep. You ain't waking up to anything."

"Coma?"

"Oh shit!" Shawn yelled. "The doctor said I wasn't supposed to talk about that."

"What Coma?" Michael persisted.

"Shit man! You've been in a coma since you were cut over that girl, almost thirty years ago."

"What girl?" Michael said, being drawn into the story.

"You know, Jackie...that bitch that use to go out with Billy Red."

Michael closed his eyes as that first fight with Billy rushed into his brain. He almost died that day, but he survived to learn of his destiny as an Osguard. He opened his eyes again, wishing the nightmare of that day would escape his mind.

"You mean to tell me, I've been in a coma since Billy stabbed me?"

"Shit, I knew it...I knew it...you telling me it was Billy who cut you," Shawn whispered. "Don't let the cops know that, or he'll come and finish off the job."

"What the hell are you talking about," Michael said, letting the frustration control his pitch.

"I'm talking about Billy Red. He controls all the shit in the streets now. He's got mad money backing him. He has the muscle too, to take care of you. Man, keep your mouth shut for the both of us."

"Shawn, what the hell are you talking about?" Michael repeated more slowly.

"Man, I won't be able to get any action if you talk, and you'll be dead."

Michael tilted his head and looked Shawn over. With lightening strike realization, Michael knew this Shawn was on drugs. He had all the signs, bloodshot eyes, sweatiness, shakiness and the lack of personal hygiene. The only question was, was he snorting it or shooting it up his veins.

"Ah Shawn," Michael chastised.

"What?"

"What!" Michael yelled. "Look at you…just look at you. You're a junkie…a dope addict!"

"No man, that ain't me. I'm no dope addict."

"Yes, you are," Michael pushed back.

"Look man, I can handle my shit. I take it when I want to…you know, to take the edge off. I can stop anytime I want to."

"Shawn," Michael exhaled, shaking his head in disappointment. He didn't realize it, but he was being sucked into this reality and losing grip on his own. For that instant he forgot this wasn't his Shawn and that his brother was safe and secure, leading USSTAP in Minor Man Galaxy as Osguard Three. "Who got you hooked on this shit?" Michael demanded.

A voice rang from the doorway, pushing the answer Michael didn't want to hear. It was familiar, but husky in its deliverance. The voice said, "Billy Red, that's who!"

Michael looked toward the doorway and saw two figures that made his jaw drop. The owner of the voice standing there was his mother, or at least his mother according to this virtual stream. She was a little heavier than the mother he knew, wearing a flowered chiffon blouse, black caprice pants and a black wig that reminded Michael of a crown. Standing next to her was the virtual recreation of his sister, Patricia Ann. She wore a plunging V-neck leopard print tunic sweater that popped out over the belly as it stretched over her overweight waist. Her blue leather skirt barely covered her rump and the make-up did a disastrous job in attempting to disguise her swollen eyes and puffy jaws.

Shawn stood up and shuffled to the corner of the room, bowing his head in shame. "Hey Mom," he greeted. "Look who decided to join us from the dead."

Elizabeth rushed in and practically tackled Michael in the bed, grabbing him up and clenching him tight in a fantastic motherly bear hug. Michael gave in to the warmth of her touch; again losing himself in what he once thought was a false virtual stream.

"Mom!" he announced.

"My baby…my baby…thank God for bringing you back to me," Elizabeth prayed aloud. "They told me you were gone forever, but I knew you weren't. I knew God didn't take you away from me…yet," she continued, while squeezing him harder.

Soon, the clench became unbearable. Michael's bedsores were busting underneath his gown. Then Michael noticed the stench of alcohol emanating from her breath.

She loosened the hug enough to stare him in the face. Michael saw many wrinkles and worry lines decorating her face. But most of all he noticed how strong the smell of liquor was springing from her breath.

The smell made him cough, "Mom, have you been drinking?"

"All day...every day," Shawn commented from the corner.

"Shut up...you crackhead," Patricia scorned from the doorway. "Don't listen to your crackhead brother, he just mad because Mom threw him out of the house after he started selling that junk for Billy Red," she reported to Michael.

"Shut up...you whore," Shawn pushed back. "At least I'm not pulling tricks for Billy Red," he muttered.

"Shut up, the both of you...right now!" Elizabeth ordered. Then she put her hand up to her mouth and blew hard, sniffing in her own breath. With a smile she said, "I just took a small drink in celebration of your deliverance back to us. The doctor said it was a miracle. One minute, he was fighting to bring you back from the dead after a heart attack, and the next minute, you're walking and talking like you just woke up from a nap."

"What?" Michael questioned, with his head still spinning from his siblings' revelations. This was too much information to take in all at once. He didn't know what he wanted to hear more about first; why his mother was a drunk, why his brother was a dope addict and dealer, or how the hell his sister became a prostitute for Billy, the man who stabbed him? And where was Daddy?

Additionally, no one had told him anything about his situation. It seemed like after his initial encounter with the medical staff, they did everything in their power to avoid him like the plague, which fed into his paranoia about this being part of a virtual stream program.

"That's right," Patricia said, coming closer and taking Michael's hand into hers. She was smacking her gum so loud; Michael could almost keep beat to it. "Dr. Pierson said he didn't understand what happened. He said anyone in your condition, being in a coma for so long, shouldn't be able to walk, talk or even move. Something about muscle memory...muscle deterioration...having to teach you to walk and talk all over...and brain damage," she explained. "But he said none of that seems to apply to you," she quickly and nonchalantly added. "How do you explain that?" she added with an accusatory voice.

Michael's mind continued to reel at the situation that he thought the program was putting him in. He closed his eyes, trying to get his bearings, but the seriousness of the information he had just learned, burned a rage in him.

"Never mind that," he said. "What the hell has happened to you three? How in the world do you two end up dealing and trick'n for the man

194

who put me in this hospital? And Mom, what's going on with you? You never took a drink in your life. And where the hell is Dad?"

The flurry of questions opened a wound as the three lowered their heads in shame and fell silent. Michael gazed upon each of them with the burning eyes of a god, his emotions bubbling to the service, mixing anguish with disappointment and anger. His body trembled, wrought with uncontrollable pain. Noticing he was being sucked into believing this virtual stream, he closed his eyes once more to cover his world with calm.

He reminded himself, this wasn't real; it was just a MARIT induced virtual stream, holding him prisoner, with the apparent objective of driving him to a nervous breakdown. He wasn't going to succumb to this objective. He told himself the people in his room weren't real, they were pieces of a program; a program he needed to figure out how to defeat.

The calm he was praying for came, bringing with it the serenity to stop his body from shaking. He took a deep cleansing breath and blew it out slowly. He opened his eyes again to see his virtual family still cowering in shame.

Then Elizabeth sighed and said, "Your Daddy is dead."

Michael remained silent, inwardly picturing his father back on Millmum Station, with his mother, happy in the joy of playing with their grandson. His father wasn't dead; it was this virtual stream trying to push him once more toward an emotional breakdown. Michael thought it was a good attempt, but the program laid it on too thick and too fast. If the objective was to break him down, the program should have rolled these pieces at him one at a time, not all together, and surely not before he had a chance to cope with his own physical problems. Yeah, whoever was running this program had done their homework alright, but they failed to optimize the psychological parameters of the program.

"Soon after we found out you were in this coma indefinitely, Dad went and figured out that Billy was the one that stabbed you," Patricia began to explain.

"Yeah, Dad pushed the cops almost every day to arrest Billy," Shawn continued. "And the cops were looking hard into it. But no one would talk…twenty people saw you get stabbed, but no one would talk."

"Well," Elizabeth breathed out, "one day, your father went out to talk to this Jackie girl, the one people said you were with when you got stabbed…and he didn't come back." She took another breath and released it. "The cops found him the next week in Waterbury, in a park…butchered…his arms and legs cut off." She closed her eyes as if she were trying to erase the sight she just described from her mind.

"They never found his murderer," Shawn said. "That's when Mom began to drink," he added with his voice trailing off. "I knew it was Billy," he continued. "So I tried to get close to him, I tried to get something on him…about you or about Dad. But I failed. To get close to him, you have to do things. Things I'm not proud to say I've done. And one of them is dealing dope for him. I've been doing it for almost twenty-five years, so long now that I've forgotten I started it to put him in jail. Now, he has enough on me to put me away for life." Shawn turned toward the window, and stared at the sun as it began to sink behind the treetops on the hills. "And even if I had something on him about Dad or you, I wouldn't be able to use it."

Patricia let go of Michael's hand and moved over to Shawn. She grabbed his arm, immersing herself in his pain while gazing upon the sunset as well. "When Shawn couldn't find out anything, I tried to get close. But like Shawn, I got caught up in this mess and I can't get out either. I have four kids, and I don't know who the fathers are. I have no ability to get a straight job anymore. All I got is this life"

Michael scratched his head, thinking how the program just pushed some psychological buttons that he didn't see coming. The new revelation almost caused him to smile, but he didn't. He needed to play along, somewhat, until he could figure a way to defeat the program and get back to Millmum Capitol Station.

He placed his hand over his mouth in thoughtful contemplation. Wondering how the programmer knew to take the first and worst enemy of his entire life and make him be the catalyst to the downfall of his family. His stabbing was a matter of public record in USSTAP. An HVP depicted it in amazing detail. But it was something he hadn't thought of for well over three decades. He shuttered at the thought that that one incident in his life may have turned out like this, if he hadn't listened to the voice telling him he had a destiny.

"You are to embrace a new world and design a new universe. The Beginning and the End has chosen you to lay out a path so humanity can begin its journey to the next level."

"Michael?" Elizabeth called, shaking him from his inner thoughts. "Are you all right?"

The displeasure of the situation wore on his face, as he snapped his attention back to Elizabeth. He started to speak, but dryness in his throat caused him to cough instead.

Elizabeth fetched the pitcher of water on the nightstand, filled the glass and gave it to Michael. Without thinking, Michael accepted the glass and sucked the water from the straw.

He shouldn't have felt it, but he did. The cool water soaked his mouth and throat, chasing the dry parched cotton taste from him. It felt good as it traveled down his esophagus, cooling the fire and refreshing his larynx. It was like Michael was dying of thirst and didn't know it. Then he stopped. He wasn't supposed to be able to eat or drink in a virtual stream. It was one part of the experience that the MARIT technology could not replicate.

He handed the glass to his mother, more perplexed than ever. "Can I have some juice, please?" he asked Elizabeth.

She took the glass, placed it next to the pitcher, and picked up the juice box to hand to Michael. After a few seconds of adjusting the straw into the juice box, she handed it to him.

Michael looked at the box, praying that if he was able to drink it, he wouldn't be able to taste it. He wanted this box to be a virtual imitation and not the real thing. He closed his eyes, put the straw in his mouth and sucked. The juice splashed into his mouth, stimulating his taste buds. It was apple juice. Michael spit the juice out onto the floor, splattering the ugly yellow tiles and somehow making it look just a little bit better.

Elizabeth jumped from the bed, shocked at first, but worried about Michael. Patricia and Shawn moved from the window watching Michael as if he had just twisted his head all the way around. Their look was smattered with fright and concern.

Michael looked up at his virtual family, wondering what was going on. He laid back in bed feeling defeated and lost. The thought of his situation being a virtual stream was the one shred of reason keeping him sane. Now he was no longer sure this was a virtual stream. Was he hallucinating? Was he dreaming? Or was it something else?

"Are you okay, honey? Should I call for the doctor?" Elizabeth asked, her motherly concern pouring out in her tone of voice.

"No Mom, I'm fine," Michael whispered. "I just got a little dizzy," he lied. Then he peered at Shawn and Patricia, who were still staring him down. "Tell me more," he requested. "I want to know everything that happened to you, especially in regards to Billy Red."

Shawn and Patricia turned to each other, bewildered at Michael's strange request. But after several seconds of painful silence, Shawn began to speak.

"Well brother, it's like this…"

***

The vigor in the room electrified the air as the sounds of ecstasy bounced off the wall. The couple was next to the bed, the woman, naked and dripping with sweat, bent at the hip, taking her lover from behind. Her breast hung down and bounced with the force of the man's raw passion. She engulfed his every stroke, with moans and groans of satisfaction, sprinkled with curses for him to stroke her harder and faster.

The words challenged and boosted the man's ego and he dutifully complied. And each time he complied he was quickly rewarded with more satisfying moans and groans and the sensation of wet warm passion squeezing his manhood in perfect rhythmic flow, which made his senses more alive and opened to her sexual pleasure. He changed the pace and force of his strokes, teasing her and making her beg for more, in which the entire exercise would begin again.

The heart is a unique but precise instrument. Its continual beat is the life force that sustains the human existence. However, sometimes that continual beat is interrupted. The intensity of a sexual climax is one of those times in which a heart can skip a beat. This man was in the throes of rapture, trying with all his mental and physical powers not to succumb to the eruption building in his manhood. But like all humans, this only delayed the inevitable.

With a bear like low growl and the fire of jet engines, the man released his nature's flow deep within the woman's soft wet cave. As he did, his heart, which was racing during the act, skipped a beat, which technically is a fraction of time one can say one has spent in death. Normally, skipping a beat would not lead to death, only an intense feeling of weakness and lightheadedness especially during sex, but in this case, normalcy did not exist.

As his heart skipped a beat and as his body released the white flow of life into another human being, a green energy bolt slithered out of nowhere and slammed with the might of a cannon ball into the man's chest; rocketing him against the wall with such force, it knocked him unconscious.

The force sent an energy shock through him and into her, before he was ejected from her body. Her love cavern pulsated and exploded in lava waves of passion. Then she shot forward unto the bed, spread eagle and faint. To her, it was the best climax she had ever experienced. The experience was unworldly, almost unholy and deviant, but one every woman wished she had in the same situation. She huffed, trying to catch her breath, eyes still closed in a peaceful cloud of bliss. Her breathing subsided to normal as the blissful cloud her mind was riding, lulled her into a deep sleep, without a care of her partner's fate.

Several weary moments elapsed before the man began to stir. He opened his eyes and spied the room. The room was not familiar to him. It was large, with a king size wood framed bed. A beautiful chocolate skinned woman was laying face down in the bed. She had a lean, skinny body with voluptuous buttocks that still begged for attention, even in her sleep. On one wall of the room was a forty-two-inch plasma T.V. Under it was a full bar, stocked with his favorite wines and liquors.

He massaged the back of his head, where he had made contact with the wall. A bump had started to rise there. He noticed he was naked and jumped up in shock. Once on his feet, curiosity rang true for him as he stepped closer to the bed. He studied the girl lying there. She was familiar, but he was sure he didn't know her name. A slight moan gurgled in her throat as she turned to her side, giving the man a fresh view of her breasts, which were just as inviting as her butt.

He rubbed the back of his head once more, again trying to massage the stabbing pain shooting through his skull. His vision was cloudy, which added to his confusion. He moved toward the bathroom, which was on the right side of the bed.

It was just as huge as the bedroom, with a Jacuzzi hot tub, full shower, and a walk-in closet. The sink was sterling silver with gold-plated faucet and fixtures. The mirror took up the entire wall over the sink. The image he saw in the mirror was a little fuzzy, so he ran some water and washed his face. He grabbed a face towel and pat-dried his face.

When he looked up, he saw his reflection in the mirror for the first time. The image beaming back to him was one of Billy Red...albeit, a little huskier, a little older, and a little grayer, but it was him. Mezhak Zyder smiled in confusion. He looked like the Billy he had created in the virtual stream he used to trap Michael. But that is the only thing he recognized.

Outside the bathroom, he heard a cell phone ringing and the young woman on the bed stirring to answer it. Mezhak ignored the sounds and continued to stare at himself in the mirror. The reflected image was a little different. There was a small scare under his left eye and his muscle tone was not as defined as he had programmed. He turned away from the mirror and began to study his arms and legs, when the young lady interrupted him.

"Billy," she called, "that was my mother. She said my Aunt Elizabeth just called her."

"Your Aunt Elizabeth?" Mezhak questioned aloud.

"Yeah my Aunt Elizabeth, my Aunt Elizabeth Genesis..." she said opening the bathroom door. She was still naked and glistening with the aura of sexual satisfaction.

"Err!" Mezhak managed to utter, now realizing who she was and who she was talking about. The girl standing in front of him was Michael's cousin, Alliyah Whitmore...all grown up and mighty fine. And from the looks of things, Alliyah was one of his bitches. "Yeah Alliyah, I know who the bitch is. What did she want?"

"Well, I'm not supposed to tell you, but I don't want you getting mad at me when you find out."

"Find out what?" Mezhak said, getting irritated at her and wondering why he was talking to her in the first place. If this was a virtual stream, he just needed to say his escape phrase and get out of there. He turned and grabbed a towel to wrap around his waist.

"She said Michael just woke up!" she exclaimed, flinching back, preparing for Billy to strike her for giving him the news.

"Michael...Michael Genesis? What do you mean he's awake? What the hell is going on around here?"

"Michael is awake from his coma," she informed him, still shying away. "The doctors revived him this morning."

"I don't give a shit," Mezhak responded. "I just want to get the hell out of here." He then pushed Alliyah out the door and closed it. He wasn't sure what was going on, but he didn't have any more time to spend figuring it out. He looked in the mirror one more time and whispered his exit phrase, "Kill the First Osguard!"

Nothing happened; Mezhak was still staring at Billy Red in the mirror. He coughed to clear his throat and then repeated the phrase a little louder, "Kill the First Osguard!" Still nothing happened. Mezhak began to worry. He coughed louder and this time he yelled, "Kill the First Osguard!"

The sound of pounding on the door punctuated the fact to him that the escape phrase had failed and he was still there—wherever there was.

Outside the door, Alliyah began screaming, "Billy…Billy are you okay in there?" She still sounded sensual, even at the top of her lungs.

Mezhak rubbed the back of his head as fright tugged at his shoulders. Something was wrong…something was very wrong.

Chapter 35 — Game Plan

The heavens in Millmum Capital Station gate portal field two lit up with the brilliant light of inner space. Two gate portals activated, opening up the cosmos. The *G.P. Nightwing* and the *G.P. Dragon Star* trudged their way into normal space through the illuminating white light. Their black slitanium skin was in stark contrast to the light, giving the appearance of two shadowy birds gracefully flying away from the sun.

After two minutes, both starships were through and the white light extinguished as the gate portals shut down. *G.P. Nightwing* carried Sharyla from the Searcy Galaxy and the *G.P. Dragon Star* carried her sister Kashara from the McNor Galaxy. Even though these galaxies were millions of light years away from Millmum Capital Station and on opposite ends of Rojam Os the gate portal system made immediate point-to-point travel to any capital station and or galaxy precinct station in Rojam Os easy. Conversely, travel between galactic clusters wasn't as simple. The gate portal system that connected the six known galactic clusters used ultra space, and travel between them sometimes took hours, almost entire days. Finally, after the approach and docking, the sisters used their gate portals to step to the unity room.

Inside the unity room, their mother, Michelle, was sitting next to their father's chamber. Her face showed signs of crying. Dry streaks of tears marred her cheeks and her eyes were dry and puffy. She had cried so much that there were no more tears left to shed. But her heartache stayed resonant on her face.

She turned to catch her grown daughters emerging from the white light. For a second a smile creased her lips as she saw the two daughters she had raised with such love and care step down wearing the same mantle of authority that her husband had worn for so long. They had truly come into their own, and if anyone were to figure out how to get Michael back, it would be her daughters. In her mind the cavalry had just arrived.

"Mom," Kashara called out, rushing to hug her.

They embraced for a long moment, no words said between them, just hugging each other, communicating through their closeness to each other. Then it was Sharyla's turn. She hugged her mother, exchanging the needed strength through their embrace. The comfort of the hug was intoxicating. However, Sharyla knew she had to get to work or they may never see their father again.

Holding back the urge to cry, Sharyla loosened her hug on her mother and turned to the chamber. Inside she could see her father's body, covered with the unity cloth. It was almost as if she was viewing his body at a funeral. The feeling was creepy and disconcerting. She looked at the ARIT monitor measuring her father's vital signs to remind her that he wasn't dead, but simply lost. Or more like his consciousness was simply lost, as if he was in a coma.

She turned to Tirana, who was waiting at the master console, for the right moment to begin speaking, "Any further news?"

"Yes Osguard," Tirana said with some excitement.

"Tirana, you know better than that. Call me Sharyla," she demanded. "There is no rank amongst family."

"I know that...Sharyla. It's just a habit to keep the formality during stressful times like these," Tirana explained. "It's been over twenty-four universal hours since your father's disappearance, which means we have less than forty-eight universal hours left before the stream starts to degrade and we lose your father's consciousness forever. Nonetheless, we did send a starguard through the gate portal a couple of hours ago, to follow your father's stream. It found another consciousness stream intertwined with your father's stream. They meet up around the coordinates the unity stream pulsates at. Then they both take a large course deviation into an energy well...an etion energy well."

"Etion energy well?" Kashara questioned. "What the hell is an etion energy well?"

"It is part of the Son Theory of Spatial Relativity," Tirana explained.

"You mean the fourth radiation of life," Kashara responded, "but that's just a myth."

"So was restion particles until one hundred years ago," Sharyla reminded her sister, "and we had no idea how to manipulate ultra space until the Tuit War."

"So, what does this mean?" Michelle asked.

"Mom," Kashara started, "it means Dad's consciousness is floating in a parallel or alternate dimension. One that doesn't exist in the same plane we do." And after a short pause, she added, "At least in theory."

"Fine...fine, but what about this other stream?" Sharyla pushed. She had already jumped to the conclusion that this was some type of sabotage, and if she could find out who was behind the sabotage, she would be able to get her father back. "Can you find where it originates from?"

"Yes we can, and yes we did," Tirana informed them. "The stream is originating from Chaktun," she admitted with some trepidation, "specifically, from the Chaktun Science Academy."

"Rillon," Sharyla pushed, "I bet he's the one behind this."

"You can't be serious?" Michelle questioned in surprise. "Rillon is from the royal house of Osguard. I'm sure he had nothing to do with this."

Sharyla's eyes squinted as she fought to control her rage, "Mom, the way Rillon has been acting, and the speech he just gave in Unity, I would not bet against his involvement in all of this...not for one moment."

"Where is he?" Kashara demanded.

"He has left for Chaktun," Tirana answered in a low voice. "He had just received word of his mother's death."

"What?" Sharyla bellowed in surprise.

"The Grand Maxim is dead," Michelle explained, "an apparent heart attack."

"But we did receive reports that after the news break of your father's situation, the Grand Maxim said some unflattering words about the Osguards in the capital square," Tirana interjected, "So much that the Maxum confined her to the Steeple."

"Are these reports reliable?" Sharyla wanted to know. In her mind she hadn't put the full picture together yet, but she had enough pieces to know that her father's fate lay on Chaktun.

"Yes, our sources are reliable," Tirana confirmed.

"Okay, then I'll go to Chaktun," Sharyla announced.

"Good," Kashara agreed. "While you do that, I'm going to take the *Dragon Star* and go visit this etion energy well. Maybe I can get some good sensor and scanner readings from it to help us locate Dad's consciousness." Then Kashara turned to her mother, "Mom, will you be alright here?"

"Yeah, I'll be fine. Your grandparents are taking care of your brother and Patricia and Shawn will be here in a few hours. They will help us watch over your father."

Sharyla and Kashara both nodded their heads in agreement, and then walked over to the unity chamber encasing their father. While holding on to each other they kneeled in front of the chamber and both place a hand on the chamber. The moment was solemn, and their spirits were full of fright.

This was the first real challenge for both of them as Osguards…one they wished they didn't have to face. But it was here, thrust upon them like so many of the challenges their father had to face as an Osguard…not expected, not wanted and certainly not easy.

After a few seconds of silent meditation, the sisters rose, hugged their mother and Tirana and exited the room through the gate portal. With them, they took the responsibility of the universe…the responsibility to get back the First Osguard, the future Chief Executive Osguard and president of the Guardian Supreme Council.

***

The bells of the Steeple rang eighty-five times every hour, signaling the death of the Grand Maxim in her eighty-fifth year of life. The word of Tishya's death had spread like wildfire, outpacing the news of her earlier escapades in the town square after the news about Michael had broken. Sorrow filled the air, like a heavy wet blanket. Laughter died as bad news continued to wiggle its way through the streets of every city, town and village on the planet. In each pocket of civilization on the planet, the bells rang eighty-five times every hour, and according to tradition, would continue to do so until Tishya was buried.

Inside the north rotunda, Tishya's body laid in state. She was in a circular white casket, arms and legs outstretched as if to make a snow angel in the flowers that decorated the interior. The flowers represented every color in the spectrum, letting off fragrances that mixed so delightfully that they chased away the air of death. Her casket was elevated five feet by several wooden steps. Over her, the glass-stained window took the sun's light and sprinkled it upon her like heaven's powder. She wore a white gown, with feathered wings attached to the back, and in her right hand, she held a sword. Her appearance symbolized her ascension into Polmeria, the land of Jus and their god. Once she ascends, she will join the Army of Jus and fight back the forces of evil for eternity…her reward for being such a faithful servant of Jus.

Rillon was kneeling on the last step in silence. Tears streamed from his eyes, echoing the pain shooting from his heart. The news of her death was more than a shock, but to actually see her lying in death brought him to another world. His mind was hazy and unclear. He was just walking…going through the motions. He had grabbed a shuttle, but that is all he remembered. From the time he walked onto the shuttle until the door opened to the rotunda revealing his mother's body, was a blank. He didn't even know how long he had been staring at his mother, or how long he had been crying.

He heard the far doors opening, but did not look to see who it was that dared violate his time of mourning. And frankly at this point he really didn't care, until he heard the voice greeting him.

"Rillon, how long have you been here?" Reppus demanded.

Rillon looked over his shoulder, catching his brother in his peripheral vision, "I'm sorry I didn't inform the great Chaktun Maxum of my arrival, but I didn't think I had to. She was my mother too."

Reppus fell silent as the gauntlet, Rillon had just thrown out, continued to build. In the tense silence, he knelt down on the last step next to Rillon and began his spiritual prayer.

After several minutes, Rillon could not stand being next to his brother any longer. He begged his mother's spirit's forgiveness and stood to go. Reppus reached out and grabbed Rillon's arm.

"Where do you think you are going?" he demanded.

"It is none of your business, but if you must know, I'm going back to my office," he responded, pulling his arm away.

"My dear brother," Reppus grunted in a low volume, "you no longer have an office here."

"What the hell are you talking about? I am still a conclave ambassador..."

Reppus cut him off, "Before mother passed, she admitted everything to me, including your plan against Michael."

"What plan? What are you talking about?" Rillon challenged.

Reppus stood and stared Rillon in the eyes, "Look, I don't know how you or mother did it, but she all but admitted that you two were behind the situation at Unity. And it won't be long before the Osguards figure that out as well. I mean, you idiot...you left a neon sign calling card with that speech of yours. The only way I can protect you from USSTAP justice now is to relieve you as a conclave ambassador and make you a Chaktun citizen only. That way I can refuse any extradition paperwork they may present me to arrest you with."

"You can't do that, I was nominated by the Chaktun Parliament and voted in by the Millmum Congress. My position is not for you to take away."

"True, your position is not for me to take away, but your office is. If you want to maintain your status, you can have your office somewhere else other than Chaktun. Which means anywhere you have your office will be in the reach of USSTAP justice...meaning, when they find out what you have done, you will be arrested, tried and convicted."

"USSTAP can't tie anything to me. I haven't done anything. I can't believe you...you heartless bastard. I can't believe you are going to kick me out of my own home before our mother is even cold in death."

"You idiot...this is your home. It will always be your home. But it will not be your office as a conclave ambassador or any other position within USSTAP."

"Fine, then I will go to my room. But hear this...I will be damned before I give up the conclave. I have nothing to hide. I had nothing to do with Michael's disappearance."

Rillon's eyes burned with hatred, punctuating the determination his words exuded. When he was finished he turned in a huff and started to walk out the door. But he stopped in his tracks when he heard his brother's communicator go off.

"Maxum Osguard, this is Osguard one–two–one...request permission to speak to you."

"Osguard," Reppus began, "Can this wait? I'm a little busy arranging my mother's funeral."

"I understand, and forgive me for not offering my condolences earlier. But this is important. It has to do with my father. We have traced evidence suggesting the incident that caused the First Osguard's disappearance originate from Chaktun. Time is of the essence. My father only has two more days before his consciousness stream is lost forever. Again, I respectfully request permission to talk to you."

"Fine, permission granted. I'll be in my office in fifteen minutes. I'll see you then," Reppus acquiesced, closing his communicator connection. Then he looked at his brother, whose jaw had dropped opened in surprise. "Are you sure you have nothing to do with this. Because a scandal over our mother's grave is the last thing I want right now."

Rillon closed his mouth and shut his eyes, wishing the last couple of hours had never happened. He opened his eyes, now scared what his brother was saying was right. Things were falling apart real fast and he didn't have his mother to tell him what his next step should be. He shook his head in disgust and made his decision after several agonizing seconds. "You will have my resignation on your desk in five minutes."

Chapter 36 — Acceptance

It took several hours, but Michael bared his soul to his uncle, Armstrong Genesis, who was a retired Methodist minister. Michael had decided that whoever was behind his predicament already knew enough about him that whatever he said would not be any news.

Michael began his story with the Chaktun-Kulusk wars that plagued the heavens for centuries. He introduced that early in the conflict the battle produced a now forgotten prison planet called Earth. He stated that over a hundred and sixty years ago, Laurona and Nausona Osguard, the heirs to the Chaktun throne, fled their beloved planet and ended up on Earth. He detailed how they reluctantly assumed the roles of slaves, but were really allies to the

Underground Railroad, ferrying runaway slaves to the North. But as slaves, they were whipped, beaten, and raped by brothers of the nearby Pathgo plantation. He then said that later they gave birth to daughters and that soon after the births, the Pathgo brothers attacked Nausona and Laurona. He told how his ancestors killed the Pathgo brothers, but both were severely wounded in the exchange. He finished this portion of the story by saying, "As luck would have it, Chaktun Sixana warriors who had been searching for the sisters, came to their rescue. However, when Nausona and Laurona were rescued, the warriors didn't know of the children and left them behind with a runaway slave family."

Then he switched the story to the turn of the century, where he spoke of two heirs to the Kulusk throne, Efas and Erif Ritchen, visiting Earth to kill the Osguard offspring. Michael told of the Ritchen brothers learning and manipulating the ways of the Ku Klux Klan in their horrid pursuit of the Osguards. Murder, lynchings, and arson were their signature modus operandi during their search and investigation. Michael mentioned that along the way, the brothers married Pathgo sisters, cousins to the Pathgos that raped Nausona and Laurona. Michael then told how the Ritchens were attacked and after being injured, the Ritchens, their wives and their mother-in-law left Earth and returned to Kulusk, where Erif exiled his family to a frozen wasteland. "This action was the catalyst to the Kulusk Civil War that brought down the Ritchen Maxum," Michael said, punctuating this portion of the story.

Afterwards he spoke about Laurona and Nausona abdicating their claim as Chaktun heirs and building the Universal Science Security and Trade Association of Planets. Then he relayed how they were about to embark on making contact with other galaxies when a gate-portal accident ripped three Tuit starships out of ultra space into Millmum Galaxy. He explained how the ensuing misunderstanding brought Nausona and Laurona to Earth where they found two of their granddaughters, but the Tuits kidnapped them and masked their DNA and the rest of the offspring's' DNA so they couldn't be found by USSTAP devices. Michael disclosed to Armstrong that at the end, the Tuit ships were destroyed trying to get back home and the Osguard descendants were lost once again.

Then finally, Michael went into detail of every aspect of his life with USSTAP, starting from the moment that he woke up in the hospital from Billy Red's attack—the point of deviation from this reality. He spoke of the voice that pulled him back to life that fateful day and the words he received from the voice that guided him through the early stages of his command. He spoke of the Mosleck, the Kulusk and the Tuit wars. He spoke of the joy his wife and children brought him, and the sense of responsibility that leading USSTAP had cursed him with. He spoke of all the battles, struggles and successes he had in USSTAP, all except for one. When it came time to talk about Talion, Michael skipped it. He blamed his selfish arrogance in causing the death of more than a third of his crew at Talion when he sired the *Galaxy Cruiser Justice*, and it was still too painful for him to talk about.

And during it all, Armstrong listened, taking notes on his notepad, which at first disturbed Michael. But as he continued talking, Michael realized he wasn't revealing anything that wasn't part of the USSTAP public record. However, he was revealing his feelings, which he had spent a lifetime hiding from the universe. But somehow, speaking about his feelings was therapeutic and refreshing. As he spoke, a great weight lifted from him that he never knew was there. It was a weight that had for years, defined his personality as moody, but determined. Even the pain of Talion seemed to lessen.

"Then I woke up here, apparently brought back to life by Dr. Pierson," Michael concluded.

Armstrong looked a little disconnected. He wiped his forehead with a handkerchief and cleared his throat. "That's a very interesting story," he said in his deep baritone voice. "It appears your mind compensated for the lack of sensory activity by creating this world you described in so much detail."

"No you don't understand…" Michael began to argue, but stopped when he questioned himself on why he was debating a virtual character in an ARIT program. He didn't know what he expected from this recreation of his uncle. It just seemed so real to talk to him. And it actual felt good to talk to him. Finally, Michael just rolled his head to the side and began to stare out the window.

"Oh Michael, I do understand. And I think it is quite amazing how your mind interpreted things in the real world and input them as part of your dream."

Michael huffed.

"No…no, really Michael, I heard you out and now you must hear me out," his uncle insisted. "Everything you described can be explained!"

"Yeah…how?"

"First of all, you always liked science fiction shows, so the nurses here kept your television tuned onto that channel that plays nothing but science fiction. Some of your exploits are very similar to some of those shows and movies that play on that channel.

Second, Michelle Katherine Goff was your first doctor, until about three years ago. Goff was her married name…I don't know what her maiden name was. It could have been Murray. But anyway, she pretty much took care of you this entire time, until she took a job in New York City. She had three kids, two daughters and a son. Now, I don't remember their names, but I'm sure they weren't the names you said. I guess there's where your mind altered perception for its own rationale.

Third, my wife, your Aunt Brenda studied our family tree, and while she was studying it, she came in here and read her research to you. Nellie Sue and Lou Ann, who you refer to as Nausona and Laurona, were real. And what your mind recorded happening to them is correct. But they were killed and their bodies were buried on the plantation. I've seen the graves myself, during our first family reunion fifteen years ago. Brenda told you about the reunion and your mind took that information and altered it to fit your world."

Michael shook his head, "No...even if that's so, the timing is still off. I knew about Nausona and Laurona well before Aunt Brenda could have told me about them."

"In a coma, the mind really has no perception of time."

"How do you know that?" pressed Michael as he turned to face Armstrong.

"My favorite nephew is stabbed and put into a coma, as a minister I trust in God, but I had to know what hell you were going through. So I researched comas. I went to the library; read books, articles and medical journals, anything I could get my hands on. I believe in the power of prayer, but I am also a realist, I needed to know what medical science could do for you."

"So now you're an expert on comas?"

"Yes, I suppose so," Armstrong answered. "I'm afraid all you think you have experienced, was just your mind trying to cope with what was happening to you. Your life, as you think you remember it, was a gift from God to help you cope with your situation."

"No, this is a virtual stream and I need to get out of it," Michael insisted.

"Come on Michael, do you really think what you said is possible. We can't even unite this country, let alone the world or the entire universe. That kind of process would take centuries and can't be accomplished in one man's lifetime."

"Well it was," Michael grunted.

"Be realistic Michael. It's not possible. Look at the conflicts in the world today: the Middle East, Muslim terrorists, organized crime, drug cartels, famine, disease, natural disasters, and poverty, just to mention a few. All these issues have been addressed by great men in the past and in the present and will be address by greater men in the future. Son, these issues are beyond you. Even if you weren't in this coma, you are a black man without a college degree with an alcoholic mother, a prostitute for a sister, and a junkie for a brother. Again, how can you think you have united an entire universe, full of galaxies, when this world is in so much turmoil?"

"I am not that Michael. This is not my world," Michael shouted, allowing his rage to bubble to the surface.

"Okay, fine!" Armstrong said, trying to calm Michael down. "If this isn't your world, what have you done for your world? According to you, in your world, you allowed these things to happen on Earth while you fought for unity in the universe." Armstrong paused to let his words sink in and then when he felt he had Michael's attention he continued. "Why is that? Is it because in your mind, even in the coma, you knew the truth that you couldn't solve these problems?"

Michael began to speak, his hands poised to punctuate his thoughts with hand gestures and then he fell silent. Armstrong's words had power. In his world he had left Earth to develop on its own, without knowledge of USSTAP. Even though USSTAP had been more active on Earth in the past four universal years, through covert contact with the United Nations, all those issues that his uncle spoke about, not only still existed, but were worsening more now than ever. While, in contrast, on other planets in his domain issues like that were rare and quickly resolved.

"That's not fair," Michael said. "USSTAP has no jurisdiction on any planet. We're not a government. We're an organization that facilitates trade, ensures security and fosters sharing of science and technology between planets. We don't police our members. We don't dictate how they should run their governments. On the contrary, there are some planets that have laws that are contradictory to ours. But they have some level of growth and maturity that is comparable and consistent to our goals. And Earth isn't mature enough to fit as a full member. Their inclusion into USSTAP would bring economic upheaval, religious bigotry, and overpopulation, which would lead to countless wars due to governmental power struggles. All the ARIT models have been consistent on this point. USSTAP would bring the destruction of Earth, not its salvation."

"What about helping the Tuits? What do you call that?"

"That's different," Michael whispered.

"Okay, what other planet in your world have you refused membership? There must be some other planets that were just as immature as Earth."

The answer caught in Michael's throat as his mind race to find a number. "Err! Ah! None ..."

Disappointment settled in Armstrong's eyes as he took a deep breath. "So, because Earth, your home planet, is deemed immature, by some standard that you really haven't explained, your organization, allows...even sits and watches, people dying from diseases you can cure, from starvation you can stamp out, from natural disasters you can save them from and wars you can stop before they even begin."

Michael shrugged, "I told you, we are working behind the scenes to mitigate those deaths."

"Mitigate...mitigate!" Armstrong cried in a raised voice. "That's a sterile way of putting it." Armstrong closed his eyes, took a deep breath and then began to laugh. It was a loud chest splitting barrel laugh that echoed and vibrated throughout the tiny room.

"What's so funny?" Michael demanded.

"I don't believe I got caught up in your fantasy," he said between laughs. "You had me going there for awhile." His laugh curtailed to a small chuckle after a minute. Then with renewed professional composure, he continued to address Michael. "The main thing I wanted to show you, was that what you think is real isn't really real. Understand?"

"Yeah, I understand that was what you were trying to do," Michael sighed.

"Okay, now that we got that cleared up, let's talk about this Messiah complex," pushed Armstrong.

"What Messiah complex?" Michael asked in surprise. He was still reeling from not being able to counter Armstrong's initial argument.

"From what you tell me, you think God has chosen you to save all of mankind. Do you really think you are the Messiah? Let me tell you, there is only one Jesus, and he has already saved us all. And even if you were the Messiah, I don't think God would approve you blasting your way through the heavens to force His will."

Michael shook his head. He never thought of himself as the Messiah, and he wasn't acting on religious convictions. But listening to his story being dissected did make it seem more unfathomable. In a way, what Armstrong was saying made sense. It probably seemed impossible to unite the universe as he had done, especially in one man's lifetime. But the Osguards did it. However, his story coupled with the fact that he admitted that his actions were guided by an unknown voice urging him on, made him sound like a first rate case for the insane asylum.

"No, I don't think I'm the Messiah," he protested. But I do know who I am, and I am not your Michael Genesis."

"Michael, Michael, Michael, you are who I think you are. You need to accept you are not the First Osguard. You're just a poor black man who has been in a coma for almost thirty years. No more...no less!"

"We're done here," Michael said with the authority of the First Osguard. "Thank you for visiting, but I'm tired and I need to rest now."

"Michael?" Armstrong begged.

"I'm sorry, can you please leave now," Michael insisted.

"Fine Michael, but we're not finish by a long shot," Armstrong countered. Then, with a slight smile and loving eyes, he gave Michael a kiss on the cheek and left.

Michael sighed, closed his eyes and rubbed his eyelids, pushing the tension from his head. Only one thought rang in his mind, time was running out and he needed to get out of this stream.

***

Mezhak was now washed and dressed, in dark slacks and a white silk shirt that he left untucked. The top three buttons of his shirt remained unbuttoned to allow the gold chain around his neck, which matched his bracelet and Rolex watch, to be seen. And to top it all off, he wore, black Italian wingtip shoes.

When he stepped out of his bathroom, Alliyah was still in his bedroom. But she too was dressed. She had on a nice snug black sleeveless cashmere sweater and white slacks that framed her body and accentuated her beauty. Mezhak froze for a second, taking in her splendor, and wishing he had stepped into this stream a few minutes earlier so he could have enjoyed the sexual pleasure he was certain she gave Billy.

Alliyah cocked her head to the side with a confused look on her face, "What are you smiling about?"

Her voice snapped Mezhak out of his daydream. "Nothing, but you baby," he chimed.

She squinted in suspicion, but said nothing further.

Moving toward what he presumed was the bedroom door, Mezhak asked, "How's Michael?"

"I guess he's okay." Curiosity rang in her voice as she stepped behind him. "Why do you want to know? I thought you hated Michael."

"Oh I do hate Michael, more than you would ever know." Mezhak pushed as he opened the door. The next room was large and open. In the middle lay a circular black leather couch. Against one wall was a full oak trimmed bar, complete with four cushioned stools. Opposite the bar was an iron hearth fireplace, spewing out the snuggly warmth of wood burning heat. Next to the fireplace was an exquisite entertainment center, complete with wireless surround sound, fifty-one-inch plasma T.V., DVD/VCR combination and other assorted electronic man-toys.

Mezhak was accustomed to state-of-the-art electronics; after all he was the scientific genius behind stream technology, which made his present predicament even more confusing. Nothing he had seen so far was anything that he had programmed in his stream or any other stream. Therefore, he had concluded that somehow USSTAP had caught him and decided to punish him by placing him in this virtual stream. Or worse, this is his stream, gone haywire.

"This week's pick-up was a little light," Alliyah began, interrupting his concentration. "It's the third time this month."

"What?" The shock was evident in his voice. Mezhak didn't have a clue about what she was talking about.

"I know it's your business Billy, but if Mr. Riccotti finds out that you've been covering the pick-ups he won't like it. And he might just find someone else to run his operation in New Haven."

"Riccotti...Tony Riccotti?"

"Yeah, Tony the 'Pain' Riccotti," she responded.

Mezhak was now starting to piece things together from Billy's past. Riccotti was an up and coming enforcer in one of the biggest crime families of New York. Billy had some dealings with him during his younger days, doing some clean-up work, collections, things that involved muscle and no sense of morality. In this stream Riccotti must have moved up in the syndicate. Nonetheless, Riccotti was of no consequence to Mezhak. What Mezhak needed to do was escape from this stream, thus he had to look for weaknesses or flaws in the programming. Thus far there weren't any.

"Billy...Billy...did you hear me?" Alliyah pleaded, trying to get his attention.

"Yeah, I heard you," Mezhak growled. "Let me worry about Tony. You worry about...whatever you usually worry about. Why don't you go see Michael? Let me know how the asshole is doing."

She moved from behind him and sauntered over to the door on the other side of the bar. Mezhak couldn't take his eyes off her backside. Her hips and buttocks still called to him, pushing thoughts into his mind, he hadn't had since the loss of his legs. *If only she was real,* he found himself wishing.

"You coming?" she teased.

"Not yet, but if you keep walking like that, I just might," he whispered to himself.

"What?"

"Nothing...I'm just talking to myself," he replied, as he moved toward the door.

On the other side of the door were stairs that led downward into an office. In the office were mirrored walls, a large oak desk, with a smoked glass top and leather chair. On the desk was a skinny chrome laptop computer; next to it was a document center housing a color laser printer, fax, and scanner.

Mezhak moved behind the desk, just knowing this was Billy's desk and plopped down in the plush leather chair. A velvet red curtain that Alliyah pulled back covered the wall behind him.

Mezhak swung the chair around and peered out the large glass window. Below him, he saw a nightclub. The club had three bars, stocked with every kind of liquor imaginable, a huge step-up wooden dance floor with floor, ceiling and beam lamps that radiated red, blue and green lights at random.

Again Mezhak was amazed. In this stream, Billy was able to amass all this. Who else but him would have credited Billy with so much in a virtual stream? This couldn't be a USSTAP stream. The more Mezhak looked for answers the more questions seemed to pop up.

"Are you sure you can handle Tony the Pain?" Alliyah questioned. "I'd hate to see you lose all of this?"

"Didn't I say go and visit your cousin," Mezhak barked.

Alliyah lowered her head, "I'm sorry."

"Good, now get the hell out of here."

Without another word, Alliyah left the room like a puppy who had just been scolded by its master. Her footsteps echoing down the wooden stairs, secured Mezhak in his knowledge that he was alone.

Using his technical savvy, Mezhak began searching the laptop computer. What he found wasn't going to help him escape this stream, but was interesting nonetheless. Billy owned this night club on Church Street called the Red Zone. It was one of the hottest spots in the area, bringing in two grand in profit weekly. But it also doubled as the headquarters for his illegal activity, which brought in another fifty thousand dollars weekly. Billy was into prostitution, drugs, gambling and anything else the Gallano Crime Family of New York City, which Riccotti worked for, wanted him to be in. However, Riccotti's cut was sixty percent, which Mezhak thought was outrages.

The electronic chirp of the phone ringing broke Mezhak out of his thoughts. For a moment, he thought not to pick it up, but after the fourth chirp, he decided it might be in his best interest to pick it up. "Yeah," he snarled into the phone.

"Billy, this is Sly," the voice on the other end announced.

Mezhak remembered Sly Jones as one of Billy's running partners, who was with him when they attacked Michael on the Fourth of July.

"Yeah Sly," he muttered trying to hide the surprise in his voice. "What do you want?"

"Have you heard about Michael Genesis?"

"Yeah, I've heard," Mezhak barked, showing his irritation.

"Well I bet you haven't heard he's fingered you as the one who stabbed him and put him in that coma."

"So...the statute of limitations has long expired by now."

"Look Billy, when Michael tells the cops you're the one who stabbed him, it will only be a matter of time before they start looking into his father's murder ... Understand now!"

Mezhak fell silent. Obviously, in this stream, Michael's father was murdered and it had something to do with Billy, and somehow the stabbing and the murder are connected in a way that will bring the cops to his doorstep. But again, all that was academic. This was a virtual stream, nothing was real and he didn't need to get caught up in the story the stream was playing out. "Fine, let them investigate the murder. I have nothing to do with that," he commented. Mezhak was for once innocent. It was the Billy of this virtual stream that was the guilty party.

"Okay," Sly mumbled, "whatever you say." Then as an afterthought he changed the subject. "You know that Callahan nurse I've been doing...well anyway she was there when Michael came out of his coma and she has a strange story to tell."

"Uh huh, go ahead," Mezhak encouraged, hoping this would be the bit of information that would be the flaw in the stream he was looking for.

"Callahan said when Michael woke up, some sort of green light, like a lightning bolt, struck him. It came out of nowhere and slapped him right on the chest. That's when he popped up like some possessed soul. She expected his head to twist all the way around or something like that. And the noise that came out of him. She said it was like the hounds of hell crying for revenge. It really scared her. She hasn't gone back in that room since. But she's close enough to it to hear things."

"Things like what?" Mezhak wondered aloud.

"Things like Michael is crazy...delusional if you ask me. He thinks he's some kind of leader in space...some kind of fuck'n king of the universe or something. I can't remember what he called himself."

"Was it Osguard?" Mezhak whispered.

"Yeah, that was it. He called himself the First Osguard," Sly confirmed like a meddlesome neighbor spreading gossip that they just couldn't keep to themselves. "I guess if he keeps talking like that, it won't matter what he tells the cops. They will think he's crazy and no D.A. will press charges against you based on the ramblings of a lunatic."

"Thanks Sly. You've been a great help. I'll take it from here."

Mezhak hung up the phone and began to stare out the window at the nightclub below. Sly's input to the problem had forced Mezhak to alter the course of his thinking and focus all his energy in another direction. He was aware of Son's Theory of Spatial Relativity, but he never quite believed in the alternate universe portion of it. He always thought that naturally occurring etion radiation was just a myth. But Son's theory purported that etion radiation particles could be isolated in a zeshion storm, if the storm was properly stripped of the other benion, trachion and restion radiation particles.

Mezhak then surmised that there must have been a zeshion storm while he and Michael were in his virtual stream. And somehow that storm caused the opening of an etion energy well, which they must have been sucked into. Thus this was not a virtual stream gone awry, but a true and factual alternate universe, in which he and Michael have somehow become inhabitants of their alternate selves. However, in this universe, Michael had been in a coma since Billy stabbed him the first time, which meant the Osguards didn't exist...which meant USSTAP didn't exist.

A gigantic smile flushed across his face. This was almost too perfect to be true. "This shit is real," he laughed. "This isn't a virtual stream. This shit is real, and USSTAP is gone."

After that the smile on his face faded as he continued diagramming his situation in his mind. Uncertainty snuck in. If he was here, where was his alternate? Did the seventy-two-hour limit still apply? How was he to get out of here? Even though the situation was sweet, the realization of it put a new wrinkle into his already complicated problem.

And then there was Michael. What about Michael? If he had figured out what was going on, he was sure Michael had already figured out what was going on and was working on a way to get back. He couldn't let that happen. He had to stop Michael, even if it meant his own death. He had to continue with the original plan. He had to kill Michael Genesis, once and for all.

Chapter 37—Murder Most Foul

Vedar Osguard II was a moody and sometimes arrogant young man. At nineteen years of age he had already alienated himself from his father, Reppus Osguard, the Maxum of Chaktun. Unlike his namesake, Nausona and Laurona's father, this Vedar was politically insensitive and socially inept. For that reason, Reppus had sent him off to the Chaktun Military Academy, in hopes to burn leadership qualities into his stubborn personality. However on the contrary, the military academy only succeeded in burning a deeper hatred of his father into his person—one he didn't try to hide from anyone.

But like his namesake, Vedar was tall, handsome, and able to sport a winning smile on command...which when combined got him into more trouble than out. As the heir apparent, Vedar took liberties with everything from money to women. His personal debt was outrageous, and more than five women had to be paid off to keep his sexual indiscretions quiet, all which were the impetus to the rift between him and his father.

But that rift was supposed to be set aside for now, with the death of the Grand Maxim. Vedar had stepped home for the funeral and was in the Steeple for the first time in four years. His mother greeted him with the love only a mother could give, but his father was nowhere to be found.

With pent up rage that had built over the years against his father, he made his way to Reppus' office. In his head the words he wanted to say to Reppus played over and over, like a broken record. He traveled past the east lounge, past the third kitchen, up the marble stairs. His boots clicked on the marble with each step. Once upstairs he pushed past the Sandson Guards and into the executive wing of the Steeple.

His anger continued to fume as he got closer to his father's office, his hand wrapped so tightly around his uniform's ceremonial sword that his fingers were going numb. He wanted to yell at him, tell him how much it hurt to be sent away like garbage, allowed back only on the occasion of his grandmother's death, a woman who he had neither the chance nor the ability to get to know or love. She was dead, and now he was expected to tow the line as part of the Maxum clan and honor an old woman who he couldn't pick out of a line-up if he was asked to. His father hadn't spoken to him for almost two years, and now he had the gall to call him…no order him to return to the Steeple to pay his respects to the Grand Maxim.

At first, he wanted to refuse. But no one refused the order of the Chaktun Maxum. So he came, but under protest. And now he was going to make his protest well known.

He reached the outer office, where the usual entourage of people was not staked out. The receptionist was missing; the Sandson Guards who are usually posted outside the office door were also missing. This little quirk did not register more than a minor note in Vedar's mind as he slammed opened the doors to his father's office. He rushed in like a lion after its prey, snarling and growling with anger. Then blackness as a red beam of energy from a pagenay blast hit him. Fire engulfed him and overloaded his axons and dendrites in the nerve cells with heat. His brain relinquished control over his body as he fell on his knees and then crashed to the floor face first.

***

It had been more than thirty minutes since Sharyla had talked to Reppus, and still he had not contacted her. While waiting in gate portal room one she paced the small space between the back wall and the control console, making the gate portal room operator nervous.

She checked her watch one more time. Another minute had past, which made her face clinch with anger. The wall next to her fist became the obstacle of her rage. The echo from the powerful blast startled the console operator, who jumped with fright.

"Sorry," Sharyla huffed.

"That's okay, sire," the operator responded. Then after a few seconds, the operator spoke again, "Do you want me to hail the Steeple for you, sire?"

Sharyla stopped pacing and sighed. "No. Forget protocol. Set coordinates for the Maxum's office. I'm going down anyway."

"Tiah," the operator said with relief. His fingers ran over his controls. Then he handed Sharyla her personal gate portal, set with the return coordinates.

Sharyla put the PGP into her alpha belt, which was the same as the delta belt, minus a pagenay, coronet pistol and mation II. On the step-up platform the glowing light of inner space radiated, inviting her to step in. She took a deep breath and walked into the light. An invisible door opened in front of her and she stepped through into Reppus' office.

Several faces turned toward her in utter surprise. Rillon's was one of them.

"Ambassador Osguard," Sharyla greeted. "What are you doing…?" Her words stuck in her throat as Rillon stepped aside, giving her a full view of the gross scene. Reppus lay on the ground in front of his desk with a sword sticking out of his stomach. By the amount of blood pooling around the body, it was apparent Reppus was dead. "What happened?" her voice quivered with confusion.

Rillon shook his head, "I'm sorry. I forgot you were to meet my brother. I should have contacted you. But as you can see, I've been a little busy."

"I bet!" she whispered under her breath, looking around the room. Three constables, two medical attendants and four forensic officers were buzzing around the room, taking care of business.

"Let's go outside and let these people do their job," he demanded, ushering her to the door. Safely out of the room, he began explaining, "It appears my nephew had his last fight with his father. I found them about ten minutes ago. From what I can tell, my nephew stabbed his father with his ceremonial sword in a heated exchange. Before my brother died, he must've knocked Vedar out with a pagenay blast, because he was lying next to his father…unconscious."

Sharyla huffed in disgust, "How convenient?"

"Okay," Rillon returned, "As the new Maxum, I must ask you to leave now, and don't bother coming back."

Sharyla's jaw dropped, "What?"

"That's right…my brother is dead and my nephew is being held for his murder. That makes me the Maxum. Granted, it's not official until the parliament says so, but it is intuitive that is what will happen." Then with a lowered voice, but strewn with determination he continued, "If you or any Osguard step foot on this planet again, I will have you arrested…understood."

Sharyla's eyes widened. She didn't know how to respond. But in her gut, she knew Rillon was the one that killed his brother, not Vedar. Her lips quivered as her mind thrust one question upon them, "Are you withdrawing Chaktun from USSTP?"

"Good-bye Osguard," he pressed. Then he turned toward the Sandson Guards guarding the doorway, "Guards, ensure the Osguard steps back to her ship." And with a smug smile, he walked back into the office.

***

The red fullness of ultra space was eerie and devilish. It was like flying in an ocean or blood, or even worse, flying in hell itself. The restion particles played havoc with all the engines, so the speed achieved by thrusters was the best speed any starship could travel. *G.P. Dragon* Star pushed through ultra space riding the wave of Michael's consciousness stream to the coordinates where the etion energy well was located. Kashara sat in the command chair, hiding her nervousness from the rest of her crew.

"Coming up on set coordinates," the navigator announced, "in five minutes."

"Great," Kashara pushed. "Can we get sensor and scanner readings on the energy well?"

"Tiah!" the science officer answered. "Sensors reading etion particles dispersed over a ten-kilomark wide area."

"Ten kilomarks?" Kashara questioned. "The starguard measured it at twenty kilomarks wide almost five hours ago."

"Tiah!" the science officer answered. "It appears the well is shrinking."

Kashara stood and moved to the screens in order to see the energy well. "Magnify by twenty," she requested. The right screen changed, displaying the green energy well in the red ocean of space like an ameba swimming in blood. "How much is it shrinking? How much time before it is gone?"

"It's shrinking exponentially by a factor of three," the science officer announced. "At this rate, we have approximately four hours before it is completely closed."

"Four hours! That means we only have four hours to find my father!" The thought sent chills up her spine. She swallowed hard and moved back to her seat. Feelings reeled inside of her, doubt crept in her mind for the first time that they might not find her father in time. Then with the vigor of an Osguard, she pushed the thought far from her mind. "Pull up at one hundred kilomarks. When set, launch a starguard into the energy well. Set it to track my father's consciousness stream." She stood again and announced, "We are going to get my father back."

***

The last forty-eight hours was a king's buffet of news, especially in Millmum Galaxy. Presently, the news links were burning with the apparent murder of Reppus Osguard and the arrest of his one and only son for that murder. Along with that, the links pushed the news of Rillon Osguard assuming control of the Chaktun government and dissolving the parliament. Many of the talking heads were speculating on Rillon's next move as images of Tishya's and Reppus' lives beamed into every living room in Millmum.

With so many planets and governments in Millmum, the death of a leader usually only brought small mention on the galaxy wide news links. But the death of two prominent figures named Osguard, with one of them being a murder, heightened the news worthiness of the story. Additionally, the mystery surrounding Michael boosted the visibility of the conspiracy theorists on the links.

Byal Vren, the Mosleck Ambassador to the Unity Conclave, had heard enough. Sitting in his quarters, he had listened with trepidation to all the news filtering in from Chaktun and decided to terminate the news link. He took out his communicator, activated it and sighed. "Unity room operator two, this is Ambassador Byal Vren."

"Unity room operator two, Captain Vejin here," shot a husky male voice through his communicator.

"Is Admiral Tirana Ritchen there?"

"Yes ambassador," Vejin confirmed.

"Open a gate portal," he ordered.

After a few seconds an invisible door slid up and open exposing the light of inner space and inviting him to step in. Once he did, he was transported from his quarters to the unity room.

Besides the operators and Tirana, Patricia and Shawn were also in the unity room, which surprised Byal. He stayed on the gate portal platform, wondering if he was about to make the biggest mistake of his life. He searched Shawn and Patricia's faces and read the mistrust radiating like a supernova.

"Osguards," he addressed, "and Admiral Ritchen," he forced a smile trying to ease the tension he had just walked into.

"Byal," Patricia nodded.

"You wanted to see me?" Tirana chimed in.

Byal stepped off the platform and moved toward Tirana, who was standing near Michael's operation console. "Yes, admiral," he replied, "and I'm glad the First Osguard's brother and sister are here. I have something to tell you I think will shed some light on all that is going on."

Fire streamed from Shawn's eyes, emanating distrust. "What can you say that will shed light on our situation? Are you going to confess?"

Byal looked around, summoning the strength to proceed. "A lot, maybe more than you want to hear. But what I have to say might very well save your brother's life and maybe save USSTAP. There's more at stake than you can imagine here." He nodded toward the table, "Can we continue this at the conference table. For what I have to say to you now is for your ears only.

And if you later attempt to attribute these words to me, I will deny them until the day I die."

"Why should we listen to you?" Shawn pressed.

Byal shrugged, "I know you don't like me because I am Mosleck, and because I led the Mosleck in battle against you some years ago. But I am not your enemy today, just like the Kulusk aren't your enemy any more. A mere eight universal years ago, you wouldn't trust a Kulusk as far as you could throw one, and not even that far. But today, you have a Kulusk, not any Kulusk, but a member of the royal house as the admiral to Millmum Capital Station. Do you not trust Admiral Ritchen?"

Patricia eyes narrowed, but she still nodded to the question, "We do."

"Your conflict with the Moslecks has been over for decades now. Isn't it time you began to trust us?"

In repulsion Shawn shook his head, "That's different. The people of Kulusk we didn't trust are no longer in charge. They are dead or in jail. The members of Mosleck, including you, who have murdered innocent people and killed many who wore the USSTAP uniform, are still around and in charge. I find that revolting, especially the fact that I have to call you ambassador."

Byal plopped down in his chair and slammed his feet on top of the table, "Nonetheless, here I am...Ambassador Byal Wren. And if you don't get past your hatred for me or my people, you will be the reason your brother dies and you will be the reason the CUC will fail. I'm not offering you a trade; I'm throwing you a lifeline. Take it or leave it...it's your call."

Patricia moved over to the table and whispered, "Why should we trust you?"

Byal cleared his throat, lifted his feet off the table and looked Patricia in the eye, "Because, believe it or not, your brother is a warrior true to his word. Even after years of conflict, he bartered a peace that benefited the Moslecks as well as the Hustains. We have lived in peaceful coexistence ever since. We owe him. I owe him. The entire galaxy owes him as we do you and the other Osguards. And now that the Grand Maxim Tishya and Maxim Reppus are dead and Rillon is the new Chaktun Maxim, I no longer am bound to silence. You must hear what I have to say, and hear it now.

Chapter 38 — Call

Michael had just finished walking around the corridor. The pain was subsiding enough for him to control. However, the looks he received from the other patients, and the convalescent home staff, were excruciatingly painful. People side stepped him, ducked away from him or just turned around all together. Others pointed and whispered as if he was a leper. Their cruel actions just fed Michael's desire to escape this nightmare. His walk wasn't just to get some exercise, but it was to execute reconnaissance.

In his mind, he was still dealing with a virtual stream…a sophisticated one, but still a virtual stream. He wasn't sure how he was able to enjoy food and drink. Just a few hours ago, he gobbled down a giant burger from his favorite fast food restaurant, along with a large order of fries and a chocolate milkshake that his mother had brought him earlier. It was delicious, just like in the real world.

Another surprise to him was he actually went to the bathroom. He was able to urinate and have bowel movements as if he was in the real world. However, when he did, he was afraid that he was going to the bathroom in the real world. He was afraid that when he woke up from this nightmare, he would wake up to a pile of feces and urine in his body suite back on Millmum Station, so he went to the bathroom sparingly.

During his walk, he observed the building structure and equipment for flaws. Each nook and cranny he examined had exquisite detail, in texture and appearance. No pixel out of place, no glitches detected. He thought that whatever ARIT was running this program must rival the network of ARITs that operated unity stream.

He had even walked out onto the terrace and observed the traffic on the road in the distance. Engine sounds, car horns and tire screeches all sounded very real. Things were so realistic that his walk back to his room was filled with fear and trepidation.

Could his uncle be correct and this was the real world? Were USSTAP, Michelle, and his kids all a wishful fantasy that God allowed him to live while he was in a coma? Was his father truly dead and were the rest his family truly swallowed up by the insanity of the streets? Was he simply a man who had slept for almost thirty years? Was he the modern day Rip Van Winkle?

But if he was in a coma, living a fantasy life, how did he know about the modern wonders of today's world. He knew about the electronic inventions of Earth, the computer, the cell phone, PDA, internet, DVDs, CDs, HDTV, and a host of other things. He was also current on news, the wars, the tragedies, the natural disasters all at least up until ten years ago.

It seems like twenty-five years ago the events in this stream diverged from the events in his reality. The world leaders were different. The political landscape was more hostile. The strains of diseases were more aggressive. The natural disasters were more punishing. From that point on, this was a different world than he knew and for some reason he concluded that there lay the flaw he was searching for. Whoever, was running this program had lost track of Earth's history years ago and had used some empirical data extrapolation program to fill in the missing years. Confidence in his world crept back into his consciousness.

It was a battle of thoughts. For a few seconds he would accept he was the Michael who had just woke up from a coma, only to have the thought replaced by feeling like he was the Michael of USSTAP. He sat in the chair next to his bed, praying for peace of mind and direction. He had less than a day left to figure it out. If he was Michael of USSTAP, the consciousness stream would disintegrate and he would die when the time ran out. If he was Michael from the coma, he would live out the rest of his days in this world.

"God give me strength!" he said in exasperation as he collapsed his face into his hands.

The phone next to his bed rang. The electronic tones of the ringing phone took a second to penetrate the dense fog of confusion that layered in his mind. After the fourth ring, Michael reached up and answered it, "Hello!"

"Michael Genesis," the voice punched through from the other line.

Michael somehow recognized the voice but couldn't quite place it. "Yeah, who's this?"

"It's Billy Red."

Michael almost dropped the phone as he sat up straight in his chair. "Billy Red...what the hell do you want?"

"Do you know Mezhak Zyder?" the voice pressed.

Michael remained silent. He had mentioned Mezhak Zyder to his uncle as the inventor of virtual stream technology, and now he was wondering how Billy Red knew that name. Was this some kind of game Billy was playing, using his uncle to pump information out of him? Or was this the perpetrator of the stream coming forth?

"Yeah, I know Mezhak Zyder...do you?" Michael challenged.

"Yes, I am Mezhak Zyder," the voice said in Chaktun.

Michael subconsciously responded in Chaktun, "I thought you said you were Billy Red?"

"I am Billy Red, I am Mezhak Zyder, I am both," the voice taunted in Chaktun. "You thought you killed me in that house...didn't you?"

Michael realized the voice was speaking in Chaktun, meaning his reality was real and this person on the line was the perpetrator of the stream he was in. "You made this stream Mezhak?" he continued in Chaktun, avoiding the question.

"Michael...Michael...Michael, you are avoiding the question. Did you think you killed me in that house?"

Michael thought for a second, punctuating a pregnant pause in his response, "I didn't kill anyone in that house. Billy Red killed himself."

"You dumb shit! I told you, I'm Billy Red. Haven't you figured it out by now? I survived it. I stepped out of the carnage before it could kill me."

Michael squinted in disbelief. "If you're Billy Red, where have you been all this time?"

"Chaktun…baby…I've been on Chaktun, your mother planet. After they put me in this wheel chair, because I had too much damage for any type of ARIT transplant, I went to school, thanks to the Maxim Tishya, and became the great Mezhak Zyder, the father of ARIT stream technology."

Michael had never met Mezhak Zyder, but knew he was disfigured and crippled from what people said was a lab explosion. But for Billy Red, the killer, to become one of the greatest inventors in USSTAP history was more than unbelievable it was downright impossible. However, somehow this person believed he was both Billy Red and Mezhak Zyder and he had to play along to get a better handle on the situation. "Okay, Billy…Do you want to tell me what all this is about." Michael demanded.

"It's all about revenge, Osguard. I was going to kill you in my stream that I attached to Unity, but I guess a zeshion storm or something like that hit us and pulled us into this alternate universe."

"What?" Michael yelled. "What do you mean an alternate universe?"

"Come on Michael! Even a self-centered, egotistical, self-aggrandizing asshole like you should be aware of Son's Theory of Spatial Relativity?"

Michael closed his eyes in self-deprecation. It all made sense now. The green light was etion energy eating a hole in his time-space continuum, forcing Zyder and him into this alternate universe. Thus, this was reality; it just wasn't his reality. It was another Michael Genesis' reality, one in which USSTAP didn't exist.

"I can tell by your silence that you are very much aware of Son's theory," Mezhak continued.

"Okay Mezhak," Michael almost pleaded, "how the hell do we get out of here?"

"Simple. Our consciousness streams are intertwined. Thus, we must be together when we say our exit phrases. Then we'll wake up in our world…you in Millmum Station and me in my lab."

"Fine," Michael interjected. "Come on down here and let's do this."

"No, I don't think so. I don't think anyone will let me near you, not after you told the cops I'm the one that stabbed you."

"Wait a minute; you're in Billy Red's body?" Michael questioned.

"Dah! I'm Billy Red, you idiot. What other body would my consciousness look for? You went into your alternate's body, and so did I. That's the second part of Son's Theory. The same individuals from different universes cannot occupy the same universe. So our consciousnesses somehow compensated and pushed into one body. The Billy Red and the Michael Genesis of this universe inhabit the stream, while we inhabit their bodies. If we don't get back in time, the switch will be complete and we will be stuck here, while they wake up in our bodies there."

"Shit…you're really Billy Red," Michael realized.

"Listen, Sly will be there in about twenty minutes. You need to get dressed and go with him. We will meet at the old house where you left me to die. There we will leave this universe together and continue this fight another day."

"Again, I ask why not here?"

"I told you why. Now you have twenty minutes. You either live your life as this Michael, or live your life as the First Osguard. It's your choice."

The line clicked dead, reassuring Michael he was not crazy, but also forcing Michael to make a decision that didn't seem to include an outcome that would end in his favor.

Chapter 39 — Nothing Stops the Political Machine

Ambassador Amierwat B'Kailine studied the CUC at his desk on Siryman Capitol Station, occasionally stopping to highlight certain ideas and marking other ideas down. He had ideas he wanted to incorporate into the CUC and others he wanted to give more weight to that were already in the CUC. At first, he was satisfied with allowing the CUC to go to a vote as is. But after listening to Rillon rant and rave in Unity, he saw many of the other ambassadors waver from their commitment to ratify it. He was especially dubious of Ambassador Jingen Tou of the Tandor Galaxy in the Gigantur Cluster.

Her lack of background before the revolution and her ambition to become chancellor was what was bothering B'Kailine. She was a formidable challenger, articulate and intelligent with recent military leadership experience…a winning mix for any politician…a mix that had afforded him all his goals thus far.

From message traffic, his intelligence was reporting that Tou was quietly garnering support from the other ambassadors in the former Tuit Consortium. The speed in which her support was crystallizing indicated to him that the CUC was more than just flawed; there was something definitely troublesome about it. But what, he did not know.

With a defeatist sigh, he decided the best approach was the direct approach. He pushed the communications link on his desk communication station. "ARIT, contact Ambassador Tou…Tandor Consulate…Gigantur Cluster…on secure connection red one…conclave ambassador level-five."

He didn't want his transmission compromised as Tou's communiqués were using normal conclave ambassador level encryption. He decided to use the highest encryption code available. It didn't matter that the use of this encryption would appear on every conclave ambassador's daily report, what he had to say was more important to keep secret than the fact that he said it to Ambassador Tou.

The transmission containing his command swept through the ARIT Portal communication center, splicing through ultra-space and pushing restion particles from its wake. It entered the Gigantur Cluster through the communications suite of Tandor Capitol Station and the office of the Tandor Ambassador from Betli.

Within ten seconds Tou answered the call, which traveled over trillions of light years of space, "Tou here! How can I help you Ambassador B'Kailine?"

B'Kailine cleared his throat, gathering the strength to play yet another political game of verbal sparring. "Good day, Ambassador Tou," he began. "I apologize for this intrusion, but I thought it pertinent for us to talk."

"What's so important that you feel it necessary we need to talk about now on a red one…level-five connection?" she challenged.

B'Kailine sighed and began to push his agenda, "Look Ambassador Tou, it is no secret that you and I are both eying the chancellorship in the conclave. It is no secret that the Millmum ambassador from Chaktun, Rillon Osguard also was eying the position. But recent events have suggested that Rillon is no longer in the running, which leaves just you and me."

"Okay," Tou said, "You are very perceptive Ambassador B'Kailine. But you have failed to see one thing."

"What is that?" B'Kailine baited.

"Out of the six clusters, five are from the former Tuit Consortium, and I being from Tandor, a former Tuit territory, have a distinct advantage over you. We just fought a war for freedom, in which I played more than a significant part. I was the prime ambassador of the provisional government that bonded our galactic star cluster back together. Thus, whereas my deeds and I are well known amongst the majority of the conclave, you and your deeds are trivial. What in the universe do you have to offer my people? You come from a cluster that hasn't suffered the way we have in the past years. And I'm not sure we as a people are ready to be ruled by an outsider, especially after we got rid of the Tuits."

B'Kailine let a second of silence permeate the conversation as he checked his mental resolve in pursuing more of his agenda. "First, I understand your popularity is prevalent in the former Tuit Consortium. Second, I understand your need to guard your new found freedom. And in that regard, I think I am the best one to help. Not long ago, the D'Ardin Empire was like you. Of course, we were just one government in one galaxy and you are speaking of multiple galaxies, but my experiences can be applied on the large scale as much as the small scale. I can teach and lead the conclave to a better and bigger vision than you can imagine. I know the pitfalls and I know who can be trusted…unlike you."

"How so?" questioned Tou with shock.

"Take Rillon Osguard for instance," B'Kailine introduced with the ease of a snake.

"What about Ambassador Rillon?" she responded, trying to sound as nonchalant as possible.

"Oh nothing much," B'Kailine pushed. "Rillon's mother suddenly died after celebrating the disappearance of our First Osguard's consciousness, his brother is killed within hours of her death and his nephew is being held for the murder…All this making him the Maxum, in a time span of what…twenty-four universal hours? Coincidences…I think not? These events have caught the eye of every Osguard in the universe, even your First Osguard Sario."

"So what does that have to do with me?" she pushed back.

"Nothing, unless you consider in your communiqués with our fellow ambassadors you quote Rillon's speech several times as a reason to vote against the CUC, giving the impression you support him or he supports you. Whichever the case, I would caution that distance from Rillon would have been the most prudent thing to do, not warming up to him."

"His situation should not impact what we do in the conclave?" she objected.

"Maybe…maybe not, but can you afford to have that connection if you wish to run for chancellor? Besides, did you know that our Osguard one-two-one, Michael Genesis' daughter, is on Chaktun now, questioning Rillon about the disappearance of her father's consciousness? I hate to think of the fallout if it is found that Rillon had something to do with our First Osguard's situation. People around him, whether innocent or not, may suffer the backlash."

Silence greeted his comments, which assured him that his agenda was working.

Then Tou spoke, "I see your point. And I suppose you will make it abundantly clear in the conclave?"

"I could, but I have something else in mind," B'Kailine offered as a peace treaty.

"Yeah, what is that?"

"Well, after further thought, I think it would be wise for us to pool our talents."

"How so?" she questioned with dread.

"I'll support you as the chancellor under certain conditions."

"Go on," she urged.

"First, I have some amendments I'd like to discuss with you. Second, you dissolve any opposition to the Guardian Supreme Council...In other words, whoever is elected as president will have your full support, even if it is Michael Genesis. And third, you chose me as your vice chancellor. That way if I chose to run for chancellor later, the people of the former Tuit Consortium will know me and my deeds."

"And if I refuse?"

"If you refuse, neither one of us will become chancellor...me because of what you said earlier, lack of name recognition...and you, because of your involvement with Rillon Osguard. I will survive to run later, no matter what, but your situation is what I would call for your political career...a terminal illness."

"Who's to say I won't double cross you?" she hinted. "I can distance myself from Rillon starting now and no one will hold that against me in the election."

"You know," B'Kailine bantered back, "I believe everyone needs a fresh start once in their life...even members of the former Tuit Consortium." Deep inside, B'Kailine knew he had no more cards to play, thus it was time to bluff. Tou's sudden appearance on a once Tuit dominated planet never sat right with him. It was more than coincidence; it was downright suspicious. And now it was time to gamble on that suspicion. "It's amazing how much information the databases on the Tuit Fireships can carry. I think we still have a couple of ships left from the Tuit attack on Rojam Os. Now if some enterprising soul were to gain access to those databases and search through them, what do you think they would find?"

Tou took a deep breath and blew it out hard, signaling a direct hit. "You know, don't you?"

"Yes, I do!" B'Kailine bluffed

"How come you haven't turned me in?" she questioned.

"Your secret is safe with me, as long as you agree to my demands and put the interest of the United USSTAP first."

"You would do that?" Tou asked in surprise.

"Do you mean the people of your galaxies any harm?" B'Kailine wondered aloud, trying to figure out what the hell he just stepped into.

"No, I only mean the best for my people," she confessed. "After my mission failed on Earth, I escaped from my crippled firefighter before it crashed in the ocean by using the ship's emergency gate portal generator. Then I used a secret Kulusk planetary gate portal to flee Earth. It took years of stowing away on large ships, eating from garbage bins and hiding from the USSTAP security machine, but I finally made it back to Betli. Once home I realized what a fool I had been following the Consortium. What I did as a sister in the consortium until then was vile and is unforgivable. I know that now. And I promised myself that I wouldn't let anyone else take the place of the Tuit Consortium and enslave anyone else, including lolwes...I mean men, as we did. But I did nothing until the fight reached my world. That's when I decided to turn against my former sisters and join the revolt. That day, I did as many in the revolt did...I changed my name, altered my appearance and began a new life. That day Lermi of Betli died and Jingen Tou was born."

"We all have secrets, some more damaging than others," B'Kailine began to absolve as he heard the honesty in her words. "But it is what is in our hearts now that counts. And I need to know your heart is in the right place, and I believe it is." Then after a moment of contemplation, he knew he needed to shore up his agenda once more. "But if you give me any reason to doubt your sincerity, I will not hesitate to announce your true identity."

"By keeping my secret, you will be considered an accomplice, in turn sealing your own fate with any announcement of my identity," she blackmailed.

"A price worth paying if need be," he pushed with earnest.

"Why not report me now and get it over with?" she wondered aloud.

"Because my dear Tou, out of all the ambassadors to the conclave, you and I are the only ones with the intellect and the will to push the United USSTAP in the direction it needs to go, no matter who or what the opposition is."

"And the Osguards?" she wanted to know.

"The Osguards are good at what they do, and we are better at what we do. Together, with us leading the ambassadors of the conclave, influencing the parliaments of the star clusters, which in turn will affect the operations of the galactic congresses and Michael Genesis doing the same to the Osguards, I see a chance for real, lasting and prosperous peace throughout the universe. Let the Osguards be Osguards, let us be the political power behind them."

"There is merit in your words, but I still fear the Osguards are empire builders and will turn against the people once they consolidate their power," she warned.

"What you don't understand Ambassador Tou, is they've already consolidated their power and the people are still free, prospering and happy. The Osguards aren't empire builders and neither are you or I. So put your fear away, I won't let that happen and I know you won't either, but we have to be in the position to see to that. So are you in or out?"

"You leave me no other choice. I guess I'm in."

"Good! Now let's look over these amendments I propose. I think you will like them."

Chapter 40—Pieces Fall In Place

"Aunt Patricia, are you sure?" Sharyla asked. What she thought she heard floored her to the point where she lost her balance and stumbled back into her command chair on the command deck of the *G.P. Nightwing*.

"Yes honey, I'm sure," Patricia Ann Genesis-Archer reassured her over the private interlink. Ambassador Vren is very clear, Mezhak Zyder is Billy Red."

"How?" Sharyla pushed controlling her anger.

"It's very complicated, but it appears the Grand Maxim was his benefactor."

"That still doesn't explain how a thug, like Billy Red, becomes one of the greatest scientific minds in the galaxy, maybe even the universe. Damned, he's even up for the Wolbo Award this year," Sharyla concluded, trying to grasp the severity of the situation.

"According to Ambassador Vren, it appears Billy Red has remnants of Omega two–four–four DNA. Vren says Zyder's DNA was degraded—perhaps by drugs—but still viable enough for the Grand Maxim to stimulate his mind with some awakening drug."

"Wait a minute...what do you mean Omega 2-4-4 DNA? That would mean he is a descendant of the Osguards," Sharyla screamed.

"Yeah," Patricia huffed. "I don't know how or even if it is true—a bastard line, adoption of an unwanted child—right now, I don't care."

"How is this possible?" Sharyla grunted.

"Honey, it doesn't matter," Patricia said. "All that matters now is that Ambassador Vren believes Zyder is behind your father's situation and he believes he is doing it from his laboratory at the Chaktun Science Academy. Since Zyder is the one who invented the unity technology, it's anyone's guess as to what technological time bomb he implanted into the system."

"Understood..." Sharyla responded.

"I can't tell you what to do," Patricia began to preach.

"No need," Sharyla interrupted, "I know what to do. And I know I must do it alone, to absolve the association of any constitutional violations."

"I know you do baby...I know you do," Patricia praised. "Right now Tirana is tracking down Ambassador Terilela, Chief Ambassador of the Millmum Galactic Congress to sign a right-to-intrude writ. I don't know how long that will take, but we won't wait. The *Vedar* and the *Nausona* are in route. We will be there in twenty galactic minutes. The writ should be signed by then, and heaven help those responsible for Michael's situation when we get there."

Sharyla nodded, "Tiah, but I will be on the surface when you get here. I'll contact you on Osguard Beta Four. Osguard one–two–one out! She disconnected the ARIT transmitter from her ear and clipped it to the arm of her command chair. "Centurion of Operations, you have the ship," she ordered as she stood. Then she turned to the sentry at the door, "Delta belt, please."

The sentry opened the arsenal closet and retrieved her delta belt, and handed it to the Osguard as she stepped through the exit.

After a quick stop in the communications lab, she made her way to gate portal room one, dismissed the operator, input a set of coordinates and activated the gate portal. Without hesitation and with her father's determination, she stepped into the light.

***

"Dad only has one more hour left before the well closes." The panic was more than evident in Kashara's voice as she spoke to her Uncle Shawn on the private interlink. "I've sent a starguard into the well to trace his consciousness. It gave me back some strange readings, so I sent in another to investigate. Preliminary readings suggest the energy well is a gateway into an alternate universe." She paused to collect her thoughts, "Millmum Galaxy is on the other side of this well," she said with shock. "Except it is different, no star traffic and no signs of dialairtic power exhaust." She huffed to cleanse her mind. "There's no USSTAP on the other side. Dad is all alone, in a universe without USSTAP!"

"Do you have a hit on Michael's consciousness?" Shawn pushed in an effort to focus the conversation.

"Yeah," she said with some glee. "My father's consciousness is on Earth…I mean the Earth on the other side of the well. The starguard will be there in about thirty minutes, giving me only thirty minutes to find him. But I don't know what to do even when I find him."

"Your sister is on that. We think Mezhak Zyder is behind all of this," Shawn pushed by way of explanation.

"Mezhak Zyder? What do you mean Mezhak Zyder is behind this?"

Shawn explained all that Byal had told them about Billy and how he became the great Mezhak Zyder.

The Moslecks trained Billy on Kulusk to kill her father in that fateful fight that started in the park and spread to that abandoned house. When the house exploded, Billy barely escaped by an emergency gate portal. However, he was severely injured, burnt and bloody, when he stepped back to Kulusk. Kie Ritchen was afraid that Billy's presence on Kulusk would bring the wrath of USSTAP on top of him so he ordered Billy off the planet, in hopes he would die in transit. But Billy didn't die; he survived, thanks to Byal, who arranged for Billy to take refuge on Chaktun and piloted the shuttle to get him there. Tishya, who was backing the Moslecks financially and with intelligence, used Chaktun resources to nurse Billy back to health, and gave him a new identity. Acting on a hunch, she had his DNA typed and to her great joy discovered Billy was the ace in the hole she knew she would be able to use later.

Tishya wanted to bring down the Osguards and place her son Rillon as the leader of USSTAP. Prior to recruiting Billy into her plans, she had orchestrated the attack on the *G.C. Justice* during Michael's first orientation flight, which ended in the death of Misul Rafinel and the destruction of his ship, and planned the Talion massacre that ended the Mosleck uprising.

When these efforts failed to kill Michael, she realized that the Osguards couldn't be brought down militarily, so she switched tactics and decided to use science and technology to bring them down. But there was no one in those fields she knew that she could trust. But she was patient, very patient…patient enough to train her own science and technology genius. That is when she called on her ace in the hole, Billy, now known as Mezhak Zyder to become a student in the prestigious Chaktun Academy.

There Billy accelerated in his studies, fueled by the notion that what he learned would someday help kill Michael. In his second year, Billy became a student teacher, and upon graduation was granted his own lab to conduct experiments that led to the creation of unity.

Kashara drank the information in with disbelief, not knowing whether to be more shocked at Tishya's duplicity in one of the most covert plans against USSTAP she'd ever heard or at Billy for hiding right underneath their nose as a respected Chaktun scientist.

"So Sharyla is going to Chaktun to take care of Zyder and break this link?" she asked.

"She's already there and she will be on Osguard private interlink Beta Four. I will relay to you," Shawn instructed.

"Okay, that's good," agreed Kashara. "I will be interfaced with the starguard approaching the alternate Earth from my unity chamber. I will have the transmission connected to the unity chamber. That way we can all hear what is going on."

***

Rillon stood in front of the mirror in the Chaktun Maxum office admiring the royal blue diamond braid across his chest, signifying he was the Maxum. In his hand he held a glass of guild; a Chaktun liquor similar to Champaign. He was in joyous celebration, smiling and giggling. In one swift move, he had solidified his position in Chaktun history. Murdering his brother and framing his nephew was a stroke of genius that seemed too good to pass up.

He took a sip of his guild, never diverting his glance from the mirror projecting the image of the most powerful man on Chaktun. Then as a thought struck him, his smile faded. Being the most powerful man on

Chaktun was not as prestigious as it once was, not since the inception of USSTAP. His mother was correct, in order for him to fulfill his destiny he had to topple the Osguards as the leaders of USSTAP. But how could he do that now that he assumed the role of Maxum? It was going to be difficult as a conclave ambassador, but as a leader of one planet out of millions of planets in the new United USSTAP it was damned near impossible. The first sign of defeat on this issue began to sneak into his head. He now wondered if he should accept his position in life as the Chaktun Maxum, or continue in his quest to become the leader of all USSTAP.

His intercom buzzer pierced the air like a jingle bell. He moved toward the desk, crossing the blood soaked carpet that a few hours ago had contained his brother's body. He activated the communication suite, "Yes,"

"Maxum," the planet's Security Chief's voice cracked through the speaker, "as you ordered, we are monitoring the USSTAP galaxy protector. She hasn't left orbit yet, and our sensors picked up possible gate portal stream activation."

"Have you pinpointed its location yet?"

"Possibly," the voice spoke with uncertainty, "the Chaktun Science Academy."

Rillon's heart jumped in his throat. In his wildest dreams, he never thought the Osguards were smart enough to connect him to the First Osguard's situation. He clicked the communications link to mute without saying another word. He checked his timepiece. Unaware that the energy well was closing around Michael's consciousness stream, he figured Michael's stream had another eighteen hours before it degraded.

He was confused on what Mezhak was doing. Whatever he was doing, it was not going according to plan. Mezhak was supposed to kill Michael in Unity and then escape. Michael's death would have been a mystery, which would require Mezhak to inspect the system. Mezhak would have then concocted some technology fantasy to explain how Michael's death was an unfortunate and unforeseen accident.

He opened the line, "Send the best Sandson guard team you have to check it out. Whoever it is, consider them armed and dangerous. The guards have permission to use deadly force."

"What if it is the Osguard?"

"Then send the most trusted guards we have and tell them...shoot to kill."

"What?"

"You heard me," Rillon screamed. "I gave you a direct order. I as the Maxum rule this planet, not any damned Osguard. And if Osguards are on this planet without my permission, they are here to spy on us, thus making them enemies of the state." He huffed to calm his anger and then with a normal voice he spoke to the security chief on the other end of the link, "So I repeat, tell them…shoot to kill!"

"Tiah!" the security chief on the other end said with doubt.

Then as if it was an afterthought, Rillon added, "Order the galaxy protector to leave our orbit…now, or they will be fired upon!"

A moment of silence was the response from the security chief.

"Did you hear me?" Rillon pushed with more anger.

"Tiah!" the security chief responded. "Will that be all?"

"No," Rillon answered. "I've changed my mind."

The sigh of relief flowing through the speaker was deafening.

"Send your two best and most trusted warriors to my personal gate-portal room and I will step with them to the science academy," he ordered.

"Are you sure?"

"Are you questioning my authority?" Rillon countered.

"No sire," the chief pleaded. "The guards will meet you in your gate portal room in five minutes."

Chapter 41—Preparing the Battlespace

Michael stepped out of the large SUV with chrome wheels. He looked back into the vehicle searching Sly's face for any signs of doubt.

Sly just smiled at him and announced, "Dead man walking!"

Michael shook his head, wondering why he didn't go after Sly and the other idiot who helped Billy attack him so long ago. It would have been two less gangsters on the street, which he was sure, would have saved someone some awful pain. Then his mind flashed to Billy and the present situation, as Sly drove away.

If what Billy said was true, that meant that Billy had become one of USSTAP's greatest minds under the name of Mezhak Zyder. As Billy, he was a gangbanger, killer and a drug dealer…a man with no intellectual future. If Michael had let him languish on Earth after the second attack he may have been arrested for something else or even better, killed by the cops or another gangster, just like the scum he was. But fate had played a cruel trick on Michael and didn't punish Billy for his deeds, but allowed him to become an intellectual genius. Even though he was an intellectual genius, he still had the blood-thirsty murderous appetite…a dangerous combination that was more evident now than ever.

The shiny SUV turned the corner and vanished from sight.

Michael took a deep breath and turned toward the house. The paint was faded, the yard overgrown with weeds and tall grass and the windows boarded by old planks of wood. But it was the same house, the same house in his world that blew up after that last fatal fight with Billy. The same house in which he thought Billy died almost thirty years ago. But here it was, standing in defiance of his realty. And inside it, stood Billy Red, a.k.a. Mezhak Zyder, the man who started his fateful journey as the First Osguard and now was ready to end that journey. Fate was such a *bitch*, he thought.

He took a deep breath and stepped through the broken wooden gate into the front yard and up to the steps. He gazed upon the house again, catching the window on the second floor which he jumped from in his reality, saving his life from the fiery hell that took the house. But the garage he landed on was gone. For a second, Michael thought this was an inconsistency that indicated a flaw in a virtual program, giving him a fleeting moment of hope. But in actuality the garage was demolished years ago to make room for an inner city garden.

Whether it was a virtual reality or alternate reality, it didn't matter. Michael knew he had to walk through that door and meet his fate. With a heavy heart and a feeling of dread wrapped in fright, Michael opened the door and walked in, allowing the darkness of the house to swallow him in a blanket of unknown.

***

At the corner, across the street, Armstrong walked out of the convenience store, sipping on a soda to help him fight his thirst on this hot afternoon. As he scanned the neighborhood he saw his nephew step onto the porch of the old abandoned house. Recognizing the house as the one Michael spoke of in the hospital, he concluded Michael had escaped the hospital in search of closure. He stood dumbfounded, trying to decide what to do next, when he saw Michael walk into the house.

He knew he had to get his nephew from the house and back to the hospital. So he rushed down and crossed the street toward the house. He flew as fast as his sixty-eight year old frame could take him, into the yard and into the door. He stood just inside the door, straining his eyes and ears, looking and listening for a sound. And just as he was about to yell for Michael, he heard voices…two distinct voices. One was Michael and the other…the other was Billy's.

***

It took all of her Sixana warrior stealth and covert training and about fifteen minutes of melding in the shadows, bypassing security locks and avoiding security imcams, but she had reached Mezhak's laboratory on the fifth floor. It was a large oval room with many intricate ARIT and MARIT devices that festooned the walls from floor to ceiling. Directly across from her was a unity chamber bed with someone in it. She scanned the area, checking for any defense ARITs she might activate in the room. Once satisfied that there was none, she rushed to the bed.

Inside the sleeve tube she saw what she assumed was Mezhak, in the same state as her father, deep inside the consciousness stream that was beaming into the heavens through a unity gate portal.

She clicked her private interlink that fit snuggly behind her right ear. She knew that even with a scrambled signaled, it would only be a matter of minutes before the Chaktun authorities would pinpoint her location once she started transmitting. But it was a chance she had to take. "Osguard two–two, this is Osguard one–two–one," she whispered.

"Sharyla, this is your Aunt Patricia," the voice of a lifeline thundered through her earpiece. "I have your uncle and your sister on two-way and the rest of the Osguards in all six clusters on monitor."

"What?" Sharyla's heart skipped a beat. She wasn't expecting such a wide audience. She wondered why her aunt and uncle found it necessary to play this episode in front of all the Osguards in the universe. She understood it playing to her immediate family of Osguards, but she hardly knew or even trusted the Osguards of the other star clusters.

"All Osguards are behind you and standing by to assist," Patricia noted with pride. Your uncle and I are entering the Gen Solar System now...ETA two minutes."

"Fine," Sharyla acknowledged, trying not to show her disapproval at the audience involved. "I found Mezhak Zyder," she announced with gleam. "He's in a unity chamber, from the looks of the readout; he's been in here just as long as Dad. It was activated at the same time Unity was activated." She took a breath while maneuvering her fingers over the console next to the unity bed. "It appears he has encoded a dominant matrix into the stream."

"Meaning what?" Shawn interrupted.

"Meaning, his stream controls the stream. It can't shut down until he shuts it down," she answered, showing her knowledge of the new technology. "It will take about five hours for me to figure this out. But I don't think the Chaktun authorities will give me that long."

"Either way, you don't have that long," Kashara's voice crackled. "The energy well in which both their consciousness streams are flowing is about to close. My Centurion of Science estimates it will completely close in fifteen minutes."

"Shit!" Sharyla cursed in English.

The door flew opened, startling Sharyla into her defensive mode. But before she could pull her pagenay from her belt and raise it, she saw Rillon and two Sandson Guards had their coronet pistols drawn and ready to fire.

"Osguard," Rillon called with the callousness of a hired assassin about to make a kill. "Please step away from the bed," he ordered.

***

The room was eerily familiar, as it should be. It was the same exact kitchen area where Michael had fought Billy for what he thought was the last time. The stove, table and all of the furnishing that were in the house in the past were now missing. Just garbage, dust, cobwebs strewn over dark moldy wood and plaster remained. The dank smell of wet old musk permeated the air, spiced with the smell of death that probably emanated from dead rodents and birds that once used the house as their home. And the biggest rodent that ever transited this house was still alive and standing right in front of Michael. Billy stood in the exact spot Michael remembered him standing that fateful day the house exploded in the past.

"So," Michael continued. "I'm here. What's next?"

Billy pulled up the front of his shirt to reveal a nine millimeter pistol. "What did you expect was next," he responded with an evil grin. "I've been waiting all my life to finish this little game between us and now I can."

Michael sighed, wondering if he had the strength in this body to fight off Billy's plan. He was still weak and barely able to function, even though he was getting stronger by the hour. He assumed he was pulling his strength from the consciousness stream and given time, he would be himself once again. But standing here with Billy he didn't know if he would get the chance to recuperate. Of all the possible situations he ever imagined that would end his life, this situation had never entered his mind, and for a quick second a feeling he never grasped before pushed its way into his awareness...defeat. Michael felt defeated.

"Tell me, Billy," Michael heard his own voice push out. "Why me...I mean with all the people you had to shit on in New Haven, why did you fixate on me?" he questioned; pushing the sound of pleading from his voice.

Billy pulled the gun from his waistband and let it hang in his hand toward the floor. "I don't know," he said. "There was something about you, I just didn't like. It was like you thought you were too good for the neighborhood. It was like you thought I was beneath you, that I was some type of bug...a cockroach that didn't deserve your acknowledgement of existence."

"What!" Michael said with surprise. "Billy, you were the *badest*, meanest ass on the street. I was trying to avoid crossing you. I was trying to stay out of your way. I wanted to fly under your radar. That is what I was doing. I was trying to stay alive." Michael took a step forward, as the feeling of defeat dissipated. He had started a dialogue with Billy, one that just might give the distraction he needed to even the situation up, or move it to his favor.

***

Unbeknownst to Michael and Billy, in the shadows, creeping up the stairs with surprising stealth and quietness, Armstrong was moving to get a glimpse of the two people he was hearing. As Michael began to move toward Billy, Armstrong found an excellent perch just behind the banister to hear and observe the conversation. He was off to the side just a bit, behind Michael seeing Michael's back, but in full view of Billy. He saw that Billy held a gun. But that didn't surprise him as much as what he was hearing.

***

"It's ironic," Michael continued, still moving toward Billy. "Because you stabbed me, Ortho was able to find me and the rest of the Osguards. It's because of you trying to kill me; I am the man I am today."

Billy raised the gun, "Stop right there," he ordered.

Michael stopped, seeing his moment of reprieve falling short of its goal.

"And in a way, USSTAP made you the man you are today as well," Michael said, trying to push the momentum again.

"Yeah, how's that?" Billy said. "If it was left up to USSTAP, I would still be rotting on that prison planet. It was the Moslecks, the Kulusks and the Chaktun Grand Maxim, who made me who I am today."

"Fate has a morbid sense of humor," Michael chimed in. "You try to kill me...twice and I end up being the First Osguard. I try to put you in prison for the rest of your life and you end up being the greatest scientific mind of our times; probable winner of this year's Wolbo Award." Michael leaned forward. "Who would have thought it; on Earth you were a killer, drug dealer and all-around scum and now you have the entire universe on the verge of using your inventions?" Michael took a stutter step forward. "Did you think you had that kind of potential in you...that kind of brain power? Man you are a damned genius...IQ off the scale." Michael took another step forward, surprised that the words he was saying to placate his captor were true. *Billy is a damned genius and the universe will be a better place with his inventions.* "If you put that gun down, you and I can go back to our lives as if nothing happened. We will call this just a glitch in the program that you needed to work out. You have paid your debt to me and USSTAP. There is no sense for us to go after retribution."

"Bullshit," Billy said, stiffening his arm and squeezing his grip on the gun even tighter, making Michael stop creeping forward. "The almighty First Osguard always looks to balance the scale. And with me, I say you have been a little bit heavy handed in your pursuit."

Now Michael was almost close enough to reach out and grab the gun from Billy, but he knew he was not strong enough to move as quickly as he needed to grab the gun before Billy could pull the trigger. He needed to get closer if he were to disarm Billy.

"You're wrong Billy," Michael said. "I haven't always pursued justice. Sometimes I let fate rule in favor of justice."

"Yeah...right!" Billy quipped with disbelief.

"I'm telling the truth Billy," Michael continued. If this was to be his last minutes alive, he might as well come clean, he thought, but what a hell of a person to confess to.

"Forget it," Billy roared. "I don't care," he said as his finger began to squeeze the trigger.

Chapter 42—The Rematch

In the heavens above the alternate world's New Haven Connecticut, the starguard that Kashara launched to find her father's consciousness stream parked in a geosynchronous orbit. Kashara was in the unity chamber onboard the *G.P. Dragon Star,* listening to her sister's plight on Chaktun and feeling very helpless.

The unity chamber was the predecessor to the unity room that the Osguards used in the past during times of emergency to communicate with each other. It was round, metallic and most of all windowless. It sat in the middle of a gigantic room, like a circle in a square hole. Over the years the chamber had been cosmetically modified, so it no longer looked like a grotesque throwback from the middle ages it once did. But it still had a feel of being out of place in the most technologically advanced starship in the heavens.

Kashara was working the controls in the seat that sat in the middle of the chamber. It was a replica of her seat at the Senate Chamber at Millmum Capitol Station, complete with an ARIT control and communications console. She integrated the feedback coming from the starguard searching for Michael's consciousness into the chair's ARIT console, so she could direct the ARIT manager onboard the starguard.

She used the ARIT to pinpoint the end of the consciousness streams. The two streams were so intertwined; they almost melded into one, which scared Kashara even more. Until she saw they broke apart once again over the skies of what she believed was New Haven Connecticut in this alternate world. A horrid look broke on her face as she read the details streaming across the screen.

"Sharyla," she called over interlink. "You've got to cut that link. It's the only way to save Dad. Billy and Dad's consciousness are too intertwined, but they separate again at the endpoint. The only way to break it is if they say their escape phrase in unison, or one link is cut."

Kashara didn't expect an answer. She knew Rillon and his guards had the drop on her sister, but she also knew that Sharyla would change that situation soon. She just wanted to let her know what to do when she reversed the tables. Until then, she knew she had to do her part.

"I'm projecting my consciousness stream through the starguard. I hope to make contact with Osguard zero–one," she informed the group.

Then she activated the unity chamber chair she was sitting in. In preparation, she had the unity program redirect itself to the starguard's ARIT program manager. The rush of energy overwhelmed her.

A black light swirled in the chamber, taking all visual clues from her sight. She was disoriented. She grabbed the armrest to steady her mind from giving her body inappropriate signals. This part always made her nauseous. Then as suddenly as the room went black, light invaded the chamber. The light was not as blinding as it used to be, when USSTAP first used the unity chamber chair ten years ago, but it was blinding enough. It took several minutes to get use to. She shut her eyes and held them shut for several seconds, and then she began squinting, trying to adjust his eyes to the light. Slowly she was able to open her eyes normally. Just in time to see Billy fire a gun in her father's direction. Kashara screamed, "Dad!"

***

The gunfire echoed through Kashara's unity stream and through the Starguard's communication console and back to Kashara on the *Dragon Star,* where it echoed through the secure Osguard Beta Four link. It was the shot heard around the universe, for every Osguard, all seven hundred and forty-nine of them throughout the six star clusters heard and recognized the sound as the archaic but effective instrument of death spouting its fury. And Kashara's scream that followed punctuated the thought that that instrument of death fired its fury into Michael. This was the last thought Sharyla entertained before she went into a blind rage. With the fleet footedness of a gazelle and the speed of a cheetah she sprang into action.

She fell to the right and raised her pagenay firing two quick bursts of red beams at the trio in the doorway. Her body slid behind a console and she braced her back against the front of the console, shielding her from her assailants. In the process, her private interlink fell from her ear and bounced under the unity bed.

Above her was a mirror, angled just right for her to see that she had hit one of the guards, and Rillon with the other guard had pushed his way to the outside of the door for defense. Without hesitation, she flipped to the side, landed on her stomach and fired a blue beam at the locking mechanism.

The door started to close, but not fast enough before Rillon dove through the opening, rolled and landed in a crouched knee position. He fired his coronet pistol, exploding the ARIT console above and just to the right of her shoulder. The flash blinded her for a split second, making her lose visual contact with Rillon, so she rolled back behind the console.

She heard Rillon scrambling for cover on the other side of the room, which fueled her anger more. But now wasn't the time to give in to that fury, but rely on her Osguard training and what her father taught her. Now was the time to let Rillon know that even if he killed her, he couldn't escape.

"Rillon," she called. "Give it up...it's over!"

"What do you mean, it's over. You are on my planet illegally and I have every right to arrest you."

"No Rillon, you are under arrest. Ambassador Byal Vren told us everything. My sister has found Billy and my father's consciousness stream and before you can celebrate this little victory my uncle will have a writ for intrusion in his hand to arrest you with," she shouted.

"No one will ever believe a Mosleck over the Chaktun Maxum, even if he is an ambassador. Besides he has the death of thousands of USSTAP personnel on his hands. I'm innocent of all that."

"What about Reppus?" she pried. "Isn't his death on your hands?"

"No, that is on my nephew's hands, not mine."

"I don't believe that," Sharyla egged on.

"I don't care what you believe," he hollered back. "So what if I killed my brother? You won't make it out of here alive to relay your suspicions to anyone else anyway."

***

Moments earlier in an old dilapidated house in an alternate universe in a town called New Haven Connecticut; Armstrong was witnessing his nephew's execution. From the shadows of the stair railing, Armstrong popped up yelling, "No Billy...don't do it!"

Michael turned and saw his uncle running toward him. Then he heard the loud thunder of a gunshot ring from Billy's gun. As if in slow motion he saw the bullet stop Armstrong in his tracks as his body flung backwards from the impact. Then Michael heard it, his youngest daughter scream Dad. He swung his head around and saw the holographic projection of his daughter sitting in her command chair. He recognized it as a projection from her galaxy protector's unity chamber.

"Kashara," he whispered.

Confusion marked Billy's face as he swung and fired at the holographic projection.

The bullet sailed through the holograph and lodged in the wall behind it with a blast of smoke and dust.

Michael took this as his opportunity and swung at Billy's gun arm, with his left hand, knocking the gun away from him. The pistol dropped to the floor and bounced twice. Before the second bounce, Michael's backhand crushed Billy's nose, knocking him backwards. Then Michael spun to face Billy and delivered a jaw wrenching right hook, further knocking Billy off balance.

Michael felt winded. These three quick moves, which he could have done with little exertion in his universe, seemed to take all he had right out of him. Before he could shift to deliver another blow, Billy managed to gather his balance and deliver a blinding swinging backhand to Michael's jaw, lifting him up off his feet and onto the floor.

In the background, Kashara screamed for her father to get up. Her yells of encouragement rang throughout the interlink and into the hearts and souls of the Osguards throughout the universe.

Somehow Michael felt energize. He sprang to his feet and spun around, releasing a wicked roundhouse kick into Billy's gut. Then he leaped like a ballet dancer and swung his other leg around and while balanced by nothing but air, kicked Billy in the face. The force of the kick toppled Billy, spinning him to the floor, where he hit with a solid thud on his neck and head.

Michael landed on his feet with his back turned to his prey, and using his Sixana warrior training, kicked backwards with his right foot, connecting to Billy's ribs.

But Billy grabbed Michael's foot and pulled it up and out, causing Michael to fall flat on his face. His head hit the floor hard, jarring his brain with a possible concussion. Billy released Michael's foot, rolled to his knees and pumped three quick blows into Michael's kidney area, bringing severe wrenching pain.

Darkness clouded Michael's vision as the pain racked him with no mercy. The taste of blood gurgled in his throat and his body no longer obeyed his commands. He wanted to get up, he wanted to stand; he wanted to keep fighting. But the energy he'd expended, along with the beating he just took countermanded his will.

Through the fog he heard Billy stand and walk over to where he had dropped the gun. He heard Billy pick up the gun and walk back toward him. In the background he heard his daughter urging him; pleading with him; and ordering him to get up and fight. But Michael couldn't move.

Billy stood above him, with the pistol pointed at his head, smiling with the grin only a devil could produce; his trigger finger poised and ready to finish the job he started so many years ago. He was about to kill Michael and the feeling of joy was surging magnificently through his body.

"Good-bye Osguard," he beamed.

***

"All ships...stealth factor ten, and jam their communications network throughout the entire damned planet!" Shawn ordered.

In his private interlink, he was hearing the rumblings of two fights --
the one on Chaktun between his niece and Rillon, and the one in some
alternate universe between his brother and Billy. In both cases he feared his
family members were losing. And to add insult to injury, upon the *Vedar* and
the *Nausona* joining up with the *G.P. Nightwing*, the Chaktun planetary
defense force ordered them to leave orbit or they would fire on them.

Upon his order, the three galaxy protectors melded into the black
fabric of space and pushed out invisible energy that in combination not only
degraded but denied the Chaktun defense system from seeing, acquiring or
targeting the ships for any possible attack.

"Has the entire planet gone mad? We are three galaxy protectors
with enough power at our disposal to surgically destroy all remnants of a
planetary defense grid," he said to no one in particular.

Then he clicked his interlink, "Patricia, I'm going down there now!"

"Not without me," she almost screamed back."

***

Sharyla's mind was moving as fast as lightening, trying to figure out
how to play Rillon to buy more time, but her sister's scream still played on
her awareness. She decided she'd had enough. She took the penlight from her
pocket and set it on the floor, all the while watching for movement in the
mirror from Rillon. She clicked the light on and shone it on the silver hook
shaped device under the bed. "Rillon," she called, "our conversation is being
transmitted to every Osguard in the universe, including my father. Kashara is
with him now. Now he is already pissed at you, think about what he and the
others will do if you kill me."

"You're bluffing!"

"No I'm not. Just look under the bed," she commanded. "I believe
what I said, a few minutes ago, still rings true. So I tell you this only once,
give it up or die."

Her words hung in the air for a few seconds before Rillon ventured
to stick his head out from around the console he was using for cover. Sharyla
studied the mirror and saw him moving. She crept to the other side of her
console, she was using for cover, to get a better angle. Then she took her
PGP from her belt and threw it against the far wall.

The PGP bounced off the wall and fell on the floor on the far side of
the room. Rillon turned, nervous that Sharyla had somehow moved behind
him. He rose to his knees and fired three shots from his coronet gun in the
direction of the noise.

The top of his head peeked over the console by about half an inch. It
wasn't much, but it was all Sharyla had. By the time he had shot his third
blast, Sharyla had stood and taken aim at her target. Knowing the target was
too small for anything less than a death blast to effect; she selected the blue

button on her pagenay and fired. The blue streak of death pierced through the air in a flash, searing the top of Rillon's head. He fell behind the console.

Sharyla jumped her console and hopped across to the other console, holding her pagenay in the ready position. Her finger slid to the red button, in preparation to knock Rillon out, just in case the blue beam only fazed him. But when she looked down at Rillon, a piece of his scalp was missing; exposing a hole in his skull and smoldering burnt brain matter. Death occupied Rillon's eyes and confusion resonated in his face. He didn't know what hit him.

Sure of her kill, Sharyla jumped down and retrieved her private interlink from under the bed. Coming across the interlink was her sister's voice screaming for her dad to get up and fight. All at once, Sharyla's heart jumped, at first for joy that her father was not dead as she thought and then in despair as she realized Billy was approaching him with a gun.

***

Billy was savoring the moment and enjoying the fact that he was going to kill Michael in front of his daughter. He prayed that Kashara was recording the proceedings through some magical ARIT contraption. He wanted this moment recorded for history. He wanted Michael's death at his hands recorded for all to see. It didn't matter the Osguards knew it was him. He didn't plan on returning to his reality after this anyway. Because even if in his reality, he was one of the brightest minds in the universe, he was still a cripple. At least here, he was the man he wanted to be, a master of his own destiny, with all the women, drink and drugs he can handle. But most importantly, he was in a universe without Michael or any other Osguard. This was his heaven.

Then his world crashed as pain jarred his head and traveled through his spine and to his extremities in a split second. Blackness covered his awareness as he went from conscious awareness to unconsciousness in that same split second. He was out cold before his knees hit the ground.

Armstrong, bloodied with a bullet in his shoulder, stood over him with a piece of board that he had used as a bat with Billy's head as the ball. It was a grand slam homerun hit.

"All right, Uncle Armstrong," Kashara yelled in relief.

Armstrong turned to the holographic image sitting in the middle of the floor, with curiosity pushing reality to the edge within his mind. "Who are you and what is going on here?"

"Oh, that's right; you don't know who I am," Kashara realized. Then as if she was speaking to a ghost she addressed the others on the interlink, "Sharyla, are you alright ... Thank God...Yes, I think Dad is alright...Uncle Armstrong saved him."

"Hey...who are you talking to?" Armstrong said, trying to calm his nerves.

"I'm your great-niece. I'm Michael Genesis' youngest daughter, Kashara. I am talking to my sister, Sharyla and my Uncle Shawn and Aunt Patricia."

"You're an Osguard?" Armstrong guessed aloud, pointing to Kashara.

"Yes," she answered. "You've heard of Osguards?"

"Only from your father, but there are no Osguards here," he admitted as he began to accept the tall tale that Michael spun from his hospital bed. He continued to gaze at her in amazement. Now he could see the family resemblance in her short cropped curly auburn hair and in her hazel eyes that held a devilish twinkle.

"Look Uncle Armstrong, I would love to chat with you, but we only have two more minutes to get my father back. I need you to wake him up and tell him to say his escape phrase now," she pleaded. Then she screamed to her sister, "Sharyla, pull the damned plug now!"

A green cloud rose from Billy's chest and hovered in the air above him for a few seconds. Then as suddenly as it slipped from his body, it streaked up and out of the room, through the ceiling and up into the heavens.

The eerie sight scared Armstrong, but he took a deep breath to hold his fear deep inside of him. Then he moved toward Michael, rolled him over and sat him up against the wall.

Michael moaned, as he started to wake from his fog. Armstrong slapped his face, bringing a slight sting to Michael's cheeks.

"Michael...Michael, it's time to wake up," Armstrong urged.

Michael slowly opened his eyes and tried to focus on his savior's face. "Uncle Armstrong?" he questioned. "You're alive?"

"Yes Michael, I'm alive. I've got a bullet in my shoulder, so I don't think I'll be playing golf anytime soon, but I'm alive."

"Thank God!" Michael praised, "I thought you were dead."

"No, I'm not dead, but I think if you don't say your escape phrase real soon, you might just die."

"What...what...what do you mean?" Michael squeaked.

"Your daughter over there in that chair said you need to say your escape phrase now, or you'll never get back to your world."

Michael looked over to the holograph and saw his daughter smiling with tears rolling down her cheeks.

"Dad, please hurry," she pleaded, "Say your phrase and get the hell out of here, or you will die or worst, be trapped here forever."

"Okay, honey," Michael agreed.

"Michael," Armstrong interrupted, "before you go, I need you to promise me one thing."

"Anything uncle…anything…I owe you my life."

"Save your Earth," he started, "…let them in. Give me the pleasure of knowing at least one of our worlds is free from strife and ruin."

Michael started to object as his lips parted but decided to hold his tongue. Then after a moment of contemplation, he nodded, "I guess it is time," he admitted. "Consider it done."

"Dad, please say your phrase," Kashara once again pleaded.

"Okay Kashara, here I come," he chimed back. Then he turned his head and whispered, "Kirk out!"

A green cloud pushed from his chest and zapped out of the room through the ceiling so fast that Armstrong almost missed the transition. Then he turned back to Michael's body and saw awareness in the eyes.

"Michael, are you still here?" he said with panic

"Uncle Armstrong," Michael called out. "Where am I?"

"Kashara…!" he screamed.

"That's your Michael…my father is back home," she said with relief. "Now I must go. Good-bye Uncle Armstrong and thank you for giving me my father back."

Then she faded into the darkness, like a disappearing mirage, leaving Armstrong cradling his favorite nephew, who was now awake from his coma.

Outside the blaring sirens of New Haven's finest wailed in the distance, signifying help was on its way. The gunshot must have caught some Good Samaritan's attention enough for them to call the police.

Armstrong looked up and with a prayerful heart he spoke, "Thank you Lord!"

Chapter 43—Healing

Sharyla was working on Mezhak, conducting lone CPR at a feverish rate, when her aunt and uncle blasted a hole through the door. The sound echoed and reverberated throughout the lab, sending a slight pressure wave sailing into the room. The blast pushed Sharyla into defense mode as she drew her coronet pistol from its holster like a masterful old west gunslinger. She had it ready and poised to blast the people on the other side of the door until her interlinked chimed in.

"Sharyla," Patricia called, "are you okay? Your uncle and I are coming in."

"Clear!" Sharyla informed them, holstering her pistol. "I need help in here, I'm losing Mezhak Zyder."

Patricia and Shawn rushed in. Patricia went to the side of the bed and checked Mezhak's pulse, and Shawn went to the ARIT console monitor to check vitals and historical signals on the monitor.

After a minute Patricia shook her head, "I'm afraid he's gone, baby."

Sharyla sighed gazing at Mezhak in disbelief, "He was alive when he got back, then he started convulsing. Blood was coming out of his mouth, eyes, nose and ears as if a balloon popped in his head."

"You pulled the plug, didn't you?" Patricia inquired.

"Yes and no," Sharyla said. "I found that Mezhak had an emergency shut-off protocol that was to have brought him back alive."

"I'm not aware of any emergency shut-off protocol," Shawn said with trepidation, while still looking over the readouts springing from the ARIT monitor. "Besides, if there were such a protocol, wouldn't we have known about it?"

"This was Billy Red," Patricia reminded her brother. "Not giving us this protocol gave him the advantage he thought he needed to kill Michael in Unity. If we had this protocol, we could have called Michael back ourselves."

"But obviously it didn't work," Sharyla admitted.

"Oh it worked," Shawn rang back. "It appears our friend Billy had suffered severe head trauma some sixty hours ago, just about the time the storm hit."

"So what are you saying," Sharyla wanted to know.

"Billy has been dead...physically since this entire episode began. So I think what happened is that his consciousness returned to a dead body and got the shock of a lifetime." Shawn went over to Sharyla and hugged her, "I know you think you murdered Billy to save your father, but you didn't. He was already dead. He just didn't know it."

"Oh!" was all Sharyla could say as she buried her head into Shawn's chest.

Behind her, Patricia wrapped her arms around them like a blanket of warm love, caressing their hearts.

"There's a fine line between killing and murdering," Sharyla whispered. "For a moment, I thought I crossed it."

"No," Shawn began to preach, "What you did here was purely self-defense. And what happened to Billy was not your fault. You murdered no one here!"

"But I killed for the first time," she pushed referring to Rillon. "And it was my flesh and blood I killed."

Patricia began to stroke Sharyla's hair, attempting to calm her nerves, "As an Osguard, you may have to kill again. It comes with the territory. And I'm sorry it had to happen now and here. But baby, you did what you had to do, and every Osguard in the universe heard it go down. I doubt if anybody will ever question this day, or your heart."

"Sharyla and Kashara," buzzed a weak but steady voice of the private interlink. "This is your father. Thank you, baby girls. Now come on home so I can give you a hug...a real hug, none of this virtual shit we just went through. Come on home...please!"

"On my way," Kashara's voice chirped across the interlink.

Shawn let go of his charge and smiled at her.

Sharyla smiled back, which seemed to wash away the false guilt that was plaguing her just a few seconds ago.

"Are you ready to go home?" he asked her.

"No, I'm not ready to go to Searcy Capitol Station yet, but I'm ready to go see my father."

Patricia smiled at them both, "Spoken like a true Osguard...stubborn and arrogant just like your father, but I wouldn't have it any other way."

"Hey!" Michael said over interlink. "Is everyone still connected?"

Shawn let out a hardy, belly-wrenching laugh that punctuated the feeling of relief that was spreading throughout the universe. Rojam Os' First Osguard had been found and he's doing just fine.

"This is Osguard zero three, close Osguard secure interlink Beta Four," Shawn said between laughs.

With that said, the three Osguards on Chaktun, walked out of the laboratory, down the stairs and out into the jungle, where the chromerion field protecting the academy ended. Five seconds after that, they were on their respective starships, pushing a course to Millmum Capitol Station, knowing the chaos they left behind on Chaktun would soon sort itself out.

Epilogue—No More Secrets

Because of the Unity incident, ratification of the CUC was delayed for six universal months. During this time the news outlets and the talking heads of the universe had a field day advancing conspiracy theories on what had happen.

The official story was that there was a glitch in the unity program and Dr. Mezhak Zyder had died trying to solve that glitch in his laboratory. But his efforts were instrumental in bringing Michael back from the program, so Mezhak was a hero, who sacrificed his life for the First Osguard.

Because Mezhak won the Wolbo Award posthumously, a statue of Billy was erected outside the Chaktun Science Academy. Additionally, Billy was buried back on Earth next to his mother with a gravestone that said, *'William E. Red, a.k.a. Mezhak Zyder. —The Greatest Mind of Our Time.'*

The official story about how Rillon and Reppus died was closer to the truth. The fact that Rillon killed his brother and framed his nephew was widely reported, but the motive behind the killing was not. The fact that Osguard One–Two–One killed Rillon in self-defense was also widely reported, but the story left out the Mezhak factor. These half-truths fueled thousands of stories and wild speculations to the point that the CUC and the United USSTAP organization became back page stories.

Now it was time for Michael to make his move, and it was a bold and daring move, even for the First Osguard and future president of USSTAP.

Onboard the *G.P. Neraka*, Michael waited for his guests in his ready room. When the door chime rang, Michael felt his heart jump out of his chest. He was nervous, almost scared, a feeling that he hadn't felt since the Unity incident. He huffed and prayed for strength.

"Enter," he said, allowing his voice to quake with nerves.

The door slid open, revealing B'Kailine and Tou, both looking a little perplexed.

"Come in, have a seat," Michael said with more strength, reaching out to shake their hands, while pointing to the two chairs in front of his desk.

The pair moved regally across the room exchanging smiles and pleasant greetings, and then they sat as instructed. Michael moved to his side of the desk and sat down. He pulled his chair up to the desk and placed his elbows on the desk, clasping his hands together under his chin. He forced a polite smile and prayed once more for strength.

"I guess you are wondering why I called you here," he began.

"Quite frankly, yes we are," B'Kailine jumped in. "Usually, we would meet at the capitol station. This meeting is tainted with covertness all around."

"Excellent read, ambassador," Michael admitted. "This is surrounded with covertness…at least for now."

"Why?" Tou interrupted.

Michael picked up the ARIT tablet from his desk and handed it to Tou. "This is a blanket universal pardon treaty, forgiving all crimes committed during the Tuit Wars," he began to explain. "Under this treaty, no one could be arrested or tried for crimes committed as part of the war on either side…USSTAP or the former Tuit Consortium." Michael huffed in an effort to continue his game plan. "The other First Osguards felt it was necessary to start the new organization with a clean slate. As you can see, everyone but me has signed a letter of intent to sign this document upon ratification of the CUC."

Tou thumbed through the ARIT pages, scanning the document and the letter of intent. When she was finished, she passed the tablet to B'Kailine. "A magnanimous proposition," she commented. "But if the CUC passes, I don't think you or the others would have the power to execute this document."

"That's what I want to talk to you about," Michael sighed. "Look, I like what amendments you two have worked out in the proposed CUC. You have made the line of legislative power for the conclave and executive power for the Guardian Supreme Council very distinct. However, you have pushed the checks and balances out of balance. It appears you have the Osguards answering to the conclave more than the conclave answering to the council. And in doing so, you have diminish the inherent power of the Osguard."

"So you want us to put the checks and balances back in balance?" Tou offered.

"Yes, I want to put the CUC into balance, which includes restoring the inherent powers of the Osguards as the executive office of USSTAP."

"Osguard…" B'Kailine began to say.

"No, Ambassador B'Kailine…Hear me out first," Michael interrupted with the same stern tone of voice. "I know you two are maneuvering for a power grab, and I admire your tenacity, but I am tired of people gunning for me, politically and physically trying to kill me. I tell you I am fed up with it. And I don't need you or any other aspiring political ass-wipe looking for my head. And I'll be damned if I support a document that would allow that to happen." Michael took a deep breath while he looked into B'Kailine's eyes. He knew B'Kailine was probably the one pulling the strings between the two of them. Then with a calmer voice he continued, "So I have a compromise, and I will not sign any intent on that pardon until you accept my compromise."

"Why should we care about your intent to sign this pardon," Tou interjected, pushing her way back into the conversation.

"Well because I wanted to give you the opportunity to do the right thing," Michael informed them.

"Do the right thing about what?" B'Kailine posed.

"Okay," Michael shot back, shifting gears a little bit. "As ambassadors, you know the real story of what happened to me in Unity?"

They both nodded.

"Well what you don't know is that while I was in that house, staring down death, Billy made me think of two things that came to my attention a couple years back. Regrettably, I just haven't been able to shake these things from my head since I've been back. And now I feel I need to wholeheartedly address them."

"Oh!" Tou manage to say, not hiding her annoyance. "What does this have to do with us?"

"I don't know…you tell me," Michael said, countering with his own annoyance. "What does an ambassador to the Universal Conclave who once was a leading member of the Tuit Consortium, and who once led a covert mission on Earth to disgrace USSTAP while trying to initiate the downfall of several key governments have to do with you?" His eyes were strong with anger and appeared to be throwing flaming darts into her soul as he spoke. "I must say Congresswoman Eldridge, you have changed. I almost didn't recognize you. If I ventured to guess, I would say you underwent what we call in USSTAP a level four ARIT surgical makeover.

The expression on her face spoke volumes, displaying the guilty conscience Michael knew she had. But B'Kailine exhibited a wide grin of satisfaction.

Then Michael, irritated by the grin, turned to B'Kailine, with the same burning eyes, "Ambassador B'Kailine, what does another Universal Conclave ambassador who spearheaded the unexplained deaths of the leaders of your prestigious government, who by the way, had traitorous ties with the Tuit Consortium during a time of war...have to do with you. The smile on B'Kailine's face faded away as the one person he thought he had kept his sin from confronted him.

"Now that I have your attention, let me describe my compromise," Michael said with reverberating authority. "I propose a third body...a review board of sorts...a body of appointed officials that the conclave can take their grievances to about the council and vice versa. Of course there will be protocol and procedures to follow before bringing anything to this review board, but in the end this body will judge all the grievances, and their word will be final. Now this board will consist of twelve members, one appointed by each First Osguard, and one appointed by each Star Cluster Prime Ambassador. And all decisions will have to have two-thirds agreement before becoming binding."

"I take it, you want our support to push this proposal," B'Kailine stammered.

Michael stretched his neck from side to side, pelting the air with cracking and popping noises as he squeezed the stress from his body. Then with his right hand he rubbed the back of his head and neck serenading the two ambassadors with more cracking and popping noises from the tight muscles in his neck.

After feeling some relief he turned to B'Kailine, "We can do this without you," he said with more bravado in his voice. "Even if these rumors...yeah, let's call them rumors. Even if these rumors are true, these incidences are no longer USSTAP's concern. However, some enterprising person could leak these stories to the press, and then multiple governments will force USSTAP to investigate the allegations. Extradition warrants would be issued that I would be honor bound to adhere to. It would be a total mess. This might push the ratification even further back and who knows what would happen if the allegations are found to be true and these ambassadors are arrested and convicted before we had a chance to come together as one organization and execute the pardon treaty. And even if later we execute the pardon treaty and it was retroactive to include these poor ambassadors, the press coverage would be so devastating that their lives would probably be worthless from then on."

Michael then leaned forward blazing his piercing eyes at B'Kailine, ensuring he had his full attention, "Now the rumors about these two ambassadors are detailed in a report I had my friend Anthony Musoto put together for me using captured Tuit databases, message traffic and news reports. And if something strange happens to me before the CUC ratification, my personal ARIT will release this report with supporting evidence and documentation to all the Osguards and news organizations throughout the universe. So whoever these ambassadors might be better pray I stay alive for the next two weeks."

"Why are you doing this?" Tou asked, swallowing her pride.

Michael smiled, giving the first sign of a diplomat rather than an authoritarian, "Let me tell you, I'm doing it for two reasons. First, I think we need you two to lead the conclave. You have the vision. You have Nausona and Laurona's vision for USSTAP. You have the vision I once had, but lost at Talion. You have the vision of unity through fairness, the vision of freedom through equality. But most of all you have the will to make that vision happen. It's just that…well; it's just that we need to temper your will a bit. Second, by instituting a review board I'm trying to show you that neither I nor any other Osguard is trying to build an empire. I'm only trying to lay out a path so humanity can begin its journey to the next level."

Michael then leaned back in his chair, reclining in relaxation. "So, do we have a deal?"

B'Kailine adjusted in his seat and with a somber tone replied, "You know, I always knew you were a great military strategist, an extraordinary visionary and an excellent diplomat, but with your words today, you have just added the not so complimentary title of a remarkable politician. And with that, I know I have been bested by one of the most preeminent adversaries I have ever faced, I concede and accept your offer."

"And you, Ambassador Tou?" Michael questioned.

She turned to B'Kailine and saw the defeat in his eyes, which translated back into her eyes. Without turning back to Michael she nodded, "I too accept your gracious offer."

"Fine, it's a deal," Michael concluded.

All three stood and shook hands, inducting the most bizarre political truce in USSTAP history.

***

A whole universal year had slipped by since Michael's incident with the unity stream and the entire landscape of the organization had changed.

The CUC was ratified with Michael's suggested amendments; Tou was the Ambassador Chancellor with B'Kailine as her second, and Michael was the president and Chief Executive Osguard of the Guardian Supreme Council. Lastly, Unity was once more activated, becoming the scientific center of USSTAP's political base.

The organization had flirted with several name changes from United USSTAP to The USSTAP Federation, to The USSTAP Coalition, and finally to The USSTAP Kelimion, where Kelimion was a Tuit word for *'owned by the people.'* However, none of them stuck, so the organization as a whole, to include all six star clusters reverted back to being called USSTAP, which was fine by Michael.

Billy Red, a.k.a. Mezhak Zyder was also credited for helping change the landscape of USSTAP. In his laboratory, the scientific community found the blueprints for a super gate portal that used inner gate portal technology within the ultra gate portal technology, allowing point-to-point instantaneous travel between galactic star clusters, which alleviated days of travel for trade and business. USSTAP pounced on this discovery and began building and testing the concept.

To Michael's chagrin, it worked, and as president he ordered the construction of one super gate portal at the main hub of each galactic star cluster for a total of six. However, with that came the daunting task of nominating Mezhak Zyder once more for the Wolbo Award, posthumously. It was no surprise when he won, bringing Michael's enemy that much closer to being immortalized in USSTAP's history books as a scientific giant, instead of the murderous thug he knew Billy really was. Oh how Michael wished he could tell the truth and let the universe know who Mezhak really was, but he bit his tongue and swallowed his pride and let the scientific community continue to celebrate Mezhak as their hero. It didn't help that Billy's autopsy confirmed the presence of Omega two-four-four in his DNA, which meant Billy was a descendant of the Osguard mothers. This shed some light on how an uneducated street thug like Billy was able to rise physically as his mortal enemy and mentally as one of the greatest minds in the universe.

The investigation uncovered a spotty and incomplete recorded lineage to trace how Billy was related to the Osguard mothers. The prevailing assumption was that Billy came from a bastard line, the product of an unknown pregnancy or a secret adulterous affair conducted many years ago. This opened up another can of worms Michael was not prepared to face. How many other people with the Omega DNA are on Earth? How many of them will tap into their Chaktun ability once the Tuit DNA inhibitor strips away? How many are already tapping into their abilities now. This was the least of several pressing matters Michael had to deal with as the president.

The introduction of the super gate portal system made the galaxy clusters of the association more reliant on each other than first expected. Tuit technology, USSTAP technology and Taiolian technology from the new Kulusk government merged into one technological smorgasbord that helped update the USSTAP fleet.

Yes, the landscape of USSTAP's domain had changed markedly. But some things remained the same. The Osguards had touched every corner of the universe and left their mark, except in one place. And today was the day that would change.

***

Michael sat at the desk in front of the communications suite on Lilly Station on Earth. Behind him was a breathtaking mosaic of space, spattered with USSTAP space stations and starships. In front of him were several ARIT imcams, surrounded by colorful stage lights. This was the first time Michael had stepped foot on the station in twenty years. He had forgotten how narrow and tiny the station was, a reminder of its Kulusk heritage.

He looked over his speech, trying to calm his nerves. He hadn't been this nervous in a long time. He could feel the sweat forming under his armpits and on his back. Beads of sweat were nestling in the small of his back, even though it was cool and he had on his temperature control uniform jacket. He felt like butterflies were playing football in his stomach.

This was odd, for he had spoken to many audiences in many forums. News links throughout the universe had broadcasted hundreds of his speeches. In fact, his presidential acceptance speech was simultaneously broadcasted through the six galactic star clusters, beamed into trillions of homes and offices. He wasn't nervous then. So why was he nervous now?

He looked up at the communications suite director, studying his coolness in this situation. But of course the director's face wasn't the one being beamed out like his.

"Captain," Michael croaked at the director. Then he coughed to clear his throat before speaking again. "Are you sure we have all the connections in place?"

"Sire," the young captain reassured him. "Every communications device will carry you. We have translators in every language standing by. They have a copy of your speech and are ready to translate it, word for word."

"How will the message get to those places without television, radio, or internet?"

"Word of mouth, I suppose sire, but we can arrange for your message to populate those sparse places afterwards. What's important is that the people, who have the technology to receive you, do so."

"I guess you're right, captain," Michael admitted.

"The world leaders are prepping their people now," the director informed Michael. "You have thirty seconds before you're on. Are you ready?"

"Tiah," Michael responded, realizing that his diplomatic corps had worked tirelessly over the past year negotiating with these world leaders for this day to happen, and that his part, even though the most visible, was just a small piece in the entire process.

Meanwhile, the thirty seconds ticked down as Michael fidgeted in his chair, imagining how the world leaders were introducing USSTAP to their people. He was wondering how the people were taking the news. Then as the director counted down the last seconds with his fingers, Michael raised his head, smiled and looked right into the ARIT camera. Today was the day he would fulfill a long-standing promise. Today was the day he would honor his other Uncle Armstrong's promise. Today was the last day of a secret no longer needed…today was the day Earth learned about USSTAP. In the past hour, Michael knew Earth's world leaders were either shattering personal worldviews or uplifting their people's spirit. What he said now would either invite chaos or soothe confusion. His task was heavy, but it was one he had vowed to take on.

"Ladies and Gentlemen of Earth, I bid you good day. My name is Michael David Genesis. I was born and raised in New Haven, Connecticut in the United States. But I come to you today as the Chief Executive Osguard and President of the Universal Science, Security and Trade Association of Planets, as the First Osguard of the Galactic Cluster Rojam Os and as the Osguard of Millmum Galaxy, which Earth resides in. But most importantly, I come to you today as your friend, as a fellow man from Earth and as your Osguard…"

ABOUT THE AUTHOR

Malcolm Dylan Petteway is a military analyst and a twenty-year veteran of the United States Air Force. He flew B-52's as an Electronic Warfare Officer and has 3,000 flight hours and 300 combat hours. In his distinguished career, Malcolm has used his knowledge in the art of war, military weapons and combat defenses in planning over 400 combat sorties. Besides his Meritorious Service Medal with three oak leaf clusters and numerous other awards, Malcolm is the recipient of the U.S. Air Force Air Medal and the U.S. Air Force Air Achievement Medal for his actions during Operation Enduring Freedom. Malcolm Petteway is a graduate of the U.S. Air Force Academy and California State University.

ISBN: 978-0-9843645-3-4